Annie O'Neil spent most of her childhood with her leg draped over the family rocking chair and a book in her hand. Novels, baking, and writing too much teenage angst poetry ate up most of her youth. Now Annie splits her time between corralling her husband into helping her with their cows, baking, reading, barrel racing (not really!) and spending some very happy hours at her computer, writing.

Karin Baine lives in Northern Ireland with her husband, two sons and her out-of-control notebook collection. Her mother and her grandmother's vast collection of books inspired her love of reading and her dream of becoming a Mills & Boon author. Now she can tell people she has a *proper* job! You can follow Karin on Twitter, @karinbaine1, or visit her website for the latest news—karinbaine.com.

A RETURN,
A REUNION,
A WEDDING

ANNIE O'NEIL

THEIR ONE-NIGHT
TWIN SURPRISE

KARIN BAINE

MILLS & BOON

First Published in Great Britain 2019
by Mills & Boon, an imprint of HarperCollins*Publishers*
1 London Bridge Street, London, SE1 9GF

A Return, a Reunion, a Wedding © 2019 by Annie O'Neil

Their One-Night Twin Surprise © 2019 by Karin Baine

ISBN: 978-0-263-26985-7

MIX
Paper from
responsible sources
FSC
www.fsc.org
FSC™ C007454

This book is produced from independently certified FSC™ paper
to ensure responsible forest management.
For more information visit www.harpercollins.co.uk/green.

Printed and bound in Spain
by CPI, Barcelona

A RETURN,
A REUNION,
A WEDDING

ANNIE O'NEIL

MILLS & BOON

This book goes, without reservation,
to my new editor Sheila.
I asked her to help make me a better writer
and she took me at my word.
Hopefully you'll enjoy the results!
May it be the first in a long list of HEAs
we craft together xo

CHAPTER ONE

JAYNE SHOULD HAVE been getting fist-bumps right now. High-fives. A group hug. Not watching a mass exodus from her operating theatre.

What on earth was going on?

She pulled off her surgical gown, gave her face a quick scrub, and deposited it into the laundry bin.

'All right there, Dr Sinclair?'

The hospital's favourite surgical nurse, Sana, didn't body-block her, exactly, but… Why was the rest of the surgical team high-tailing it out of there?

Peculiar.

Maybe they all had hot dates. Or on-call rooms to collapse in.

Ten hours of heart transplant surgery was tiring. For most people, anyway. Sana looked as energetic as ever. Maybe it was the dancing unicorns on her scrubs.

Sana fixed Jayne with her bright smile. 'Somebody's frown is upside down. And we don't do that here at the London Merryweather Children's Hospital. Not after a successful surgery.'

'I'm not frowning.' Jayne fought to smooth the furrow between her eyes.

Okay, fine. The surgery had been tough…but it wasn't as if she wanted to *talk* about it.

'The Jayne Sinclair I know doesn't frown. So…' Sana popped her hands on to her hips. 'Are you going to explain to me what's broken your smiley face or am I going to have to start pulling teeth?'

Jayne tried to look away and couldn't.

Oh, crumbs. So this was *The Sana Look.*

Five years at the Merryweather and she'd never once seen it. If the rumour mill was anything to go by it was pointless to resist.

The Sana Look, as it was known in hospital parlance, was something to actively avoid. It was responsible for all sorts of madness. The Head of Paediatric Surgery had buckled under its strength, finally fulfilling a life-long dream to climb Mount Kilimanjaro. Registrars fled to cosy cottages in Devon to tackle long-neglected 'To Read' piles. Nurses skipped around theme parks in Florida. Even the aptly named Dr Stayer, who was rumoured never to have once taken a day of holiday in his thirty years of practice, had handed in his notice and was learning how to surf in Bali at this very moment.

No one was immune.

When Sana gave *The Look*, the HR department listened. As did the hospital's Chief Executive. It was that powerful. It meant one thing and one thing only: *someone needed to take a holiday.*

Jayne shuddered. Already she could see her six weeks of unused holiday waiting to pounce and attack.

Nooo!

She didn't do breaks. Or downtime. She certainly didn't casually hand in holiday requests. She did surgery. And extra shifts. And proactively offered a helping hand wherever she could in the hospital so that she could become the best paediatric cardiologist possible. This was her happy place. Here she could fix things. Out there she... Well, she and London had never exactly bonded.

She swept her hands across her face and turned her frown into a smile. 'Nothing to worry about on this front, Sana. See?' She struck a jaunty pose. 'Happy face!'

Sana gave her one of those slow head-to-toe scans that said, *Girlfriend...try telling that to the judge.*

Jayne shifted uncomfortably.

'You did a great job...' Sana said, in a way that had a big fat 'but' lying in wait.

'Always a good day when I can fix a heart.' *If only she could fix her own.*

Sana arched an eyebrow as if she'd heard the silent plea.

It had been one tear. Just the one! A tear that had been shed *well* after the critical part of the surgery had been finished. Jayne's hands had been clear of the patient. The other surgeons had been closing under her supervision. Nothing for Sana to get all *Looky* over.

Sana crossed her arms over her chest and started humming. She was patient. More than that... She was well-versed in cocky young surgeons lying about their feelings after particularly tough surgeries.

If only she knew just how tough this one had been...

Jayne's patient—a gorgeous, bright and very funny fourteen-year-old called Stella—had been on a mechanical heart for five months now. An epic stretch of time for anyone to endure that level of heart failure, let alone a kid. Her family was exhausted from putting on a brave face. Not to mention bearing the weight of constant fear that came with the simple fact that one day Stella's body simply might not be able to handle being put through the mill any more.

When a donor heart had become available early that morning Jayne and her team had been elated. They'd pulled in every favour in the book to get it to London and into the patient's chest, where it was now beating away all on its own.

It should have been a landmark moment. For Stella, obviously. But for Jayne, too.

She'd spent over ten years of her life training, studying, and fine-tuning herself to become a paediatric cardiologist—just as her twin sister Jules had imagined *she* would be one day.

Her heart seized so hard and tight she could hardly breathe. She needed to get out of here.

Her eyes darted to the doors of the operating theatre and once again Sana's brown eyes appeared in front of her. *Looking.*

This wasn't how she'd pictured this moment. Completing a full heart transplant surgery was meant to have been an epically happy day for her. The day that she finally fulfilled her sister's dream.

As she shrank under Sana's unblinking gaze she felt her blood begin to chill in her veins. Maybe fulfilling someone else's destiny didn't work that way.

If she were Jules she'd be leading a parade to the pub right now. Buying the first round. Toasting her team of fellow surgeons, nurses, nephrologists, immunologists and all the other medical professionals who'd helped make this critical surgery a reality. Daring everyone to join her in a charity skydive.

Not being stared down by Sana.

Okay, fine! Blubbing over a patient wasn't the done

thing in transplant surgery. Which was why there were rules in place. And yet the one rule…the *only* rule…of her operating theatre when she was about to place one person's vital organ into another person? Oh, *that* rule had been well and truly broken.

No. Unnecessary. Details.

A good heart was a good heart. Origin stories weren't necessary. They made her emotional. There wasn't a person on earth who was served well by an emotional surgeon.

Committed? Passionate? Intense?

Absolutely. Jayne admitted to all those things. Proudly.

Sure, it was important to know *some* things about donor organs. Suitability. Viability. Accessibility. Jayne always checked the facts. She also ran a slew of tests. Bloods, X-rays, tomography, MRIs, ultrasounds. Not to mention the coronary angiography and the cardiac catheterisation. She'd done each and every one of them with the exacting scientific precision they had required. And then asked for the flow of information to stop there.

One of the junior surgeons on her team simply hadn't got it. Just as she'd lifted the heart into her hands he'd blurted out the origin story of the donor.

That was when the first sting of tears had hit.

She'd crushed them, of course.

But it had been tough.

The donor heart had come with strings attached. Strings that went all the way back to the worst day in Jayne's life. The heart she had successfully transplanted into Stella had belonged to a young woman who'd been out for a bicycle ride on a country lane.

Just like Jules. Jayne's twin.

Neither young woman had returned home. Neither had heard their sister calling frantically for the car to stop. Neither one had lived to fulfil their destinies. Because both of them had been declared brain-dead at the scene. So if Jayne's smile wasn't hitting her eyes she had a damn good reason why.

She heard a page on the intercom and made a dash for the door. 'Pretty sure that's Stella's room.'

Sana started laughing and body-blocked her. 'Easy there, tiger. That was for Dr Lewis. It's his wife.'

'How do you even *know* that?' She'd not heard a single word of the page.

Sana's face softened with one of those warm, all-knowing smiles of hers. 'She always rings around now, to find out whether or not she should put his supper on.'

'Ah.'

A twist of envy squeezed the air out of her chest. She could have had that too. Someone who loved her enough to make her supper…cared enough not to burn it…cared if she came home at all…

An image of Sam popped into her head and swiftly she swept it away. No point in swan-diving into ancient history. Even so, she'd bet *he* wouldn't be fazed by Sana's *Look*. He'd shoot her one of those crooked smiles of his. Give her a wink, a hug, and promise they'd sit and talk all she wanted over a cup of tea and a scone down by the river.

He was one of those men who made time for everyone and the expression on his face when she'd handed him back his ring…

Sana gave Jayne's arm a gentle squeeze. 'Go home. Take a bath. Do whatever you do to unwind. Then take some *real* time off. You've dedicated yourself to Stella for months. This is when you let the rest of the team look after her.'

Jayne bristled. 'No way. Until her body accepts that heart I'm staying.'

The Look reared up, strong and powerful. 'When's the last time you took a holiday? And I'm not talking about the two days a year you take off to throw some Christmas presents at your parents, either.'

Ouch.

'You cried. In surgery.' Sana rolled her finger. 'And the reason why was…?'

Jayne tried to turn away, but it was as if Sana's eyes were pouring invisible cement into her trainers. Lemon juice into her seven-years-old wounds.

Was this what *The Sana Look* did? Brought things to the surface that you'd tried for years to hide?

Sana blinked. Deliberately.

The tiniest hint of perspiration broke out on Jayne's forehead.

Suddenly Jayne was beginning to see the advantage of taking a break. A chance to regroup. Get her emotions back under control. She could go to a boot camp. Or a Mastering Your Inner Ninja week.

The flash of another option sent a complication of emotions pouring through her heart. Maybe she could just…*go home*?

Sana had a point. Everyone's life needed balance, and her life was one hundred per cent devotion to her job. She had no life outside the hospital. She'd tried clubbing, rock-climbing, wild city breaks in Europe's party places, and yet, years later it turned out partying till she dropped, terrifying herself with adrenaline-laced activities and fixing someone else's heart, was never, ever going to bring her sister back.

Which meant…maybe going home to heal some wounds might be a good thing.

Oh. My. Word. What was *happening* to her?

It was *The Look*. No doubt about it.

Sana put her hands on Jayne's shoulders, forcing her to meet her eyes.

'Jayne.' Sana's voice was kind—loving, even. 'You need some time off. What about your parents? They're out near Oxford somewhere, aren't they? Surely they'd love a visit from their surgeon daughter?'

Jayne shook herself free of Sana's hands. Her relationship with her parents had altered irrevocably the day Jules had died. She knew they loved her, but Jules had been one of those rare souls who'd taken people's breath away for all the right reasons. Beautiful, vivacious, crazy, smart…

Risk-taker. Unsettled. Adrenaline junkie.

All the things Jayne wasn't.

'My parents tend to go away in the summer.'

It was Scotland this year. Was it the Outer Hebrides? Somewhere remote, she knew. The fewer cars the better. She had the address in her phone, but the remit was always the same. No cars. Her mother, who'd once shone with a bright passion for life, had been all but literally wrapped in cotton wool ever since the accident.

'Friends, then?' Sana persisted. 'Surely you've got someone back in Whitticombe who'd love to see you?'

'Not really,' she lied.

Her bestie, Maggie, would put her up in a heartbeat.

As if Sana's inquisition was wringing the truth out

of her, she silently admitted there were two very simple reasons she hated going home.

One: she couldn't think of Whitticombe without thinking of her sister's death. A death that never would have happened if she hadn't asked Jules to come home that day to celebrate her engagement. Which led to reason number two. The only thing more painful than helplessly watching the life slip away from her sister had been handing her engagement ring back to Sam.

Urgh!

Sana's suggestion was impossible. Six whole weeks of avoiding The Romance That Might Have Been? The Marriage She'd Always Wanted? The Life She Could Have Had?

Impossible.

She'd missed that boat a long time ago—had practically thrown him the oars. Besides, if Maggie's newsy emails were anything to go by there'd been a whole lot of water under Sam's bridge over the last few years. A marriage. A divorce. His mother's death.

And yet here she was, still stuck on *That Day...*

If she shut her eyes she could see it all in fine detail. It had been sunny. Tourists had been beginning to flood into town to enjoy the iconic sandstone cottages and, of course, the beautiful stone-lined river that lazily wound its way through the heart of the village. It had been early June, as it was now. The usual riot of flowers had been in bloom.

She'd had a shiny new diamond solitaire on her finger.

Jayne had come home from med school to see Sam and he had proposed. Of course she'd said yes. He was the love of her life. Had been since the first perfect kiss they'd shared the day she'd turned sixteen.

Jules had dropped everything and raced home from London. The family's golden girl. They'd all adored her. As usual, she hadn't wanted to settle for anything simple like a toast to celebrate. Jayne had suggested they ride their old bicycles down the lane and on to the pub they'd visited when they were in pigtails. Only this time they'd order a glass of fizz instead of the squash they'd used to ask for.

Jules had been pulling out their bicycles as soon as the suggestion was out there.

Their father had thrown them a distracted wave from his easel—another landscape. Their mother had laughed from her sculpting table and, before waving them off, had done what she'd always done—kissed them each on the cheek, then told them to be safe.

Then she'd thrown in an extra warning to Jayne, as though they were still kids rather than grown women, 'Keep an eye on your sister. You know what she's like.'

Stop at the end of the lane. Check for traffic a hundred times. Proceed to pub. That was the procedure.

Only this time Jules hadn't followed it. She'd taken off at high speed and turned it into a race.

Three hours later…after the ambulance had gone and neighbours had flooded the house to make her parents cup after cup of sweet, milky tea… Jayne had slipped the sparkling ring on and off her finger.

A few months later she'd taken it off for good.

She'd changed in those months. No longer had she been the carefree, optimistic girl Sam had asked to marry him. In her place had come someone more steely-eyed, driven, determined to fulfil the dreams her sister never would.

Jules had always been a bit mad. Her interests wide

and varied. But the one thing—the *only* thing—that had captured Jules' high-octane energy had been her desire to perform a paediatric heart transplant.

As the days and then months of grief had built and festered after her death, Jayne had felt every bit as helpless as she had performing CPR on her sister, waiting for help to arrive. Her failure to overcome her sister's catastrophic injuries had set something alight in her that had steered her away from the life she'd planned. A fierce, intense need to make amends for causing her sister's death. To live the life her sister wouldn't. Perform the surgeries her sister wouldn't. Save the lives her sister wouldn't.

She had done that today. Fulfilled her dream. It was meant to have drawn a line in the sand. Loosened the reins on the strict, driven intensity with which she had pursued this goal. Instead it had only proved what she had feared all along—that she hadn't moved on at all.

'Dr Sinclair.' Sana's voice forced her back into the operating theatre. 'If you don't take care of this…' she pointed at Jayne's heart '…you aren't going to be able to look after your patients with *this*.' She pointed at Jayne's head.

Jayne shifted from one hip to the other, then pretended her phone had buzzed.

'Dr Sinclair at your service!' Jayne gave Sana a cheeky wink and mouthed *Sorry*, pointing at the phone. 'Yes! Absolutely. No. No… Nothing on my schedule. I have all the time in the world.'

Sana rolled her eyes.

A code red sounded. Their eyes clashed. They both knew whose room it belonged to. They both knew exactly what it meant.

* * *

Three days later, when Jayne heard her own hollow voice call the time of death at the end of Stella's bed, she looked straight into Sana's eyes. She saw everything she needed to know.

It was time to go home.

Sana was right. She had to heal her heart before she could care for any more patients. They deserved her absolute focus, and Stella's death had thrown her right back to the starting line of a race she'd thought she'd finally finished.

Trying to outrun her past was impossible. She almost laughed as she thought of the advice she regularly gave her own patients.

If you ignore the problem it will only get worse. If you face it head-on you have a chance to live the rest of your life with a few scars. Scars that will make you stronger.

Sam read the final page of the report, then put it on his desk. He turned and looked at his patient. 'So, if I'm reading this right, it's bedrest for the next couple of months, then…eh, Mags?'

'Madness! I can't do that,' his patient wailed. 'There are the children, first of all. Connor's got all sorts of things on, and Cailey's set to have her first ever sports day. The teashop has Dolly, of course, but that place needs my cake-baking skills. Then there's the village fete. I'm on the committee. Obvs.'

Sam smiled. Maggie was on *all* the committees.

'And then there's the fundraiser for the automatic external defibrillator that the village desperately needs. The art fair that I haven't even *begun* to—'

'Whoa! Slow down. What's most important here,

Mags? You and the babies. The ones in there.' He pointed at her generously arced tummy. 'Everything else we'll get it sorted, all right?'

Tears pooled in Maggie's eyes as she pressed her fingers to her mouth and nodded.

It was at moments like these that Sam Crenshaw understood exactly why some GPs preferred to start their practices in villages where they *hadn't* known their patients since they were toddlers. Delivering bad news to someone he used to make mud pies with wasn't easy.

Maggie had been to the maternity and children's hospital just outside of Oxford earlier in the day, and had come to him in tears with a sheaf of paperwork detailing just how complicated her pregnancy had become. She'd also told him she'd come up with a solution, but they hadn't quite got to that part yet. Sometimes a patient needed to vent before they could listen…so for now he'd listen. And dole out tissues.

Wiping away a friend's tears was hard…and yet it was precisely why he'd wanted to be a general practitioner right here in Whitticombe. Just like his grandfather.

Their shared love of medicine wasn't genetic. He'd been adopted. Too early to have remembered otherwise but even so the generosity of the Crenshaws, bringing a stranger's child into their already full home, lived in his heart like a beacon. Their credo was to treat people as you wanted to be treated. Lovingly and honestly. That way you never had to hide anything. He liked that.

His family's honesty, openness and love were his foundation. The reason why he'd decided to pursue medicine in the very building where his grandfather had worked for the last forty-odd years. The very building his grandfather refused to retire from!

The bright-eyed rascal loved it. Said he'd have to be dragged from the building rather than retire. Sam was the last person to suggest otherwise. His grandfather was still a highly valued member of the community, and even though Sam had been a GP here for three years now some people still thought of him as the little boy in shorts who'd used to refill the boxes of cotton buds and tongue depressors.

All of which culminated in moments like this. If a person felt vulnerable they should have someone they trusted to come to. If they were frightened or scared? Same thing. And if they were going to hear some very bad news it should come from someone who knew them.

Which was why now he wheeled his chair over to Maggie, took her hands in his and looked her straight in the eye. 'Maggie. I know you're Wonder Woman, but you cannot do this alone. Pre-eclampsia is serious. You need someone who *knows* you to help out. With your parents in Australia, I'll do what I can. We can set up a rota to help with the kids. I can make some calls about your committees—'

His very pregnant patient cut him off with a roll of her eyes. 'You think I haven't thought of all that? I've got it covered. Someone's coming to stay. She's just…' She picked up her phone and gave it a couple of swipes with her finger. 'She should be here any minute. I was hoping you might be able to talk her through everything. With Nate gone and all—'

Maggie's voice hitched and she only just managed to stem another sob. Sam's heart ached for her. Her day had been riddled with bad news. Pre-eclampsia. Danger of premature birth for her twins. Enforced bedrest. And all of this with her Air Force pilot husband stuck in the

Middle East until the twins were due. Not to mention taking care of their two little ones.

He hoped this friend of hers had stamina. He could already tell that Maggie was going to run whoever it was ragged.

He went to the supplies cupboard to get a fresh box of tissues and gave himself a stern look in the mirror as he passed. He should carve out more time for Maggie. He was meant to be going for a casual drink with his receptionist's niece tonight. His divorce had gone through over a year ago, so technically it was time to move on. Old news. Today's fish and chip paper, as his grandad would say.

His mum's death earlier in the year had really kicked him in the teeth. Cancer wasn't kind to anyone, and the only blessing that had come from it was that his mother was no longer suffering.

'So who's this friend, then? Why don't you tell me about her? It is a she, right?'

'Yup. Yes.' Maggie suddenly refused to meet his eye. 'She's female all right. Um...'

A quiet tapping sounded at his door. Maggie sat as bolt upright as a woman pregnant with twins could.

'That might be her now.'

Sam crossed the office, opened the door—and there, looking every bit as perfect as she had the day she'd handed him back his diamond solitaire, stood Jayne Sinclair.

She gave a shy little waist-height wave and then, as if they'd rehearsed it, she and Maggie said in tandem, 'Surprise!'

CHAPTER TWO

IF ONE OF Sam's patients had called in with the same physiological responses to a surprise he would have rung an ambulance. Immediately.

Heart slamming against his ribcage. Pulse hitting the red zone. Blood pumping to all the wrong places.

Great. In a little less than the blink of an eye Sam's well-worked theory that the next time he saw Jayne Sinclair it wouldn't so much as register on his heart monitor was blowing up in his face.

He slammed on a mental emergency brake and pulled a sharp U-turn.

Jayne had caught him unawares, that was all. The collapse of their relationship wasn't the only hurdle he'd overcome. He had a marriage, a divorce and his mother's death under his belt now. Making peace with his mountains of emotional baggage had been tough, but he'd done it. Maybe he had a few more grey hairs than he would have thought average for a thirty-one-year-old, but, *that which does not kill us…*

Jayne had had to tackle her own set of emotional hurdles, but time hadn't touched her Snow White aesthetic. Glossy black hair. Bright blue eyes. An English rose complexion that was looking slightly pale considering it was early summer. The Jayne he'd known would have had the kiss of the sun and a smattering of freckles appearing on her nose about this time of year. Twenty-three at the last count.

He forced himself to update his memory banks.

She wasn't the woman he knew any more. That Jayne had all but disappeared the day her sister had been killed.

The 'new' Jayne only came at Christmas. She spent an hour at the pub. No more, often less. Years back they had chatted. Awkwardly. How else could a man exchange Yuletide greetings with the girl he'd thought he'd marry? It wasn't as if he'd asked for the ring back.

At the time—over seven years ago now—he'd actually suggested she keep it. Think about it. Consider the consequences of giving up everything they'd dreamed of. He knew she'd been grieving. Trying to wrap her head round her sister's senseless death. But in the end he'd run out of suggestions. Realised with a cold, numbing clarity that she'd chosen a new path. One that didn't involve him.

As the years had passed their strangulated chit-chat had become a wave. Then a nod. Three years ago, when he'd met and married Marie, it had dissolved into nothing at all. Last Christmas he'd stayed at home because his mum had been so ill. He hadn't let himself consider the option that seeing Jayne so soon after his divorce might reopen wounds he wasn't ready to examine.

Jayne's smile was as unnatural as his own felt. 'Hey, Sam. I hope it's all right that Maggie invited me along?'

As Jayne and Maggie exchanged a quick glance he flexed his hands, willing them not to curl into themselves. He wasn't this guy. Tense. Edgy. Protectively defending his decision to live the life he'd—*they'd*—always dreamed of having.

The life his wife had left behind.

The last three years of his life flashed past in an instant. He'd thought he and Marie were happy. They'd enjoyed a year-long courtship when he'd finished med school. A classic country wedding. A solid year of marriage. The next year hadn't been quite as rosy, but he'd thought he'd made it clear to her that he'd be busy. Extremely busy. The house to build... The medical practice to haul into the twenty-first century... His mother's cancer in full attack mode.

Sure, he'd been vaguely aware of hairline fissures in their relationship, but when Marie had told him she wanted out it had shocked him. She'd said getting married so soon had been a mistake. She'd laid out the truth as she'd seen it.

Sam's priorities were the surgery, refurbishing the old barn and his family. She didn't feel she factored anywhere on that list, and for that reason she wanted to cut her losses before the wounds ran too deep. She'd told him this as she'd served him with divorce papers.

He'd had a card from her after his mother had died, and from the sounds of things she'd already found her special someone.

The fact that he was genuinely happy for her spoke volumes. Nothing like an ounce of truth landing like a ton of bricks in your gut. Which all circled back to the here and now, and the fact that Jayne Sinclair was still registering on his personal Richter scale just like she shouldn't.

He scrubbed the back of his neck and pasted on what

he hoped was a passable smile. His focus should be on Maggie, not his debacle of a love-life.

'Come on in.'

He ushered Jayne in, showed her to a chair, accidentally inhaling as that all too familiar scent of sweet peas and nutmeg swept round his heart and squeezed a beat out of it. The way it always had.

The Jayne Sinclair Effect.

How could he have forgotten about that?

You didn't. You put it in a box and hoped it would never get opened again.

'Ta-da!' Maggie waggled jazz hands. 'Here's my friend!'

Jayne put out her hands and heaved her friend up for a hug. Maggie's head just about reached Jayne's chin. Jayne's eyes met and locked with Sam's. A familiar energy that he hadn't felt in years shunted through him. The type of energy that came from being with the person who made him feel whole again.

'You look good,' she muttered above Maggie's pile of auburn curls.

She did too. Different. But good. She was all woman now. As if she'd finally grown in to all five feet nine inches of herself. Still slender. Still with a quirky dress sense that spoke of a woman whose life revolved around a children's hospital. She wore an A-line skirt embroidered with polka dots. A well-worn T-shirt with a unicorn on it. Flip-flops with red satin roses stitched across the straps.

Her black hair was still long. She had a chunky fringe now. The rest of her hair was pulled back into the requisite 'doctor's ponytail'. A brush or two of mascara framed those kaleidoscope blue eyes of hers. Ocean-blue one minute. Dark as the midnight sky the next. Nothing on her lips apart from a swoosh of gloss. They didn't need anything else.

Except, perhaps, for him to find out if her gloss still tasted of vanilla and mint.

He smashed the thought into submission.

That type of impulse was meant to have died a long time ago. Right about the moment she'd handed his ring back to him.

Jayne blinked and hitched her nose against an obvious sting of emotion. When she opened her eyes again they held tight with his.

Oh, hell.

What he wouldn't give to be able to read all the secrets she held in those jewel-like eyes of hers.

They'd used to light up when they were planning their wedding. Dreaming of finally refurbishing the old barn. Talking about Jayne's plan to specialise in paediatrics. Sam in geriatrics. They'd used to light up when she saw him come round a corner.

Her sister's death had knocked the light out of her eyes. Even so, he'd refused to believe her when she'd said she didn't love him any more. She'd been through a trauma. She was bound to be different for a while.

Jayne had loved Jules as he loved his own family. Fiercely. Protectively. There was no fighting with a ghost. He got that. He'd thought he could wait it out. Be there for her. But she'd refused his support, again and again. Months had gone by before he'd finally seen the change of heart she'd said she felt. The change that had seen her handing him back his ring for good.

That was the day her eyes had lit up again. Glazed with tears, sure, but he'd felt the flare of life return to her as acutely as he would have felt a lightning strike. And it hadn't been him who had put it there. Holding the ring between them, she'd told him she'd changed disciplines. She wanted to be a paediatric cardiologist. She didn't want to move back to Whitticombe. She'd taken over Jules's flat in London. She'd told him it was time for him to find someone else to run the surgery with.

That had been the blow that had struck the deepest. She had always known more than anyone how much he valued his family and how important running his grandfather's surgery was to him. His family was his adoptive family—they'd never made any secret of it—but he'd never felt anything less than family. When he'd finally been old enough to register that his future might have been completely different—alone in an orphanage—he'd vowed to stick with them as loyally and as lovingly as they'd stuck with him as they'd brought him up. With all of his heart.

It was then that he'd known he had no choice but to walk away from Jayne and get on with his own life. It had broken his heart to do it, but doing anything else would have been living a lie.

Their intense eye contact broke as Maggie pulled back from the hug and hooked her arm round Jayne's waist so that the pair of them were facing Sam.

'Can you believe it? Jayne rang a few days ago and said she had some time off. So I was all *You've got to come back to the village! Nate's away. We've got the cricket tournament on. And the fete. And the art show.* She was supposed to come tomorrow, but when I rang her from the hospital this morning, to tell her about the pre-eclampsia diagnosis, she dropped everything and came straight away.'

Wow. That got his attention. Jayne didn't drop *anything* to leave the hospital. He dipped his head so he could look into her eyes again. See if he'd missed anything.

As his eyes met hers she looked away and said, 'I have a lot of accrued holiday HR were threatening to give away, so...' She gave a half-shrug and a smile that didn't quite meet her eyes.

Something was off here. Had something gone wrong at the hospital? In her private life? Whatever it was, his gut told him she wasn't here for a bit of R&R. She'd come back to Whitticombe because she *needed* to.

She'd been back before. There were the annual Christmas trips, and he had seen her at his mum's funeral in January. Right at the back of the church, flanked by her parents. He hadn't been surprised when she'd disappeared before the wake, even though he knew as well as she did that his parents had all but considered Jayne part of the family. More so, he was beginning to realise with hindsight, than they ever had Marie.

Anyway... She'd made the gesture. It had been noted.

He forced his thoughts back into their cupboard and slammed the door shut. His complicated past with Jayne wasn't the priority in this scenario. Maggie was.

Maggie who was now talking and laughing as if years of history *wasn't* humming like electricity between her two childhood friends.

'I just can't believe you had holiday *exactly* when I needed you. It's like *kismet*!'

She threw a smirk at Sam, as if he'd spent the past half-hour pooh-poohing her choice rather than being blindsided by his own past.

He felt Jane's eyes on him, met them and held her gaze. *Kismet.* That had been 'their' word.

They'd known each other from school, of course, but they had been busy being kids and, as a twin, Jayne had been pretty inseparable from Jules. The magical 'click' had come when their secondary school teacher had decided to throw out the alphabetical seating plan and change things around. They'd shared a table from that day on. Along with a whole lot of other things.

As he dragged himself along memory lane he could hear Maggie saying something about the cricket tournament. He only managed to tune back in when Jayne mock-admonished Maggie.

'We are doing no such thing, young woman! You're meant to be resting.'

'What are you talking about?' he asked.

They both looked at him as if he'd just missed a large gorilla walking through the room in a tutu.

Jayne put on a gently disapproving face. 'This minx here thinks we should take the kids to the cricket tournament tonight for their supper. Ridiculous, right?'

'Uh...not if we want to eat properly,' Maggie said, as if it were obvious.

She had a point. For all her plus points, Jayne was *not* a cook.

Sam and Maggie looked at Jayne as one.

Her cheeks pinked up. 'What?'

'Well, let's see... How I can put this gently?' Maggie teased. 'I can barely reach the counter and I'm meant to be on bedrest anyway.' She feigned fanning herself like a French countess. 'And, as I remember, your cooking skills are about as good as your ability to stick around in Whitticombe.'

'Ouch, woman! Kick a girl when she's down!'

Jayne poked Maggie in the arm, then threw a quick look in Sam's direction. One long enough for him to see the comment had hit its mark. A protectiveness he hadn't realised he still possessed flared in him. What did that mean? 'Kick a girl when she's down'?

Maggie realised she'd gone too far and started apologising, blaming her hormones, blaming Nate for being gone, blaming life for making her pre-eclampsic at her busiest time of year.

Speaking over her apologies, Jayne was trying to accept the blame herself. She was being too sensitive. She knew Maggie was teasing. It had obviously been a joke. She was here. Maggie could rely on her. Please, please, *please* don't worry.

'Maggie's right, Jayne. About supper,' Sam intervened, before everyone's blood pressure went in the wrong direction. 'The cricket club is putting on a proper barbecue tonight and it would be a shame to miss it. The kids will love it. There's going to be a minis' match to kick things off. Sausages. Burgers. I think there are even marshmallows.'

He resisted the temptation to reach out as he would have in the old days and put a reassuring hand on Jayne's shoulder.

'You've had a long drive, no doubt. And Maggie's *definitely* supposed to be taking it easy. Amongst others, my sisters are cooking. I heard one of them mention potato salad at the coffee shop this morning.'

He nudged this comment in Jayne's direction. His sisters made Jayne's favourite potato salad. Unless that had changed, too.

'Sounds good,' she conceded with a grateful smile.

But that playful look in her eyes was missing. And then it hit him. It hadn't been there since she'd walked into the room.

Sure, there was the whole awkward 'running into your ex' thing, but they'd seen each other before since they'd split up, at the pub over Christmas, and had just about hit the casual acquaintance kind of comfort level. A quick *Hi, you look well. So do you. Well...happy Christmas, then!* and off they'd go and live their lives for another year.

He narrowed his eyes as Jayne fussed about, picking up Maggie's bag and the paperwork she'd left on Sam's desk. She looked a bit tired, but that wasn't it.

The spark in her eyes had only gone once before, and that had been at her darkest ebb.

A thought jammed itself into place and stuck. This spontaneous trip to the country was definitely loaded with something heavier than just getting HR off of her back. She'd managed to dodge the village for the past seven years, so...why now?

Jayne waved the paperwork at him. 'All right if I pop in another time to talk through these?'

'Yeah, sure. Absolutely.'

He caught himself smiling. They'd always enjoyed doing that. Going over patients' notes together had been one of the myriad reasons they'd planned to work together. *Live together. Love together.*

Well... He supposed he'd see how much things had changed when she came in. Things he would remind himself of when she left again. Because this wouldn't last. *Couldn't* last. Jayne Sinclair had made it more than clear her future was not in Whitticombe. And not with him.

Jayne bundled Maggie towards the corridor and Sam automatically moved forward to put his hand on the small of Jayne's back. He saw her notice the movement out of the corner of his eye and pulled it away. Which was ridiculous. What were his fingers going to do? Catch on fire if he touched her?

He gave himself a few extra seconds to regroup before going out to the waiting room to get his next patient. Tommy Stark. A ten-year-old boy who looked as though he'd had a bit of a run-in with a fist in the playground.

'Oof. That looks sore.'

'Yup.' Tommy grinned as he followed Sam into his office with his mother in tow.

His mum explained how her son had managed to insert himself between the school bully and the school chess champion, a rather shy girl called Molly.

'That was a brave thing to do,' Sam said.

'Nah,' the little boy explained. 'I did it for love, so it doesn't hurt.'

Sam hid his rueful smirk as he checked the boy over, then showed them out of the room. If only it were that easy.

'Have you gone completely mad?'

A blade of guilt swept through Jayne as words flew out of her mouth and steam poured out of her ears. What was Maggie *thinking*? The whole point of bedrest was doing just that. Resting. Not pole-vaulting them both straight into the heart of village life.

Maggie was totally unfazed. Perhaps it was the promise of grilled food on the horizon. Or maybe it was the foot-rub Jayne was giving her. The only successful lure to get her active friend to sit down.

'Ow! Not so hard. It's the *cricket*,' Maggie offered amiably in explanation, then pointed to her foot. 'You missed a bit.'

Jayne arched an eyebrow. 'It's not just "the cricket", Mags. It's the whole of freaking Whitticombe coming out to play!'

'So?'

'So... I just...'

She didn't want the entire universe to know she was back. Not *en masse*, anyway. It was hard enough being home at all, let alone at this time of year. Only two short weeks away from the anniversary of the day her sister died. If they knew it had been her fault they'd... Ugh... It didn't bear thinking about.

'It just seems a bit awkward, you know?'

'Why? You're a Whitticomber. So's near enough everyone else. Think of yourself as a stand-in for your parents. Cheer for them, too.' Her voice softened as she asked, 'How are they, anyway?'

Another blade of guilt sliced through Jayne's conscience. 'They're all right...'

She'd sent a couple of texts, telling them she was going to be staying with Maggie, and had received a short message in return. They were fine. It was quiet. They were both working a lot.

Nothing more personal than her patient notes.

Brief, informative texts seemed to be the only way they could communicate since Jules had died. As if her twin had been the glue that had held them together. Jayne had stayed home for a couple of months afterwards, but whenever they'd looked at her she'd seen the emptiness in their eyes. They all knew but they never spoke the one simple truth.

If Jayne hadn't rung Jules…if Jayne hadn't asked her to ride to the pub…her sister would be alive and well today. If only she'd screamed loud enough. Fast enough.

The sports car had been moving so fast when Jules had whipped round the corner on her bicycle. Jayne's screams had stayed lodged in her throat. When her sister had been pronounced brain-dead it had been as if they would never stop sounding inside her own head.

As best she could, Jayne conjured up a smile and put away the massage cream, rubbing the residue into her hands. The tingle of the minty gel reminded her of how she'd felt when, just for a nanosecond, Sam had reached forward to put his hand on the small of her back as they'd left his office—until he'd caught her noticing and pulled it back. Fire then ice.

'Apparently it's not much of a summer as far as the weather is concerned. They're up in the farthest reaches of the Scottish isles.'

Maggie pulled a face. 'I couldn't live up there. Although I suppose the communities must be close, what with the weather and all. I was talking to the McTavishes—'

Jayne lifted her brow questioningly.

'They're the ones who are doing the house-swap with your parents. Really nice couple. They *love* my kids. Said they don't have grandkids of their own, so they always pounce on a chance to play with them. Mrs McTavish has been teaching Connor how to sketch. It's pretty cool!'

It sounded cool. Just the sort of thing her father would have done with her own children if she'd lived down the road in The Old Barn with Sam, as they'd planned. Bundled a child upon his knee and pulled out a huge sketchpad, as he had done with each of them. Jules had taken to it like a duck to water, but Jayne's artistry had always lain much more firmly in the surgical field. In fixing things.

That was why she spent all her spare time in the other hospital departments. No way would she ever again fall into the 'helpless maiden' category. Not after that horrible day.

Kneeling on the pavement next to Jules after she'd been hit, not caring that her own knees were scraped raw, Jayne had felt so *helpless*. She'd done CPR, but her sister's injuries had been so severe the only thing she'd been able to do was keep her heart beating until someone else had told her otherwise. There had been no way she was going to call her own sister's death.

She hadn't even thought of becoming a surgeon at that point. It had been general practice with a specialty in paediatrics all the way. Sam would do the 'oldies'. She'd look after the little ones. And between the two of them they'd take care of everyone ese. It had been a perfect plan for a perfect life.

'Woo-hoo? Earth to Jayne?' Maggie pulled back and then suddenly went wide-eyed, as if a lightbulb had gone on inside her head.

'You aren't being weird about the cricket because of Sam, are you?'

Jayne made a scoffing noise. 'No.'

'Ohmigawd, you totally *are*.'

She wasn't. Okay. She was. A bit. But what she felt for Sam was just one piece of a bigger puzzle. Something had been ripped open inside her when she'd called Stella's time of death. Something she'd thought had healed.

Maggie gave her belly a double-handed rub. 'You're not still in love with him, are you?'

Jayne did not dignify the question with an answer. Of

course a part of her was. Always would be. Their's had been a love that ran so deep it could never be completely erased. Even if she'd told him otherwise.

'Jayne…' Maggie's voice held a warning note. 'If you're here to win Sam's heart again you should tread very, very carefully. The man's been through a lot. His divorce was only a year ago, and of course he's had to cope with his mum passing. He's strong, of course. He's Sam. But—'

'That's *not* why I'm here,' Jayne snapped, a bit too defensively.

She looked into her friend's eyes and saw twenty years of friendship shining back at her. Why was she lying? She knew why she was back. She was here because calling Stella's time of death had made her feel as if she'd killed her sister all over again.

Pain. Anguish. Guilt.

Feelings she wasn't meant to be having. Not as a top surgeon, anyway. She'd thought placing that heart in Stella's body would salve the torment she'd been carrying with her all these years. When Stella's body had rejected the heart Jayne had felt as if it had rejected her too. All of which boiled down to one simple truth: if Jayne didn't find a way to make genuine amends for her sister's death, and the emotional wreckage she'd left in her wake, she could not continue as a surgeon. And that was a future she was completely unwilling to imagine.

Maggie tipped her head to the side, looking not unlike the twelve-year-old version of herself who had befriended Jayne after a particularly rough round of netball. 'Whatever it is that's brought you back… I just want you to know I'm glad you're here. If you ever need to talk…'

It was an offer Maggie had given her countless times. But the only person Jayne had come close to confessing the full story to was Sam. No matter how close she felt to Mags, he'd always been the sounding board she'd needed. He was wise beyond his years. Always gave her perspective on things without making her feel stupid.

When she'd handed him back his ring she'd seen every emotion in his eyes. Pain. Anger. Hurt. Frustration. Disbelief. But instead of lashing out he'd leant in and given her cheek the softest kiss.

'No matter what it is you're going through,' he'd said, 'I want you to know there is a light at the end of the tunnel. You may not see it now, but you will find the way. You'll survive this. Believe me when I say you are so much stronger than you think you are.'

If she had believed him would they be together now?

Back then it had seemed impossible. The only path she'd seen was to pursue her sister's dreams with blinkered, exacting energy. A path so narrow there had been no room for anyone else on it.

It had taken Stella's death to make her realise just how wrong she'd been. No amount of lives saved would ever bring her sister back.

She forced herself to pop on a smile and clapped her hands together. 'Honestly—I'm good. Just…you know… it's always a little bit weird seeing an ex, right?'

Maggie gave an apologetic shrug and automatically gave her wedding ring, now hanging from a chain around her neck, a quick rub. She wouldn't know. She and Nate had married pretty much straight out of school, before he'd headed off to boot camp. Theirs had been a very similar romance to Jayne and Sam's. Childhood sweet-

hearts making good on their teenage dreams. Well...
Not so similar. But Jayne was happy for them.

She cocked her head to the side at the sound of children laughing. 'Why don't I round up those kids of yours
and get us to the cricket ground?'

Maggie peered at her for another moment, obviously
trying to decide whether or not she should try and force
Jayne to talk, and then thought better of it. 'Let's do that.
The doctor said I was supposed to keep my calorie con-
sumption up—so bring on the burgers!'

CHAPTER THREE

HALF AN HOUR LATER Jayne was still steeling herself for some sort of retribution.

The beautifully manicured cricket ground was bustling with activity. Sam was nowhere to be seen, so that was a bit of breathing room, and the McTavishes had shown up and were every bit as lovely as Maggie had said. They'd taken Connor and Cailey over to the minis' match, before the main Whitticombe team faced off against the neighbouring village.

The villagers were every bit as nice to her as they were on her annual Christmas visits. Lots of hellos and delighted smiles of surprise. She supposed her usual fleeting visit and toast to the festive season never gave anyone a chance to do much of anything else, but the villagers were loyal.

Sam's family were particularly well known for their huge hearts and charitable ways—Sam's adoption being a case in point. His parents had already had three girls, but Sam's mother—a social worker—had been helping a Fire and Rescue team when they'd found Sam abandoned in a rubbish skip as an infant. They'd never made a big fuss of the fact he was adopted, and she knew Sam's heart burnt bright with love and loyalty for them. From his grandad all the way down to his sister's children.

He had always been aware of how fortunate he was to have found his way into the Crenshaws' lives as the son his adoptive parents had always dreamed of having. And when she and Sam had got together, they'd treated her with as much love and kindness as they did their own children.

She wondered how kind his family would be to her now.

She physically shook the thought away, reminding herself that they, too, had offered nothing but love and support after Jules had died. *She* had been the one to turn away from them.

Well, she was here now, and life had moved on. It was time to try and see the village through fresh eyes.

The clubhouse was festooned with bunting. Of course. This was a village that loved bunting. A few dads were getting the huge barbecues up and running. Clusters of children who weren't in the minis' match were running round playing tag, just as the adults had done as kids.

This was nice. Maybe enough time had passed that some of the rawness of the past had genuinely begun to heal over.

'Jayne Sinclair—is that you?'

Sam's sister Kate appeared in front of her, carrying a huge bowl of potato salad. Behind her was the rest of the Crenshaw clan. Jess and Ali. Their husbands. Their children. Mr Crenshaw and his father Ernest—Sam's grandfather. The family she was meant to have been a part of. The family whose secret potato salad recipe would be tucked away in her head by now if she'd married Sam. Memorised. Cherished.

And just like that the few precious seconds of contentment she'd felt dropped away.

Instinct caught her seeking Sam out amongst the melee. His Irish Wolfhound, Elf, was keeping a watchful eye on him as he lifted one of his nephews onto his shoulders so that he could unhook a bit of bunting that had snagged on the corner of the clubhouse. It was a simple act of kindness, but one that drove home exactly the sort of man he was.

He cared. About the big things, the little things and everything in between. Her heart almost exploded from the pain of acknowledging that he had always been everything she'd wanted in a man and the only one she couldn't have.

There was no coming back from the catalogue of nightmares she'd put him through. When a girl took a man's ring off her finger and said goodbye she had to mean it. She *had* meant it at the time. Hadn't been able to see the wood for the trees. But now that seven years had split the difference... Only she was too late to make those sorts of amends.

'Jayne?' Sam's sister was looking at her curiously. 'Everything all right? It's good to see you outside your normal visit.'

'Yes...um...' She shook her head distractedly and flicked her thumb over her shoulder. 'I'm here for Maggie. For a few weeks, in fact.'

'Oh, gosh! I hadn't realised.'

Together they looked across to where Maggie appeared to be organising some sort of impromptu three-legged race.

Jayne rolled her eyes and huffed out what she hoped

was a comedy sigh. 'She's meant to be *resting*. I'd better go lend her a hand. Get her on to a picnic rug or something.'

And avoid this very awkward conversation.

'Of course.' Kate gave her arm a quick pat. 'And Jayne…just to let you know… Sam's been thinking about dating again, so…' She crinkled her nose and gave her a smile that was hard to interpret. 'Just be careful how you tread if you're back for a bit, yeah? He's already been through a lot.'

A warning. A nice one. But a warning nonetheless.

'Absolutely. Got it.'

She fought a ridiculous impulse to curtsey and instead did what she was brilliant at doing. Turned round and walked away.

'Hey!' Sam ran up behind Jayne as she strode up the small hill that overlooked the pitch. 'Everything okay?'

She whirled round and their eyes caught and locked. Crackles of electricity snapped between them like a summer storm. She stared into his eyes like a deer caught in headlights.

'My sisters said you looked upset. What's going on?'

'What? I'm fine.'

She punched him on the arm. A classic playground flirtation move. Proof, if she needed any, that the plethora of feelings she'd hoped had faded were still alive and kicking.

'Nothing to see here!'

He frowned at her. An uninvited whorl of heat unleashed itself in her belly as goose pimples skittered up her arms.

Sam's frown was kind of sexy. How could she have forgotten how perfectly green his eyes were? That thick,

straw-coloured hair…a bit wavy, a bit not. Lightly stub-
bled cheeks and a jaw that just begged a girl to trace her
fingers along it before landing on that remarkably full
pair of lips of his.

She pressed her fingers against the rough bark of a
tree and dug in, praying it was enough to stop her from
wrapping herself around him.

Unexpectedly, he flipped his frown into a variation
on a smile. A wary one. But still that same sexy, slow
smile that lit her up from the inside out.

He'd never fixed that slight overlap of his two front
teeth. Funny how the tiny imperfection made the whole
picture perfect.

He hooked his thumbs on his hips. Hips barely holding up a pair of chinos that were only just keeping purchase on the hem of a white shirt that brought out his
early summer tan…

Grown-up Sam was…*mmm*…extra-nice. The little
crinkles by his eyes and the tiny hints of white hair at
his temples unleashed a whole new set of butterflies
and fireworks…

Just as quickly they were extinguished.

Those crinkles and the white hair hadn't been there
before he'd moved on from their disastrous relationship.
Time had taken its toll. Or, more accurately, life. A divorce. The loss of his mother. A pair of body blows there
was no proper consolation for. Especially when the divorce had been finalised just a few months before his
mother's death.

She wanted to hug him. She *should* hug him. Their
shared past held her back.

'Sorry about your…um…you know… Things.'

Sam looked at her long and hard, those green eyes of

his boring straight through to her soul. He didn't dignify her paltry commiserations with a response.

She had attended the funeral with her parents but hadn't stayed to pass on her condolences. She regretted that because she *was* sorry for his loss. And for so much more than she would ever be able to stuff into a *Thinking of you at this difficult time* card.

'You planning on hiding up here for the rest of the match or are you actually here to help Maggie?'

The challenging spark in Sam's eyes made mincemeat of the oxygen in her lungs. There was definitely an edge to him now. Something hard and unyielding that she hadn't expected.

He shifted and gave her a look that was almost edged with respect. 'I'm impressed that you came. It's got to be tough. Especially this time of year.'

This time of year. What a loaded phrase.

Fifteen days and about eight hours away from the moment of impact.

She threw on a smile Jules would've given her stamp of approval. The type of grin that said the world might have given her a kick or two, but she was going to keep on keeping on.

'Ha! You and me both, mate.'

They both flinched at the use of the word 'mate'. He'd been her childhood sweetheart. First kiss. First dance. First love. She'd said yes when he'd gone down on bended knee and presented her with a perfect diamond solitaire. Wept in solitude when she'd returned it. Sam Crenshaw was not a casual buddy.

No matter how many times she'd told herself leaving him was the right thing to do, each time she saw him her heart had begged her to change her mind.

Jayne nodded her head towards the table where Maggie was sitting, receiving the full adoration of the villagers now that news of her tricky pregnancy had spread.

'I've scanned through the notes you gave me. It reads worse than she's acting. How is she really?'

He ticked Maggie's diagnoses off on his fingers. 'Preeclampsia. Gestational diabetes. Twin pregnancy. She's on a bit of a tightrope walk, if I'm honest. She's all right now, but...' His voice took on a warning note. 'She won't be if she doesn't start putting her feet up properly. You know as well as I do how quickly these symptoms can take a turn for the worse.'

She did. There was a specialist unit in her hospital for mothers who were experiencing difficult pregnancies. Too many times her colleagues had been forced to call a time of death. She wished now she'd done a few more shadow shifts in that department. Maybe she'd give one of her colleagues a call. Get a few key notes on what to look out for. There wasn't a chance in the universe that Maggie was going downhill on *her* watch.

Jayne gave a jaunty salute to cover up the fact that her insides were jelly. 'Ready and on high alert. My sole remit is to keep those babies right where they belong. And Mum healthy. And, of course, make sure her children eat more than toast. Toast that isn't burnt. Can they *make* toast?'

She was wittering now. She couldn't help it. Sam's entire visage spoke of a man who believed she'd keep her word about as much as he believed in the Tooth Fairy.

He lowered his voice and leant in. She tried her best not to breathe in. One whiff of warm skin and that spicy man scent of his and her knees would start misbehaving.

'She needs this, Jayne. She needs *you*. If you let her down I'll—'

'You'll what?' she challenged.

His voice hardened. 'I'll pick up the pieces. But I will *not* have your back. You'll have to ride this one out on your own.'

She wanted to protest. It wasn't as if being here was easy for her. If he had even the slightest clue of just how difficult...

Why not tell him? A burden shared...

No. If Sam knew that their engagement had led to her sister's death... No chance. She wasn't letting him take any of the heat for this one. Jules's death was solidly on her. *She'd* been the one who'd agreed to race her sister. She'd been the one who hadn't got Jules's helmet to her on time. The one who hadn't screamed loud enough in warning when that sports car had raced round the corner.

She looked him in the eye. 'I've promised to help. I'll help.'

The crinkles round his eyes narrowed. Enough to send a wash of ice water through her veins.

'Don't you trust me?' she asked quietly.

Sam didn't say anything. He didn't have to. The number of times she'd seen that same flash of emotion in his eyes was the number of times her own heart had broken.

Talk about 'open mouth and insert foot'. She might as well shove both her feet in there and have done with it.

Sam eventually broke the awkward silence. 'I guess you've probably heard the news?'

Her mind reeled for a second, then landed on the most recent thing she'd heard about Sam.

'Yes! Absolutely. Your sister told me. Um...well... good luck with the dating thing!'

Both his eyebrows shot up and he barked a tight laugh. 'That wasn't the news I was talking about. I meant the news that Kate is pregnant again. I saw you two talking.'

Oh. And, *ouch.* No, Kate had only mentioned that she had better watch herself with Sam. Then it hit her. Maybe he hadn't *wanted* her to know about the dating. Her tummy did an involuntary flip.

She sought his eyes for any signs of lingering affection. But just as she sensed those creases by his eyes might be about to soften a pixie-haired woman Jayne didn't recognise swooped in, bearing a pair of wine glasses.

'*There* you are, Sam! I wondered where you'd got to. I thought we were going to sit down by the pitch? Hope it wasn't too cheeky, but I've brought you a glass of Pinot from the bar. Mmm! Delicious. I am *parched.* So...' The woman—petite, blonde, and with huge fawn eyes— looked at Jayne then back at Sam. 'Friend of yours?'

'Something like that,' Sam said, his eyes still glued to Jayne's. 'Blast from the past.'

Another burst of fireworks exploded in Jayne's belly. *That was one way to put it.*

Sam shifted his weight and touched the woman's arm. 'Jayne Sinclair—allow me to introduce you to Nell Pace.'

Her heart sank straight to her toes. Sam wasn't *considering* dating. He was *on a date.*

The fireworks went out in one swift move.

'Hi! Goodness... Well!' Jayne's voice was getting a bit screechy. 'Nice to meet you.'

Sam threw her a peculiar look as Nell launched into an explanation as to how they'd met.

'My aunt works with Sam. I'm new in the village and

she thought we'd hit it off, so when I heard about the cricket match I thought I'd come along and say hello.'

Sam looked about as uncomfortable as Jayne felt. So Jayne did the only thing she could think of to fix it.

Scarper.

She threw a frantic wave in Maggie's direction. 'I really should get going. Maggie's waiting for me, and I'm the last person to stand in the way of a budding… um…friendship…'

She was. Absolutely she was. But if she hadn't been cringing before, she was properly mortified now. It was as if she were wearing an invisible scarlet letter on her chest. *A for Abandonment.* If only it were absolution.

Nell waved one of those fingertip waves as Sam, who was now standing behind Nell, gave Jayne a quick nod that said a thousand things.

First and foremost it said *Don't you dare let Maggie down.* He was watching her.

Her heart suddenly weighed about a million pounds. It looked as if Whitticombe wasn't the time machine she'd thought it might be after all.

Jayne slammed the ladies' room door shut and headed straight to the sink. She threw cold water on her face, willing it to help the heat fade from her cheeks.

She'd known coming back would be tough, but talk about out of the frying pan and into the fire!

She caught her own eye in the mirror and saw things through the chinks in her armour that she barely wanted to acknowledge. Loneliness. Loss.

Maybe you don't want to be alone as much as you think you do. Maybe that's why you came back here instead of running even further away.

She quelled a frustrated howl and stamped her foot. She was living the life she wanted to live. The life her sister couldn't. If that meant sucking it up in London and trying to do the things her adrenaline junkie sister would normally have had to beg her to do, so be it.

So she didn't like bungee jumping? She could get over that. And the constant hum and buzz of city life. And the late night clubbing. And, and, and...

What she *did* love was her job. While there were no silver linings in losing Jules, her sister's death had brought out a love for paediatric surgery Jayne would have never known she had. She genuinely, one hundred per cent, loved what she did for a living.

Which begged the question why had she come running back to Whitticombe instead of perfecting her techniques at the hospital?

Helping children at their most vulnerable moments was one of the most rewarding things in the world. *Except when it wasn't.*

The truth brought streaks of red to her cheeks.

Losing Stella had thrown her right back to that day when she'd lost her sister. And feeling that level of pain and loss meant being in Whitticombe. So here she was dodging her ex—in the loo.

Now what? Stay in here until everyone had gone home?

Hardly.

She blinked away a couple of tears and forced her brain to take part in the conversation.

Losing Stella was a loss...but not a failure. She knew that intellectually. Her heart took a nose-dive as memories flooded in. But losing Stella with *that* particular heart and then crying about it... That was proof—as if she needed any—that she was still wrestling with her sister's death.

She forced herself to look at the mirror again. She'd sometimes pretend she was looking into Jules's eyes when she looked into her reflection. Sometimes she genuinely thought she caught glimpses of her. Especially when she was scrubbing in for surgery. They'd been identical twins, after all.

But lately it had been harder to drum up that vital, energy-charged version of herself. The version that was part Jayne and part Jules. She had no idea who she was looking at right now. Seven years was a long time to keep a ghost alive.

She stuck her tongue out at her reflection, then forced a silly grin. She was here for Maggie. Sure, it might not have started out that way, but it was a chance to prove she could do something good in the world.

An image of Sam's dubious expression popped into her head. She quickly shook it away.

Six weeks. She could do just about anything for six weeks.

She pushed through the door, determined to make a better go of it, and bashed straight into a chest. A chest that smelt of grass and wood and a kick of grapefruit as the perfect olfactory chaser.

In other words it was a chest that smelt of Sam Crenshaw.

Couldn't a girl get five minutes on her own to wrestle with her past?

Trying to keep her voice light—fun, even—Jayne looked up into those green eyes of his and joked, 'Look, Sam, I know I don't have a great track record in sticking around, but I'm pretty sure you can count on me not to climb out through the window of the ladies' loo.'

He tilted his chin to the side and gave her a confused look. 'I was just checking that you were all right. You looked upset.'

Score one to Sam for still being able to read her emotional barometer.

But she couldn't accept sympathy from him. Not with her yo-yoing emotions.

'Aw… You wanted to make sure my heart wasn't breaking because you're on a date? Don't you worry. I'm not jealous.'

Sam's arched eyebrow made a reappearance.

Oh, sugar. She was *totally* jealous.

If Jayne could have thrown herself into the world's deepest pool of quicksand she would have done it. Immediately.

She pulled her ponytail across her eyes, unwilling to read what was going on in Sam's. 'Sorry…sorry. I'm happy for you. Of all the people in the universe, you deserve happiness.'

'And you don't?'

She dropped her ponytail and felt it swish between her shoulder blades as her eyes met Sam's.

Now, *that* was a loaded question.

His eyebrow dropped back into place. His tight smile softened. He lifted his hand up and swept the backs of his fingers against her cheek.

Against everything her brain was screaming at her to do, she leant into them. A cardinal sin if ever there was one.

Sparks flooded her bloodstream and her heart bashed against her ribcage so hard she was sure the unicorn on her T-shirt looked as if it was galloping. Not that she could tear her eyes away from his and check. It might have been raining diamonds at this very moment and she wouldn't have noticed.

'Miss me?' he asked softly.

'Yeah…' She only just managed to deadpan. 'Something *awful*.'

She did actually. Always had. More than she'd ever admit. To *him* anyway. Each Christmas at the pub she'd seek out his dog, Elf, and whisper it into his ear. Elf always licked her nose as if he got it.

Sam took a step closer towards her.

'How much?'

Her heart skipped a beat. And then quite a few more. She hadn't been this close to Sam in years. Being touched by him…her body wanting nothing more than to be just that little bit closer…they were just the beginning of a myriad reasons why coming home had never been on her to-do list.

She felt the space between the two of them diminish.

Maybe it was the failed surgery. Maybe it was seeing him with another woman. Maybe it was the simple fact that she'd loved Sam Crenshaw for near enough her entire life and being here with him and not touching him was next to impossible.

They were going to kiss. She could see it in the angle of his chin. Feel it in his fingers on hers. Her heels lifting off the ground so she could reach his mouth.

Just as her feet felt as if they were going to begin floating Sam pulled back. He scrubbed his hands through his hair and looked about as confused as she felt.

What had *that* been about? Another test?

If it had been an experiment to see if there were still

a few sparks flying between them, Jayne was pretty sure they had the answer to that.

'I'm guessing that wasn't meant to happen.' Jayne made a couple of comedy noises to show Sam she was willing to pretend it had never happened if he was.

He cleared his throat and rubbed his hand along the back of his neck. 'Right, um...'

Sam didn't seem to know which way to look. Anywhere but at her seemed to be working for him.

'I was just on my way to put some orders in at the bar. Want anything?'

'No, I'd better not. I'm driving Maggie and the children back.'

When he turned around she skimmed her fingers across her lips, as if they had actually been bruised by the kisses that never came, then scraped the sensation away with her nails.

She watched as he strode swiftly to the bar, taking note of all the waves and back-slaps and hellos he received on the way. Just like his father and grandfather before him, he was a valued member of the community. Someone people respected. Someone people loved. Someone they'd protect...

All of the sudden the low hum of activity from the playing field burst into cries of dismay, quickly followed by loud calls for Sam.

Sam ran as fast as he could. Faster when he saw it was his grandad lying stretched out at the far end of the cricket pitch.

Calls to clear the area and to give Ernest some air wrapped round him as he knelt down by his grandfather, who was trying to push himself up to seating.

'It's all right, Sammy. It's just a sprained ankle.'

Sam knew his grandad wasn't critically injured, but the wince and the quick breaths he was taking told him the seventy-eight-year-old had taken a proper fall.

Ernest gave his wrist a tentative back-and-forth bend which indicated that would need a look as well. If he'd been looking up into the air for the cricket ball, then tripped and stumbled, he definitely would've used his wrists to blunt the fall.

Sam sat back on his heels and grinned. 'What sort of stunt move was it this time, Grandad? Did you think you were playing for England today?'

His grandfather waved him off and reached out to pull up his trouser cuffs. His knees weren't stained green, which meant they hadn't taken any of his weight either. At his age there were also his hips to think about. Bone infection if there was a break. Nerve or blood vessel damage. Arthritis.

It was a long list.

Sam was just about to start in on the stream of questions that followed an injury like this when he felt rather than saw Jayne kneeling by his side and sliding a first aid kit into place between them.

His grandad's eyes brightened.

Despite the intense moment they'd shared earlier, Sam found it strangely reassuring to have her there. Sure, it wasn't a critical injury, but Sam had cared for his mother whilst she was dying of cancer and that had been tough. A blunt reminder of exactly why doctors treating their own family was not a good thing.

It made his heart stop for a moment as he reminded himself that Jayne had been all on her own when her sister had been struck by that sports car. She must have been absolutely terrified. He'd been over and over the scenario a million times and it always ended the same way. With a diamond ring in his hand.

Had he been so blinded by the way she'd shut him out that he'd genuinely not realised how helpless she'd felt?

His family had drawn even closer together during his mother's illness. The opposite had happened to Jayne's. As if the injuries Jules had sustained had had a ripple effect. Little wonder... They'd had no time to prepare.

As awful as it had been to see his mother so ill, they'd had time to prepare. To attack her bucket list. To say they loved her and to say goodbye. Jayne and her parents hadn't had any of that. The world as they'd known it had changed in the blink of an eye.

'Jayne? What on earth are you doing here?' Ernest dropped her a wink, then winced. 'They didn't drop you in from some sort of helicopter ambulance, did they?'

'Oh, no—that's the sort of thing my sister would—' She stopped and gave her head a short shake. 'I've brought along the cricket club's first aid kit. Someone mentioned a stretcher and they're having a dig around for that.' She made a quick scan though the medical kit. 'I'm guessing we should start with some ice packs.' She held one out to Sam. 'Shall I play nurse to your doctor?'

It should have been a loaded question. She was a surgeon. He was a GP. In this scenario this kind of injury was his proverbial bread and butter. But Sam knew Jayne wasn't pulling any sort of rank. Injuries like this needed to be treated quickly.

Sam's grandad might have been born and raised in the heart of World War II—and might be the poster boy for stiff upper lips—but he was going pretty pale.

It was easy to see they needed to get him to hospital for a thorough check.

'Are we going to go straightforward P-R-I-C-E on this one?'

Sam nodded. *Protect, rest, ice, compress and elevate.* The easiest and most effective guidelines for a minor soft tissue injury. 'There are no obvious breaks. Not from what I've seen. Want to double-check his ankle for me?'

'I hope you two aren't forgetting I *am* actually a doctor,' Ernest piped up.

'Not at all,' said Jayne. 'You're the reason I wanted to become one in the first place.'

Sam smiled and accepted a stretchy bandage to wrap round his grandad's wrist.

He remembered when Jayne's mum had used to bring bright flushes of red to her daughter's cheeks as she told the story of Jayne bringing a cloth dolly to the doctor's surgery as a little girl. She and Jules had become embroiled in a tug of war and the doll had been its victim. Her little cloth hand had been torn off and Jayne had been inconsolable. Ernest had taken the doll, put it on the exam table and asked it a few questions. Then carefully inserted an IV before pulling the curtain round him while he deftly stitched the hand back on and handed the doll to Jayne as good as new.

He refocused on his grandfather's wrist. 'The way the swelling's ballooning on your wrist, Grandad, I'm afraid you're going to need an X-ray.'

'The ankle as well,' Jayne said apologetically as she gingerly lifted his grandfather's foot.

The exposed area between his trousers and his sock was already visibly swollen, and taking on some rather unnatural hues.

'I'm just going to take your shoe off, if that's all right?'

''Course it is! I'd do it myself if my grandson here would quit his fussing over my wrist. It's only—*ouch!*' He pulled his arm protectively to his chest. 'Well… maybe an X-ray would be a good idea.'

After a couple of men had shown up with the stretcher, and they'd rolled his grandfather on to his side to load him up, Ernest began grumbling—a good sign that his injuries weren't too serious.

'I have a load of patients on the roster tomorrow,' he protested. 'So the sooner we sort this the better.'

Sam barked a laugh. 'You're not going anywhere near a patient for at least a week.'

'What?' Ernest squawked. 'There is *no* chance you can run that surgery on your own.'

Sam got ready to launch into a well-rehearsed speech about how he'd been getting himself up to speed for the past three years so he could do precisely that. He would leave out the part about how they had always meant for there to be two of them in the surgery. But before he could say anything Jayne's voice filled a brief lull in the general hubbub.

'I could help.'

He felt as if the entire village had taken a collective breath. Of course it wasn't true, but as most of the people here knew their history it felt that way.

'You've already got Maggie to look after—and the children.' If there was a grateful way to wave off an offer of help he hoped he was doing it.

She shrugged. She clearly wasn't going to push it.

'Fair enough. But Maggie lives three doors down from the surgery. I'm pretty sure I could run down any time you need me.' She pulled her mobile phone out of her pocket. 'I think that's what these are for.'

Sam was about to protest again, but before he could say anything Jayne put her hands up.

'Don't worry about it. Just saying… The offer's there if you need it.'

Then she walked away.

It was a view he should be used to. And not in a sexy way as her thighs and bum swished against the fabric of her skirt, either.

He never should have touched her. Feeling the soft skin of her cheek had brought back countless good memories when he should be focusing on the bad ones. The reasons they weren't meant to be together.

'It's all right, Grandad. I can hold the fort for a few weeks if necessary.' Before his grandfather could protest he added, 'It'll only be a week if they really are just sprains. Two at most.'

His grandfather shook his head. 'You've had an offer of help, son. You'd be a damn fool not to take it.'

Sam knew what he was saying. It was hard to admit to needing help. But sometimes you simply had to do it.

If only Jayne had accepted *his* offers accepting hers now would be a moot point…because she'd already be by his side.

CHAPTER FOUR

A FEW HOURS into his work day and Sam was regretting refusing Jayne's offer. His grandfather had sustained a fracture in his wrist and a sprain in his ankle. The fractured wrist meant he would be off work for a few weeks, whether he liked it or not. Their patients' care was first and foremost and a doctor in a sling wasn't ideal.

Greta, the surgeon's long-time receptionist, was run off her feet, trying to reschedule non-urgent patients and Sam was trying to dispense with the 'take all the time you need' philosophy he prided himself on.

He jotted down a couple of numbers then turned to his current patient. 'The blood pressure pills definitely seem to be doing the trick, Mrs Greenfield.'

'No!'

Sam laughed. Denial wasn't the usual response he got when something was going according to plan. He turned the blood pressure monitor towards his sixty-something patient. 'See for yourself. Lowest blood pressure you've had in years.'

'I can see it well enough, Sam. My eyesight's never been the problem. Oops. Sorry. *Dr Crenshaw.*' The grey-haired woman tittered at her mistake. 'I'm still just so used to your grandfather being the only Dr Crenshaw in town.'

'I've been your doctor for three years now, Mrs Greenfield,' Sam reminded her playfully.

'I know…but you're also the same little boy who used to mow my lawn.'

Sam grinned. 'If memory serves, I'm *still* the same boy who mows your lawn.'

Mrs Greenfield smiled. 'Yes… You've been good to me since I lost my Daniel.'

She gave a quiet little sigh and pressed her hands to her heart. Her husband had died some fifteen years ago and she still wore her… *Wait a minute.* Where was her wedding ring?

As if she'd read his mind, Mrs Greenfield turned her focus to her hands as she wove her bare fingers together on her lap. 'Dr Crenshaw, I'm curious. Do you think that, rather than the pills, *love* might have something to do with lower blood pressure?'

'Love?' This appointment wasn't going in the direction he'd anticipated.

Mrs Greenfield nodded, but didn't meet his eye.

Love as an antidote to high blood pressure? *His* blood pressure had just about shot off the scale when Jayne had walked into his office yesterday. Double that when they'd nearly kissed. He didn't know what sort of divine intervention had pulled him back from that mistake, but… It was a path best left unexplored.

'I'm taking it from your silence, Dr Crenshaw, that there is no scientific evidence to suggest that love might lower blood pressure?'

'Apologies, Mrs Greenfield.' He scribbled a few numbers on a notepad to make it look as though he'd been doing some calculations. 'Your question caught me off guard.'

'Made you think of romance, did it?' Mrs Greenfield teased, and then she pushed the blood pressure cuff towards Sam. 'Should we be checking out *your* stats? From what I hear, things were very lively at the cricket ground last night.'

Sam suddenly saw where this was going and did his best to steer the conversation in another direction. 'Jayne is back in town to look after Maggie. Nothing to do with me.'

Mrs Greenfield's looked perplexed. 'Jayne? Jayne Sinclair's back in town? I was talking about Greta's niece—Nell. The shy one? Greta was telling me all about it before my appointment.'

Terrific. Greta was the most proactive contributor to the Whitticombe grapevine. And Nell had clearly not passed on to her aunt the 'I'm not really in the market for a relationship' talk he'd had with her when she'd suggested they have a second drink. It had been a white lie on his part, but one he'd thought would protect them both.

'Yes…well…it's always nice to show someone new about town.'

Mrs Greenfield sat back in her chair. 'Ooh, Jayne Sinclair… Now, that takes me back to when I heard that awful screech of tyres just outside on the lane.'

Sam didn't need to ask for embellishment. Mrs Greenfield was talking about the day Jayne's sister had been killed. Things like that didn't happen all that often in Whitticombe, so when they did the scars ran deep. Too deep, in Jayne's case. But he hadn't been there. Didn't know first-hand what she'd been through. He'd certainly treated enough retired servicemen to know that watching someone die wasn't just something you forgot about.

'Such a shame, that was,' Mrs Greenfield continued. 'Her poor parents… How they soldiered on here in Whitticombe is beyond me. I would've moved if I were in their shoes. Would never have been able to set foot in this village ever again.'

A lightbulb pinged on in Sam's head. A few months after Jules had died, Jayne had announced that she wanted to become a paediatric cardiologist. She'd said the only way to pursue her dreams was to live in London. He'd been utterly thrown, because she'd always wanted to be a GP and paediatrician right here in this very surgery.

He'd taken what she'd said at face value. As a slight, even. As if she'd been saying that living in Whitticombe equated to settling for second best rather than seeing it as he did—total life fulfilment. Whitticombe had everything the two of them had valued. Family, friends, a strong community that came together in time of crisis. There were hospitals nearby if Jayne wanted to pursue more advanced paediatric care. Research facilities in Oxford. But mostly…it was *home*.

A community, family and friends Jayne had closed the door on when she would surely have needed them most.

Had he been focusing on the wrong thing all these years? Had Jayne been running from the nightmare of her sister's death rather than pursuing a dream?

That look of pain in her eyes when he'd asked her whether she thought she deserved happiness… Had Jayne been punishing herself all these years?

It had been an accident. Yes…an accident that she would be constantly reminded of every time she came home.

Half of him wanted to pull Mrs Greenfield up into his arms and kiss her. The other half wondered why it had taken him so long to see something so obvious.

'So…about this love theory of mine…'

'Yes. Sorry, Mrs Greenfield.' Sam scrubbed a hand through his hair, hoping it would release all the Jayne-centric thoughts and allow him to concentrate on his patient. 'What's this theory?'

'Well…' She threw him a coy look. 'I have been enjoying visits from a certain gentleman caller lately.'

Sam's eyebrows shot up. 'Oh?'

Mrs Greenfield's cheeks pinked up. 'It's nothing too racy, Sam. Don't worry.'

He wasn't worried. He was delighted for her. If a bit surprised. He'd thought Mrs Greenfield to be a one-man kind of woman. The same way his father was and his grandfather before him had been. Crenshaw men seemed to pick a woman early on, set his heart at her feet and then get about the business of loving her for the rest of their lives.

Sam gave his jaw a scrub. He obviously wasn't quite as successful as his forebears. It probably worked better when the woman you loved was a willing participant.

'So, who's this fancy man of yours, then?'

'Oh, Sam. He's no fancy man!' Mrs Greenfield chided. 'He's a *gentle*man.'

The way her voice and features softened spoke volumes. She was in love.

'And may I ask how you met this gentleman?'

Her cheeks flushed a soft pink. 'Oh! Well, we were sweethearts back in the day.'

'What? I thought you and Daniel had been an item from the get-go.'

'Oh, no. Not at all. I had what they used to call "a past".'

'Mrs Greenfield! You're shocking me.'

She batted at the air between them. 'Oh, you... I am not. It was nothing, really. Just a flirtation in the school playground. It never amounted to anything. Not back then, anyway. Flirtations were definitely much more conservative back in those days.'

Despite the patients waiting out in Reception, Sam's curiosity overrode the ten-minute window he was supposed to have for each patient. 'So...how did he go from being a bit of a playground Lothario to the gentleman who's lowered your blood pressure?'

'The Lothario's name is Colin.' Her gaze went a little soft focus and dreamy. 'Colin was ambitious back then. *Very* ambitious. Big plans. Big dreams. He didn't want to stay in the tiny little village where we'd grown up and I did. So...he went off to seek his fortune.'

'And came back to Whitticombe to claim it?'

'Something like that.' Mrs Greenfield laughed. 'It wasn't Whitticombe. Smaller, if you can imagine. Anyway, Colin moved all over the world. Made his fortune. Lost it. And his family.' She leant forward and explained, 'His wife turned out to be a bit of a fair weather wife. She didn't like Poor Colin as much as she liked Rich Colin. Anyway!' She swept Colin's past into the bin with a flick of her hand. 'He's started again. New business. New lifestyle choices. New girlfriend.' She made a *ta-da* gesture with her hands.

There were about a thousand things Sam wanted to examine from Mrs Greenfield's story. The childhood romance. The pursuit of dreams. The lessons learnt. The love that was given a second chance. The trust it must take to believe he'd stick around.

Trust.

There it was. The elephant in the room, standing between him and Jayne. He didn't trust her to stay. She didn't trust him to give her the life she wanted.

A perfect impasse.

Sam did his own version of flicking his romantic failures into the bin, opting to stick to his patient's needs. He made a few notes and came to a decision. 'I think we can thank Colin for this.' He ripped up the prescription for more blood pressure pills he'd started making earlier.

'Looks like it.' Mrs Greenfield beamed, then patted his hand. 'Do help Greta transport all those cakes and stews queuing up in Reception to your grandfather, won't you?'

Sam smiled and nodded. Village hospitality at its finest.

He stood, and as he did so Mrs Greenfield said, 'Sam, you know we're all here for you, don't you? In whatever way you need.'

He did. But he wasn't about to fall on his romance sword in front of the entire village again. Not with Jayne anyway. Maybe not ever again.

Butterflies were swooping all around her tummy as Jayne walked down the Victorian tiled corridor to the second door on the right, as Greta had instructed her. She'd come for entirely professional reasons, but everything about being home felt personal.

Home.

What a loaded word.

She started as she heard that rich, all too familiar voice come through the door, then trickle down her spine like warm honey. Her fingers drifted up to her un-kissed lips and, despite trying not to remember just how much she had wanted it, she swept out her tongue to soothe the heat away.

'Come on in, Maggie. Why aren't you putting your feet—?' Sam pulled open the door and stopped dead in his tracks when his eyes met Jayne's. 'Ah. It's you.'

Not quite the response she'd been hoping for, but she supposed it was a response she should get used to. He was moving on with his life…and she was a blip from his past.

Sam crossed his arms over her chest. His lovely, warm, solid chest.

'What are you doing here?'

Okay. Someone's bedside manner could do with a bit of work today.

'I brought some cake for your grandad. Don't worry. I didn't make it.'

'Jayne. It's incredibly busy and you know you could've just brought it to the house. Why are you here?'

Swallowing back a sharp retort that went something along the lines of *I told you I would help but you refused in front of everyone*, she said, 'I wanted to go over Maggie's notes with you, *as she requested*, but if you're too busy I can just ring some nameless, faceless person at the hospital.'

Sam ushered her in. 'Apologies.' He didn't sound all that sorry. 'I— The appointment was in Maggie's name so I was surprised, that's all.'

He looked tired. He hadn't shaved. The mix of gold and auburn stubble suited him, but she could tell by the way he scrubbed at it uncomfortably that he wasn't used to it.

'How's your grandad?'

'Good. Well, sore and bruised, and already driving my sisters batty, but… It's a fracture in his wrist and a sprained ankle. He'll be the size of a house if he eats all the cakes that have been flooding in.'

Jayne stifled a laugh as she thought of Sam's sisters flying round Ernest, tending to him with all the fuss and bother Sam's mum had been so good at. They were a family of natural comforters. Unlike her own who—when tested—had discovered that they preferred to lick their wounds in private.

Or maybe you sent yourself to purgatory and didn't give them a chance.

She sat down in the chair Sam hadn't yet suggested she sat in even though she was pretty sure that's how the whole doctor-patient thing worked. *Come in. Sit down. How may I help you?*

Sam let his chair accept his full weight and started tapping away on his computer. He had yet to meet her eyes again.

Her heart split wide open for him. She got it. Having her show up out of the blue had to be awful for him. If the tables had been turned she probably would've run away.

Just like you did after Jules died.

No. She hadn't run away. She'd changed. Doggedly poured her energies, her determination…her *grief*…into becoming the best paediatric cardio surgeon she could. One who could do transplants, so that the next time she was in a seemingly impossible situation she could do something about it.

A sick feeling washed through her as she thought of Stella's grief-stricken parents. The loss they must be feeling because of her.

The organ didn't take. It wasn't your fault.

She desperately wanted to talk it out with someone. And not just any anyone. She wanted to talk it out with Sam. He would get it. When they'd started out in med school they'd used to talk on the phone for hours about just that very thing. The cruel randomness of illness. The limits of medicine. The power of talking things through.

He doesn't want to talk to you.

Sam tapped his desk. Presumably so that she would get on with it. She closed her eyes to regroup and opened them just in time to see him lick his lips.

Damn, the man was sexy. She crossed her legs again and sat up straight.

His eyes flicked up to the wall clock. 'Jayne...? There's a waiting room full of patients—what do you want?'

She pulled a notebook from her tote bag. 'I wanted to get your take on everything Maggie's been experiencing. I've read the hospital notes, but I thought you'd know better than her part-time doctor there.'

'Or her part-time friend?'

Ouch!

The barbed words had hit their mark. This definitely wasn't going to be the breezy chit-chat about Maggie's health she'd been hoping for.

'We text. *And* email.'

Sam's lips thinned.

Fine. She could have been a better friend. Come home more regularly. Not counted on pure happenstance to put her in Maggie's path when she needed her most.

Questions flooded in where she should have had answers.

What if she'd stayed? What if she'd finally opened up to her parents, Sam—everyone—and admitted what she and she alone knew. That she was responsible for her sister's death.

If she had stayed…and by some miracle been forgiven… she might be married now. To Sam. Maybe even have children of her own. But that was a big *if.* Before forgiveness must come the courage to admit her failures. Failures that gnawed at her conscience every single day.

She was alive. Her sister wasn't. And there was no one else in the world who could make her sister's dreams come true.

She pressed her hands to her face and peeked at Sam through her fingers. If only she was brave enough to tell him her deepest, darkest secret.

She rubbed her fingers along her closed eyes and saw flashes of light where she usually saw her sister, flying round the corner from their small lane to the larger one…a mane of jet-black hair flying in her wake…the oncoming rush of a yellow sports car.

If she was going to do this—stay here, help Maggie, not fight with Sam—she was going to have to fall on her sword.

'Sam…' She dropped her hands, trying to control the waves of emotion ricocheting around her insides. 'I know I hurt you—'

He huffed out a humourless laugh. '*I'm* not the one we're talking about here.'

'I think we are,' she countered. 'If you don't trust me to do what's best for Maggie then this is going to be really difficult.'

His eyes flashed bright. She knew what they were saying. He didn't trust her. He was braced for her to be difficult. He was braced for her to leave again.

Something deep inside her—something so deep she rarely let herself acknowledge it—surged into her heart. *Longing.* A longing to bring about that soft look that used to pour through his features when he turned and saw her. The complicit wink he'd used to throw her way that only she had understood. The smile she knew was especially for her.

Her fingers instinctively moved to her lips and shifted across them.

'Can you not do that, please?' Sam shifted uncomfortably in his chair and looked away.

'What?'

'Touch your lips like that.'

'Well, then you shouldn't have almost kissed me,' she snapped, instantly regretting it.

His features hardened. 'I think it was the other way round, actually.'

She was the one who'd gone up on tiptoe. He was the one who'd sought her out in the first place.

Doing her best not to sound defensive, she looked Sam straight in the eye. 'Let's focus on Maggie, shall we? I'm here today. I will be here tomorrow. And the next day and the next. I will be here right up until Maggie has those babies. Longer if need be.'

Sam shook his head and waved his hands for her to stop. 'Jay...'

Her heart leapt to her throat. He hadn't called her plain old Jay in years. 'Yes?'

When he met her eyes again she caught a glimpse of all the heartache she had caused, and then, in the blink of an eye, it was gone. 'Look. You're partly right. About *"the moment"* yesterday.'

At least he was admitting it was a moment.

He looked down at his desk and continued. 'I shouldn't have come after you. You looked upset. Gut instinct kicked in. But... I should've let you be. You're your own boss now.'

A lead weight hit her gut like a wrecking ball. *Wow.* That stung. She was too late even to win his friendship. Had something happened between yesterday and today that had turned him so hard?

Yes, you idiot. The moment.

'Why did you do it? Follow me?'

'I wanted to see if anything was still there.'

It was about as honest an answer as a girl could ask for.

From the look on his face, he regretted the admission. As they were being so blunt she decided to get the whole truth, whether she liked his response or not.

'And was there?'

Sam scrubbed his hand across his chin, then fixed her with a look she would never forget. It was hard, unforgiving and set in stone.

'No. Nothing.'

Then he turned to his computer, printed out a few contact numbers at the nearby hospital in Oxford, handed the piece of paper to her and suggested she call Maggie's obstetrician in future.

Well, then, she thought numbly as she left his office, at least she knew where she stood.

Three days later Sam was still kicking himself for being so awful to Jayne.

Sure. She'd broken his heart back in the day. She had also apologised. Countless times. None of them had ever stuck because he'd never truly believed she was following her heart.

Maybe it was time to believe it. It had been seven years. If the medical journals he'd accidentally-on-purpose pored through were to be believed, she'd hit some stellar professional heights. You didn't work at the London Merryweather because you were in a slump. You worked there because you had a dream. Of being the best.

An image of the hurt lancing through Jayne's eyes popped into his head so vividly he sucked in a sharp breath. Emotion had got the better of him. He'd needed to make a point. Re-draw that line in the sand.

But there had been no need to be so cruel. Or to lie.

He'd felt something. Of *course* he'd felt something. That same old surge of flame licking at everything that made him a man had hit hard and fast the second her lips were within centimetres of his own. And it had hurt. He had wanted to feel nothing.

But no amount of hurt should reduce him to lashing out at a person for a nanosecond's pleasure. And he hadn't even got that. If anything, the hurt he'd caused her had only made him feel worse.

Which was why he was standing outside Maggie's house with a basketful of truce croissants. Jayne's favourite. At least they had been back in the day.

He rang the bell and half considered leaving them on

the stone doorstep, before reminding himself that grown men didn't run away from self-made conflict. Grown men took calculated risks...with a bit of a buffer if they needed a quick escape.

Offer gift. Apologise. Agree to move on. Go back to surgery where there's a ton of paperwork to tackle. Get on with life.

Easy-peasy.

The second Jayne opened the door he instantly knew his plan had flaws. The Jayne standing in the doorway of the chocolate box cottage was the Jayne he'd fallen in love with.

Her inky black hair was falling free from a pair of messy topknots. Her bright blue eyes were made up all smoky and mysterious. Her nose was painted black and she had a full set of cat whiskers fanning out across her cheeks, as well as a pair of bright red lips. A curve-hugging cat suit with a zipper that sat just below that delicious divot at the base of her throat and ran right the way down to her belly button completed the outfit.

'Interesting look.' Not really the opening gambit he'd been going for, but...

She looked confused for a minute, then realised he was referring to her face. 'Ha! Yes. Um...the kids and I were having a bit of a practice session this morning and I got distracted. Did you know having children in the house equals about nineteen times the amount of laundry I'm used to?'

She looked nervous. Bracing herself for a repeat of their last fractious encounter, no doubt.

'Are you planning on spending the summer as a house cat?'

Whether she said yes or no, she looked completely endearing. And very, very sexy.

'We were going to put on a play for Maggie. Ears.' She pointed to her topknots and then to the kitchen table, where an array of children's costumes were spread out. 'They dressed me up this morning, while Maggie was having a lie-in. I thought I'd go through the children's costumes while they were at school to see if I could come up with something inspired.'

'Apart from doing your own version of *Cats*?'

'Ha! No. I think you'll remember my singing voice is more like a feral cat than an opera singer. Maggie's the only one with talent in that department.'

She opened the lower half of the barn-style door and stood to the side so he could duck under the thick beam of a doorframe and come into the kitchen.

She pointed at her face. 'This was Cailey's handiwork. I let her raid Maggie's amateur dramatics make-up box before school. To help alleviate the boredom.'

'Cailey's or Maggie's?'

Jayne laughed. 'Maggie's. Definitely Maggie's.'

'She's bored already? I thought she'd be thrilled to tackle a few boxsets.'

He didn't really. Maggie was *always* doing something. Experimenting with new cake flavours for the tearoom. Setting up the village fete. Cheering on her husband at the annual Whitticombe river football match. When her obstetrician had rung Sam and recommended Maggie be put on bedrest for the final few weeks of her pregnancy, the first words Maggie had uttered were 'House arrest, you mean.'

Jayne cracked a proper smile this time. The type that

could put a movie star to shame. Resisting that smile was like stopping time. Impossible.

'Last night she started watching online videos to teach herself how to crochet, because she's already knitted three new baby blankets.'

'What? Since last week?'

Jayne leant against the wooden kitchen counter and drew her top teeth over her lower lip. 'You might not know this, but Maggie doesn't really do relaxation all that well.'

Sam was about to say he was pretty sure he knew Maggie better than Jayne did, seeing as he saw her near enough every day, then stopped himself. He wasn't here to nark. He was here to offer an olive branch. Not stare at her teeth, or her lips, or her adorable button nose.

Big breath in...big breath out.

That was something he hadn't had to do in a while. The old trick of counting down until he'd made sure he wouldn't say something he was going to regret. His grandad had taught him that one when he'd had one too many patients asking to see 'the *grown-up* Dr Crenshaw...'

Three...two...one.

Coming here was meant to return him to an even keel, not throw him further off-course. Three days of trying to pretend Jayne wasn't in town had shredded his relaxed demeanour to bits.

He had hurt her with his unnecessary—and untrue—remark about having felt nothing when they had nearly kissed. Of *course* he'd felt something. He'd felt *everything*. And that was precisely why he'd denied it. Because for every ounce of pleasure he felt when he was with Jayne, he felt an equal serving of pain.

As if they'd made a decision to move on from small

talk about Maggie, Jayne gave a shrug and pointed at his hand. 'What's in your basket, Goldilocks? Are you stealing things from your grandad's growing pile of get-well baked goods?'

'Believe it or not...' He lifted up the basketful of croissants. 'These are expressly for you.'

'Really?' She shot him a look of disbelief as she accepted the basket and inhaled deeply. 'Did you get these at the Vanilla Bean Bakery?'

'Is there anywhere else to buy croissants in Whitticombe?'

He wasn't going to tell her about Carla's raised eyebrows when he'd ordered them. Sam had near enough kept her bakery afloat back in the day, sending croissant care packages to Jayne when she was in med school. After she'd broken their engagement, sales had plummeted.

Jayne danced her fingers over the basket, selected a croissant, then took a huge bite. 'Ooh, almond. My favourite.' She blinked a few times, then looked up at him as her cheeks pinked up. 'You remembered?'

Of course he did. He remembered a lot of things. The first time they'd gone to the cinema and she'd pretended to be scared so they could hold hands. The first time they'd kissed. The first time they'd made love. Watching her pack to go to a different university. Standing beside her at her sister's funeral.

Just about all of the big firsts that mattered in life he'd done with Jayne.

He stopped himself from reaching out and brushing some icing sugar off her cheek. Instead he said, 'I was hoping we could maybe have a do-over. Pretend the other day down at the cricket ground went a bit more...

platonically. It was a bit of a shock to see you when you showed up at the surgery the next day. I—'

'Aftershocks?' she said, not unkindly.

She got it. She was feeling it, too.

Her tongue dipped out between her lips and licked away some of the sugar at the corner of her mouth. He felt a match-strike run the length of his zip.

Damn, this was harder than he'd thought.

Jayne's brows cinched closer together as she chewed on her lower lip and then, as if she'd made a decision, released it. 'Shall I put the kettle on?'

'Depends on whether or not you want to draw up a treaty.' Why was he kicking up those flames again?

Jayne bristled. 'I thought you were here to apologise.'

'I was. Am. I'm trying—'

He *was* trying. Trying not to pull his heart out of his chest and simply hand it to her, as he had all of those years ago.

He pulled his phone out of his pocket instead. This was obviously going to take longer than he'd thought.

'Go on. Put the kettle on.'

CHAPTER FIVE

JAYNE TRIED NOT to earwig too much while Sam called Greta at the surgery, but it was hard not to sit down, plop her chin in her hand and grin at him as he rattled through all sorts of complex details about his patients without a single note.

When he asked after a woman they'd both gone to school with, who'd just found out she had cancer, she went into the washroom and tried to scrub her face clean.

She scrubbed as hard as she could. The way Sam dealt with everyone he'd known since he was a boy so professionally and compassionately was…exactly what she'd expect from him. He'd been born to do this. Not literally, of course, as he was adopted, but when Mrs Crenshaw had insisted on bringing that little abandoned baby boy home there had to have been a touch of the angels about it.

She looked into the mirror to check if her face was clean. No good. Maggie's daughter had used a permanent marker for the whiskers and the nose. *Nice.*

She came back into the kitchen just as Sam was thanking Greta for saying she'd pop in on his grandad as he'd need the afternoon off after all.

Nerves bunched in her belly. She'd meant for them to

have a chat, not spend the rest of the day together. Especially if he had work to do.

Stream's Edge Surgery was his pride and joy. He'd never been shy about wanting to follow in his grandfather's footsteps—saw it as the best way possible to show his adoptive family just how much he loved them. It wasn't a duty. Or a penance. It was love. He would do absolutely anything for them. It was one of the most appealing things about him beyond his being *him*. His loyalty.

When he saw she was not so covertly looking at him, Sam cupped his hand over his mobile's mouthpiece and explained to her that today was his catch-up day.

'Is that code for playing golf?' she joked.

Of the many things Sam Crenshaw was, a golfer was definitely not one of them. He'd be a bit like her in the kitchen. All thumbs and no taste buds.

He rolled those gorgeous green eyes of his and returned to his call.

The hammering in her heart slowed down a tiny bit. At least he was relaxed enough to roll his eyes at her lame joke. But if she was ever going to pull herself out of the past she was going to have to accept that things had changed—that Sam had changed.

Sure. He had a bit of a white-haired thing going on around the temples. But it was more than that. The fact he was here at all spoke volumes. When they'd split up he had protested. Said he didn't believe she didn't love him any more. But when she'd insisted that her calling was to become a surgeon at London's top children's hospital he'd finally stepped back. Not happily, but he understood a calling more than most.

His was to work in the surgery. To be with his family. To support the community that had nurtured him as he'd grown up. The Sam she'd known had let sleeping dogs lie for seven years. But this Sam—the one who'd weathered a divorce and the death of his mother…the one who'd proactively accepted a role as a caretaker for his community…this Sam was an adult. An adult asking her to confront their unfinished business.

One way or another, he looked determined to finish it.

Jayne tried to fight the nerves jangling round her insides as she filled the kettle, put a few of the croissants on a plate and then rearranged them about nineteen times. Having what was shaping up to be a serious conversation with Sam while she was dressed as a cat was…well, *awkward* was one way to put it.

Just as she was about to see if washing up liquid might take away some of the ink, he finished the call and pulled out a chair at the kitchen table.

'Shall we?'

Sam didn't miss the hint of nerves in Jayne's laugh as she slid the mugs of tea onto the table, pulled out a chair and sat down.

'This all seems very formal.'

'Well… I think I probably owe you more than a few croissants.'

She shook her head. 'Sam, you don't owe me anything.'

'I do. I shouldn't have tried to kiss you and I definitely shouldn't have lied about the way it made me feel.'

'Ah.' She teased a flake of croissant away from the edge of the plate with her finger, then steered it round the wooden table top. 'So, what are you saying?'

He took in a deep breath. This moment had been

seven years in the making. 'I'm saying it's time we each moved on.'

'What?' She looked shocked. 'You want me to leave?'

'No. Of course not. Bad choice of words. Maggie is counting on you. I just mean…there's obviously some unresolved—' He sought for a word that would capture the myriad of emotions he felt on seeing her. He settled on, 'Unresolved history. We've got to find a way to let go of the past. Move forward.'

His phone pinged, and as he was the only doctor on call he apologised and glanced at the screen.

'Anything serious?'

Sam gave her a knowing grin. 'Depends upon how having lunch with my sisters sits with you.'

Her eyebrows shot up. 'Really? They want to talk? With me?' She gave him a sidelong look. 'How do they even know you're here?'

'Greta.'

Jayne's eyebrows lifted. *Of course.* The Whitticombe Grapevine herself.

She shook her head. 'I don't know. I saw Kate the other day and I didn't really get the impression she wanted to talk to me.'

'Of course she does. Listen.' He read out the text. '"Would Jayne fancy a girlie lunch sometime? Maggie welcome. K xx".' He turned the phone towards her. 'There's even a smiley face. No daggers.'

Jayne's shoulders stiffened. Fair enough. Kate had already confessed to him that she might have accidentally-on-purpose brought up the dating thing at the cricket ground. Protective older sister. He loved her for it, but he was a grown man now. Just knowing his family were behind him in good times and in bad was all the backing he needed.

'Jay—it's not for an inquisition. They haven't seen you properly in ages and they want to hear everything that's been going on in your life.'

Precisely what he was trying to do. She'd said she wanted to become a certain type of woman…but he'd never really sat down with her and found out if those dreams she'd been pursuing so doggedly had actually come true. After he'd reluctantly taken the ring back he'd closed the door on her every bit as much as she had on him. He could see that now.

'So…what do *you* want, Sam? From me?'

Mostly he wanted the past not to have twisted up his present so much. He wanted to be happily married. To be going to the school play and watching his own children be starfish or trees or King George III. He wanted to be *living* his life, not ricocheting between the past and present every time Jayne came to town. Had he wanted the woman he did all that with to be Jayne? Of course he had. A long time ago.

All of which meant… 'We need to find a way to become friends.'

She sucked her cheeks in sharp and fast. From her tight wince as she took a sip of tea he was guessing she'd bitten the inside of her cheek. Her go-to reaction when she was stressed.

'You all right?'

'Yup. Good. I'm…'

He watched as her eyes searched his face for something more. Eventually her shoulders dropped down and back, as if she were opening up her heart to him.

'I'm sorry, Sam.'

His own heart was rammed tight and fast in his throat. This wasn't an ordinary apology. 'For what?'

'Everything.' She put her hands up before he could say anything. 'I mean it. You're one of the kindest, bravest, most generous men I've ever known. The last thing I ever wanted to do was hurt you, but…'

Sam gave a rueful laugh. She *had* hurt him. Hurt him more than anyone else had. As much as he'd like to say his failed marriage had cut him to pieces, Jayne's departure had hurt him far more.

'That's a rather large apology.'

She blew some air up at a few stray hairs to get them out of her eyes. 'I've made a rather large hash of things. I…' Her mouth stayed open, the words she was trying to say never finding purchase.

Sam took a croissant, teased apart a flaky layer from the rolled pastry, then put it back on his plate. 'Is everything all right back in London?'

Jags of pain darkened her eyes. 'I had a surgery go wrong at the hospital.'

His eyebrows lowered together. Now they were getting somewhere. He'd *known* this wasn't just a holiday lark.

'What kind of surgery was it?'

'Heart transplant.'

Jayne wasn't surprised to see Sam's eyebrows shoot up towards his hairline. He wasn't to know she'd finally reached her goal.

Reached her goal and failed, more like.

It isn't a failure. Sometimes things just go wrong.

Sam pushed his plate away and said, 'Impressive. You took the lead?'

She nodded. 'First time.' She went on before he could leap to any conclusions. 'As you know I've been training in paediatric cardiology.' She looked away from Sam as she continued. 'I wanted to add transplants to my skill base, so I did the general surgical rotations, paediatric training, acute medicine, neonatal paediatrics—'

When she paused to take a breath, Sam continued for her. 'Six months in transplant, hepatobiliary, cardiovascular collapse, cyanosis...'

There was more. A lot more. And he rattled through it all. Not the usual syllabus for a GP. Not that she'd thought he'd spent his time in med school learning only basic diagnostic skills then called it quits, or anything, but...

'Samuel Crenshaw! Have you been following my career?'

He feigned a casual shrug. 'I read the medical journals. I just might occasionally read up on what's happening at your children's hospital. To keep myself up to date medically...for my patients' welfare. Obviously.'

There was a glint in his eye now. A humorous one. That fuzzy warm feeling that came from knowing someone special cared lit up her chest. *Oh, Sam.*

'So, what happened with this surgery?'

She stared at him long and hard. Sam had used to be the one person in the world she could tell anything to. The embarrassing stuff. The fun stuff. The things she wished she had or hadn't done. He never judged. Only listened. And on the occasions he gave advice it was always thoughtful. Considerate.

This was her chance to take a leap of faith that he was still that man. That he really did want them to be friends.

And just like that she opened her heart to him.

Once she started talking she couldn't stop. She told him all the details. About Stella's heart failure. About keeping her alive with an artificial heart for months. The opportunity to finally do a transplant. The offer for her to take the lead.

'So…did something actually go wrong? Or do the parents want someone to blame?'

Typical Sam. Able to cut through to the quick of the matter like a hot knife through butter.

'No. The parents aren't why I took the break.'

They'd been amazing, actually. Had actually thanked her for giving Stella those precious few five months, as harrowing as they'd been.

She took another leap. 'Mind if I just unload everything on you?'

'Absolutely,' he said. 'That's what friends are for, right?'

If hearts could crumple and expand in the space of a millisecond her heart did just that. Above and beyond any romance they had shared, they had always been friends. And that was what she'd missed the most in those dark months after Jules' death.

His lips, his body, his lovemaking… Oh, they all ranked up there in Things She Missed Most in the World, but it was this…being able to just sit and talk and make sense of something with someone she could trust…that she missed more than anything.

So why can't you trust him with what you know about Jules?

She kicked the thought back into her Cupboard of Dark Things and focused in on the surgery.

'Is there something that makes you think you might have made a mistake?' he asked.

Reluctantly, she nodded.

The gesture visibly caught Sam by surprise.

She scrambled to right it. 'No. Not technically. It was textbook. But as a surgeon… Yeah. Absolutely. I messed up.'

He looked perplexed. 'How?'

'One of the junior surgeons told me where the donor heart was from.'

'Isn't that protocol?'

'Yes, but he told me the back story. The whole entire back story.' She hoped her voice carried enough weight that he would be able to figure it out on his own.

He spun his finger round. *Keep on talking*, that gesture said. He wanted to hear it from the horse's mouth.

'It was a young woman's heart. A woman who'd been riding her bicycle out on a country lane and been hit by a car.'

He let out a low whistle. 'Hell, Jay. It's a coincidence, but…'

He was saying it was out there. But not impossible.

'But of all the surgeons in the entire world…that heart ended up in *my* hands.'

Didn't he see? The fact that it had affected her so much meant she might not be equipped to do it again. There would be more hearts. Perhaps more from girls who hadn't looked right and left before they careered into oncoming traffic.

'Did Stella die in surgery?'

It was strange hearing Stella's name coming from Sam. It felt…*intimate*. The first thing she'd shared with him since she'd left Whitticombe all those years ago.

Jayne shook her head. 'The surgery went perfectly. She died two days later. Rejection.'

Sam pushed back from the table as if the matter was

settled. 'So—a straight-up rejection. There isn't any-thing you could've done about that. It's not nice, but it happens.'

'It shouldn't have happened to *me*. Not with *that* girl! Not with *that* heart.' The tears she'd been holding at bay for days began to flow.

Sam had her in his arms before she knew what was happening. It felt unbelievably perfect to be there. To let someone comfort her. She was so used to pushing people away. So used to pushing Sam away.

She cried and cried, accepted tissue after tissue, even-tually laying her heart against his chest until the sound of her sobs abated and all she could hear was the steady thump-thump of his heart.

'Hey, you two!' Maggie appeared in the doorway.

They pulled apart as abruptly as if they'd been caught naked. Maggie's eyes glinted mischievously. She loved a bit of gossip.

Totally unfazed, she popped a finger on her chin and said, 'Oops. I'm not interrupting anything, am I?'

They both shouted, 'No!'

Maggie clicked her tongue. 'I'm obviously interrupt-ing *something*. What's going on?'

Jayne had no idea what to say. She was supposed to be looking after Maggie, not morphing into a blubber-ing emotional wreck who sobbed her heart out into her ex-fiancé's shirt.

Sam swept a few stray locks of Jayne's hair behind her ear, then turned to Maggie. 'I think our Jayne, here, might need as much looking after as you do.'

Sam was just about to shoulder his messenger style bag when a knock sounded at his front door, quickly followed by a, *'Yoo-hoo... Sam-u-el?'* that could only belong to his older sister Kate.

He walked out into the hallway with his coffee cup, only to find his sister already inside, as ever 'casually' inspecting the place. A finger across the oak beam framing the inglenook fireplace... A quick tidy of a stack of medical journals beside the deep-cushioned sofa. A wrinkled nose.

'Are you still drinking that horrid coffee in the morning?'

He laughed. 'If by "horrid" you mean the Vietnamese beans I would sell my left arm for, yes. Yes, I am.'

'Sammy, that stuff will—'

'Keep me awake all day,' he finished for her.

That caught her attention. 'Haven't you been sleeping? I told you—you should get someone in to help you at the surgery.'

'It's not a problem. I love my job. Double the work means double the joy.'

His sister made a noise suggesting that she didn't believe him. No surprise there, then. It was a common trait amongst his sisters. Why believe their little brother when they could go with feminine intuition instead? Mind you, his gut was telling him a few things he was trying to ignore as well, so perhaps she had a point.

'Grandad is going to be in his cast for another five weeks, Sam. Maybe longer if he keeps insisting on bashing open doors with it.' She looked him straight in the eye in only the way a sister could. 'Be honest. How's the clinic?'

'Great,' he lied.

It was busy. And about to get more so. It was the beginning of hay fever season, tourist season, sports day season, and there would be the inevitable injuries that came with long jumps, high jumps and potato sack races. Not to mention the usual extensive list of coughs, check-ups, aches, unusual bumps, infant earaches... Maybe his sister had a point.

'A little birdie tells me you've been popping over to see Maggie after surgery.'

And by 'Maggie' he knew she meant Jayne.

'Yup.' He stuffed a stack of papers into his bag, try-ing to give his sister the hint that he really did have to get going. 'Maggie's got a pretty serious condition.'

'I get it that you like doing the whole country doctor thing with house calls, Sam, but Maggie has an actual *surgeon* living under her roof who just might be on top of all that—am I right?'

'Yeah, well... She's—'

His sister did one of those *Oh, don't bother lying* flicks of her eyes.

Fine. He went there because of Jayne as well. How could he not? What had come through loud and clear the other day was the fact that she was still dealing with her sister's death as if it had happened yesterday. The part of him he'd thought would never leap to her rescue again turned out not to have got the message.

Talking to her, holding her, laughing with her and Maggie over cups of tea and a board game after work... For the first time in he didn't know how long he had felt one hundred per cent whole. And if he was being really honest it felt as if he was getting a second chance.

Not with the romance side of things—he didn't even know what to do with the chemistry buzzing between them—but something deeper was at work. Something he felt they'd never had a chance to deal with all those years ago.

'You aren't trying to do your knight in shining armour act again, are you?'

'What act?' He bridled. Sometimes sisters didn't know when to leave well enough alone.

'Oh, come on, Sam.' She pointed at one of the and sat down on the other.

Here we go. Another Big Sister Talk. As much as he loved her, she was properly off base.

'Sam.'

'Kate.'

'You know as well as the entire village does that the whole reason you got together with Marie was to rescue her.'

'What on earth are you talking about?'

'Oh, come on. She was great. I'm not saying otherwise. But...'

Sam rolled his eyes. *Here it comes.*

'She had a horrible ex-boyfriend. Moved out of the city to escape him. Came to Whitticombe to start over. You had the perfect life all sketched out, with this house, your work at the surgery... All you were missing was a woman to do it with.'

'You make me sound like a real arse.'

'Don't be silly. We know you loved her. We also know you've never really got over Jayne.'

Oh, for heaven's sake! No wonder Jayne had looked nervous about the 'girlie' lunch. Just one sister was enough to drive him round the bend, let alone all of them at once.

'Jayne and I are ancient history.'

Kate pursed her lips at him. 'You know I do not usually swear. But that is total *crap*, Samuel Crenshaw. We loved Marie. Every bit as much as you did. But the two of you… It was never the same as it was with you and Jayne. You're the only one who didn't see it.'

'Oh, c'mon, Kate. I think I'm a bit better than that.'

'Look… No one blames you for wanting to be someone's hero after what you'd been through with Jayne. You tried everything you could to help her.'

'Thanks for the reminder. I think you'll also remember that she told me to go and live my dreams because she wanted to live hers. Alone.'

He'd tried talking to her. She'd hardly responded. He'd told her he was there to listen. She'd said there wasn't anything to say. For the first couple of months she'd practically been a zombie, so it had been a shock when she'd announced she was heading back to her studies as per normal.

And on the handful of trips she'd taken back to Whitticombe since only a fool would have failed to notice she had become a different person from the one he'd fallen in love with.

Kate sighed and gave his hand a squeeze. 'After Jules died she was a lost soul. She had no idea *what* she wanted. You knew *exactly* what you wanted. And at that age it's hard to take your eye off the prize.'

He was taken aback. 'Are you saying I chose my life here over Jayne?'

'Not at all. I'm saying you were a young man. A young man who'd set his heart on living the life the two of you had always dreamed of. For Jayne that life didn't exist any more. *Couldn't* exist any more.'

She had a point. When Jayne's sister had been killed she'd been completely shell-shocked. He'd had no idea how to help someone enduring that level of grief. He'd never called a time of death at his training hospital, let alone seen someone he loved pass away.

If Jayne had clung to that pain of course it would have been traumatising for her to perform a transplant with a heart that had come from a woman who'd had a similar accident. There had been something else, though. When she'd spoken about Stella's death he'd seen something in her eyes that had looked...*haunted*. As if by pursuing paediatric surgery she'd believed she could put a stop to all bicycle accidents. Or...more to the point... feel she was bringing her sister back each time she fixed a child's heart.

'Why are you frowning?' his sister asked.

'I'm not frowning.' He was. He was totally frowning. He pulled her into a bear hug and acquiesced, 'Maybe you've given me a bit of food for thought.'

'You know I'm right, don't you?'

He parted his lips, poised to protest, and instantly knew there was no point. Kate had been the one who'd driven him to complete his medical degree all those years ago, with the ring box burning a hole in the corner of his duffel bag. He still had it. Hadn't thought it right to propose to another woman with Jayne's ring, just as...

Oh, God. Kate was right. He had tried to make Marie's dreams come true with his own vision of the future. The future he'd planned with Jayne. He looked round the big open house. Marie had often said she'd felt as if there was a ghost living in the renovated barn, and he'd always told her she was being silly, but honestly... Maybe she'd been right.

That ghost was Jayne.

She'd been the one who'd stared at the derelict yellow

brick building and said, 'That would make a nice place to live one day.' She'd been right. It was great. Vaulted ceilings. Thick oak beams. Windows two metres high that saw the sun rise in the master bedroom and set in the open-plan family area.

Family.

'Who made *you* so smart?' he asked.

'Mum and Dad,' she said, giving his hand a pat. 'And a splash of sisterly intuition.'

He rolled his eyes at her.

'Sammy...' His sister stretched across the kitchen island and began picking at a bowl of grapes. 'You be careful.'

'What? With Jayne? She's fine. We're just friends.'

He wondered if she could see his nose growing. Technically they weren't anything else...but there was that *thing* that hummed between them.

'Okay,' she said, suddenly changing tack. 'If things are so chummy between the pair of you, why don't you ask her to help you at the clinic. We all heard her offer. She's probably desperate to put a bandage on someone or look down someone's throat.'

Sam scoffed. 'I don't really think it's her kind of thing.'

'Why not? She's a doctor, isn't she?'

'Obviously. But she—' He checked himself.

It wasn't Jayne's surgical career that was the problem. It was the idea of having her a metre or so down that corridor where they'd planned to work together. It would be like playing at something he could never have, and in all honesty he was still at the baby steps phase of this supposed friendship.

His sister gave him another one of those X-ray vision

looks of hers, then said, 'Why don't you let her decide? You're big kids now.' She patted his head in the way only a big sister could. 'If you really are friends she'll want to lend a hand. If you're not…you'll see the back of her by the end of the day.'

She briskly wiped her hands back and forth, as if she'd sorted out yet another one of the vast problems of the universe.

'Have her do a children's clinic or something. Go on,' his sister said, popping another grape into her mouth, a mischievous glint to her eye. 'I dare you.'

When Sam got to the surgery and saw the patient list bursting at the seams he knew his sister was right. He needed help. And it was just a few doors down the lane. Maybe it was time to take a chance.

CHAPTER SIX

'YOU'LL BE FINE.'

Sam handed Jayne a cup of strong coffee. Thick and black with a couple of lumps of sugar, just the way she liked it.

'And you're absolutely sure you're cool with this?'

Jayne's nerves were pinging all over the place. Not about seeing patients, but about doing it here. At Stream's Edge Surgery. They might as well unfurl a banner that said *Jayne's Back in Town! Why not get your blood pressure checked and give her a quiz while you're at it?*

Or maybe that was just her nerves at work.

'Greta's going to send all the paediatric appointments your way, but since your training did cover all the basics you'll be completely fine to handle anything else too.'

She pulled a face. 'I don't know anyone as well as you.'

He shrugged. 'Sometimes that's a good thing. People often hide the whole truth if they know you well.'

All the air left her lungs and she looked away. Did he know she'd kept something from him all these years?

He took a long drink of his coffee, then smiled. 'I know you two are friends, but maybe a bit of distance explains why Maggie wanted you to look after her and not me. She's loving those foot-rubs you're giving her, by the way.'

Jayne disguised her relief that he wasn't referring to something darker with an airy wave of the hand. Foot-rubs were the least she could do for her friend, who seemed to run the village singlehandedly from her arm-chair. She'd do more if required. Much more.

If she'd been able to reach in and fix her sister's heart that day she would have, but…

She shook the image away. *Work.* Work was good. Es-pecially with the anniversary of Jules's death coming up.

Sam escorted her to his grandad's examination room. The walls were covered with family photos and scads of hand-drawn thank-you cards. And in pride of place, on the centre of his desk, a huge family portrait with all the Crenshaws, their spouses, their children…

Looking at it made her realise just how much she'd missed by staying away.

'I'm going to be right next door. If you need me call or knock or—'

'Oh! Can we have a secret knock?'

Sam laughed. He was obviously a bit nervous, too, so adding a bit of playfulness to the day might take off a bit of edge.

'Sure. Let's have a secret knock.'

She knocked on the wall.

'Sounds like tachycardia.' He grinned.

'You knew I was doing a heartbeat?'

He shrugged. Of course he knew. He'd known every-thing about her once upon a time.

'Okay…how about this?' She did it again, but with the slow, steady cadence of his heart that had steadied her when she'd had her little meltdown the other day.

'That's good.'

He stuck out a hand and she gave it a solid shake.

'Good luck, Doctor. Enjoy.'

He dropped her a wink, then headed into his office.

The wink! It was *their* wink! Just the confidence boost she needed.

Before she could think about it any further, she picked up the phone and buzzed Greta. 'I'm ready for the first patient.'

Two minutes later a little pixie-haired girl called Poppy was giving full vent to the fact that she had a slightly ingrown toenail.

'Mummy says I can't wear my favourite shoes to the concert!' she wailed.

Poppy's mother gave her a weary smile. She was around Jayne's age, but hadn't grown up in Whitticombe.

'How long has this been bothering you, poppet?' Jayne asked.

'It's *Poppy*,' the little girl said grumpily, crossing her arms over her chest.

'She's been like this for the last couple of days,' her mother explained. 'In a mood... So I suspect her toe's been hurting more than she's let on. And...well...it does look rather swollen.'

'It *doesn't* hurt. I just want to wear my fancy sandals!' Poppy insisted.

Jayne pulled a small set of steps over to the exam table. 'Why don't you pop up on here and tell me all about the concert?' Distractions always helped when children were in pain. Focusing on an injury could often make them more distressed. 'What instrument do you play?'

'My voice,' Poppy said proudly, and then began to

sing a catalogue of show tunes as Jayne eased off her shoe and looked at the very swollen toe. The nail was slightly ingrown, but not so badly she'd need to see a podiatrist. Unless she insisted upon wearing her favourite shoes non-stop.

After Poppy had finished a remarkably skilful rendition of a song from *Matilda*, Jayne applauded. 'That was great. Now… Here's the good news. You don't need an operation or to see a podiatrist.'

Her mother heaved a visible sigh of relief.

'What you *do* need to do, however, is give this toe a bit of extra TLC.'

She wrote down a list of recommended treatments, talking through it as she did so, making sure her mother and Poppy understood. Kids were always smarter than a lot of adults gave them credit for, so it was best to include them in the conversation if at all possible.

Poppy pulled a face. 'You want me to put apple cider vinegar on my toe?'

'No need to pour it straight on the toe. If you give it a soak in warm soapy water, or warm water with apple cider vinegar, it will help draw out the infection.' She went on to explain that she would prescribe an antibiotic cream and that, despite Poppy's desire to have a few practice runs in her closed-toe shoes, she'd probably be better off in flip-flops or something similar for the next week or so.

'And if it gets worse?' asked her mum.

'Come back in and we'll get you referred to a podiatrist. And let us know if she gets a fever. Then she'll need a proper course of oral antibiotics.'

The pair thanked her, and after that small triumph the rest of the day whooshed by. A bloodied nose from a scooter accident. A deep cut that required a few stitches. A little boy who was presenting with some pretty serious allergies... She referred *him* to a specialist unit at the nearby hospital.

By the time the lunch hour rocked round she was feeling as though that little bit of her that had shut down the day Stella had died was starting to spring some green shoots.

'Someone looks pleased with themselves.'

Jayne reached out to take Sam's empty coffee cup from him as she was already washing hers in the small kitchen at the back of the surgery. The building was an old house so it was a proper kitchen, with room for a table that had clearly seen its share of hastily eaten lunches.

Sam reached into the refrigerator and pulled out a plastic container with a rice dish in it. He caught her looking and held it out. 'Paella. My sister brought it by this morning. Want some?'

'No, I was going to head back to Maggie's and make her some lunch.'

'Ooh...' Sam sing-songed. 'So she's given you access to the kitchen, has she?'

'Hey!' Jayne protested feebly. 'My cooking's not that bad.' There was no malice in Sam's laugh so she conceded. 'I told her I'd pop by the teashop. Dolly is making some bespoke sandwiches.'

'I'm surprised Maggie hasn't installed secret cameras in the teashop.'

'Are you kidding me?' Jayne joked. 'If she could, she'd have them over the whole village. The more pregnant she gets, the crankier she is about everyone's follow-through. My inability to cook tops the list. I think we've eaten our way through every healthy café and takeaway in the village.'

Sam laughed good-naturedly. 'How about I come over one night and cook?'

A rush of warmth flooded through her as their eyes met. A wink and then an offer to cook? Was this *flirting*?

'Maggie would like that. And the children.'

'And you?'

It should have been a leading question. In some ways it was. For her, anyway. More proximity to Sam meant more chances that she'd fall right back in love with him and—

Wait. What?

She pulled her eyes away and began scrubbing the mugs a second time around. Of course there was a part of her that would always *love* Sam. And there had been some serious sizzle when they'd nearly kissed at the cricket clubhouse. But…*in* love? No. She couldn't do that. There were too many demons and too much guilt swirling away in her soul to plonk on a man whose heart she'd already broken once.

'I could make my roast chicken.'

That got her attention. 'The one with garlic?'

'The one with tons of garlic.'

She couldn't say no to that. She put on her best doctor voice. 'It'd be extra good for Maggie's pre-eclampsia, wouldn't it?'

There were a list of other benefits for pregnant women in garlic. Garlic boosted baby weight, reduced mum's cholesterol, helped prevent cancer and shielded them both from infections or colds.

Sam took the mugs and began to dry them, to save

them from yet another sousing. 'I wasn't suggesting it because of its medicinal properties, Jayne.'

Their eyes caught and meshed as they both had the same memory. A glitter rush of sensation washed through her chest and her heart did another one of those insane dance moves inside her ribcage.

Sam had made it for her the night they had first made love. His parents had been out of town. He'd been living in a little annexe flat above their garage. His sisters had all been out on dates. She and Sam been eighteen years old and on the brink of heading off to different unis.

After giggling about kissing someone who'd had so much garlic, they'd both grown very serious. They'd promised they'd stay true to one another despite the distance. It was the night they had begun openly planning for a proper future together, here in Whitticombe.

A bittersweet memory if ever there was one.

'That'd be really nice, Sam,' she heard herself say.

He looked as shocked as she felt. 'Oh! Great. Well... see you back here for the afternoon rush, then I'll go shopping and meet you back at Maggie's.'

'Perfect.' She gave him a smile and slipped out through the back door towards the towpath that led to Maggie's cottage.

Maybe this was how forgiveness began. Revisiting old history and offering it a fresh layer to weave into the fabric that made up their shared past. Baby steps.

Her pace picked up at the thought. If she was able to make peace with her past, and all the people she'd hurt along the way, maybe then she could build some balance into her life. Balance she'd so obviously lacked the day she'd called Stella's time of death.

Patients weren't stand-ins for her sister. They were

individuals needing her utmost respect and care. Not the emotional fallout from a loss she'd experienced so long ago. Look at Sam. When she'd come back to town he might easily have refused to be as open and kind as he had been. He was rising above what had happened between them and was truly making an effort to start afresh.

With that thought in mind, she vowed to start saying yes a bit more. To Sam. To the friendships she'd let fade. To life. Even if it was scary. Even if it meant testing the limits of her heart.

Sam looked out of the window and smiled. He was one of the only people he knew who liked a good summer rainstorm. Not so much because of the rain, but because of what came next. The rich flush of growth that came after it.

Or…maybe he was smiling because he had a date with Jayne tonight.

He checked himself. Definitely *not* a date. And it was also with Maggie, Connor and Cailey.

He gave his freshly shaved jaw a scrub as he ran through the details of his final patient of the day before calling her in.

He'd shaved. *Was it a date?*

The conversation he'd had with his sister poured ice on that thought. The last thing he should be doing was putting a romantic spin on time spent with Jayne. He had offered a fresh start for *friendship*. So he should play by the rules. But just one day of working together had teased away years of tension.

Medicine had always been a shared love of theirs. As teens they'd used to do odd jobs for his grandfather and the now long-retired doctor who'd used to work with him. They would fill up all the supplies. Restock cotton buds. Bandages. Make sure all the white rolls of sanitary paper for the exam beds were replenished. Simple jobs that had made them feel important.

A knock sounded on his door.

'Sam? It's Jayne. I think you'd better come quick. Greta's calling an ambulance.'

Jayne's tight tone had him up and out of his chair in a flash. Three long-legged strides and he'd caught up to her as she jogged back towards the waiting room.

'What is it?'

'Mrs Maynard from the greengrocers. It looks like she's having a stroke.'

His heart sank. Mrs Maynard had been to him a couple of times over the past few months, complaining of symptoms that sounded a lot like TIAs. Transient ischaemic attacks weren't as bad as a stroke, but they were indicators that a stroke might be lurking on the horizon. He'd referred her to the hospital, but perhaps she'd been stuck in a backlog of appointments.

The second he saw her being propped up in a chair by her niece, Deanna, he knew Jayne was right.

F-A-S-T pinged into his head. Face. Arms. Speech. Time.

From the confused expression, and the odd way Mrs Maynard was holding her body, Jayne was right to have asked Greta to call an ambulance.

He gave a reassuring smile to Deanna and knelt in front of Mrs Maynard. 'Mrs Maynard? How are you feeling?'

She tried to answer but her words were slurred, and one side of her face was now visibly drooping.

Deanna spoke at a rate of knots. 'We were coming in for her regular blood pressure appointment and to check on her diabetes when she started acting a bit funny. Said she felt a bit nauseous. Then she stumbled as if she was having a dizzy attack. Luckily we were only a few steps away, and by the time we got to the waiting room…' Deanna made a helpless gesture. 'Is she going to be all right?'

Sam's gut instinct was to assure her that everything was going to be fine, but strokes were peculiar territory. Some were minor and others put people in comas. Or worse.

'It looks like she might be having a stroke. It's difficult to tell how serious it is, but help is on the way.' He refocused his gaze on Mrs Maynard. 'Try as best you can to answer my questions. No stress. No pressure.'

She gave a half-nod and then her hand slipped off her lap as if it was a dead weight, indicating possible paralysis.

'Can you smile for me, Mrs Maynard?'

She did so, and the droop that was apparent in her face became even more pronounced.

'How about putting your hands out in front of you on an even plane? Can you do that?'

She lifted one arm, but the one that had slid off her lap remained where it was. A hint of panic entered her eyes.

Sam gave her shoulder a gentle rub. Poor woman. Blood-flow to part of her brain was being cut off or reduced, and ensuring she didn't go into panic mode was essential.

Jayne appeared by his side. 'Here's some aspirin and some water.'

'Brilliant—thanks.' Aspirin within the first forty-eight hours of a stroke always helped. 'Do you think you can take this without being unwell?'

Mrs Maynard nodded her head and with a bit of help was able to take the pill.

He took her blood pressure, which was high, but not off the charts. Her blood sugar level was a bit on the low side. Not so good. What she really needed was a CT scan, to determine if there was any active bleeding in her brain. And if there was she'd need medication. And fast. Within three hours of the stroke was the recommended timeline.

About ten minutes later they heard the sound of approaching sirens, and shortly afterwards the paramedics were loading her on to a wheeled gurney.

Sam took the lead in rattling through the patient's symptoms and the handful of stats they had to hand. What she needed was a neurologist and an emergency centre. When Deanna explained she needed to collect her children from school Sam volunteered to go along with Mrs Maynard to the hospital.

'I'll sort out Maggie's children—get them something to eat—then come and pick you up.'

Jayne was standing just outside the ambulance. She looked in complete control. A woman who dealt with high-pressure situations on a daily basis. The kind of doctor you'd want treating you when the ground seemed to be slipping out from beneath your feet.

'That'd be great. Tell Deanna I'll text with updates.'

She nodded and smiled. The hum of connection felt magnetic, and even as the doors of the ambulance closed between them Sam knew he'd been right when he'd thought of their dinner together as a date.

Because everything he did with Jayne Sinclair involved his heart.

How he dealt with it was going to be another story.

Having been informed that Mrs Maynard had only suffered a minor stroke, Jayne arrived at the hospital a few hours later—and her jaw literally dropped at the sight of the cottage hospital's lush surroundings.

The facility had been built since she'd lived in the area and she'd not yet visited it.

To call it a cottage hospital wasn't entirely fair. According to the website she'd searched to get the address, the recently refurbished facilities might look old-fashioned, but inside the three traditional Georgian buildings they housed all the bells and whistles a doctor could dream of.

This particular building was the critical care unit. Another housed a maternity and paediatrics unit. The third offered cancer and hospice care. The place where she imagined Sam's mum would've received care in the end.

She squished away the feelings that came with that. The fact that she hadn't been brave enough to come back and say goodbye, to thank her for all the love and support she'd given her through the years, had always been a thorn in her side.

She sighed and thought of the long list of regrets that festered away in her Dark Place. Being outside London was actually giving her the emotional breathing room she needed to look at her life with a clearer perspective. She appreciated there was nothing she could do to change the past, but maybe she could start making steps to change her future...

She parked the car and strode inside.

Sam was leaning against a central reception desk,

speaking with a couple of doctors in blue scrubs. They were laughing at something he'd said. She enjoyed seeing him this way. At ease. Not with that little hitch in his shoulders he pretended didn't exist when she entered the room.

He turned at the sound of the doors opening and smiled. It was the first genuinely relaxed, peaceful smile she'd had from him in years, and it filled up her heart with squishy, gooey good things.

He said something else to the doctors, then waved goodbye.

'Friends of yours?' she asked.

He nodded. 'Sort of. In this neck of the woods we all get to know each other one way or another.'

She scanned the brightly lit waiting room, complete with a children's play area filled with soft toys. There were the obligatory rooms off to each side, where loved ones often received the worst sort of news. She'd sat in a room like that with Stella's family. She'd sat in a room like that when the emergency doctors had asked her parents if Jules was an organ donor.

Though she tried to turn away, she knew Sam had seen the inevitable sheen of the tears she couldn't seem to keep at bay these days glossing her eyes.

Much to her surprise, he put his arm round her shoulder and gave her a gentle squeeze. His hugs were like a cosy duvet on a winter's day. Perfect.

'You did well today. Calling the ambulance. Seeing the signs immediately. I'm just sorry that we're going to have to take a rain-check on that garlic chicken. I never got the chance to go and buy the ingredients.'

'Well... It was standard protocol.' She turned her

fingers into pistols and did a quick draw. 'You gotta act *fast*!'

They both laughed, and Sam's hand dropped from her shoulders, then rested briefly on the small of her back as they left the waiting area and went out into the warm summer evening air. The rain had disappeared as quickly as it had arrived.

Jayne was still missing the warmth of his touch when he suddenly spread his arms wide and inhaled deeply.

'Don't you just love it?'

'What exactly are we loving?'

His eyes met hers and his smile softened. And just like that it appeared. That look she'd thought she'd never see again.

Butterflies took flight in her belly. Did this mean Sam was feeling what she was? The inevitable draw of attraction coupled with a deep, mutual respect?

'The summer, of course,' he said, his eyes still glued to hers. 'Don't you love it?'

'Yes,' she whispered. 'Very much.'

CHAPTER SEVEN

MAGGIE LET OUT a roar of frustration. 'If I sterilise the washing up gloves, could you reach in and pull these babies out?'

'Is that what you would advise *me* to do if I'd had a cake in the oven for only three-quarters of the baking time?' Jayne replied evenly.

When her friend made a *'gah!'* noise, pushed herself up and stomped off into the garden, to languish on a cushioned bench in the shade, Jayne knew that the baking analogy had had the desired effect. Leave well enough alone!

As Jayne stuffed yet another load of laundry into the washing machine, and caught a glimpse of a brightly coloured canal boat loaded with happy holidaymakers drifting past outside on the river, she had to admit she couldn't blame her for feeling so frustrated.

The weather was lovely. Everyone was out and about. Maggie would normally be scurrying around the village, organising about a zillion activities. Not to mention kitting out the seating area outside her tearoom with bunting and her annual display of sunflowers. Just last night Maggie had sobbed for a good two hours about the shop's impending demise.

'Balderdash!' her business partner—the rather fabulous Dolly Johnson—had cried when she'd come round with a basket of butterfly-themed fairy cakes. *'It's doing better than ever.'*

Maggie had only become grumpier with that little nugget of information.

This morning it was Nate. She missed him desperately. She hadn't had a good snog in over two months and she wasn't sure she could survive any longer without a kiss from her man.

Jayne knew exactly how she felt.

Not about snogging Maggie's husband, obviously, but now that she and Sam had their 'give friendship a chance thing' going on she was really struggling to keep her body's responses in check.

Working at the surgery was brilliant, but each time their hands brushed, or their paths crossed, she had these *saucy stirrings*. The man was sparking up all sorts of engines she'd forgotten she possessed.

It was an excruciatingly frustrating reminder of just how long it had been since she'd had sex. She'd had a couple of half-hearted flings over the course of her time in London. Maybe three. Maybe a couple of ill-advised one-night stands. But…nothing had stuck. No one seemed to have that special something.

Except Sam.

The truth was she wanted him. He was sexy. And they had sparks aplenty.

She flicked on the washing machine and stared out of the window towards the surgery.

Was that such a bad thing?

Yes…if you're trying to be friends.

She caught herself running her fingers across her lips,

her stomach feeling all glitterball sparkly at the memory of that near-kiss. It was like being a teenager all over again. Giggling and swooning and…her eyes flicked to the calendar…*two more days.*

All the fizz in her tummy flattened. Two more days and it would be seven years since her sister had died.

Busywork. She needed busywork. It was the perfect time to lay out the surprise she'd been working on for Maggie. Since she couldn't really go far, Jayne had thought she'd bring a project to her.

A while later she had her friend blindfolded and was leading her up the steps.

Maggie burst into laughter when Jayne finally allowed her to take the blindfold off. 'What did you do? Buy the entire craft store?'

'Pretty much. I also popped in on Mum and Dad's. The McTavishes let me have a little dig around the art studio for some watercolours *and*…' She masked how weird that had felt, being in the studio without them, by pulling something out of a drawer with a flourish. 'Their trusty glue gun.'

Maggie looked shocked. 'They didn't take it to Scotland?'

Jayne laughed. Her parents weren't really glue gun artists.

'Have you called them yet?'

Jayne sheepishly shook her head. She would. Maybe on the anniversary? Maybe after.

'So. Operation Artwork. What do you think?'

Jayne and Maggie surveyed the kitchen together. There wasn't a single surface that was visible. Glitter. Sequins. Canvasses. Piles of cloth. Reams of coloured paper. Scissors. Paints. She'd gone absolutely mad.

'I thought we could get a head start on that Home-made Art Fair of yours.'

Maggie's eyes sparkled with delight. 'Quick—I've got an idea for the glue gun.' Maggie wiggled her fingers at Jayne, then abruptly pressed her hands to her belly.

'Cramp?'

'Mmm… Nothing serious, I don't think.'

'Any bleeding today?'

'Nothing beyond the usual.'

Maggie had been spotting every now and again, which wasn't unusual. And there had been a bit of am-niotic fluid. But at thirty-two weeks the more symp-toms she was presenting, the greater the likelihood of the babies coming out before their due date. It wasn't insanely early, but the longer the little ones could stay put, the better.

After the cramping had passed, Jayne handed her the glue gun. A few minutes of concentrated silence later Maggie held up an abstract of buttons and glitter glue. 'What do you think? Would your parents be able to pass it off as one of theirs?'

'Ha! You know as well as I do my parents are into landscapes and sculpture.' And into leaving town at this time of year. A time full of memories.

As difficult as it was for Jayne to admit, easing back into life in Whitticombe was the tiniest bit easier with-out them here. Every time she looked at them she saw the loss in their eyes. Loss *she* had to own, all because of a silly desire to relive a childhood game.

If only she'd waited to tell Jules her happy news until she'd been back in London. And then what? Dealt with the wrath of her sister for keeping the happiest day of her life a secret? That hadn't been an option either. Jules and Jayne had shared everything.

Which was why becoming a paediatric surgeon had been a no-brainer. Not that it had eased relations with her parents. If anything, they had become even more distant.

Maggie and Sam's parents had all but adopted her in the weeks following Jules's death. At that point she was still meant to be becoming family, and they'd treated her as one of their own.

She'd done her absolute best always to smile, never to cry. It hadn't elicited sympathy from her own parents, so why she had thought it would work with anyone else... And yet when she'd cried about Stella in front of Maggie and Sam a few days ago he hadn't thought her weak.

She realised now that it took *strength* to open up in that way. It took power to be the honest version of herself in front of people who mattered. Well...mostly honest.

Perhaps this was the beginning of that journey. Step by step. Day by day. Could she finally allow herself to grieve? To believe in the possibility of forgiveness one day?

As if on cue, Sam rapped on the frame of the half-open barn-style door. She became swiftly and vividly aware that she was wearing only a string-strapped summer dress. As he propped his arms on the bottom half of the door and locked eyes with her goose pimples skittered up her arms.

'Mmm...smells like...'

Jayne rolled her eyes. 'I know. I know. Burnt toast. We all know I'm not winning a cooking contest any time soon. Thanks to you lot, I'm beginning to realise just how much I relied on my local deli to stave off malnourishment.'

'You don't cook at all?'

Jayne shrugged. 'I'm hardly ever home. And with every cuisine of the world on offer…no contest. Take-away every time!'

He and Maggie both looked at her as if she was mad. They were right, of course. Her private life was pitiable. If anything, her flat was a near replica of how Jules had left it. Empty fridge. A couple of tins of date-expired tomato soup in the very bare cupboard. Two plates, two cups, two forks—and that was only because Jules had once had her over. They'd had a takeaway.

Why settle in, Jules had asked, *when all I want is to be out there?* She'd pointed out to the sparkling lights of central London with the same glimmer in her eye Jayne knew she'd had herself when she'd thought of moving into the Old Barn with Sam one day.

No wonder she hadn't learned how to cook. She was living in Jules's flat. Trying to live Jules's life. The only thing she'd managed to make her own was her job—and look how well *that* had turned out.

Maggie unsuccessfully tried to press herself up and off the chaise longue Jayne had dragged into the kitchen so Maggie could direct in comfort.

'I'm off on a walk.'

'What? I thought you wanted to make art!'

Jayne and Sam rushed over to her. Sam started taking Maggie's pulse, none-too-subtly, and Jayne knelt to help Maggie slide her very swollen feet into the only pair of flip-flops that would accept them. Nate's.

Maggie's eyes darted between Sam and Jayne. 'No way. Not with you two fussbudgets hovering over me.'

'We're not hovering!' they said as one. Then laughed. Then sobered.

Sam gave her shoulder a squeeze. 'Mags… Are you sure you should be walking about?'

'Stop your fussing. I'm just… I'm going to go down to the teashop.' Her hands slipped under her enormous bump. 'If I don't get to boss someone around who isn't one of the two of you I'll go crazy! So help me up and let me unleash some of my pent-up crankiness on Dolly.'

'It's warm out,' Sam cautioned. 'Maybe you should carry a parasol or something.'

'This is not the nineteenth century, Sam!' Maggie pursed her lips. 'The only fan I want is Nate, and I can't have him.' Her forehead crinkled and her lower lip stuck out, just as her daughter's did when Maggie insisted she finish her vegetables.

Sam and Jayne exchanged a look behind Maggie's back. Nate's absence was really beginning to stress Maggie out. And the higher her stress levels the more danger she was in.

'Don't be too bossy,' Jayne warned as Maggie waved goodbye without even turning around. 'I'm coming to get you in an hour if you don't reappear!'

Maggie slowly waddled round the corner, at which point Sam launched into a barrage of questions. How was her blood pressure? Had there been any bleeding? How were the headaches, the nausea, the swelling?

Jayne pulled out her phone and wiggled it in front of his face. 'I'm tapped in to some of the world's best obstetricians over at the London Merryweather. We've got an entire clinic of staff devoted to mothers experiencing difficult pregnancies. I've been stalking them. Making video calls. Demanding research papers. It's the only thing I do at night.'

She made the mistake of looking into his mossy green

eyes. Okay. Fair enough. There was a bit of fantasising going on at night as well...but she was trying not to let that world collide with the real one.

'The point being...' she pocketed her phone '...if anything goes wrong I've got a hotline to some of the best doctors in the country.'

'London's much further away than Oxford.'

She touched Sam's arm. 'Hey... When and if Maggie needs to be in hospital she'll be in hospital. We've got weekly appointments from here on out, so I can start doing speed drills.' She crossed her heart and put her fingers up Girl Scout-style. 'I promise. I'm here for her.'

The lines of concern crinkling at the edges of his eyes smoothed out, and as they did so she saw his eyes travel round the kitchen and a smile twitch at the corners of his mouth. Underneath the extravagance of crafting materials there was a haphazard stack of children's cereal bowls, a rack of incinerated toast, and some of last night's congealed macaroni cheese. Balanced on the sink's edge was a plate of... What had that been again?

Bacon! She'd burnt the bacon, too.

Sam turned to her, with a full smile this time. 'Apart from takeaway places, doesn't London also have loads of places where you can learn how to cook?'

More flirtatiously than she'd intended, she parried, 'I've not got anyone to impress in London.'

Sam leant against the counter and shook his head. 'I don't believe that.'

She debated whether or not to be totally honest. A friend would disclose just how pants her social life was, so... *Here goes nothing.*

'I have *zero* social life.' She laughed.

She sort of did. The kind of social life that was

jammed in between surgeries and forty-eight-hour shifts and trying to get a few hours of sleep. Nothing that stuck. Nothing that mattered…

'I don't believe that for a second. You're a beautiful woman. Suitors must be queuing up at your door.'

A flush hit her cheeks and Sam gave himself a silent boot in the bum. Why was he quizzing Jayne about her love-life? He wanted details of the men she'd been with just about as much as she wanted to hear him talk about his ex-wife. Not at all.

She picked up some yarn and began twirling it around her finger so tightly that the blood ran out of it.

She didn't meet his eye, but said, 'I've gone out with the odd person, but they were set-ups mostly. The type that make up a foursome when a mate doesn't want to go on a blind date on her own. It's not really my thing. Dating. Getting to where I am on the surgical side of things has been my real goal, so…'

'Snap.'

Her eyes widened with surprise. 'Seriously? I thought you had the whole work-life balance thing covered?'

'Ha! Not so much.'

He swirled his finger in a few drops of water on the counter as his ex-wife's words echoed in his head. *There's a ghost in this house.*

'I think my ex would disagree with you on that one.'

He met her wide-eyed response straight on. It was the first time he'd properly mentioned his wife to Jayne. Obviously she knew about her, had seen her at Christmas, but even so…

Even so nothing. You're just friends.

'It used to drive her crazy how much time I spent at the surgery.'

'That wasn't very fair! You were just setting up!'

He smiled at the note of defensiveness in her tone.

As if she feared she'd been a bit too defensive, she playfully tacked on, 'Didn't she realise how much time it would take to steal all your grandad's patients?'

He laughed. 'All work and no play made Sam a very single boy,' he said, twisting the oft-repeated phrase to more factual effect. 'The truth is, hindsight is making it pretty clear I married her too soon.'

Once again he met Jayne's eye.

'Too soon...?' She spoke barely above a whisper.

'Too soon after you.'

Jayne's cheeks drew in swiftly as she registered what he was saying. He hadn't been over her when he'd got married. His sister was right. His ex had been right. There'd been a ghost in his house and another woman in his heart. He hadn't realised it at the time. He'd truly thought he'd moved on. But here he was, and his heart pounding against his chest was telling him what he should have known all along.

Jayne Sinclair was the love of his life.

Maybe he'd never get over her. But he sure as hell had to find a way to live with it.

Jayne scrambled to fill the awkward silence. 'Well... I obviously didn't know her...but she should've known you don't do things by halves. It's a shame she didn't stick around longer. Getting through tough times takes a while.'

Jayne stopped talking, clearly realising the words she spoke could just as easily have been about the pair of them. The words hung heavily between them.

'Has it been worth it for you?' He nudged her elbow. 'The all work and no play?'

She snorted. 'I think you know the answer to that one. The first transplant surgery I led ended with me having a bit of meltdown, so... I hate to admit it, but Sana—the nurse I told you about—she was right. I did need a break. A chance to get some perspective on things.'

She swept her tongue across her lips. Those stirrings he'd been trying to keep at bay reared up strong and vital.

She looked straight into his eyes and said, 'Sam, I—I just wanted to say... I know you and I have history... and it makes everything a bit more complicated...but I owe you a thank-you. You've been amazing since I came back. More than I deserve.'

His eyes dropped to her dress. Fresh cherries dotted across sage-green fabric. Its flimsy straps were all but begging him to reach out and just slip one off a silky-soft shoulder, then the other off the other silky-soft shoulder...

A wave of lust swept through him like wildfire. Surged past any sensible, logical lines he might have drawn in the sand. He lifted his eyes as her dark lashes fluttered against her cheeks and unapologetically she met his gaze.

The atmosphere between them shifted. The space between them hummed. Instinct took over. Before he could think better of it Sam was cupping Jayne's face in his hands, drawing her in close enough to breathe her in. Cotton. Sweet peas. Sugar.

'What is it you want from me, Jayne?'

Instead of answering she went up on tiptoe and accepted the kiss she knew he was waiting to give.

What followed was swift, carnal, and utterly satisfying. His brain barely had time to catch up with what his body was doing. Kissing. Tasting. Touching. Everything about Jayne's body language mirrored his. The same old spell that had first drawn them together unleashed itself. Nestled right back into place as if not a solitary day had passed since they'd last made love.

He wove his fingers into the hair at the base of her neck and pulled her even closer to him. His body was consumed by the need to taste her. Her lips, her tongue, that sweet spot at the base of her throat. He dropped kisses the length of her collarbone, dragged his teeth along her earlobe until he heard her moan.

The sound of her pleasure shot straight to his groin. His hands swept along her curves as he unleashed swift flicks of his tongue into that sugary nook just below her ear. The way he knew would instantly made her grind her thighs together with longing and press her hipbones into his.

Close wasn't close enough.

He wanted skin on skin.

He stepped back long enough for her to see the heat in his eyes—heat that soared in temperature as he took one of those flimsy spaghetti straps in each of his fingers and slipped them off her shoulders. He barely waited for the fabric to puddle on the floor before he was cupping her breasts, skating his hands along her stomach, feeling her shivers of response as he tugged her panties down to meet her dress.

It was insane. All of it. But it felt so good. A hot, intense reminder of just how magic the sexual chemistry between them had been. He could see it in her eyes. She hadn't forgotten it either. She wanted him every bit as much as he wanted her.

The phone rang.

'Don't answer it,' Jayne groaned.

'Not mine...' Sam growled.

She batted at the counter—presumably trying to switch the phone off—took hold of it and held it up behind his shoulder even as he swept a stack of fabric off the counter and replaced it with the two curved cheeks of Jayne's bum.

Mmm... She felt good. Each and every ounce of her.

He began unbuckling his belt as her free hand swept along the length of his erection—then abruptly stopped.

'Everything okay?' he asked against her lips, his body primed for her to fling the damn phone away so they could get back to devouring one another.

'It's the hospital. They want me to phone in.'

He could already hear her calling. And just like that the volcanic heat in him turned icy cold.

Jayne started at the sound of footsteps. She'd thought she had the small churchyard to herself, but it appeared that Monday afternoon was rush hour at the cemetery. A rush hour of two.

She looked up.

Her breath hitched in her throat.

Sam.

They'd not really talked since that super-awkward lust-fest she'd destroyed by taking that call from the hospital. It had been gut instinct.

Hospital rings. Jayne responds.

She'd tried to explain. Had insisted he would've done

the same if a patient had been in need... But at the end of the day he'd left without saying anything.

Of course it was more complicated than her simply taking a phone call. Perhaps he'd come to the same conclusion she had. The phone call had been a cruel divine intervention, pointing out the obvious: they weren't meant to be together.

She'd gone into the surgery that morning, as discussed, but when her last patient had left the building she'd needed to come out here and see her sister. Offer amends. Ask for forgiveness.

'Thought I'd find you here.'

Sam's voice wrapped around her like a cashmere blanket. Soft and protective.

'Well... I figured it was safer than visiting the lane where it happened, so...'

He nodded.

She shot him a grateful smile. Despite the complication of feelings pinballing between her heart, head and gut it was comforting to have Sam here.

It was the first time she'd been in Whitticombe on the anniversary of Jules's death. She'd thought she wanted to do it alone, but it was nice to know there were other people thinking of Jules as well.

Would her parents benefit from this? Seeing their daughter's grave and the flowers those who had also known her had left?

Jayne gave Sam a grateful smile as he nestled the potted plant he was carrying at the base of Jules's grave, then stepped back to where Jayne was kneeling and sat on the ground.

'Mind if I join you?'

She shook her head. ''Course not. The flower's lovely.'

'It's an aster. I thought it suited Jules's personality.'

'What?' Surely the aster was a symbol for patience. If there was one thing her sister hadn't been, it was patient.

'It means star,' Sam said into the silence.

She started. 'But that's—'

'Greek. I know about the patience thing, but it also stands for love of variety, and the Jules I remember loved variety.'

Despite herself, Jayne laughed. 'That was definitely Jules, all right.'

Sam's laugh blended with her own, and as their eyes met she knew he was here for all the right reasons.

He crossed his legs and leant back on his hands, his long fingers disappearing in the thick early summer grass. 'She would've liked a patient I had today.'

'Oh, yeah?' Jayne picked a dandelion and plucked at the petals.

'Definitely. An eight-year-old girl who's as devoted to her trampoline as Jules was to racing around the lanes on her bike. A real adrenaline junkie.'

Jayne tried not to sound stiff as she asked, 'Why was she in?'

'A tib-fib break after a particularly enthusiastic somersault session on the trampoline.'

Jayne sucked in a sharp breath. 'Did her parents not have one of those protective guards around the springs?'

Sam nodded. 'That and more. They had it dug into the ground so she wouldn't fall off. They had protective padding. They even had padding for her. But Carlee is her own spirit.'

'Which means…?'

Sam reached over and gave Jayne's knee a squeeze.

'It means Carlee is probably going to be a familiar face up at Grandpont's A&E.'

'The hospital up the road?'

'One and the same.' He smiled. Not gleefully, of course, but nor was it grim.

She wondered if that was how his grandfather had thought of Jules. A live wire who, no matter how much padding she had, would have found herself at the wrong end of a poorly calculated risk at one juncture or another. Which might mean...

No. She could have stopped Jules. Laid out the rules more clearly. End of the road and *no* further.

Sam picked his own dandelion and began plucking off the petals one by one.

She loves me...she loves me not...

He abruptly ripped off the rest of the petals and sprinkled them on the grass. 'I'm sorry things got a bit hot and heavy the other day.'

'Hey. No need to apologise. It takes two to tango.'

They weren't looking at one other, but she could feel the energy buzzing between them tighten.

'I'm glad you're here,' he said eventually. 'I know there's a lot of awkwardness to sort through, but with the surgery being so busy, and Maggie needing your help, it's been a Godsend.'

She tapped his foot with her flower. 'I feel like we've spoken more honestly in the past two weeks than we have in years.'

Sam laughed. 'To be fair, we haven't really talked since we split.'

True. She'd been too frightened to. Too scared to confess to Sam that she was the reason they were kneeling

at the end of this grave. She should have trusted him
enough to tell him. She knew that now.

After a few more moments of silence Jayne stood and
stretched. 'Guess I'd better get back and check on Maggie. The kids'll be back soon, moaning about whatever
gruel I manage to dish up for them.'

Sam's eyes lit up. 'Hey, want to take a look at the Old
Barn on the way?'

Jayne's felt a whoosh of anticipation unfurl in her
heart. 'Absolutely!'

Sam couldn't believe how nervous he was. He *knew* the
house was beautiful. He and his architect father had
spent years designing it. And they'd paid even more attention to detail once they'd started putting it together.
The exact tiles. The precise woodcuts. The perfect window frames. He knew every inch of the place in detail.

It had been a true bone of contention with his wife.

'You love that house more than you love me!'

He'd protested. *Of course he didn't. The house was a
thing...she was his wife.* He'd told her she was being ridiculous, but when she'd gone the house hadn't felt any
different. Which, of course, was when he'd realised it
had never really been *their* home.

As Sam and Jayne turned the corner into the cobbled
barnyard Jayne's hands flew to her mouth. He watched
as she soaked in all the details. The peaked roof. The
dark beams standing out against the golden sandstone.

Her eyes practically glittered with delight. 'Oh,
Sam...it's perfect. It's exactly how I imagined it.'

In that moment he realised just how right his ex had
been. He hadn't built this house for her. He'd built it for
him and Jayne.

CHAPTER EIGHT

GRETA GRINNED AS Sam whistled his way into the surgery the next morning. 'Well, would you take a look at who the lark brought in?'

'An early night and a perfect cup of coffee works wonders.'

It was the truth. After Jayne had left he'd made himself a light supper and spent the evening reading medical journals. Lately, his time at home had felt like filling a void until he could go to work again. Last night he'd really enjoyed being in the house.

He'd loved seeing it through Jayne's eyes instead of seeing it as the time-waster his ex had pronounced it to be. The poor woman. The more he thought about it, the more he wondered how they'd ever thought they were right for one another.

You wanted to be her knight in shining armour.

She'd wanted stability. Village life. A guy with old-fashioned values. He'd given her all those things and married her with the absolute best of intentions. With love.

But in the end the love he'd had to offer her hadn't been enough. Hadn't been on the same scale as the love he'd had for Jayne.

The thought dropped a lead weight in his gut, and he was relieved when Greta handed him a full patient list. Jayne was taking Maggie to the hospital, so he wouldn't have that extra pair of hands he'd come to rely on a bit too quickly.

A few hours, a stack of paperwork and a dozen patients later, Greta rang through. 'You all right if I squeeze in an extra patient this morning?'

'Absolutely! Send him in.'

'Dr Sinclair…?'

'Ah! Mr Sedlescombe.' He got up and ushered in the elderly maths teacher. 'Come on in. Here, let me grab you a chair.'

He took one of the man's canes and held on to his elbow as his former teacher eased himself into the chair.

When Sam sat down again he did a quick scan to see if there was anything visibly wrong. A bit of dry skin on the backs of his hands… There was an aqueous cream for that. His eyes were the slightest bit watery… Nothing too out of the ordinary for an older gent.

'So, Mr Sedlescombe, what can I do for you today?'

'Well, it's a tad embarrassing.'

'Nothing to be embarrassed about here. You know as well as I do that anything you disclose to me in this room will stay right here.'

'Well…' The old gentleman, whose blue eyes still glinted brightly, leant on one of his sticks and threw a quick glance at the closed door. 'I suppose you've heard about my upcoming retirement party?'

'I certainly have. It's going to be part of the fete, isn't it?'

Mr Sedlescombe's thick silver hair caught the light as he nodded. 'Yes, that's right. They're unveiling a long-service plaque for me and the new village AED, if I'm not mistaken. A geriatric and a heart-starter. What a double bill!' Mr Sedlescombe winked.

Sam laughed. 'I'm sure it's more coincidence than a message from above.'

'That may be… But what I'm wondering about is…' He dug into his pocket and pulled out a blister pack of little blue pills.

'Oh!'

Sam's eyebrows near enough shot off his forehead. After a morning of arthritis pills, earaches and blood pressure tests, he certainly hadn't expected this. It was one of the reasons he loved his job. Constantly kept him on his toes.

'So you're interested in a bit of lovemaking after your retirement party?'

'Something like that. But the AED has got me thinking…' He pushed a newspaper clipping onto Sam's desk and tapped it. 'Says here I might have a heart attack if I take these pills.'

Sam quickly scanned the article. 'Well, this poor chap appears to have taken more than the recommended dose.' He picked up the blister pack. 'Mind if I have a look?'

A quick scan revealed they were on the level. He'd obviously ordered them through the post, but they seemed legitimate enough. Sam would be happy to prescribe some through the local pharmacy, but something wasn't sitting right… Sometimes being a GP was a bit like being a detective. A detective with particular sensitivities about people's health and emotional state. Their generational leanings… Social class…

Mr Sedlescombe had taught maths at the village school for as long as Sam could remember. He was often in the local light opera performances. He made a mean Christmas punch. There were some dots he was failing to connect…

'Mr Sedlescombe. Is there something else that's bothering you about taking these pills?'

The elderly gentleman stroked his chin, then finally met Sam's eye. 'Please, call me Terry. And, well… I know this isn't strictly how things are done in the medical profession…diagnosing by the internet and all…but the truth is I was hoping to give them to Vera.'

'Your wife?' Vera, the retired English teacher at the village school, had had a stroke a couple of years back, but regular appointments indicated that everything was pretty much back to normal. 'Why?'

'She thought they might help her.'

The penny dropped. 'Have you been looking into clinical trials about memory loss?'

Relief flooded Terry's features. He'd clearly been uncomfortable disguising the real reason he'd come in.

'Okay. So, what we're really talking about are the clinical trials that are being done on vascular dementia?' He'd read about them too. They were testing people in their fifties and sixties who had had a stroke or were experiencing memory loss. 'If I remember correctly, they're about increasing blood flow by dilating blood vessels?'

Terry nodded. 'Vera ordered these things.' He picked up the packet. 'She did it in my name, so luckily I was the one who opened them up when the post came. I was hoping if you agreed with me that taking these pills is the wrong thing to do, I could dissuade her from taking them.'

'Perhaps the best thing to do would be to bring Vera

down here and we can all talk about it. These aren't the pills they're using in the trials and... Well, it's still a trial.'

Terry nodded in agreement. 'I know. That's what I told her. But she won't come down. No offence to you or your grandfather, but she's taken a notion that she'd like to talk to a woman.'

There was a female GP in the next village, who came in once a week to take appointments for just such a reason, but she and her husband had decided to pack up a caravan and drive across Mongolia for the summer. Sam had been so busy he'd not had a chance to find a suitable replacement.

An idea struck. 'Do you remember Jayne Sinclair? We were in the same maths class.'

Terry's forehead crinkled as he thought back. 'Of course I do. The twin who lost her sister.' His gaze drifted to the church spire, which was visible through the window. 'Her poor parents...not quite sure how they stuck around after that.'

Sam nodded. There it was again. Disbelief that Jayne's parents had stayed in the village.

He was struck by the fact that people still remembered Jayne as 'the poor sister who survived.' What a cross to bear. No wonder she wanted to live somewhere else. The past was shackling her to the worst time in her life.

An uncomfortable feeling tightened in his gut. Was he guilty of the same thing? Had he ever really sat down and thought of her as a leading paediatric surgeon? A woman getting on with her life the best she could?

Maybe he'd been so busy reeling from rejection he'd refused to look at things from her perspective. It was obvious from her reaction to Stella's death that she took her work incredibly seriously. Stepping away from the surgical ward to ensure she only gave her patients her A-game must have taken some serious strength.

It was something he prided himself on when it came to his own patients. Being there for them with nothing less than his best. So why hadn't he been able to do the same when it came to his personal life?

The answer was as plain as the hand in front of his face.

He'd tried to fix Jayne by insisting they keep following their dreams. The engagement, the wedding, Stream's Edge Surgery, The Old Barn... He'd completely missed the fact that everything had changed for her the day her sister had died. Just as he'd missed the signs from Marie that he wasn't including her in the life he'd become so determined to live. The life he'd planned to live with Jayne.

What a pattern! Truly loving someone meant being there for them. Good times. Bad times. It didn't mean trying to jam a person into a predetermined mould. People were malleable. They changed. Love had to be every bit as flexible.

Just as Terry was trying to be with his wife as they approached old age.

He shifted in his chair and gave Terry a *We can do this* smile. 'Jayne's in town for a spell. Now, she's not a GP, but she *is* a highly respected doctor. I'm sure she would be more than happy to speak with your wife.' He glanced at his watch. Jayne should be back from the hospital by now. 'I can ring her right now, if you like. See if she'll pop in some time this afternoon?'

Another wash of relief softened his maths teacher's features. 'You'd do that for me?'

'Of course, Mr— Terry. It would be my pleasure.'

After Sam had reassured himself that everything was okay on the health front for Mr Sedlescombe, he showed the gentleman out of the office. He was completely surprised to see Vera sitting in the waiting room. Her eyes lit up when her husband appeared, bright with expectation. Terry whispered something in her ear and her eyes shot over to Sam. She gave him a brisk nod and a hint of a smile.

Crisis averted.

As he called in the next patient a familiar satisfied feeling filled his chest. *This* was why he did what he did. Now, if he could just convert that to his personal life maybe there'd be some way to see if he and Jayne could find an opportunity to give each other a second chance…

'Everything go all right at the hospital?'

Jayne nodded. 'Yup. Well, as good as can be expected. Maggie isn't taking it quite as easy as they'd like, but the babies are still where they're supposed to be. I've tied her to an armchair and put on a reality show on extreme cake baking. I'm hoping it will hold her interest for the next hour or so.'

'Tied her to a chair?' Sam deadpanned.

'Yeah.' She shrugged. 'It's how we roll in London Town. Now, about Mrs Sedlescombe…'

She was feeling strangely nervous. She prided herself on the personal touch with her own patients, but it wasn't as if she'd learned about split infinitives from any of them. Talking to her former English teacher's wife about whether or not to take erectile dysfunction pills for memory loss felt...*intimate*. A bit like going through her granny's underwear drawer. Something you didn't really *do*.

It's something GPs do, you idiot!

She locked the thought away in the drawer marked 'Yet Another Reason to Respect Sam'.

As if he'd been reading her mind, he gave her shoulder a squeeze. She shook off the little crackles of response she felt at his touch and focused on the words coming out of his mouth. Or was she just staring at his mouth? She'd been kissing that mouth a couple of days ago. *Mmm*...it was a lovely mouth.

Wrong point of focus, woman!

'Don't worry. They know you're not a dementia specialist. Mrs Sedlescombe just thought it would be a bit easier for her to speak with a woman. I think she's more embarrassed than anything.'

Fair enough. It wasn't your everyday conversation about how to stave off the effects of aging.

'And you said Mr Sedlescombe's coming too?' She'd learned fractions from Mr Sedlescombe. And Algebra. The foundation for a lot of the science courses she'd taken in med school.

Sam threw a kind smile towards the waiting room. 'They've been married for ever. He's worried. And, as he's finally taking retirement at the end of the year, I suppose it's just another reminder that they're both getting on. He should've retired about fifteen years ago. I think Vera only retired because she had the stroke. It's sweet, really. He wants to make sure the woman by his side stays the way she is as long as she can. Even if means a bit of embarrassment at the local GP's.'

Wow. If that didn't tug at her heart strings nothing

would. This was village life. In and out of each other's pockets in the best way possible.

'You lot need a female GP on staff.'

Sam shot her a look. *Whoops.* She was meant to have been that person.

'We do have a doctor who comes over from Farmstone once a week, but she's on an extended holiday. You're right, though. With Grandad getting on we probably need someone on a more permanent basis.'

She avoided his eyes just in case they were saying what her brain was... *It could've been you.*

Sam clapped his hands together, as if he was trying to dodge the awkwardness as well. 'All right. I'll call them in, shall I?'

'Sure. Fine. I'll just...' she flicked her thumb towards the office '...I'll just wait in here.'

She went into the homely room and sat down. Then stood up. Then struck what she hoped was a casual pose by the examination table.

Why was she feeling so awkward? Her patients in London were every bit as important to her. Up until a handful of weeks ago her world had all but revolved around them.

A thousand reasons played out in front of her. They hadn't known her when she was in pigtails. Their parents hadn't driven her home from sleepovers. Not one of them had been to her sister's funeral.

She swallowed down the inevitable lump in her throat. So many of Sam's patients had been there for her family that day. Helping Mrs Sedlescombe was the least she could do.

Maybe that was how Sam felt. He could have ended up anywhere in the world. With any other family. Or in another orphanage. He knew how fortunate he'd been, and serving his community was a pleasure, not a penance.

The truth whipped in and shunted through her. Paying penance was the reason why Stella's death hurt so much. She'd put so much pressure on that one surgery to make her world right again, when the truth was nothing would bring her sister back.

As she heard Sam and the Sedlescombes walking down the corridor she made a quick vow to herself. From here on out she'd treat her patients the way Sam did. As individuals with their own journeys. Not stepping stones in her medical career. Maybe she'd never been *that* clinical with her patients, but... The truth hurt. She'd been on a mission, and that mission had failed because she'd had the wrong goal.

Once Sam had shown them in, and the couple had sat down, everything slipped into place as if she'd been having this sort of chats all her life.

Jayne showed Mrs Sedlescombe that the pills she'd bought off the internet weren't the same pills they were using in the trials. She also pointed out to Vera, as she insisted she call her, that the full results from the second stage of the trial had yet to be released.

When it became clear that Vera still had yet to be fully convinced that taking the pills would be risky, she pointed out the potential side effects that might be experienced if she took the pills she'd purchased: sudden and sharp memory loss.

The couple looked at one another in shock. And a little relief.

'I had no idea more memory loss was a side effect.' Vera looked at her husband and gave his wrinkly hand a squeeze. 'I could've made things worse if you hadn't insisted on coming in.'

'That didn't happen, though, love. Did it? We came in and Dr Sinclair set us straight.'

Vera batted at the air between them. 'I feel so silly.'

'Don't,' Jayne insisted. 'Who doesn't want to fix something that seems out of your control?' The list of things *she* wanted to fix wouldn't have fitted on a scroll that circled the earth! 'If you're genuinely worried about memory loss there are a few things I suggest for my paediatric patients.'

Terry tightened his grip on his wife's hand. 'I didn't realise children had strokes.'

Jayne sobered as she explained that anyone could have a stroke. 'The trick as regards memory loss is to keep your brain stimulated. I appreciate you both had a shock when Vera suffered her stroke, but I hope it hasn't changed how you live your life in terms of mental stimulus.'

'Well, no. I still read as much as I ever did.'

Jayne smiled as she remembered Vera's classroom. It had been filled to the brim with books. 'It was you who built her all those bookshelves, wasn't it?'

Terry smiled proudly. 'It was. I got a class who were struggling with the practical application of maths to design them. Couldn't have been prouder.'

'Right. So, that's exactly how you need to continue. Stimulate your brain. Do you play chess?'

Vera nodded. 'Sometimes we pull the board out at the pub.'

Jayne smiled. There was a stack of board games at the pub. Being social would help as well.

'Great! Keep on doing that.' She printed out a list of

other exercises and habitual practices that would help. As she handed it to Vera she said, 'These are actually just wise tips for anyone who's…'

'Who's getting old and wrinkly?'

Jayne laughed. 'I wasn't planning on putting it quite like that—but, yes. As you start to get on in years, looking after yourself gets a bit trickier.'

'Well, it's a good thing I've got this one by my side,' Vera said proudly as she helped Terry up from his chair. He took both canes in one hand, linked his free arm with his wife's.

'Any more questions?'

'Only one,' Terry said, and he reached into his pocket and took out the box of pills they'd been there to discuss. 'Would you mind disposing of these? Safely,' he added with a wink. 'We wouldn't want to put the village's new AED to work any time soon, would we?'

'That we would not,' Jayne said with a smile.

She waved them off, then wandered back along the corridor. She suddenly realised a couple of her father's wildflower meadow paintings were on display there. She should call her parents. Make a better effort. Report on the news from Whitticombe for once, rather than the other way round. A sea-change from their seven-years-old habit of ignoring everything.

Sam popped his head out of his office. 'How'd it go?'

'Good! Great. They're such a lovely couple.'

Sam grabbed hold of the doorframe with one of his hands and leant out further, so he could watch as Mr Sedlescombe let his canes take his weight while he opened the door for his wife.

Jayne watched Sam watching them. He looked so

happy for them. The little crinkles by his eyes were soft with affection.

'What a gentleman,' Sam said.

'You're a gentleman, too!'

'Why, Jayne Sinclair...' He made a half-bow and as he dipped low she was sure a sentimental look washed across his features. When he came back up to his full height he grinned. 'You almost sound as if you're defending my honour.'

He swept the backs of his fingers across her cheek. That crackle of electricity swept through her body in double-time as her heart did a swirly dance around her chest.

Sam's honour didn't need defending. *She* was the one who was the problem. How could she lumber someone so perfect with a girl who hadn't told her own parents about the role she'd played in her sister's death? She couldn't. And nothing would ever change that. Except, of course, taking the risk of a lifetime and coming clean.

She squeezed her eyes tight and tried to picture hell freezing over. Nope. Still bubbling and hot and awful.

'Hey, there.' Sam slid his hand along her arm and dipped his head so he could look directly into her eyes. 'What's going on? You look as though your thoughts have gone dark and broody.'

'Don't be silly.' She gave his chest a little pat, ignoring just how lovely it felt beneath her finger-pads. 'I'm fine.'

Sam stretched his arms out and pressed himself back and forth in the doorframe to his office. It was very distracting. His blond hair just about grazed the top of the frame and her eyes couldn't tear themselves away from his forearms as they went through round after round of cord and release.

The very same forearms that had lifted her up onto the kitchen counter as if she were no heavier than a cotton bud...

Before she could stop herself she lowered her voice and asked, 'Want to meet up later?'

The husky quality of her voice didn't leave any room for interpretation, and in the blink of an eye the atmosphere between them hummed with the same pent-up sexual chemistry that had launched them at one another in Maggie's kitchen.

Sam's eyes raked the length of her. He was so up close and personal he might as well have been doing it with his hands. Her skin felt tingly with anticipation of his actual touch. Blood started roaring round her body and flash flood warnings pounded in her ears.

He gave his jaw a swift scrub. 'How about I take you out instead? A good old-fashioned date? Dinner? Movie?'

She couldn't help it. She did a double-take. 'What?'

He nodded. 'Yup. We're obviously not very good at the friends-only thing, but...' He tipped his head towards the space where the Sedlescombes had just been. 'As far as relationships go, I want what they have. Always have. I wanted that with you. I thought I wanted it with Marie, but it was you all along. So... *Lord.* I can't believe I'm saying all this.'

His opened his palms wide, as if he were baring himself to her.

'I don't want to be your *I'm having a crisis* fling before you head back to London. I want more. And more starts with less. Honesty. Talking. We're human. We've made mistakes. We need to find out if they're mistakes we can forgive one another for.' He dropped her that familiar wink of his. 'So what do you say? Do you fancy a date tonight?'

She bit down on the inside of her cheek. Hard. Her body was vibrating from the bombshells Sam had been dropping all around her in a heart shape.

Commitment.

Mistakes.

Honesty.

She felt as if her insides were being ripped in two. She wanted a second chance with him. Plain as day. But second chances wouldn't work if she didn't tell Sam about Jules.

Would he still want her if he knew the truth?

There was only one way to find out. To pull her socks right up and be brave.

The words that came out of her mouth were totally different, but she hoped he would see she was trying to say yes. Yes, she was willing to try.

'Maggie will need some help getting the children sorted with dinner and bedtime…'

Sam tipped his head back and forth, then smiled that broad, happy smile of his. 'How about we cook them dinner together? That can be the first part of our date and then I'll take you to the Golden Acorn.'

She laughed nervously. 'What? The pub in the centre of the village?'

The one where she'd tactically avoided him for the past seven Christmases?

'That's the one. Great burgers.' He grinned. His tone was still light, but there was something different about him. As if a switch had been flicked. 'We've been dancing around each other for years, Jay. I don't want to do it any more.'

The heated tingles turned cold.

'No. Don't *do* that,' he said.

'What?' She took another step back and bumped into the wall.

'Back away. It's what you always do.'

Yeah. So what? It was her thing.

Determination lit up those green eyes of his. 'I care about you, Jay. Deep in here.' He pressed a hand to his heart. 'I'm pretty sure you feel exactly the same way. But neither of us really knows each other any more. So, from here on out, if you want some of this…' he drew one of his big hands down the length of that sexy body of his '…you're going to have to come out with me. And *talk*. We've got seven years of catching up to do.'

Before she could say it was too much, too soon, too big an ultimatum, Sam ran his finger along her jawline. 'I'm not asking you to marry me. I'm asking you to do what normal people do. Date. We're not the same happy-go-lucky kids we were way back then.'

True.

'We might have changed so much we aren't a match any more.'

Oh. She would put money on the fact that wasn't true, but Sam had a point…it was a possibility.

'If the dates go well, maybe we can enjoy something a bit more…' his tongue swept across his lower lip '…*intimate.*'

Her insides went liquid. In an excruciatingly lovely way. And he still wasn't finished talking.

'And if that goes well… We carry on dating.'

'For how long?' Her voice came out breathless, even though she hadn't so much as moved a muscle.

'For as long as it takes to find out what grown-up Jayne and Sam want. From life. From each other.'

Strewth.

He wasn't saying it straight out, but she got the sub-text. She needed to come clean about why she'd broken their engagement. And *then* they'd decide whether or not to continue.

'What about once Maggie's had her babies and my holiday runs out?'

Everything in her seemed cinched tight as he tipped his head back and forth.

'We'll cross that bridge when we come to it. Look. Jayne…' He pressed his hands to his chest. 'I have a life here. An adult life. With friends. My family. I'd love you to see it. Properly. This is where I want to be. Where I'm happiest. It's all well and good, us living in a little bubble while you're here, but… If you go back to the London Merryweather and decide your life is there, then we go our separate ways. For good.'

'That sounds a bit final.'

If this was what being a bundle of nerves felt like then she was a bundle of nerves. Sam, on the other hand, looked more calm, cool and collected than she'd seen him in ages. Master of his own destiny. It was power-fully attractive.

He moved the pads of his thumbs across the furrows in her brow. Smoothing them out as if he had all the time in the world.

She could barely breathe as he leant in and said, 'I need you in or out of my system, Jayne Sinclair. Ignoring you didn't work. Being mates sure as hell isn't working either. So how about we try a bit of immersion therapy? See if that does the trick?'

It was the most insane invitation she'd ever had. And completely irresistible. Saturate herself with all things Sam so that they could both officially move on...

'You'll cook up a chicken tonight for Maggie and the kids?' she asked, her cheeks pinkening at the breathlessness in her voice.

Sam's voice dropped straight down into the heart of the *come-hither* register. 'I plan on doing more than cooking things up.'

There was no way she could say no. Not with that voice pouring through her system like hot butter.

'Okay.'

'Okay, what?'

'Let's do it. The dinner. The date. All of it.' She bit down on her lip again, trying to keep the panic from her eyes.

'You're sure? There's Maggie to consider. If this is going to send you running for the hills, forget it. It's an all-or-nothing deal.'

'Absolutely.' She bumped into the wall again, then play-punched it as if it was its fault that she'd reversed into it. She took a very definite step towards him. 'I want to go out on a date with you. *And* I will stay here for Maggie.'

The only question was...would she ever have the courage—the strength—to open up completely to Sam about the past?

'Well, then...' Sam's smile was slow in coming but worth the wait. 'It's a date.'

It was a risk. Just the sort of thing Jules would've done. Risked everything for one single perfect moment.

Like the kiss Sam was planting on her cheek at exactly this moment.

'See you at six. I'll bring the chicken.'

CHAPTER NINE

'ARE YOU DICING that shallot or trying to murder it?' Maggie called from the chaise longue.

Sam looked at the poor shallot. 'Bit of both. Doing it this way brings out the natural sweetness,' he fibbed.

He didn't know. He was still wondering what the hell had possessed him to ask Jayne to go out on dates. For the rest of the summer.

Either he was a glutton for punishment or he had actually finally hit on something. Whatever it was, he felt they were finally being open and honest with one another.

He loved her. Always had. Always would. What form that love took… Well, that was still up in the air. But it certainly felt nice to know he was finally doing something about it other than drawing invisible lines that they both kept moving.

He looked over at Jayne, who was distractedly quartering some cherry tomatoes at the table where the children were colouring. Her hair, as usual, was coming loose from the French twist she'd pulled it into. Her blue eyes kept darting up to meet his. Her lips had that extra deep red flush that came from one thing and one thing only: heightened emotions.

It was taking all his brain power not to pull the mostly cooked chicken out of the oven, pop it on the table then take Jayne by the hand and walk very, very quickly down the river lane to his house.

Just as well giving Maggie and her family salmonella was on the no-no list.

He popped the bowl of salad he'd just filled onto the table. 'Tomatoes can go in there when you're done, love.'

All the eyebrows in the room shot up at that one. He'd not called Jayne 'love' before. Judging from the streaks of red on her cheeks and the flash of her smile, she didn't mind all that much. Perhaps a bit of good old-fashioned wooing was what they needed. Courtship. Manners. Respect.

'Nice pinny, Sam,' said Cailey, Maggie's littlest.

'Do you think it matches my eyes?' Sam tugged at the edges of the apron and struck a pose.

Maggie's children applauded. Apparently pink roses and frills suited him.

He didn't know why he was being such a show-off. Maybe to counterbalance just how quiet Jayne was being. Not in a weird way, as if she was going to bolt or anything. It was more…she was being *shy*. Though he knew that at heart a lot of her bluster and bravura was a front, he hadn't seen the shy girl he'd fallen in love with for years.

Maggie's wolf-whistle broke through his thoughts. 'Gorgeous!'

He caught her throwing Jayne a saucy wink.

'And I'm not just talking about the chicken.'

Jayne, much to his satisfaction, flushed even more deeply.

He chopped up a few bits of bacon and slung them in a

small frying pan. Maggie claimed her children wouldn't
eat peas. Today they would. Today he could do anything.

'Where did all the village fete artwork go? I thought
you lhad a gallery's worth of artwork in progress?'

'We did.' Maggie shrugged. 'Jayne's moved everything.'

'Where?'

'To our bedrooms,' Connor said as he finished his
drawing of a tree with a flourish. 'She said she didn't
want you to think she always lived like a heathen.'

His eyes shot to hers. 'Oh, she did, did she?'

She licked her lips. 'As if… We just needed room at
the table.'

'You normally just push everything to the side,' Cailey said, as she too wrapped up a drawing of abstract
bunny rabbits.

Maggie was cackling away in the corner.

'I'm glad my cleaning attack has amused you all so
deeply,' Jayne sniped imperiously.

'Oh, is *that* what we're calling it?' Maggie teased.

'Why? What would *you* call it?' Jayne asked, then
immediately looked as if she regretted doing so.

'I'd call it trying to impress a boy,' Maggie said
through another wave of laughter.

At which point the children began singing a song
about going on a date. 'A date! A date! Jayne's going on
a date! She's going on a date and the boy is *Sam*.'

Jayne dumped the tomatoes into the salad and announced that she was going upstairs to change. 'I'll meet
you at the pub.'

'What? I thought I'd walk you there, just as soon as
I set supper out for this lot,' said Sam.

The children and Maggie turned to her as if they were watching a tennis match.

She shook her finger back and forth. 'No can do. If this is going to be our first proper date then I want to make an entrance.'

For the next fifteen minutes, while he pulled Maggie and the kids' meal together, he whistled.

Jayne stared at her reflection, then grabbed the make-up remover and swiped off her third attempt at casual, sexy, smoky but not too horny eyes. Maybe she should simply give her lashes a swipe of mascara and have done with it.

She closed her eyes against her reflection, trying to figure out what on earth had possessed her to go along with Sam's hare-brained scheme.

Hormones had obviously played their role, but basically she'd agreed to date him for the rest of the summer. *Madness.*

An image of Mr Sedlescombe opening the door for his wife as he teetered along on his canes popped into her head, along with Sam's voice. *'I want what they have.'*

Had she said yes because somewhere deep inside her she did too?

He'd been right about one thing. She cared for him. Deeply. More than that. She loved him. But loving him and doing right by him were two totally different things. The last thing she wanted to do was break his heart again. If she had any sort of bravery she'd rip the plaster off and tell him tonight. *She* was the reason Jules was dead. Her guilt was what had fuelled their break-up.

The only mercy had been falling in love with surgical paediatrics. She adored her job. But being back here was a vivid reminder of how she had absolutely no life beyond the hospital walls.

As strange as it was to admit, she was really enjoying being back in Whitticombe. Running all Maggie's errands. Taking the children to birthday parties and play-dates. Working at the clinic...

Being here had thrown a spotlight on a side of village life she'd never experienced as an adult. Maggie was right. It was nice knowing you could actually borrow a cup of flour from your neighbour, or tap on the window of a shop that had just closed if you needed a pint of milk. People here were kind. Thoughtful. Generous.

The same people who didn't know that *she* was the reason her sister wasn't alive and well in London instead of her.

It's your life. Live it. She heard the words as if Jules herself had said them.

Fault lines had begun to appear in the narrative she'd been telling herself for years. Though she'd been through it a thousand million times, was there even the slightest chance that Jules would have slowed down even if Jayne had been able to catch up with her? Jules had always been a daredevil. She had always thrown caution to the wind. She'd never played it safe.

It's your life, that voice in her head said again. *Live it.*

'What do you mean you're *off the market*?' Ethel was looking at Sam as if he'd just grown an extra pair of ears. And feathers.

'I mean, thank you, Ethel for offering to set me up on a date, but... I think I'm okay for now.'

Ethel's eyes narrowed. He knew that look. It was her I-might-be-your-publican-but-I-am-also-your-friend look.

'It wasn't your manners I was quizzing you about, young man. I was quizzing you about your nous. You won't be finding yourself a wife by holing up at the surgery or in that big house of yours.'

'I know. I'm not saying that's the plan.'

'Oh! So you have a *new* plan now, do you?' She pursed her lips at him and started pulling a pint. 'Are you going to let me in on this new plan of yours?'

She handed him the pint and didn't wait for an answer, which was fine. He didn't want to say. Not just yet. Ethel was about as protective as his sisters when it came to his love-life, so picking The Golden Acorn to show rather than tell everyone his plan was bordering on insanity.

He smiled and took a long draft of his pint. He was obviously infuriating Ethel, but she'd see what he was talking about in a matter of minutes. Seconds, if he was lucky.

Ethel swiped at the counter with a cloth before he put his pint down. 'What's this really about, Sam? It isn't like you to be a quitter.'

Oh, he wasn't quitting… He was—

Oh, hell.

The front door to the pub had opened and framed by a million summer roses was Jayne Sinclair.

A hush fell over the place, much the way it did in Wild West films when a woman with all the right curves in all the right places walked into a saloon in a town that hadn't seen so much as a flicker of a feminine touch in years.

Sam swallowed. Hard.

Jayne's hair was down. Flowing over her shoulders

like liquid silk. Her blue eyes were clean of the make-up she often wore. Maybe a swoop of mascara. Nothing on her lips. She didn't need it.

And her dress…

It was a knock-your-socks-off number.

The blue fabric matched her eyes to a T, and the nineteen-fifties style was modest…but it was making the most of her beautiful figure. The cuffed sleeves weren't so much covering her shoulders as offering a bit of a tease of the soft, creamy skin it was resting on. The bodice hugged her torso just so, before arrowing in to a slim belt where the skirt flared out from her hips.

In the driest tone he'd ever heard from Ethel, she intoned, 'I think I understand what your plan is a bit more clearly now, Sammy boy.'

He nodded at her, still waiting for the air to return to his lungs. Jayne certainly knew how to knock a man sideways.

That shyness he'd noted earlier was still wafting round her like a brand-new perfume. He crossed over and leant in to give her a kiss on the cheek. *Mmm.* Cinnamon…and something else. Orange? Whatever it was, it *was* a new perfume, and it smelt about as delicious as she looked.

He looked at the lemons dotted all over the fabric of her dress, then back up at her.

Jayne smoothed her hands along her skirt, then said, 'I decided to make lemonade.'

Wow. There was a lot in that simple statement. He hadn't ever thought about life handing her lemons, but there was the obvious. No one would have equated her sister's death to anything *good*, but he'd always presumed she saw her sister's accident as just that. An accident. Cruel, bad luck. A tragedy.

But tonight was about fresh starts. And making lem- onade. He put out his arm, just as Terry Sedlescombe would for his wife. 'May I?'

Jayne smiled and tucked her hand in the crook of his arm. 'Don't mind if I do.'

They stopped by the bar and got a glass of wine for Jayne. Ethel shot her a difficult to read look. Half smile, half don't-you-dare-mess-with-our-boy. To Jayne's credit, she smiled and complimented Ethel on how nice the pub looked—which, of course, immediately put her back in the good books. Ethel's life was this pub, and anyone who lavished it with compliments couldn't go wrong.

'I'll send someone over with a couple of menus,' she said as they picked up their drinks.

After they'd sat down and ordered Sam lifted up his glass. 'Cheers, my dear.'

'Cheers to you, Sam.'

They clinked glasses and drank.

'So,' Sam said, suddenly very keen to make good on his silent promise to court Jayne, 'tell me about yourself.'

Three hours later Jayne couldn't remember when she'd laughed so much. She'd forgotten what a good story- teller Sam was, and life in Whitticombe had given him anecdotes in spades.

She loved watching him relive the stories as he told them. The way his green eyes lit up bright when it was a happy one…the way they darkened when it was sad.

She nearly spat out her wine when he embarked on a story about a woman who'd got her arm caught in her daughter's hamster cage, had been bitten by the hamster, then walked into the surgery with the entire thing still attached!

'She was screaming away. Swearing she'd build the hamster a little raft and set it loose on the river. Her daughter was with her, sobbing, "No, Mummy. No! Fluffy doesn't know how to swim!" Poor Greta was beside herself.'

'What did you do?'

'Washing up liquid.' He mimed easing the mother's arm out of the cage door. 'Her hamster bite was treated and her tetanus jab was boosted and the little girl carried her fluffy pet home, scolding it all the way for being so mean to her mummy. The next year it won Best In Show at the village fete pet show.'

'Hilarious.' She wiped away a couple of tears. 'We don't get too much in the way of that sort of drama at the London Merryweather. At least not in my department.'

Sam's smile dimmed. 'I suppose things are a bit more of the life-and-death variety there?'

She nodded. They are. The last thing a parent would want is for their child to be admitted to the London Merryweather because it means only one thing: it's their only hope.

'But you enjoy it, right? It's your dream?'

She took a sip of her wine to delay answering the question. The London part? Not so much. The work part? She loved it. But discovering it wasn't enough had been one hell of a knock to her blinkered quest to do a heart transplant.

Admitting as much? She wasn't quite there yet. So she did what she always did. Changed the topic.

'How's your dad getting on? You know…on his own?

It must be weird, knocking around that big house on his own.'

Despite the sombre topic, Sam laughed. 'You think my sisters let him knock around the house on his own?'

Jayne didn't have to think about it that long. 'No.' She grinned.

He cleared his throat and rubbed his hands along his chair's armrest. 'When Mum died he volunteered to look after Elf. Now whenever I come to pick the dog up he looks as though I'm tearing him away from his bestie, so it's looking like I'll be in the market for a new dog soon.' He gave a little laugh. Half wistful. Half sad.

Her heart ached for him. It was easy to see how much he missed his mum. She reached across and touched his arm. 'I am so very sorry about your mother.'

'Thank you, that's kind.' His voice was gruff.

'And very, *very* overdue.' She was about to apologise for not staying for the wake, but even making it to the church service had taken a Herculean effort. Funerals and Whitticombe weren't her thing.

Sam stopped playing with his beer mat. 'Have you heard anything from your parents?'

She shook her head, almost feeling the weight of her conscience dragging her chin down to her chest.

'Are you planning on calling them?'

'Yes. Yes, I am. But it's…complicated. Once I left for London we…' Oh, God. Her voice was beginning to crack. 'We found it easier, I guess. Moving on from things in our own way.' Which begged the question… 'Why did *you* never come to London? We'd talked about it. You doing a year or so in one of the hospitals there.'

'You *know* why,' Sam said, his eyebrows doing that

little swan-dive towards the furrow between his brows. 'You told me not to. *"Don't follow me. Do your thing. We're through."'*

'Crikey.' She covered her face with her hands, then dropped them. 'I was pretty horrible to you.'

'I won't disagree with you, but it wasn't as if life was a bed of roses for you either. So long as you're happy in London, I guess it's all turned out for the best.'

She blew some air up at a few errant hairs, then blurted out the truth. 'I love the hospital. I *really* love the work. But...'

He took hold of her hands and gave them a squeeze. 'But...?'

She saw everything she'd always wanted in his eyes. Kindness. Love. Trust.

Here goes nothing.

'I don't really have a life.'

'What?'

He dropped her hands and instantly she felt the loss of his touch.

'I thought you were always out and about. Going to the clubs. Dating. Living the life.' He did a little dance move as if that would make it all true. Sparkly and delightful.

She *was* out. She was out a lot. At the hospital.

'There might've been just an itty-bitty bit of fibbing about how social I've been.' She pinched her fingers together, then squished them tight.

She'd tried to do a few of the things she'd thought Jules would love when she'd first got her job at the London Merryweather. Clubbing. Zany charity events. Skydiving... The mere thought of that last one sent shivers rippling along her arms. None of them had stuck. No matter how hard she'd tried, they'd scared her silly.

'Looks like someone should've brought a sweater.' Sam tipped his head at the goose pimples skittering all the way up to her neck.

Jayne took the comment as a chance to skip over the obvious follow-up question. *Why do you stay in London, then?*

It had used to be super-obvious.

Because Jules couldn't.

Because Jayne needed to live the life Jules never would.

But she wasn't exactly doing a stellar job of it, was she? Would Jules have settled for second-best if there had been a better fit for her somewhere else?

She looked towards Maggie's cottage. 'You're right. It is cold. Maybe we'd better head back so I can help get the kids to bed. Give Maggie her night-time foot-rub.'

Sam pulled out Jayne's chair and held his arm in the direction of the rose-covered path that led to Maggie's.

As first dates went it had hardly been the stuff of rainbows, unicorns and floating cupids. They'd covered his ex-wife, his recently deceased mother, his widowed father and then—skirting it, but touching on it—what sounded like her not entirely happy life in London.

But, hey. They were on a date and speaking to one another. Openly and honestly. It wasn't as if he had been expecting her to tell him she was going to give notice on her job and move back for good.

Communicating this way felt healing. It was a hell of a lot better than the hollow-eyed looks he'd received when he tried to talk to her after Jules had died.

When they reached Maggie's, Jayne gave him a soft smile. 'Thanks for dinner?'

They laughed.

'That wasn't really meant to come out as a question.'

He pulled her to him and they shared what felt like their first proper 'just like the old days' hug.

Sure. There were differences. They'd both seen and experienced things that had left marks on each of their hearts. But sometimes those scars made a person stronger.

He crooked a finger and tipped up her chin so that they were looking into one another's eyes.

'As first dates go I think it was pretty good.'

Jayne huffed out a *yeah, right* laugh.

Okay, fine. It had been weird. What *wasn't* weird was this. Holding her in his arms. Feeling her thighs brush against his. Her breasts pressing lightly into his chest. Her lips just inches away from his own.

'Was it good enough to go on another one?' she whispered.

He saw it then. The vulnerability in her eyes. And everything that made him the man he was wanted to reassure her that whatever was going on between the pair of them would work out for the best. Even if neither of them knew right now what form that might take.

'Absolutely,' he said, then dipped his head to kiss her ever so softly on the lips, the nose, the forehead. 'Sweet dreams, love.'

She smiled and blew him a kiss as she climbed the steps to the door. 'And you.'

He waited until the door had closed behind her before turning to go. It was early days, but maybe now would be a good time to feel a bit of optimism.

* * *

'You're looking rather cheery today,' Maggie observed as Jayne wiped the crumbs from the unburnt breakfast toast from the table.

How could she not? That one solitary sweet kiss at Maggie's front door had given her the first night of restful dreams she'd had in years. Sure, the evening had been unusual in terms of conversation topics, but—tempting as it was to live in a happy romantic bubble—they were doing their best to address real issues. Otherwise, how on earth were they ever going to trust one another? More to the point, how was Sam ever going to trust her.

'You're humming,' Maggie said.

'I just *love* keeping a happy, tidy home,' said Jayne on a *tra-la-la*.

Maggie snorted. 'Yeah, right…' She made a show of lumbering over to the kitchen window and looked out towards the river. 'How were my little rascals when you sent them off to school this morning? Sorry I couldn't get up.'

'Rascally.' Jayne laughed. 'And don't worry about not getting up. That's why I'm here.'

They'd been great, actually. Now that they were used to having someone else get them sorted for school. She was also enjoying being called Auntie Jayne. Before, when Maggie had had them do it, it had felt false. As if everyone were putting on a show that this stranger was a part of their lives. Now she felt connected to Maggie in a much more real way. They were proper friends again. Friends who were *there* for one another.

'Right, girlie! You ready to make some more bunting for the fete?'

'Ugh. Why did I decide it needed to be handmade?'

Maggie waddled back to her chaise longue. 'Are you sure this thing can handle me?'

Jayne laughed. 'It's been handling you for the past few weeks. I don't see why it should stop now.'

Maggie flicked her thumb in the direction of the downstairs loo. 'I just stood on the scales.'

'Oh...?' Jayne kept her reaction neutral. Weight gain during pregnancy was normal. A rapid weight gain— especially with Maggie's diagnosis of pre-eclampsia— could indicate something much, much worse. 'How much was it this time?'

'About three kilos.'

'Okay...well, let's check again in a couple of hours. See if there's any change.'

It was a lot for an overnight weight gain, but nothing to get too concerned over. Not yet, anyway.

Maggie sat down and, with Jayne's help, swung her legs up on to the cushions. 'Mmm...nice. Okay.' She started issuing instructions. 'Pull that table over here. I need a the polka dotted fabric and the one with the butterflies. And the ribbons, too, please.'

After Jayne had set Maggie up with her tower of material, ribbons and a wealth of needles and thread, she sat down at the kitchen table and poured out a jar of buttons. This huge old oak table had seen a lot of action lately. Family meals, crafting, planning for the fete, Sam's roast chicken...

She wondered if she might ever share a table with Sam that would become embedded with their own memories.

It's still early days, yet.

'Throw the scissors over, would you, Jayne?'

Jayne mimed hurling them across the room, and then

presented them to her as a courtier might bring a gift to a queen.

'Thanks, friend.'

Maggie's thank-you flew straight into her heart. It was one of those special thank-yous. The type that actually meant *I knew I could count on you.*

A thought spiralled round her brain, then clattered into her heart. Had she got the trust thing wrong?

Sharing the details of Stella and the surgery had been painful, but Sam hadn't judged her. Hadn't pushed her away. He'd pulled her in closer. Told her she would heal. Told her that everyone would help, that they were there for her. In good times and in bad.

Then why didn't you trust Maggie when Jules died? Your parents? Sam?

She rammed a button onto her canvas and succeeded in gluing her finger to it. Served her right.

Living with her secret had driven such a thick wedge between her and the life she now knew she wanted to live. One with balance and friends and, most importantly, love. Sam was the love of her life, and keeping this one simple truth from him made the whole idea of a fresh start a joke.

Her mother had told her to look after Jules. When her daredevil sister had insisted they do something to celebrate her engagement, pulling out their bicycles had just popped into her mind. She'd never once thought it would lead to Jules's death. She'd pictured the two of them tootling along to the pub for a celebratory glass of fizz. Not high-tailing it down the road as Jules led, shouting over her shoulder about needing to feel the wind in her hair and the rush of danger in her veins.

As button after button went down on her canvas Jayne relived the scene.

She'd tried to catch up with Jules. Her lungs had burnt with the effort. She'd pushed and pushed her pedals as hard as she'd been able to, but despite her efforts she hadn't been as fast as that sports car had.

Since that day her life had become an endless race. A relentless push to catch up with a girl who had died because of a longing to feel the wind in her hair.

Jayne fought the urge to close her eyes, knowing the scene would play itself out yet again if she did. Instead she glued button after button.

So much good had come of the last few weeks. The renewal of friendships. The gentle healing of old wounds with Sam. She didn't want to lose that. But would honesty do more good or make her biggest fear come true? That the family and friends she loved would turn their backs on her the way she'd turned her back on them so they wouldn't see her pain.

Maggie looked up from her project and saw Jayne furiously working away. 'Show me.'

Jayne held up her canvas. A dog could have done a better job. 'What do you think?'

Maggie tried her best not to smirk. And then she couldn't hold it in any more. She laughed until tears began to roll down her cheeks.

'That bad?'

Maggie's hands moved to her swollen tummy. 'Let's just say the apple didn't fall very close to the tree when it comes to artistic abilities.'

Jayne didn't take offence. She'd never been artistic. But the comment hurt. Not only was she not anything like her parents, she had failed them in the most epic way possible.

She made a vow then and there to ring them tonight. Tell them everything. Fly up and see them if need be. Maybe face to face would be better…

She started making a to-do list in her head. The children would need help if she went. Maggie would need looking after. There were Sam's sisters… They might help. And after the surgery closed perhaps Sam could make his famous roast chicken again—

'Jayne?'

Maggie was swiping away tears with one hand and holding her stomach with the other.

'Yes, honey? What's up?'

Jayne went over to her in case she needed to be handed something. When she got there the crimson stain of blood told her all she needed to know.

She didn't need art supplies. She needed an ambulance.

CHAPTER TEN

'WHEN IS THE ambulance coming?'

It was about the fifteenth time Jayne had asked since she'd rung him.

'Soon.'

Sam snuggled the quilt up to Maggie's back as Jayne held her on her side. It would be a makeshift stretcher if the paramedics couldn't get their gurney into the old-fashioned kitchen. It would also be a protection against the hard stone floor if she had a seizure.

Once they'd got the quilt in place Jayne put a cool cloth on her friend's forehead. A distraction, really.

'Mags, try not to twist and turn so much, all right? Sam needs to insert a cannula in your forearm.'

There was no hint of panic in her voice, but Sam could see fear in her eyes. Maggie's pregnancy was going rapidly, dangerously wrong. The paramedics' arrival time might very well be a question of life or death.

'Magnesium should help with the cramping, Mags, okay?'

Jayne stopped still for a second, swept her hair away from her shoulders and cocked her head to the left. 'I think I hear the ambulance. Shall I go out and flag it down?'

'No. They know where to come. Hold Maggie's arm

steady… On my count I'm going to insert the cannula. And one…two…three. Job done.'

'The cramping's getting worse!' Maggie screamed, paled, then whispered, 'The children. Don't let the children see me like this.'

Jayne shot him a grim look.

'You stay with Mags. I'll go. There's diazepam if she starts to seize or the cramps get too severe. I've already drawn a five-milligram injection.' He pointed to where he'd put it, within arm's reach, and then headed for the front door.

He'd rung the village school, but hadn't been able to get through to the head teacher before running out of the surgery and along the river to Maggie's cottage. Seeing their mother like this would be terrifying.

Jayne mouthed a quick thank-you as she calmly and quietly continued to make Maggie as comfortable as she could.

This, he realised, was the Jayne her patients met. Serious, compassionate, and committed to seeing things through no matter what the circumstances. Her hospital had one hell of an asset in her.

He ran out onto the lane just as the children appeared with another mum. He took her to one side and quietly explained the situation. She immediately insisted on having them over at her house for the night.

When he got back to the house Jayne was taking Maggie's blood pressure again. He raised an eyebrow instead of asking the obvious. *Too high?* Her tight expression was all the answer he needed.

Hypertension was the last thing Maggie needed. She was already on tablets for high blood pressure. They had obviously stopped working. The consequences were almost impossible to take on board. Stroke, heart failure, aneurysm…and the list went on.

'I'm not going to lose my babies, am I?' Maggie's voice was breathy and the words came out in individual gasps.

Sam knew as well as Jayne did that she could absolutely lose the twins. They could even lose Maggie.

'I think it might be H E-L-L-P Syndrome,' he said in a low voice.

'What's that?' Maggie wailed.

Not low enough.

He and Jayne shared a sharp look. Simply put, it wasn't anything she wanted to have.

'It can complicate a pregnancy,' Jayne said as she used a fresh cool cloth to wipe away a sheen of sweat from Maggie's forehead.

She was putting it mildly. H-E-L-L-P was a life-threatening pregnancy complication. It struck hard and fast. If she didn't get to a hospital soon the outcome was grim.

Sam had been so jacked up after that sweet, simple kiss with Jayne last night he hadn't been able to sleep. So he'd read medical journals instead. Fate, or luck, or whatever it was had led him to articles about pre-eclampsia and its equally nasty cousin H-E-L-L-P.

Sam forced himself to slow his thoughts down, focus in on the details.

H-E-L-L-P. Haemolysis. Elevated liver enzyme levels. Low platelet levels. Maggie's red blood cells would be breaking down. Her liver enzymes would be damaging the cells in her liver, leading to organ failure. All this while her platelet count would be plummeting, leading to internal bleeding. The long and the short of it meant that her life and the babies' lives were at serious risk.

Sweat was running off of Maggie's forehead as fast as Jayne could wipe it away. Her breathing was becoming tighter—a sign that fluid was filling her lungs.

'It's only a guess, honeybun. We need to get to the hospital before we know all the facts.' Jayne was soothing. She caught Sam's eye and he saw the doctor in her take over. 'She's been gaining weight over the past week. All fluid, from the look of things. It shifts when she rolls on to her side. She's also been complaining of a bit of tingling in her hands. I thought it might be because she was doing too much. Miss Arts-and-Crafts, here, doesn't *do* idle.'

'You're not blaming the *bunting*, are you? We *need* it! The village needs it!' Maggie gasped.

'No, love. Don't worry about that now.'

He nodded at Jayne. He understood what she was saying. Getting Maggie to rest properly was as easy as getting a puppy not to wag its tail.

Then Jayne delivered the punchline. 'Right before I called you she started complaining of shoulder pain and blurred vision. Then the cramping hit, big time.'

Classic H-E-L-L-P. Although it was a difficult syndrome to diagnose. Especially without blood and urine tests.

They did the best they could to make Maggie comfortable as the wail of sirens drew closer. Sam shot outside and ran the paramedics through the scenario as they jogged towards the house, flanking a wheeled stretcher.

They entered the kitchen just as Jayne was giving a very pale-faced Maggie a cervical examination.

She looked directly at Sam. 'We need to get her into Theatre ASAP. Otherwise we're having twins right here.'

Together they swiftly shifted Maggie to the trolley and fitted her with an oxygen mask. Sam ran through the symptoms again, and then medications they'd need to counterbalance premature labour as they hurried Maggie into the ambulance.

When it was time for one of them to jump in with her Jayne deferred to Sam. 'You're her doctor.'

'No.' He shook his head. 'You're her *friend*.'

She squeezed his hand tight and hopped in alongside her.

Just as they were about to close the doors Jayne stopped them. 'Are you coming too?'

His heart slammed against his ribcage. She didn't need him there, but in those blue eyes of hers he could see it as plain as the hand in front of his face. She *wanted* him with her.

She didn't need to ask him twice.

He drove his own car behind the ambulance and ran from the car park to catch up with them as they hurried Maggie straight into an operating theatre.

When Jayne moved to follow the surgical team, one of the surgeons held his hand out as they shifted Maggie on to the surgical trolley. 'I'm sorry. We've got this now. Friends and family have to wait outside.'

One of the nurses called out. 'Blood pressure's rising. Two-ten over one hundred!'

All the blood drained from Jayne's face. *Maggie could die.*

The surgeon put his hand out again as she lunged towards the open doors of the operating theatre. 'Sorry. We need you to leave. *Now.*'

Sam wrapped his arms around her from behind and held her tight. The surgeon was right. She was too close. Far too close. Although he could feel the fight in her, he also sensed acceptance. And if she was going to have to wait with anyone, fight with anyone, grieve with anyone, she could do it with him.

And that was one hell of a sea-change from seven years ago when her sister had been killed.

All they could do was watch and wait.

Surgeons were pouring into the operating theatre. More trolleys were wheeled in, and lamps, IV stands and meds were all steered into place around Maggie.

Jayne's eyes shot to Maggie, who was being hooked up to a fresh IV line. 'Look. She's scratching at her hands.'

They all knew what that meant. Liver failure.

'Please,' she pleaded. 'Let me scrub in.'

One of the surgeons shook his head. 'You should be calling the father. He'll want to know as soon as possible.'

'We're on it.'

Sam shifted his hold on Jayne and wrapped an arm firmly round her shoulders. She was living her worst nightmare all over again. Watching someone close to her fight for her life. Maggie was his friend, too. He got it. This was terrifying. But part of surviving was knowing when to step back.

'He's right, Jayne. We should leave them to it.'

The surgeon gave him a quick nod of thanks and then disappeared behind the swinging doors.

Jayne whirled round, her expression a mix of anger and confusion. The cool, calm, collected surgeon had quite clearly left the building.

'I should be in there!'

'No.' Sam knew he was on solid ground here. 'You shouldn't. You're like family to Maggie. Why do you think she wanted you back here in Whitticombe?'

Jayne flicked her thumb towards the operating theatre. 'Uh…that's pretty obvious, isn't it?'

'Tell yourself whatever you want, Jayne. But she didn't ask you here to be her doctor.'

She shook her head. 'Of *course* she did. We all know I've barely been home over the past seven years. I hardly knew her kids before now. I've failed her. I've not been a good friend to her. To *any* of you.'

As refreshing as it was to hear her being so honest, she was really missing the point. Hadn't she yet realised that true friendship had a way of skipping over the glitches in times of trouble?

'Good? Bad? Doesn't matter now, Jayne. You're the friend she wanted with her. And you delivered. You've been here for her.'

He put his arm round her shoulders again and led her towards the waiting room. It was directly across from a handful of smaller, quieter rooms. The rooms where they delivered the news no one wanted to hear.

When they reached the chairs she shook his arm off her shoulders. 'Sorry, I just—'

She didn't sound apologetic. He got it. She was reliving bad memories. Falling back into old habits. But he wasn't about to let her dive back into that rabbit hole again. Not after the huge strides they'd made.

'I know you're hurting. That you want a chance to fix something. But this isn't work and it definitely isn't the past.' He took her face in his hands and looked her straight in the eye. 'This is *family*, Jayne. Right here and now. And family stick together. Especially when times are tough.'

He stopped her when she started to protest.

'She called you because she was scared—and having you here helped reduce that fear. You are *not* the person who should be in there delivering those babies. You are the person who should be out here, praying and hoping and doing everything else a friend who loves someone does at times like these.'

It was tough love at its cruellest.

He knew she'd been in a waiting room much like this before. Hoping. Praying. Covered in blood just as she was now.

This was a make-or-break moment for her. One he was going to have to stand back and watch even if it pulled his heart straight out of his chest.

She could either choose love, family...*him*...and all the messy joy that came along with that, or go back to the treadmill in London. Fixing and fixing and fixing tiny little hearts and hoping that one day it would heal the wounds she was so obviously still nursing.

As the seconds ticked past, and her eyes flicked again and again to the wide surgical doors, Sam realised that the foundations of friendship and healing they'd built over the summer would either come true...or she'd run again. Run as if her life depended on it.

Jayne's lower lip had begun to quiver. She was visibly fighting the emotion, swiping at non-existent tears. There was a battle raging between her heart and head and he had no idea which was winning.

She blew out a shaky breath, and in the most fright-

ened voice he'd ever heard from her asked, 'Do you
think she'll be okay?'

It was an awful thing to admit, but Sam didn't know.
She was asking him for moral support, not false assurances, but... By God, he would have given anything in
the world to say yes.

This was one of those awful cases where medicine
and nature were fighting one another. It was a race
against time. For Maggie. For the babies.

It might be that there would be three coffins at a funeral.

It might be that there would be one hell of a chris-
tening party.

Only time would tell.

As they sat, silently waiting, he tried to put himself
in Jayne's shoes. Imagine what it must have been like
that day all those years ago, sitting and waiting, covered
in bloodstains as she was now.

Though Jules had been declared brain-dead at the
scene they had still brought her in. Triple-checked that
there wasn't the slightest hint of neurological activity.

Jayne had sat in a chair like this. Hoping and praying.
She'd seen doctors appear, fresh from the operating theatre, sombre expressions on their faces, asking her parents to come into one of those quiet rooms. She'd heard
their wails. Their cries of despair. Their pain.

Something he hadn't remembered for years suddenly
pinged to the fore. It was hardly the silver lining they
were looking for, but he thought it was something worth
remembering.

He enclosed her hand with his, rubbing the back of
her palm with his thumb. She didn't try to yank it away,

so even though she wasn't looking at him, he knew she was listening.

'You know, I don't know if this is any solace to you, but when I think back to Jules and you and me, and all the things that went wrong after she died, I try to remind myself of the good that came from that day.'

'What are you talking about?'

There was a coldness in her tone that scared him, but he persisted. 'The lives Jules saved.'

'Again.' She tugged her hands free and balled them into fists on her lap. 'I have no idea what you're talking about.'

'Jayne, c'mon… You remember. The organ donations.'

'What?' She looked at him as though he was telling her a story about aliens taking over the village, not recounting actual facts.

'You must remember. The only reason your sister lived as long as she did…the reason she was able to become an organ donor…was because of *you*.'

Jayne's look of disbelief had never been more complete. 'No, it wasn't. The reason she *died* was because of me.'

Now it was his turn to be confused. 'What are you talking about? You two were out riding your bikes. It wasn't your fault that sports car came by when it did.'

Jayne looked him straight in the eye and said, 'It was my fault that she was there when it did.'

'What are you *talking* about?' he repeated.

The words came tumbling out. 'She came home to celebrate our engagement. You know Jules… She couldn't do it in any ordinary way. A huge hug and a kiss weren't enough. She wanted to *do* something. So I suggested we race our bikes down to the pub. The winner had to buy the other a glass of fizz...'

Sam's stomach turned. He knew which way this was going.

'She wanted to race. I didn't. So I was dawdling. I was frustrating her. Which always made her want to go faster. She said she wanted to feel the wind in her hair so she took off her helmet. Threw it in a hedge. It took me a minute to pick it up and then I couldn't catch her. I tried so hard but I couldn't catch up.'

Sam felt his skin go clammy as the information sucked the oxygen from his lungs. Jayne held herself responsible for her sister's death. If Jules hadn't come home to celebrate their engagement...

Hell. What a load to bear.

Losing someone you loved was hard enough. But feeling *responsible* for it in the wake of what should have been the happiest time of your life... How did a person crawl out from beneath that sort of guilt?

She had to be made to see it from a new perspective. It was the only way she could allow herself to live again.

Jayne *wasn't* guilty of Jules's death. If the logic she was using applied it would mean *he* was complicit too. If he hadn't proposed...

Oh, God. Had she been trying to protect him from owning any of the guilt by heaping it all upon herself? But if that sort of logic worked it would be never-ending. *Everyone* would end up being involved.

If they hadn't been at the same school... If her parents hadn't moved to Whitticombe... If his parents hadn't adopted him...

No. Life didn't work like that. Jules had been an adrenaline junkie and that car had been speeding.

Plain as.

There was no way he was going to let her carry this on her own any more.

'Jayne—you *created* life that day…you did not destroy it. You did CPR. Kept the blood pumping through Jules's heart. To all her organs. That was why she was able to be an organ donor. You saved at least three other lives that day.'

'It doesn't matter how many lives were saved that day!' She looked up to the ceiling, dragged her fingers through her dark hair and shook her head. '*Urgh.* I don't mean that. Of course I don't. What I mean is, I destroyed the one life that mattered to my family. To *me*.'

She may as well have stabbed him in the heart. The *one* life that had mattered?

Again, life didn't work like that. His father was a case in point. His world had completely revolved around Sam's mum…but had her death stopped him from living life? For a while. Yes. But not for ever. Grief slashed wounds into souls. But souls and hearts healed. The scars made them stronger. More resilient. Capable of a fiercer and more determined love.

Jayne had obviously never let those wounds heal.

Her blue eyes were savage with grief. A grief he was powerless to salve. Forgiving herself was the only way she could move on from this. Just as he suspected he was going to have to forgive himself for putting his heart on the line again with her.

He didn't just 'feel deeply' for her. He knew that now. He loved her. He wanted to be with her. But there was no chance of that love flourishing if she was going to prioritise her baseless guilt over their battling life's tougher moments together. So it was time for him to start asking the questions he'd been afraid to ask all those years ago.

'Is this why you gave my ring back?'

She nodded in the affirmative. 'I didn't want you to be burdened with someone who'd done something so awful. I know. I know. It wasn't fair on you. But I wasn't exactly seeing things straight, and once I got back to London…'

She sighed heavily as memories weighted her to the chair.

'I guess I stopped seeing everything from my point of view and only saw it from hers. The clubs she would never go to. The nights out she wouldn't have. The surgeries she would never complete. It reached a point where I couldn't bear knowing her dreams were going to go totally unfulfilled.'

'So that's why you stayed in London?'

She nodded. 'I know. It's horrible. And it was cruel to you because I loved you so much. But…'

Her eyes jumped to the surgical suite. A sickening feeling swept through him. The gesture spoke volumes.

Jayne had changed track on her medical studies because she had been following Jules's dream. No wonder she'd fallen to bits when Stella had rejected the donor heart. It hadn't been just a surgery gone wrong. It had been much bigger than that. She'd failed at making her sister's dreams come true.

A sour taste ripped through him. The bitter taste of finality. Whatever happened with Maggie and the twins would make or break her. Make or break *them*.

He could walk away now. Admit defeat. Or he could hold his ground and stay true to his conviction that they belonged together. Either way, no one—not even the girl who might break his heart twice—deserved to carry that much grief around with her.

'Jay, listen.' He waited until she met his eyes. 'You are *not* to blame for Jules's death. Just as you aren't to blame for what is happening today. A speeding driver killed Jules. And that man is living with the consequences of his actions at this very moment. The last person who should be taking the blame is you. It is not your fault.'

She shook her head. 'No. You're wrong. If I hadn't called her she wouldn't even have been in Whitticombe. She'd wanted to go rock-climbing that weekend but she cancelled it.'

'Rock-climbing?'

'Yeah. If she'd gone rock-climbing instead she'd be here right now.'

Seriously?

Jayne was spiralling. Not seeing the wood for the trees. Jules had always courted danger. As awful a thought as it was, if it hadn't been the cycling it might've been the rock climbing. Or the abseiling…or old age. They'd never know. What he *did* know was Jayne was going to have to find a way to stop blaming herself for Jules's death.

'Do your parents know you feel this way?'

Her shoulders moved up to her ears and then dropped heavily. 'We haven't ever really talked about it. They were so… I don't know…' She drew in a jagged breath. 'My mum specifically asked me to look after her. They knew she was a daredevil. They knew she needed looking after and I didn't do it.'

'Have you *asked* them if they blame you?'

Tears glazed her eyes as she shook her head. 'Let's just say actions speak louder than words.'

She didn't have to explain. Jayne's parents had never really been the touchy-feely type, and after the accident they'd kept to themselves more than ever. Even hired someone to run their art gallery so they wouldn't have to.

No wonder Jayne was afraid to speak to them.

All her life her mother had appointed her as Jules's wingman. The one person who would keep her safe. Hence the surgical career. And now even that had let her down. And little wonder. As much as Sam knew that Jayne loved medicine, the destiny she was trying to fulfil wasn't hers. How could she be truly happy if she spent the rest of her life trying to make her sister's dreams come true at the expense of her own?

But what did a man say to the girl of his dreams when all this truth came tumbling out?

He did the only thing he could think of. He reached out and held her hand.

Jayne shifted in the increasingly uncomfortable chair. It felt as if days had passed since they'd arrived at the hospital, but it had only been an hour. Maybe two. Still too long for the news they were waiting for to be good.

She tried Sam's method of hunting for a silver lining.

They were in the right place.

Nate was on his way.

Sam's dad had rung to say the base in the Middle East had put him on a helicopter to the nearest airbase and he would be back in the UK as soon as humanly possible. The Royal Air Force was pretty dependable on that front.

'Through adversity to the stars' was their motto. Through adversity to Oxford would do for today. If the heavens shone down on Maggie and her family it would show that the stars—maybe even Stella and Jules—had been playing their part, too.

She should go and get coffee. Or biscuits. Something. Make a show of thanking Sam for not bolting when she'd poured out her blackest thoughts to him. For reaching out and holding her hand when she'd needed it most.

As good as it had felt, there was still a parent-sized hole in her heart. Until she spoke to them as honestly as she'd spoken to Sam she wasn't sure she could begin the journey of grieving and forgiveness she so longed for.

'Hey…' She gently nudged Sam, who was staring blindly at a two-years-old magazine. She knew he wasn't actually reading it because he had yet to turn the page and they'd been here for two hours.

He looked up at her, his eyes impossible to read. She tried not to react. They were both going through the emotional wringer right now.

'I'm going for a walk.'

He nodded. Unsurprised. Didn't meet her eye. 'I'll call you if anyone comes out.'

She gave his shoulder a squeeze. 'Thanks.'

He flashed her a quick smile, then went back to staring at his magazine.

As she wandered the corridors no matter how hard she tried to clear her head her thoughts kept circling back to Sam. He was such a good man. When she'd poured out her story to him he hadn't recoiled. Or judged. He'd done what she had always hoped he would do, but had been too frightened to find out.

He'd soothed her. Assured her she'd done the best she could in an impossible situation. He had been awfully quiet since then, though. Something had shifted in him now that he knew the whole story. She saw it in his eyes. Felt it in the change of his demeanour.

The truth hit her hard and fast.

She'd chosen her grief over Sam. Over a *life* with Sam. Maybe it was even deeper than that. She'd chosen grief over life.

Sure. She was a top-rated surgeon because of it. She saved lives. But the one place…the one *heart* that mattered the most…she'd left behind.

Of course Sam wouldn't meet her eye. By revealing her secret—the most important secret of all—she'd shattered the fragile trust they'd been building together over the past few weeks.

He'd all but handed his heart to her on a plate. And she hadn't reciprocated even when she knew damn well she loved him with every cell in her body. She'd been too afraid to burden him with the guilt she'd never wanted him to own.

She'd held too much too close.

Was it too late to put things back together again? Being here, waiting on a knife's edge for news of Maggie and the babies, had pulled everything into crystal-clear focus. She had to confront the truth that had been staring her in the face for years.

She couldn't live Jules's life for her. Jules was gone. Unless she lived her own life she would never be happy. And the life she wanted included Sam. It included Maggie. It included Whitticombe and all the bunting and the sunflowers and the village fetes and everything else that came with it. Namely…her parents. The two people who had taken Jules's death every bit as hard as she had.

She pulled to a halt outside the maternity unit window. That same spot she regularly found herself at in the London Merryweather when she needed to give her heart a bit of a boost.

She needed to see her parents. The things they had to talk about were far too big for a phone call.

A list of priorities snapped out in front of her with military precision.

Be here to see Maggie and the babies come out of surgery.

Ensure Nate was by her best friend's side.

Give in her notice at the London Merryweather.

She still wanted to be a surgeon. But she also wanted a life outside of the hospital. The London Merryweather had been Jules's jewel in the crown. It didn't have to be Jayne's.

Yes. She'd do that, then get on a plane to Scotland.

Until she made her peace with her parents she would be unable to give herself completely to Sam. It was possible she wouldn't get any resolution from them, but until she tried she couldn't give her entire heart to Sam.

A baby began to wriggle in its tight swaddling, her tiny fingers peeking out from the edge of the blanket, clasping and unclasping as if searching for her mother.

She heard someone approach, but didn't turn.

'Gorgeous, aren't they?'

Sam's voice trickled down her spine just as it always did. Warm. Comforting. Loving.

She bumped her shoulder against him, knowing that if she spoke her voice would crack and she'd tell him right then and there just how much she loved him.

She needed to speak to her parents first. Then she'd tell him. Tell him every day for the rest of their lives if he was up for it.

Just then two surgeons appeared from round the corner.

Maggie's surgeons.

Her heart leapt to her throat as they approached.

They looked exhausted.

She felt Sam's hand take hold of hers. They both squeezed tight.

CHAPTER ELEVEN

BLOOD POUNDED SO LOUDLY in Jayne's ears she had to lip-read the surgeon's words.

When she saw Sam's smile near enough hit each of his ears, there was no doubt she'd heard properly.

'They all made it.'

Sam whooped as he picked up Jayne and swung her round, both of them laughing as happily as a pair of newlyweds.

Looking into his sparkling green eyes, she realised just how many times she'd imagined moments like these. Being held in his arms, being swung round with nothing but joy in their hearts. At their wedding. When they had their own babies. At the start of one of the good old fashioned lust-fests that seemed to come so easily to the two of them.

A flicker of something she couldn't identify flashed across Sam's eyes, as if he'd been thinking the same thing and then remembered they weren't a couple.

He put her down as quickly as he'd picked her up and turned his focus on the surgeons.

He was right, of course. Maggie was who was important here. Not her bag of mixed-up feelings.

She heard all the words. *Emergency Caesarean...*

Catheters... Epidural... Anaesthetist... High blood pressure... Cords around babies' necks... No oxygen deprivation... Mum was awake to hear them both cry.

Jayne pressed her fingers to her mouth to stem a small sob. Sam punched the air as if he himself were the proud father.

Almost everything that could have gone wrong, had. But the things that had gone right were the ones that counted.

'The little ones are in the NICU,' the surgeon said when Jayne asked if the babies were with Maggie now.

'Boys? Girls?'

Maggie hadn't wanted to know. She had always loved a surprise.

'One of each.'

Jayne shot a look at Sam. Just as Maggie had hoped. They shared one of those smiles that helped everything slide into place. She loved this man. Loved him to within an inch of her life. Maybe more. And she wanted what he wanted. Love. Marriage. As many babies as they could handle. Holding hands when they were eighty. Fighting each other's corners.

And yet she could see the reserve in Sam's eyes. A reserve that spoke volumes.

He knew she hadn't forgiven herself, and until she did...

How could everything she dreamed of be so close and still so far away?

She forced herself to tune in to the surgeon as he updated Sam. 'The babies are a bit small, but as you know a lot of twins come early. Not all of them under this much stress, but if they're anything like their mum, they're fighters.'

Jayne shot a quick look up at Sam, then asked the question on both their minds. 'So, Maggie...? She's definitely all right?'

The list of things that might have caused permanent damage was long. Too long.

'She will be. The water weight obviously wasn't helping. She lost a lot of blood, and the C-section took a lot out of her, but the fact she made it this far is a credit to the pair of you.'

Jayne refused to take the praise. 'I think all the credit can go to Maggie on this one.'

They sobered as their thoughts turned to the many women who'd died in the same situation. The fact that the three of them were safe and sound was little short of a miracle.

The surgeon shrugged. 'Have it your way, but it sounds to me as if she had a pretty good support team.' He tipped his head towards the far end of the corridor as if the matter were settled. 'As I said, the little ones are in the NICU for the night. We want to keep an eye on them. And Mum is obviously going to need time to recover. Any word on Dad's arrival?'

Sam pulled out his phone and checked his latest text. 'Looks as though he'll be here in a few hours. By sun-up.'

One of the surgeons cracked a joke about speeding tickets and the RAF.

'They probably had to strap him into the cargo hold to keep him from the flight deck.'

They all laughed, picturing a wild-eyed Nate trying to commandeer a jet so he could get to his wife and hs new babies and hold them all in his arms.

Jayne's eyes caught and held with Sam's. He itched to wrap his arms round her and hold her again. He saw strength in her gaze. Love. Love she wasn't yet prepared to admit she felt. That was fine. He had time.

He reached out and took her hand in his.

Her breath caught and his gaze dropped to the base of her throat, where he could see her pulse pound. Oh, she could see it. all right. See the love in his eyes.

He squeezed her hand, willing the heat streaking across her cheeks to be shared passion and to make their love the real deal. Complex. Supportive. Honest.

They'd been down this road before. Sam offering her a lifetime of love. Jayne running for the hills.

Her blue eyes glistened with everything he'd seen the day he'd asked her to marry him: hope. Hope and love in equal measures.

Oblivious to this silent exchange of information, the surgeons shook hands all round, then showed them where Maggie's room was. As expected, she was sound asleep, with one of Nate's T-shirts clutched in her hand. His way of being there, Maggie had said. As long as she could smell him she could get through anything. And she had.

At Jayne's suggestion, she and Sam walked to the NICU for a peek at the babies. They weren't allowed in, as they weren't the parents, but one of the nurses wheeled their incubator over to the window so they could see the infants. They were holding hands.

Sam reached out to take Jayne's hand in his and together, hand in hand, they walked back to Maggie's room.

'Probably time we got some sleep,' he whispered, standing at the end of Maggie's bed.

'This chair flattens out into a bed.' Jayne pointed to a large recliner by the window. She handed him the thick blanket she'd found in the room's cupboard. 'Why don't you take the first shift, seeing as you were at work all day?'

'You sure?'

'Absolutely.' She did a little jog in place. 'You know me. Always a bit restless. I'm going to call Cailey and Connor's sitter. Let them know everything's okay.'

That wasn't the full story.

'Jayne. What's going on?'

It was a loaded question and both of them knew it.

She sucked in a sharp breath, as if she were building up courage, and then said, 'I need to leave. There are a few things I need to sort in my "other" life.'

All his senses shot to high alert. 'What does that mean? Are you going back to London now your job here is done?'

'No. That's not it. Not right away, anyway.' She wouldn't meet his eyes. 'I just… I know it's hard to put your faith in me, with all we've been through, but unless I do this I… Oh, Sam.'

Pain had replaced the love he'd seen shining in her eyes.

'Please just trust in me. Believe that I'm doing what's best. For both of us.'

She gave his cheek a quick kiss. Kissed Maggie's forehead, then left the room.

Staying awake wasn't much of a problem for Sam, with a thousand new questions burning holes in his head.

It was his own damn fault. He'd let himself become immersed in a 'Whitticombe love bubble' way too early. She had a life in London. What had he expected her to do? Drop it all and come running back to him for a life of wedded bliss? She also had unresolved issues. Shaking off seven years of pent-up guilt wasn't something that happened overnight.

He shook his hands open, as if the gesture would take his dark thoughts with it.

This was life. This was love.

The only thing he could do now was pray that Jayne found the strength to forgive herself. If that didn't happen they really would need to draw a line in the sand.

As the plane came in for landing Jayne could hardly believe how beautiful it was up in the Outer Scottish Isles. Azure crystal-clear water. Sandy white beaches. If it hadn't been so chilly and a palm tree or two had been dotted round the place she would've deemed it tropical.

It was remote. Very remote. There wasn't much further north a person could travel to 'get away from it all' unless the North Pole and thermals was their thing.

A part of her hated the way she'd up and left Sam, but she'd seen the way he'd looked at her once they'd found out Maggie and the babies had made it.

He was ready. Ready to embark on the rest of his life. She wanted to be the woman who went on that journey with him, but until she'd come clean to her parents and had their forgiveness she wouldn't ever be able to forgive herself for the pain they'd all endured.

It had taken her a couple of days to build up the courage. There were other steps she needed to take to try and face her future—with Jules still in her heart, but with enough room for her to pursue her own dreams. One of those was to be back in Whitticombe.

With her heart on her sleeve, she'd gone to the London Merryweather and told them she was going to apply for a job at the paediatric unit in the hospital in Oxford.

They'd been surprised, but had said they understood, and they had told her there would always be an open invitation for her in those 'extra-tricky' cases. Cases like Stella. Then they'd handed her a letter of thanks from Stella's parents that had near enough broken her heart.

She'd read it on the plane.

In it they said the only way they had survived those five awful months with their daughter in hospital was knowing that Jayne had been the one looking after her. They knew transplants came with risks. They also knew they'd had five extra months with their daughter they wouldn't have had if Jayne hadn't been her doctor.

It was a powerful letter to read on the way to see her parents. A pair of people who experienced a similar loss. Without the chance to say goodbye.

The captain was asking the stewards to prepare for landing. She took in a deep breath.

Ready or not, she was about to embark on the rest of her life. As Jayne. Living Jayne's life. No more trying to live someone else's dreams.

After leaving the small airport and walking through the small village, she hit upon a low row of stone cottages, just as her instructions from the McTavishes had detailed. She walked to the cottage at the end with bright red window frames. Flowers tumbled out of boxes, much as they did in Whitticombe. She wondered whose personal touch it might be. Mrs McTavish's or her mother's.

Only one way to find out.

She lifted her hand and knocked.

'Do you think we should put the bunting up a day early or on the morning of the fete?'

Sam stared blankly at the village's mayor and

shrugged. He didn't know. The love of his life had disappeared. Again.

Okay. This time there was a proviso, but...

Back on Sunday.

Who the hell sent a text like that?

A woman who hadn't found a way to forgive herself.

'Right,' said the mayor when Sam didn't answer her question. 'Why don't we do this with a show of hands?'

Sam distractedly raised his hand as his brain tried to connect one dot to another. No matter which way he tore the message up and put it back together again, he didn't like what his brain was telling him.

History repeats itself.

'Sam? Are you voting to keep the cake stands over by the river?'

Oops. They'd moved on from bunting. 'Absolutely,' he said, a bit too jocularly. He sounded falsely cheery, and from the look on everyone's faces they'd heard it too.

'Even though the swans stole Mrs Johnson's crumble cake last year? We almost lost two Victoria sponges as well,' Dolly reminded him sternly.

Hell's bells. How could he concentrate when one measly text was all he had to work with?

Was Jayne coming back to cut her ties for good? Or to beg him to unearth that ring he'd never quite managed to return to the jeweller's? Or none of the above?

When he'd walked into the village fete meeting today, as Maggie's proxy, questions had been lobbed at him like arrows on a battlefield. How was Maggie? The babies? Any names yet? How was Nate? Over the moon or flat-out exhausted? When were they coming back? Would they make it to the fete? Where was Jayne?

That was the one question he couldn't answer.

London was his best guess.

Realising that Jayne blamed herself for her sister's death had been a revelation. He'd had no idea. He'd also seen the weight of guilt ease…just a bit…when she'd un-burdened her heart and had seen he wasn't going any-where.

He wished he'd known years ago. A burden shared and all that…

Blaming herself for a death that wasn't her fault… Trying to live the life her sister couldn't… No won-der she'd found coming home so hard. Living a happy, contented life with her childhood beau in Whitticombe would have seemed like dancing on her sister's grave.

There was only one way out of this endless cycle of pain for Jayne. Forgiving herself. Whether or not she was capable of it… He guessed he'd find out on Sunday. Forty-eight incredibly long hours away.

In the meantime here he was, trying his damnedest to decide whether or not the three-legged race should come before or after the egg and spoon race. Or were they still on cake theft by swan?

'Sam? Do you think we could count on one of your sisters to keep tabs on the cake competition and perhaps put Jayne in charge of the three-legged race?'

Back on Sunday.

'Sam?'

He forced himself to focus on Mrs Sedlescombe as she repeated the question.

'Will Jayne be on hand for the fete?'

He didn't know. 'Maybe... She said she would be.'

She'd also once said she'd marry him.

No. That wasn't fair. Life had thrown one hell of a spanner at the pair of them. She'd gone to a far darker place than he'd thought. And he'd let her go. Hadn't fought for her as intensely as he might have. Hadn't seen the point. He'd been too young to know better. Too un-equipped to deal with rejection.

He thought he'd moved on. He'd dated. Met and mar-ried a terrific woman. He had loved Marie. He truly had. But he saw now that the love he had given her had been far from complete. How could it have been when he'd been so busy pouring himself into the two things he had meant to do with Jayne? Without hearing what his wife had been telling him.

They needed their own dreams and goals. Not to try and live out someone else's.

Ha. That was rich. The same thing that had hobbled Jayne's happiness had hobbled his own.

As painful as it was to admit, his ex-wife had been a rebound. A rebound from the love of a lifetime.

The only saving grace was that he knew how happy Marie was now. Their brief shambles of a marriage had led her to her own happy ending.

Silver linings.

Unbidden, he heard Jayne's voice in his head the night they'd had their date at the pub. *'Why didn't you come to London?'* she'd asked.

He had thought she was talking about work. But what if that hadn't been it at all? What if she'd been asking why he hadn't come after her?

He glanced at his watch. If he left now he could be in

London within a couple of hours. Maybe even before she put herself back on the roster at the hospital.

She didn't belong there. Not by a long shot. She belonged here in Whitticombe. With him. He'd seen how happy she was here. How much she loved being with Maggie's children. The soft look in her eye when she pressed her nose up against the glass at the maternity unit. She wanted what he wanted. She was just scared to reach for it.

Well, who wasn't? He sure as hell was. But this time he wasn't going to let fear stand in the way of their happiness.

'Sam?'

The villagers were all giving him that sympathetic look again. The one that said they weren't quite certain about what was going on, but they were pretty sure it involved Jayne.

Right! He'd vowed once not to be the guest of honour at a village-wide pity party and it looked as if he was going to have to do it again.

Everyone jumped as he clapped his hands together and gave them a swift rub. 'Egg and spoon first. Three-legged race after. It's always funnier. Cakes away from the river. Decision made. So.' He scanned the group. 'What's left?'

Oli Dickinson, the local butcher, pulled a rather grubby-looking piece of paper out of his pocket and slowly began to read. 'We've got yer Whack a Mole, of course…'

'That's always a winner,' chorused the committee members. None of whom could clearly imagine a village fete without one.

'Ethel's bringing over the skittles from the pub. I'm bringing the Hook a Duck.'

'Good.' Sam was barely registering anything the poor man was saying. Time was a tickin'. 'Anything else?'

Oli listed a few more things—a human fruit machine, a ring toss and a few other things Sam didn't quite catch. How could he? He was about to change his life for ever.

'Of course we're going to need one more volunteer for Dolly's stand.'

'I'll do it,' Sam said.

The sooner they wrapped this up the better. Presumably Dolly was setting up a baked goods stall selling scones and cakes from the teashop, with all of the proceeds going to the hospital looking after Maggie and the babies.

Everyone looked shocked.

'What?'

They all shared complicit glances, then smiled benignly at him.

'As long as you're happy, Sam,' Dolly said. 'I'll bring a couple of spare towels and some wet wipes.'

'What for?' he asked absently.

He gave his jaw a scrub. He supposed he could have shaved a bit more neatly. And probably worn a nicer shirt, given he was about to make a massive declaration of love, but he wasn't looking too scruffy, was he?

'You *do* realise you just volunteered to be on the cream pie stall?'

He hadn't. He pretended he had. 'Got it. What's next?'

'That's about it!'

'Great!' He had to get to London, find the girl of his

dreams, get a ring on her finger and then bring her back to Whitticombe, where she belonged. 'See you on Sunday afternoon.'

Four hours in rush-hour traffic and a speeding ticket later, all Sam's hopes plummeted to the core of the earth.

Jayne had been to the hospital. Just long enough to hand in her notice.

No forwarding address. Not for a scruffy-faced man running in off the street, anyway.

It was private information, the HR secretary had said. *Family only.*

He'd wanted answers.

He'd received them.

If only they were the answers he'd wanted to hear.

CHAPTER TWELVE

JAYNE COULD HARDLY believe what she was hearing. Her parents didn't need to apologise to *her*.

It seemed they'd all gone through their own form of torture and, with the clarity hindsight always offered, she could see they'd all unnecessarily gone through the pain alone, when they could have come together as a family.

They'd lost one of the family. Who was equipped to handle that sort of devastating loss with grace and an eye on the future?

Now that they were here, together, one thing was very clear. It was time for them all to let go of the pain. It was time for them all to heal. Together. As a family.

Her mother took Jayne's hand in hers—the first time she'd done so in years. It felt warm and comforting. Tears filled her eyes as she spoke.

'We handled it so poorly. The more we withdrew, the more we saw Jules in you. That fighting spirit that carried on no matter how tough things were.'

Jayne's mum reached out to hold her husband's hand too.

'You seemed so much better equipped to take care

of yourself and...to our shame...we let you. We failed you, Jayne.'

As much as the little girl in Jayne needed to hear that her parents knew they should have reacted differently, she knew now that the blame didn't lie in anyone's camp. The apology that had been lodged in her throat for the past seven years finally came out.

'You didn't let me down. If I'd spoken to you then, told you what really happened, maybe we could have gone through it together.'

Her parents looked at her sharply. 'What do you mean?' asked her father.

Her voice shook as she spoke. 'I'm the one who suggested we ride our bicycles.'

Her father paled and her mother stemmed a small sob.

Jayne forced herself to continue. 'Jules said we should go to the pub and get a celebratory glass of fizz, so I suggested we race our bikes there like we used to. She threw her helmet off so she could feel the wind in her hair. You know what she was like...'

They both nodded. There was no need to remind them how much of a daredevil Jules had been.

'I picked it up for her, but fell behind. I saw the car coming, but I didn't scream loud enough. I tried.' Her voice cracked straight down to her broken heart. 'I tried so hard. But I wasn't fast enough to help.'

At long last she wept. Wept with her parents' arms around her as they soothed and held her.

After who knew how long, they finally pulled apart.

'Jayne, darling. Have you been blaming yourself all this time?' her father asked.

'Of course. It *is* my fault. If I hadn't suggested it things might have been different.'

'It wasn't your fault,' Jayne's mother said solidly.

Her eyes were red. Her cheeks were still wet with tears. But there was a resoluteness in her Jayne hadn't seen in years.

'It was an awful, awful accident. Nothing more. You did everything you could.'

Jayne's father rubbed his wife's back and turned soft blue eyes to his daughter. 'I think what we've learned is that we turned away from each other at exactly the moment we should have turned *to* each other. You coming here has helped us see that a bit more clearly.'

'Even now that you know everything?' Jane tugged a tissue out of the box and swept away her own tears.

'It brought you to us, didn't it?'

She nodded. 'Yes... I have to admit that when I got back to Whitticombe and you weren't there, even though I knew you were here, I... I felt as though I'd driven you away.'

'What?'

Her parents looked shocked.

'That's not true at all,' her mother protested. 'We love you. And do not think for one second that we have ever blamed you. It was not your fault. We just... We found being in Whitticombe difficult. Looking down the lane every single day, tensing at the approaching roar of a car. The whole reason we loved the village was how safe it had made us feel, and without either of you girls there it...'

'It didn't feel the same,' her father finished for her. 'But maybe it was *us* that wasn't the same, rather than the other way round...'

He began to apologise again, but Jayne held up her hands. They were beyond playing Pass The Guilt. 'I absolve us all. We're…' Her voice shook with emotion. 'We're all *human*, aren't we? There are a lot of things we could've done better. Sticking together was one of them.'

And telling Sam she loved him. She should have done that before she'd left. She could do it right now, but even sending him that paltry text had seemed wrong, somehow. Particularly when coming here had been so powerfully healing.

She offered a silent prayer that she hadn't messed things up with Sam. Hadn't ruined them for ever.

Her father tucked a stray strand of hair behind her ear, just as he had when she was a girl. 'We're so proud of you, darling. So very proud of everything you've done with your life. We just hope you live the rest of your life for *you*. Jules was a bright, beautiful star, and we were so lucky to have had her, but now we're going to have to carry her here.' He pointed at her heart.

In that instant a lifetime of distance and misunderstanding was erased. The courage to make the final change barrelled into her heart like a beautiful racehorse surging towards the finish line. Jayne knew what she wanted. She knew where she was going and what she was doing. And she knew who she wanted to do it with.

'You two up for taking a spontaneous trip to Whitticombe?'

'C'mon, old man! Show me what you've got!' Sam was doing his best to bait everyone who came along to the pie throwing stall. Even poor Martin Cainen, the butcher. One of the nicest chaps he'd ever met. And one of the vainest.

Sam knew any reference to his age would throw him off.

'Bring it on, you old wrinkly! Do your best to hit the Pie Man!'

Martin threw him an odd look. Fair enough. He wasn't exactly exuding charm. Reeling from being too late to find Jayne was more like it.

Family only.

She *was* his family. Was meant to be his *wife*. He'd even dug the ring out of his drawer and felt it searing through the fabric of his pocket straight through to his skin. Ah, well. She clearly wasn't coming back. It would be onwards and upwards from here on out.

Seeing as his face was already covered with cream pie, he figured he could scowl all he wanted till his bad mood decided to take a hike and let him get on with it.

Back on Sunday.

They were already thirteen hours into Sunday and so far there was no sign of Jayne.

'You going to throw that pie or eat it?'

Sam made a wild face and Martin took the bait. He missed by a mile.

A new punter stepped up to the plate. A woman holding a pie in front of her face. A woman he would have known if she'd been holding an armful of pies and wearing a Victoria sponge on the top of her head.

Jayne Sinclair.

The way his heart slammed against his chest was all the confirmation he needed to know that he hadn't expected her to show.

Especially with such a big smile on her face.

A number of people fell into line alongside Jayne. Maggie. Nate. Each with a baby strapped to their chest and holding a child by the hand. His father was there. His sisters. His grandad. Jayne's mother and father.

He let out a low whistle. *That* was a surprise. And it explained Jayne's mysterious absence. They were holding hands. Smiling. Wearing the same light glow of serenity that he'd been praying Jayne would wear one day. The luminescence of a woman at peace with herself. The warmth of forgiveness.

Her hair wasn't combed. Her clothes were wrinkled. She looked as though she'd been travelling all night. She was absolutely beautiful.

'You going to take a shot?'

'Maybe. But first I think you'd better know that I love you.'

His heart skipped that same old familiar beat. She loved him. But was it the kind of love that meant sticking around?

'Yeah? Well…what are you going to do about it?'

She grinned.

Everyone took a step in.

'Stick around for a while.'

'Uh-huh?' He needed more than 'a while' before he bit.

'For a lifetime, if you're good with that?'

'What about the London hospital? They told me you'd handed in your notice.'

Her eyes widened. 'You went to the hospital?'

'Of course I did. Let the woman of my dreams run away to the big smoke twice? Wasn't going to happen.'

A complication of emotions washed across her features. 'I should've told you. A girl should definitely *not* withhold information from her boyfriend.'

'Your boyfriend?' He was being cheeky now, but if

he couldn't be cheeky with the love of his life when she was holding a cream pie in her hand and her heart in the other when could he?

'If you'll have me.'

Damn. There was a hitch in her voice.

'Of course I will, woman. You're the love of my life.'

The smile came back. 'Well, since that's the case... I thought I'd ask you a question.'

'Go on, then.'

Everyone leant in.

'How would you feel about being more than a boy-friend? Maybe...a fiancé?'

Blood shot to his brain so fast he saw stars. When he regained his focus what he saw up close and personal was Jayne. Those blue eyes of hers brimming with hope. Her cheeks all pinked up with nerves and anticipation. This was Jayne with her heart on her sleeve, in front of all the people they loved most.

Could a lifetime of happiness be as simple as saying yes? They had a past. A complicated one. But they could have a future. A beautiful, rich, fulfilling future. So long as he could trust that she would stick it out with him.

She bit down on her lower lip and then released it. 'I know I have a pretty dodgy track record, so I thought maybe this would help.'

She knelt down in front of the ridiculous wooden cut-out they had him posing in and held up a piece of paper.

'What's that?'

'It's a contract.'

'For marriage?'

He was about to tell her he hadn't really expected things to move quite that quickly when his eye caught a few of the words on the contract. It was a job offer for Jayne from the children's hospital in Oxford. Just up the road.

Was this enough? Enough to prove she would stay for good this time?

Jayne's heart was pumping so hard she could practically see it pounding through her shirt.

What she was feeling right at this very instant was what she'd been waiting for her entire life.

Hope.

Hope that her love for Sam could finally blossom. In the light. In front of everyone she loved. Everyone who mattered. Hope that they could work through their problems together, no matter how painful it might be. Hope that they would have a family of their own.

She knew change didn't happen overnight, but she was ready to try. Right here. Right now. In front of everyone who cared enough to hold her accountable to the vows she hoped she would one day make in front of them all. To love, value and cherish the love that Sam felt for her.

She stared into his face, trying to read the mix of emotions sending flashes of dark and light through those green eyes of his.

Trust was the biggest problem. She hadn't done anything over the years to win it. Quite the opposite, in fact. But she was ready and willing to do everything it took to win it back and hold it dear.

So she would tell him as much.

In as loud a voice as she could manage, she said, 'Samuel Crenshaw. I love you. I love you with all my heart. I know I haven't been the most consistent part of your life, but if there's one thing I've learned it's that honesty is the best policy, and the biggest lie I've been telling myself all these years is that I could survive without you. I was wrong. Crazy wrong. I love you. And there isn't *anything* that will stop me from loving you with all my heart for the rest of my life, if you'll have me.'

He looked at her. Blinked. Then disappeared out of sight.

Her heart plummeted to her gut. He didn't believe her. She had known it was a grand gesture that could go wrong, but she had hoped with every fibre in her being that he would say yes.

All of a sudden Jayne felt herself being lifted up off the ground. Before she had a chance to exclaim, Sam was kissing her. Kissing her right there, in front of the entire village, as if they were the only two people in the world. As her body arched to meet his kisses she finally began to understand what was happening.

He was saying yes. Sam was saying yes. He'd be her fiancé. And one day he'd be her husband. Together they would do whatever it took to stay together. Openly. Honestly. And with the loving support of their community.

And that was exactly when the pair of them began to be pelted by cream pies.

They kissed through all of them. Banana cream. Lemon meringue. Chocolate cream. Every flavour under the sun. They were a mess. They were also crazy in love.

Sam swept a blob of meringue away from Jayne's forehead. 'Fancy jumping in the river to make this engagement official?'

She felt as if a thousand roses were blooming in her heart. A jump in the river? It was the *perfect* way to make a new beginning.

'Why not?'

They clasped hands and together, as a couple, they jumped into the river, laughing and whooping. Because with love everything had a silver lining.

CHAPTER THIRTEEN

'OH, MAGGIE...IT'S PERFECT.'

Maggie beamed as she twisted another cupcake into a just-so position on the massive tower. 'Nothing less for my bestie!'

'Right. So...' Jayne's fingers moved to her throat to touch the pear-shaped necklace Maggie had worn to her own wedding. 'Thank you for the "something borrowed".'

'Absolutely. The "something new" is that amazing dress.'

They both grinned as Jayne did a twirl in the pleated, tiered maxi-dress, sending layers of white tulle fluttering.

'"Something old"?'

Jayne poked her toe out from beneath the hem of the maxi-dress. 'Mum's wedding shoes.'

Maggie gave them a round of applause.

'And "something blue"?'

Jayne held out her wrist to show off her bracelet.

'Ooh...that's pretty. Is it new?'

'No. I found it in Jules's jewellery box. We bought them together years ago but I lost mine. I thought it'd be a nice way to share my wedding day with her.'

Before she had a chance to cry, a knock sounded on the doorframe of the village hall.

Maggie squealed. 'Sam Crenshaw—don't you know it's bad luck to see the bride before your wedding?'

'There are a whole lot of things that we haven't done by the book, so why start now?'

Sam strode in, swept his hands across the white gown stretching over Jayne's curved belly and dropped a kiss on her cheek.

'You look beautiful. I've brought you a present.'

'You didn't have to do that, love. You're all the present I need.'

Maggie rolled her eyes. 'I'm going to leave you two alone. You've got that lovey-dovey look in your eyes again.'

'How could I not have when I'm minutes away from marrying the man of my dreams?' Jayne parried.

'Good point. Get on with it, you two... The pub is stuffed with well-wishers, waiting to see the happy couple make their way down the aisle.'

'Have Ethel tell them to get inside the church and we'll be there when we're good and ready!' Jayne laughed.

When Maggie had gone, Sam pulled Jayne as close as her pregnant belly would allow. 'Are you good and ready to become Mrs Crenshaw?'

Jayne pulled a face—a frown-grin. 'Hmm... I was thinking something more along the lines of Sinclair-Crenshaw.'

Sam unleashed a slow grin of his own. 'I don't care what you call yourself so long as you're going to be in the church to let me put a ring on your finger.'

Jayne answered with a soft kiss. Of course she would

be. Nothing would stop her. 'So what's this present of yours, then?'

'Go on. Open it.'

Tears sprang to her eyes when she unwrapped it. It was a plaque.

'The Jules Sinclair Bicycle Trust?'

Sam nodded, his own eyes glassing over. 'I thought, as we're on our way to having little ones of our own, we could have their Auntie Jules helping them out when they're ready to start riding bicycles.'

He told her he'd already organised for the charity to offer free helmets and cycle training to all the children in Whitticombe, as well as put up new traffic awareness signs around the village.

'Oh, Sam, it's perfect.'

'I'm glad you like it.' He leant in to give her a proper kiss, then pulled back.

'What?' Jayne laughed. 'Am I so fat with Baby Crenshaw you can't kiss me any more?'

Sam shook his head. 'It's not that. When I kiss you again I want to be kissing the bride...not the bride-to-be.'

'Well, go on, then.' She shooed him out through the door towards the stone church across the green. 'I think we've both waited long enough for that kiss.'

A few minutes later, with her father on one side and her mother on the other, Jayne stood at the entrance to the church, smiling at her husband-to-be, waiting at the altar.

It had taken them a long time to get to this point. But if she'd learned anything she now knew that some risks were worth taking. Especially the risk of falling in love.

* * * * *

THEIR ONE-NIGHT
TWIN SURPRISE

KARIN BAINE

MILLS & BOON

For Jane xx

PROLOGUE

IZZY FITZPATRICK RAN blindly out into the night, uncaring about the rain soaking through her clothes and bringing goosebumps out over her skin. She didn't know where she was going, only that she no longer felt safe in her own home. Her whole life as she knew it seemed to have unravelled completely over the course of the evening.

It was bad enough she was still mourning the loss of the man she'd thought she was going to marry and raise her much-longed-for family with, but to discover Gerry had sold her a lie all along was something she knew she'd never recover from.

Now she needed to be somewhere she felt protected, be with someone she could trust. It was no wonder she found herself standing outside Cal Armstrong's house. He was her friend, her colleague, and a man she knew she could turn to in a crisis.

She jabbed at the buzzer on the gate, desperate to get inside and close the door on the nightmare haunting her out here.

Eventually the voice of a sleepy-sounding Cal came over the intercom. 'Hello?'

'Cal?' The sheer relief of hearing his familiar voice was enough to completely break her and the dam broke on the tears she'd been trying to hold at bay with every revelation she'd uncovered tonight.

'Izzy, is that you? What's wrong? I'm coming down.' The gates swung open and she ran towards the house as though she was still being chased by Gerry's invisible demons.

He was pulling on a T-shirt as he opened the door and Izzy launched herself at him, making him stagger backwards into the hall. 'Oh, Cal, I didn't know where else to go, who else to turn to.'

'Calm down and tell me what's wrong. You're safe now.' He kicked the door closed behind her and she was inclined to believe him. His solid presence was just the reassurance she needed right now.

She let him hold her, enjoying being cocooned in his strong arms and the heat of his body warming hers as the cold reality of Gerry's betrayal hit home.

'There was a man at the house…he said Gerry owed him money…something to do with a card game.' Her teeth were chattering now with the shock of having a visit from the kind of people she'd thought only existed in gangster movies.

'Did he hurt you?' Cal tensed beneath her, his biceps bunching and flexing as he demanded the truth.

'No. He was just…intimidating. I told him about the accident, that Gerry had been killed, but he didn't seem to care. He wanted the debt paid. I had to give him every penny I had in the house to make him leave.' She shivered, remembering Gerry's associate standing with a foot inside her door, knowing she was there alone and terrified he'd want more than cash from her.

Cal swore and pulled her tighter into his embrace.

'You're freezing and soaking wet. Go inside and get warm by the fire. I'll get you some towels and warm clothes.'

He led her into the living room, put a blanket around her shoulders and handed her a glass of amber liquid. 'For the shock,' he said, making her drink it before he went to get her the dry clothes he'd promised.

Her throat burned as she downed the alcohol, but she was grateful as it took the chill from her very bones and warmed her from the inside out. That unpleasant house call had only been the start of unravelling Gerry's secrets and lies and now she was afraid there could be a string of debtors turning up on her doorstep looking for recompense.

'I'm sorry I didn't have more in your size,' he said with a half-grin and she appreciated he was still trying to make her laugh even at a time like this. She needed Cal's stability, this normality, to prevent her from tipping completely over the edge.

'That's fine. Thank you.' Izzy took the fresh towels and Cal-sized outfit from him, but she didn't have the energy, or the inclination, to leave the room to get changed. She simply sat and stared at the pile of laundry on her lap, unable to move.

'Let me.' Cal knelt at her feet and gently tugged off her shoes and socks, followed by her sodden trousers and blouse. He moved swiftly and efficiently to strip her of her wet things, leaving just her underwear before wrapping her in a warm, fluffy robe.

He took one of the towels, sat beside her on the sofa and began to dry her hair. She closed her eyes as he massaged her scalp, finding comfort in the intimate gesture. It had been a long time, if ever, since anyone had done that for her.

'I'm sorry for imposing on you like this. I know I'm making a habit of turning up here unannounced.'

'There's no need to apologise and as for your previous visits, I think they were more of an intervention for my benefit. If I hadn't had you chivvying me along after Janet left me I'd either still be in bed, unable to face the world again, or in rehab for jilted men whose fiancées had run off with the *actual* fathers of their babies.' Cal's dark humour failed to disguise how much Janet had really hurt him by stringing him along, pretending they were going to have a baby together.

Izzy understood his pain more than ever since Gerry had essentially done the same thing to her. He'd promised to marry her one day and give her the family she'd always dreamed of but that would never have happened.

'Well, if we're playing who had the worst relationship, I'll see your lying fiancée and raise you a gambling addict.' That was the only way she could see him now, tonight's revelations overriding everything she'd thought she knew about Gerry.

Cal's soothing hands stilled on her scalp. 'Oh, Izzy. I'm so sorry.'

She shrugged but the tears made a resurgence as she thought of all her hopes and dreams for the future that had been doomed from the first time they'd met. 'I've been mourning him for two months, but I wasted my grief on a stranger. That knock on the door tonight prompted me to finally look at all the post and paperwork he left behind. He'd taken out bank loans in my name, forged my signature on goodness knows what and racked up debt wherever he went. It's going to take ages to sort through the mess he's left behind. I just feel so alone, Cal.'

With no family to turn to and her best friend, Helen, living miles away, those old feelings of rejection were surfacing again. She was lucky she had Cal to lend her a shoulder to lean on.

'You're not alone. I'm here for you, day or night, the way you were for me.' He put his arms around her neck and kissed the top of her head.

'What did we do to deserve Janet and Gerry?' Izzy had seen him in the depths of despair where she was currently languishing, and it just didn't seem fair.

'Absolutely nothing.' He tipped her face up and made her look at him. 'None of this is your fault. Okay?'

'I remember saying something similar to you not so long ago…' Somehow just being in Cal's company was enough for her to stop panicking and provide her with some comfort. She hoped she'd managed the same for him in the aftermath of Janet's departure, even though turning up, unwanted, with home-cooked meals and taking the beer out of his hands had seemed like a thankless task at the time.

'Well, I think I needed reminding then and now so do you. You're a good person, Izzy.' Izzy snuggled into the crook of his arm, gazing into his eyes and realising how special he really was.

She'd never looked at him in a romantic way before but now, wrapped in his embrace, her body was responding to him altogether differently from what she was used to. The comfort she'd found with him had turned into something new and thrilling, desire stealthily making itself known so she was aware of every spot where his body was pressed against hers, that tingling sensation electrifying every inch of her skin.

He was looking at her now with the same hunger in

his eyes as she was currently experiencing and the atmosphere between them was suddenly crackling with sexual tension.

She tilted her head up to his, stopped when she thought it might be an unwanted advance, then rejoiced when he bent to meet her lips with his.

They sealed the strange new dynamic with an exploratory kiss that soon obliterated Izzy's doubts that he might only be offering her comfort. She could tell from the increased passionate intensity of his kisses that Cal wanted her as much as she wanted him at that moment. Their mouths were clashing together, they were tugging at each other's clothes in their frantic need to make that ultimate connection, and Izzy knew things between them would never be the same again.

CHAPTER ONE

Three months later

THE MINUTE THE call came in Izzy knew it was going to be a tough one for her.

'We have a thirty-one-year-old pregnant woman badly hurt after a car accidentally reversed through a shop window.' She paused to clear her throat before she continued relaying the harrowing details to the rest of the crew on board the air ambulance. 'The patient was shunted through the glass and has suffered severe lacerations and potential crush injuries. Her wrist and main artery have been severed but police on the scene have applied a tourniquet to her arm and require immediate medical assistance.'

'What about the driver of the car?' Cal's voice came over the headset and she knew, as the attending doctor, he was concerned for everybody's safety at the scene.

'Superficial injuries and shock, as far as we can tell. The ambulance can take him to hospital by road, but time is of the essence for our pregnant lady.' Depending on how much blood she'd lost and how long it took for them to get her to the hospital, there was a chance both mother and baby might not make it. Unfortunately, death was a part of the job but under current circumstances this one felt a bit close to home when Izzy's hormones were already all over the place.

Once the pilot found a clear place to land they hurried towards the melee of people and flashing lights. Thankfully the police had cordoned off the area so they could get to work without interference from the general public who were watching the drama unfold.

'This is Tara Macready. She's four months pregnant and has sustained substantial wounds to her left arm. We've been applying pressure to the wound since we arrived on scene.' One of the young police officers talked them through events as his colleagues did their best to stop the patient bleeding out. With their first-aid training they'd known to elevate the arm and apply pressure to reduce the flow of blood and had probably saved her life in the process. They'd done their part and now it was up to Izzy and Cal to get her transferred to the hospital as soon as possible.

Despite the police officers' good work, the ground was heavily stained with the scarlet evidence of the patient's trauma and Izzy had to fight against the unexpected emotions welling up inside her. 'Tara, we're with the air ambulance crew. We're going to take over now and get you transferred to the hospital.'

'What about my baby?' she mumbled, battling against unconsciousness.

'We're going to monitor you both, but we need to do a few things first, Tara. Izzy, she needs a bilateral cannula as quick as you can.' Cal set to work getting a pressure bandage on to replace the makeshift tourniquet that had been applied to Tara's arm and Izzy inserted the cannula so they could administer fluids. Once she was at the hospital they could do the blood typing necessary for a transfusion.

'I'm giving you some morphine for the pain, Tara.' With the bleeding halted Cal went ahead with pain relief. In this situation, even though they wanted to save both lives, the mother took priority.

Their portable kit enabled them to monitor Tara's blood pressure and heart rate and Izzy made sure everything was in place before they transferred her to the helicopter. They both climbed into the back with their patient so they could keep a close eye on her for the duration of the flight.

'I'm going to take a listen to your baby while the doctor checks your progress. Okay, Tara?' Izzy kept talking her through what was happening, reassuring her everything was going to be all right, even though she was slipping in and out of consciousness.

With a special stethoscope she was able to put her ear down to Tara's belly and listen for the baby's heartbeat. Hearing that faint rhythm felt like winning the lottery and Cal mirrored her smile when he realised the baby was still hanging in there too.

'Your baby is fighting right along with you, Tara. We'll get you both to the hospital as quickly as we can.' It was all down to timing now and Izzy was taking this one more personally than anything she'd ever witnessed before. Apparently, the prospect of becoming a mother made a woman fight harder than ever and that was one symptom of pregnancy she could get on board with.

Izzy could have kissed the tarmac when the helicopter touched down back at their Belfast base after transferring their patient into the hands of the emergency staff at the hospital.

'Are you okay, Fizz? You're looking a little green around the gills there. Don't tell me you've developed a sudden fear of flying? We'd have to ground you and then who would I have to wind up on a daily basis?'

She rolled her eyes at a grinning Cal. He knew she hated that nickname he'd foisted on her when they'd first met at air ambulance training and she'd let her temper get the better of her, striving to prove she was better than any of the men there.

At least, she used to hate it. In the five years of working together it had grown on her and she'd missed it of late when things between them had become awkward, to say the least. Things weren't going to get any easier between them once he heard her news.

They'd both been hurt by people who'd purported to love them. Cal's pregnant fiancée, Janet, had run out on him with the man who was apparently the *real* father of the baby she was carrying, leaving double the void in his life and double the hurt.

Izzy knew the heart-stabbing pain of betrayal, thanks to Gerry, the man she'd thought she'd spend the rest of her life with. She'd put all her hopes and dreams into their relationship, believing he was the one who was going to give her the family and stability she'd never had growing up in the foster system, only to have everything cruelly snatched away from her when he'd been killed in a motorcycle accident.

The only thing worse than losing someone she loved had been discovering he hadn't been who she'd thought he was at all. A parade of nefarious debt collectors and loan sharks who'd bankrolled a gambling addiction she'd been oblivious to and a bank account emptied as a result of his addiction had merely fuelled the notion that she would never have anyone in her life who loved her unconditionally. The realisation that had sent her running to the one person in her life she knew she could trust.

In Cal she'd found a kindred, wounded soul and she'd needed him to comfort her. They'd shared that one incredible night together but they both knew it could never be more than that when they were too raw to even think of getting involved in any sort of relationship. It was difficult enough going back to work as though nothing had happened between them when every erotic memory of sharing his bed was still so vivid in her mind.

And that one night of seeking solace in Cal's arms had ended in the life-changing consequences she was yet to tell him about. She didn't know how he was going to react to the news he was going to become a father so soon after his break-up and, to be truthful, she didn't want to lose his friendship if he resented the fact she was pregnant with his baby instead of Janet.

'I'm perfectly fine,' she bristled, as they ducked under the still spinning blades of the air ambulance.

This pregnancy might have come as a shock, but she wasn't going to let it get in the way of doing her job. The time would come soon enough when her bump would encroach on the limited space inside the chopper and prevent her from being as physically involved in the rescues as she was used to. At which point in time she'd probably have to become more involved in ground operations and hospital transfers, but not before then.

She was sure the odd bout of nausea would pass soon now she was reaching the end of her first trimester. Although she'd been unaware of the little person growing inside her belly for most of that time. Since she and Cal had agreed to put their indiscretion behind them, it hadn't entered her head that she might be pregnant and had blamed the stress of finding out about Gerry's secret vice as the cause for her missed period. Now everything was going to change between them.

Those tears, which never seemed far away, blurred her vision once more and she rested her hand on the slight swell of her belly to reassure her little bean it still had her, even if Cal decided he didn't want to be involved. She needed to confide in someone and the closest she had to family was Helen, her childhood friend and the only person she'd had growing up who had seemed to genuinely care for her.

Helen still lived in the Donegal area, where Izzy had spent the last of her teenage years before moving to Belfast to study nursing. She was a shoulder for Izzy to lean on when she needed one and though there was a vast geographical distance between them, hearing her voice would be enough to comfort her. Once she got over the shock herself, Izzy resolved to make that phone call. There was just one other person she had to inform first.

'Seriously, though, are you sure you're all right?' Cal stepped closer, his frown wiping away all traces of joviality, his pale blue eyes full of concern.

Izzy dropped her hand, so he wouldn't guess her secret.

'Low blood sugar, I expect. I haven't eaten all day.' A complete lie. Her blood was probably ninety per cent sugar due to the number of biscuits she'd been wolfing down lately.

'Why didn't you say? I'm sure we can do better than a cup of tea and a stale bun in the canteen. After what we've just been through we could probably do with something a lot stronger. Pub?' He began to unzip his bright orange flight suit and let the sleeves drop to his waist, revealing the lean frame encased in a tight black T-shirt beneath the bulky protective layers.

Izzy told herself it was pregnancy hormones making it impossible for her to drag her eyes away. That was the bonus side of her condition, being able to blame recent impulses, including an apparent spike in her libido, on the changes going on inside her body. Although her intimate knowledge of that hard body and the pleasures it could bring a woman was making her temperature rise steadily with every flashback of that night they'd spent together.

It was a loss to womankind that because one of their sisters had been blind to what a great man he was, all the rest would be denied the privilege of getting close to him. Except her, of course, but then they'd agreed it would never happen again, no matter how physically compatible they'd turned out to be. It was ironic that they hadn't wanted to complicate their relationship by getting romantically involved when they were now going to be tied together for the rest of their lives.

Izzy watched him climb out of his suit and flash her that cheeky grin of his.

'Enjoying the view?'

'You wish,' she shot back with just as much sarcasm before he realised how true his observation had been.

Given the physical nature of their work, it was important to keep up their fitness levels, but Cal was the type who could never sit still anyway. His trim, nicely muscled physique wasn't the result of hours spent at the gym. He wasn't the slightest bit vain enough to spend time staring at himself in the mirror whilst he hoisted weights. No, this perfect specimen of the male anatomy was a pleasant result of his busy life as a doctor in the field and the manual labour he did in his vast garden in his spare time.

She shivered as some particularly erotic memories sprang to mind of this handsome man with his tan, sun-bleached mop of hair and that mischievous glint in his eye, lying naked next to her.

'Are you sure you're all right? You've got that hungry look in your eyes again.'

Izzy blinked away inappropriate thoughts and images of her colleague, her friend, and the one constant she'd had in her life here in Belfast before she'd screwed up and potentially lost him for ever too.

'Just starved.' Apparently for more than food. Not that he'd ever shown any interest in her as a woman apart from as another one of his mates until that night.

It hadn't been planned. Izzy had just needed to be with someone who cared about her. Through the tears and shared stories of heartbreak they'd found themselves kissing and searching for some feeling of peace. She didn't regret anything. It had been a beautifully raw expression of their affection and compassion for one another. They simply should have taken adequate pre-cautions for their evening as friends with benefits.

'Let me get the paperwork out of the way and we'll head to the pub before you get hangry. I know what you're like when you're so hungry you turn into a red-headed hulk.'

If she'd had any doubts that he only saw her as a mate, they vanished. She was so completely friend zoned he didn't expect her to take offence at that comment.

'Do not,' she huffed, regardless she knew very well her fiery temper reached boiling point when there was a lack of food close to hand. He hadn't drawn a pretty picture of her when she'd created a sexy centrefold out of him. 'I'm not keen on the pub idea either.'

She worried he'd be suspicious if she sat in the bar nursing an orange juice instead of her usual glass of wine.

'Dinner at that new Italian place, then? Although it'll probably mean having to go home and get changed first. I'm not sure sweaty work clothes will fit their dress code.' He was being unnecessarily concerned. Cal always managed to smell amazing no matter how stressful their shift proved or how energetic he'd been.

'Hmm, I fancy something stodgy and greasy.' She didn't.

'I'll die of starvation if you make me go home first.' She wouldn't. However, if they went to that posh place and Cal changed the habit of a lifetime by not offering to pay the entire bill she'd be mortified because she couldn't afford it.

Even before she'd discovered there'd be a new mouth to feed in the future, she'd been struggling to cover the bills. Gerry had never officially moved in, but he'd used her place as a base when not travelling around the country as a pharmaceutical rep. It wasn't that she was missing his financial contributions to household expenses, quite the opposite. He was the reason she had no savings left to furnish her nest now.

She'd invited him into her heart and her home without the knowledge of his gambling habits. Gerry had had no family or friends either to call on for help and the cost of his funeral on top of his other financial mismanagement meant money was tight for her and nothing short of a miracle would change that now. Wages would have to stretch as far as possible and that would mean cutting back on luxuries like fancy Italian restaurants or any sort of social life.

Izzy should have known better than to think she was sitting pretty at any stage of her life and keep herself protected. Being a kid bounced around the care system had taught her never to rely on anyone except herself and never to let her guard down. Once too often she'd imagined she'd found her forever home, only to be returned like an ill-fitting shirt. Too young, too old, too opinionated, too red, she'd been a nineties Anne Shirley, without the lovable Matthew and Marilla Cuthbert giving her a happy ending at Green Gables.

Meals and board had been provided along with whatever basic material possessions she'd needed, but that all-important element had been missing, as it had for most of her life. Love wasn't something given or received easily for her, even with Gerry.

It had been a slow burn for them but eventually she'd learned to trust, to open up her heart and believe him when he'd promised her a future and a family together.

Even though Cal knew about Gerry's betrayal since it was the reason she'd been driven to his arms, the extent of her financial struggles was another secret she was keeping from someone she considered a friend. With good reason. He'd insist on riding in on his white steed, waving his fat wallet, to save her and she wasn't going to be indebted to him or anyone else. She had to get used to managing on her own when she had errands to run or do the night feeds when she was exhausted beyond belief. The stakes were too high now for her to let anyone into that armoured heart again.

'The "caff" it is, then.' Cal took the lead from Izzy's clues as to what she could afford, not necessarily what she craved. Which, at this moment, didn't go beyond a chance to kick off her shoes and sit down with a cup of builder's tea.

'Do you think they're going to be okay?' Izzy cradled the chipped mug in her hands, drawing comfort from the heat as a chill fluttered over her skin.

'Who?' Cal sawed off another chunk of sausage and popped it into his mouth. It had become a tradition to go for a meal when their shift had ended. Not only because they'd worked up an appetite, but they needed that time to come down from the adrenaline high and process what they'd gone through at the scene of whatever medical emergency they'd just attended.

'Tara Macready and her baby—you know, the woman we just saved.' She set her tea down and poked the sausage and bacon on her plate with a fork. A fry-up was the standard fare in this particular establishment, but the smell of grease was making her feel queasy again. Rather than make him suspicious she'd ordered her usual, but she'd only managed to nibble at the toast so far.

'We did our best and they're in the best place to recover.' Cal carried on eating, but the image of the blood and knowledge of Tara's condition wouldn't leave her. Most people probably wouldn't have realised she was pregnant, but Izzy would've noticed even if it hadn't been in her notes. These days she was aware of every new change in her body and she'd recognised Tara had the same slightly swollen belly as she did.

This kind of accident wasn't an unusual sight, given the nature of their work, and it was vital they kept a certain detachment when attending these scenes. They weren't supposed to take the emotional trauma home with them and usually she didn't, other than a phone call to check up on a patient's progress.

This one was different as it was a mother and her unborn child in jeopardy. Perhaps they'd all be different now she was going to be a mother herself. The idea of setting off in the helicopter alone was making her question her own mortality these days. Until now she'd never worried about her own safety up there, but in the not-too-distant future she was going to have someone depending on her coming home from work day after day.

The sound of cutlery clattering onto the plate made her jump and the touch of Cal's hand as he settled it on hers didn't help soothe her nerves.

'They would never have made it at all if they'd gone by road and she might lose the use of her hand but they're still alive. Now, are you going to tell me what's going on in that head of yours today? You're not yourself at all.' It wasn't that Cal didn't have sympathy for them, but he knew, as well as she did, that they had to do their job and move onto the next one without looking back in case it affected future call-outs.

That had taken some getting used to, although she'd had years of experience as a nurse in A and E. Cal too, a consultant in emergency medicine, had found those first cases difficult to walk away from at the hospital doors. They'd often talked into the wee hours about their day, much to his fiancée's annoyance.

These pregnancy hormones were making her feel as though she'd taken a step back, seeing everything in a new, terrifying light. Not that she had any intention of giving up her job. She loved being part of the team being whisked up into the air at a moment's notice to save people in trouble. This was simply a blip and one she couldn't wait to get over, along with this nausea.

'Sorry. I'm not the best company at the minute.'

He squeezed her hand. 'You know I'm here for you anytime.'

His misplaced concern caused her eyes to prickle with tears. Recently she'd suspected her eyeballs had been replaced by tiny hedgehogs, that was happening so often. He was so considerate it pained her, knowing she was about to turn his world on its head again.

'Thanks,' she said, withdrawing her hand from the safety of his. It wasn't going to do her any good to expect Cal to prop her up every time she had a wobble, no matter how comforting it was. They hadn't planned this baby and whilst she was reconciled some way to the idea of becoming a parent there was no guarantee he would. There was every chance she would end up raising their child alone and she was fine with that. If that's what Cal wanted.

'Perhaps you came back too early—you know, after Gerry,' he said softly with some hesitation, and she knew he was half expecting her to kick off at the suggestion. Which she usually did when anyone tried to tell her what to do, thinking they knew her better than she knew herself.

She didn't agree with him on this occasion either but she'd no other way to explain her current mood without spilling the beans about the baby.

'You could be right.' She pushed her plate away before she vomited.

* * *

Now Cal knew something really was wrong with Izzy. She usually fought him over the smallest difference of opinion, so daring to suggest something as huge as she'd returned to work too soon warranted all-out war.

Between that and her roller-coaster appetite he was beginning to worry about her. One minute she was eating everything in sight, including his emergency chocolate stash he kept for those occasions they didn't have time for a meal break. The next she was sitting staring at her rejected fry-up as though she was about to burst into tears at any second.

He hadn't noticed until today how emotional she'd become, having taken her stoicism and ability to bounce back from any eventuality for granted. Caught up in the sorrow of his own break-up, he hadn't seen past the front she'd been putting on since Gerry had died, accepting her assurances she was fine too easily. Probably because he didn't want to over-analyse what had happened between them that night when she'd come to his place in a state about Gerry.

He'd been committed to his relationship with Janet, even if she hadn't considered it a priority, but when Izzy had come to him seeking support and comfort, any thoughts of his ex had been obliterated by his all-consuming need for her. Once he'd tasted desire on her lips, all those suppressed feelings he'd apparently been harbouring for her had been tangled in there right along with their limbs and tongues. He never considered that she might've been down in those depths of despair all this time.

Yes, Janet had betrayed him in the worst possible way, stringing him along with that dream of his happy family, only to snatch it away for ever. It had been partly his fault, so desperate to set up a loving home like the one he'd grown up in he'd clung onto the wrong person, ignoring all her flaws in favour of the family he'd envisaged having with her. Now he was worried he'd taken advantage of Izzy when she was obviously still emotionally vulnerable.

They'd been close for years and that bond had irritated their partners at times, but they'd only crossed the line that night when their relationships had forcibly ended. Ever since they'd fallen into bed together he'd found it difficult to rein those feelings back in and pretend nothing had happened. They'd agreed that was the best course of action, but it was impossible to put their indiscretion completely out of his head when he saw her every day and was reminded how incredible that time together had been. As though they'd finally stopped pretending their chemistry was nothing more than camaraderie and had expressed their feelings for one another physically.

How was he supposed to forget something so amazingly honest after his recent experience of deceit?

'I've been a bad friend to you lately. I'm sorry.' There'd been a distance between them recently, which he'd created as a coping mechanism to protect himself, never thinking about the support Izzy needed. He thought back over these past horrendous months and thought of all the support she'd offered him after Janet had left.

Izzy had been a constant on his doorstep despite his repeated warnings he didn't want to see or talk to anyone in the aftermath of his ex's revelation. She'd been the provider of home-cooked meals when he hadn't wanted to eat and the confiscator of alcohol when all he'd wanted to do was drink. Ignoring his bad temper, she'd fought past his defences and dragged him out of the quagmire, so he'd been able to get on with his life when he'd truly believed it was over.

That was the true definition of a friend. Not someone who muttered his sympathies and accepted her grieving was over because it suited him better than having to dig beyond a fake smile and talk about feelings. Now, seeing her here, eyes glassy with unshed tears, biting her lip to keep up the façade, he wanted to finally step up and be there for her. The way she'd done for him. She was the closest thing he had to family now. The only one who'd been there with him through the darkest hours of his life, and he owed her.

'Don't be daft. Aren't you here, putting up with my mood swings?' There was that smile again that he was learning not to trust when her eyes were cloudy with uncertainty and something else he couldn't quite decipher but which made him feel guiltier than ever.

'I wasn't there for you after Gerry died.'

'Um, I think you were.'

He wasn't expecting her to reference what had happened between them but there was a suggestion of that passionate encounter flickering like erotic flames in her eyes. Rather than complicate matters more between them, Cal chose to ignore the reminder. In conversation at least. 'If something's wrong I expect you to tell me and let me help. Okay?'

'Understood. Now, shall we get the bill?' She wrestled out from his grip and waved to the waitress.

Cal sighed and pulled his credit card from his wallet. 'I'll get this. It's the least I can do.'

Izzy made her usual protests as she fished in her bag for her purse, but he grabbed the bill first. 'Let me pay my half at least.'

'You can leave a couple of pounds for the tip if you want.' It was then he caught a glimpse inside her purse to see only a few coppers resting in the lining. Rather than embarrass her further, he tossed the loose change he found in his pocket on the table and made to leave.

Something wasn't right with Izzy and he wasn't going to rest until he discovered what. And if he wasn't the friend she needed he knew how to find the one who fitted that description.

CHAPTER TWO

'THIS IS SUPPOSED to be fun,' Cal called back to Izzy, who was doubled over trying to get her breath back and looking as though she was hating every second of this.

'I'm sure you're enjoying yourself, but I'd rather be vegging out watching the telly on my day off.' Izzy straightened up, pulled a hairband out of her pocket and tied her wild mane of red hair away from her face. Despite her protests, he thought she looked happier than she had in days, hiking out here in the County Down countryside, in the shadow of the Mourne Mountains. To be on the safe side he'd contacted Helen, who she often talked about, and suggested she might want to check in with her friend. It hadn't been difficult to make contact when Helen's phone number was on the birth announcement she'd sent Izzy after her son was born. The picture of mother and baby with the time and date of arrival took pride of place on Izzy's desk at work.

'I think we've both done our fair share of moping around. The fresh air will do you good.' He'd been keeping a closer eye on her lately and had noticed how withdrawn she seemed to have become compared to the old, devil-may-care Fizz he'd come to know.

There was always some excuse post-shift now about

why she couldn't come out for a meal or even a quick drink, and he hated to think of her shut away in that empty house with nothing but memories to keep her company. After Janet had left him he'd thought he'd never venture over the doorstep again, afraid to face the world outside. Izzy had gone through a lot and was bound to have been changed by it, but he was determined not to let her retreat from civilisation altogether.

Since she didn't seem keen on spending time in crowded places he'd gone to the other extreme and dragged her out on one of his walks in the countryside with him.

'You can sit still and enjoy the fresh air. I think they call it sunbathing.'

'With your colouring?' He snorted as she tried to convince him her pale skin did anything other than freckle and burn.

Izzy shrugged off her jacket and tied it around her waist. Although he'd been concerned she wasn't eating properly, as her white T-shirt drew taut he could see she'd filled out a bit over these past weeks. He was glad. She looked better with a little meat on her bones, healthier, and as the sun shone through her shirt, silhouetting her figure, he could see exactly which parts of her had blossomed.

'Enjoying the view?' An amused Izzy echoed the words he'd teased her with the other day and snapped Cal's attention away from the soft round breasts he so clearly remembered palming in his hands.

'I was doing this for your benefit. I prefer a hike in the mountains myself.' He dismissed her comment, instead of confirming where his gaze had been lingering.

This walk was small potatoes for him when he preferred the challenge of a hill climb, whatever the weather, where he was focused on every step lest he end up at the bottom of a ravine. It was good for him to keep busy, his mind and body too active to entertain thoughts of his broken dreams, and he wanted to do the same for her.

'Yeah, 'cause we don't see enough of this at work.' Izzy rolled her eyes and started walking again.

'Who could ever tire of this?' He held his arms aloft in celebration of today's beautiful blue skies. They weren't always blessed with such favourable weather in Northern Ireland, even during these summer months, and he was of the opinion they should enjoy every second before the rain made another appearance.

'Me. Pretty. Damn. Quickly,' she huffed out as she climbed the slight incline of the bluebell-lined pathway, her slim legs flexing below her shorts with every step.

Cal let her reach the top first, determined to see her do this at her own pace in case he scared her off altogether. Today was about re-forging that bond between them so she'd be comfortable enough to share what was really going on in her life now, without any awkwardness coming between them.

She stood above him, hands on hips, face tilted towards the sky, eyes closed and soaking up the heat of the sun. This was what he wanted for her, to find peace and be free of the stresses she was under. Studying her from here, he could see why his ex had always seemed so threatened by her. He'd laughed off Janet's bouts of jealousy when he'd mentioned Izzy's name because at that time he'd never thought of her as anything more than a friend. Now it was difficult to think of her as anything other than someone he wanted to share his bed with again.

As he stood there, appreciating the dusting of freckles across her nose and the stunning red hair most women would pay a fortune to try and replicate, she suddenly crumpled to the ground.

'Izzy?' His heart leapt into his mouth and he sprinted towards her, their perfect day shattered at the thought of something happening to her.

She was spread-eagled on the grass, her eyes still closed.

'Izzy?' He dropped to his knees and called her name again, before throwing off his backpack in case his medical skills would be required. Perhaps he had asked too much of her in coming here when she hadn't been herself recently, but he'd wanted to do something for her since it was his fault she felt she couldn't confide in him any more. He was sure it was because she regretted sleeping with him, but he couldn't change what had happened between them, even if he'd wanted to.

He leaned over her, his face close to hers, listening for signs she was still breathing. Her chest continued to rise and fall, and he could feel her soft breath on his cheek.

Suddenly, her eyes snapped open and he was staring into the depths of those sea-green pools. In that moment he was transported back to that night-which-should-not-be-named, when they had been lying in his bed together, naked and wanting. Izzy was looking at him the same way she had then, her eyes and her body asking him to hold her, kiss her, love her. He didn't think he'd be able to resist any more now than he had then, and it was only the impact of those past actions on their relationship that made him pull back. Today was about improving relations between them, not making their working environment more awkward.

'I hope you're happy now you've almost killed me.'
Izzy sat up and brushed off any suggestion that she'd
ever wanted him to do anything other than feel guilty
about bringing her out into the wild.

He sat back on his heels and whistled out a quivering breath. 'Don't ever do that to me again. You nearly
gave me a heart attack.'

'Now you know how it feels. I'm not moving again
until we've refuelled.' She rolled over onto her side and
reached for the food supplies stashed in his bag.

'There are kinder ways to let me know you're hungry
than fake fainting, you know!' He pulled out a bottle of
water from the side pocket in the rucksack and flicked
the condensation from the cold bottle at her, getting
them back on the pranking friends track rather than the
almost kissing past lovers one on his mind.

She let out a shriek before dissolving into a fit of adorable giggles. It was good to hear her laugh again and
for him to do it with her. He realised then it had been a
while since he'd found the fun in anything. Izzy in any
capacity was good for his soul.

'I'll get you back for that when you least expect it,' she
vowed, eyes narrowed as she took a bite of her sandwich.

Cal stretched out on the grass beside her. They did
spend the majority of their time in isolated countryside,
going to the rescue of those in mortal danger, but there
was no time to enjoy the surroundings. It was nice to
chill out here in the open and better still with company.

Izzy handed over the parcel of sandwiches she'd
made. He'd suggested a pub lunch, but she'd insisted
on a picnic. Come to think of it, she'd been doing a lot
of that recently, bringing her own lunches, forgoing their
usual coffee runs in favour of her ever-present water bot-

tle. He harked back to that day in the café when she'd struggled to scrabble together a few pounds for a tip. The awful realisation of what was going on made it hard for him to swallow his mouthful of food.

'I hate to sound like a broken record but is there something wrong? I'd really hate to think you were suffering and hadn't come to me for help.'

He saw the flicker of anxiety on her face as she gulped at her water, but it didn't give him any pleasure to know he'd been right. That withholding of information illustrated the decline in their friendship over these past months since they'd slept together when before that they'd used to share everything going on in their lives. He'd feared the repercussions of that intimacy so much it was possible he'd created that distance between them. Worried about getting hurt again so quickly after Janet that he'd backed right out of Izzy's life when she'd needed his support most.

'I, er, I'm just having a few money troubles at the minute. The funeral and everything else has left me a bit strapped for cash, but I'll get by. I always do.' She gave him a bright smile before quickly looking away again, but he didn't believe her problems were as straightforward as she was making out.

He was grateful she'd finally confided in him because he'd never considered the financial implications of losing her partner, regardless of the gambling debts he'd apparently accrued before his death. For one thing he would've imagined Gerry had had some sort of life insurance policy in place to ensure she was protected for this kind of eventuality. Then, of course, there were the everyday practicalities of losing a second income.

When Janet had moved out he'd had to cover the mortgage and household bills himself.

He might not have been great at providing Izzy with the emotional support she'd needed but this was something practical he could help with.

'There's no point worrying yourself sick or depriving yourself over the sake of a few pounds. I can give you a loan if that would help dig you out of a hole?' He'd be happier to write her a cheque with no desire to see the money returned but she would never entertain the idea. She was already shaking her head at the alternative suggestion.

'That's a very kind offer but you know I couldn't do that. Taking money from friends always gets messy and I've had enough of being in anyone's debt. Thank you but I'll get through this myself.' Izzy wrapped up the leftovers, tucked them back into the bag and got to her feet, discussion over.

Cal wasn't surprised she'd turned him down because she was notoriously as stubborn as hell but so was he. He was sure there was more to the story, more he could do to help her.

They'd often partnered up on social occasions with their significant others and he'd never believed Gerry good enough for his Fizz. Where she had been the fun and friendly half of the two, Gerry had been her complete opposite. Often sullen and reluctant to be drawn into conversation, he was a closed book and hard to like. He'd never known what Izzy had seen in him but respected her enough not to question her judgement.

Izzy was trying to pick up the fractured pieces of her life in order to move on and Cal was going to be there for her every step of the way. It was about time someone was. Now he knew there was a problem he wasn't going to rest until he knew she was going to be okay. He could be every bit as obstinate as Isobel Fitzpatrick when it came to helping a friend.

'Ten-year-old girl suffering severe burns after falling against a barbecue.' Izzy recapped the few details they'd been given on the emergency call and directed Mac, the pilot and operations manager, to a clear landing site near the address they'd been given.

Although she didn't wish harm on anyone, never mind a child, the distraction of work was good for her. She had let slip more than she'd intended about her problems to Cal but telling him her money woes was preferable to surprising him with the news he was going to be a father. They'd both messed up, and Cal had enough of his own personal issues to deal with. There was no way she was bringing a child into the world expecting to have someone bailing her out at every hint of trouble. That would be asking for more heartache. She loved him for the offer all the same.

His ex didn't know what she'd thrown away. Cal deserved someone who loved him as much as he'd obviously loved Janet. There was nothing he wouldn't have done for her. Including bringing up someone else's baby as his own if she'd been honest with him instead of stringing him along until she'd been sure her other lover did want her after all.

If he hadn't, Izzy suspected she'd still be letting Cal play happy families with a child who wasn't his. He'd been broken by the betrayal, as anyone would've been, and Izzy had been crushed on his behalf because she knew how important family was to him.

Izzy needed a friend right now, someone who could provide some normality for her when her life was falling down around her, but as soon as he found out about the baby she knew that would change. Things would become untenable when he'd lost the family he'd always dreamed of, only to be left with one he hadn't planned. It was bound to cause some resentment or tempt Cal into interfering in some way, directing that focus from Janet's baby onto hers. She wasn't going to fool herself into thinking anyone had her back any more now than they had before. If there was one thing she excelled at it was picking herself up and dusting herself off after being left in the lurch.

Apart from not wanting to hurt him with her news, she also wanted to avoid him becoming over-protective where she was concerned. When he'd discovered Janet was expecting he'd practically dressed her in bubble wrap, afraid to let her lift a finger to keep mum and baby as safe as possible. Janet had been happy to put her feet up and let Cal run around after her but that was exactly what Izzy didn't want.

She intended to carry on as normal for as long as she could. Being pregnant wasn't a disability, millions of women had gone through it time and time again. Besides, she was almost at the three-month mark and out of the danger stage. If Cal had any inkling he wouldn't have suggested a country ramble, never mind let her carry on with the physical side of her job.

Fitness and strength was a huge part of being air ambulance crew and she loved her job. If nothing else, she needed every penny she could put aside before her maternity leave. She didn't want to think about the cost of childcare for the next eighteen years. From now on she was going to take one day at a time. It was the only way she'd get through these next belly-blossoming months without going doolally.

'Earth to Izzy. I asked if you were ready for this.' Cal's eyes were on her instead of the lush green scenery whizzing past below. The last thing she needed was him getting distracted on this call with her. There was no room for error when every second counted.

''Course. Why wouldn't I be?' She frowned at him, a warning to mind his own business at work. He knew better than to let personal problems encroach on this already too-small space and make it even more claustrophobic. The pile of bills he thought was her only problem was definitely not something that warranted a discussion here. Especially when she was doing her best not to think about the little bundle who was about to throw her life into more chaos.

Cal gave her the thumbs up as they landed, and she considered the matter closed for now when there was a patient needing their help.

They hiked up the street with their gear to the house with the door already lying open.

'Let's hope someone had the foresight to administer first aid.' It was Cal who said it, although Izzy was thinking the same thing. Providing that immediate care in the aftermath of a burn could make all the difference to the long-term damage.

'I'm sure the switchboard operator would've given them instructions on cooling the burn under tepid water.' They didn't know how serious the burns were but with a child involved the stakes were that much higher. Skin grafts, infection and plastic surgery were all possible, depending on the extent of the burns, and not something a parent would want their baby to go through.

'Hello. Air ambulance crew here,' Cal called into the house as they made their entry.

'We're upstairs in the bathroom.' A woman appeared at the top of the stairs and beckoned them up where there was a group of adults crowded around a sobbing child.

'Okay, could we ask everyone to give us a bit of room, please?' The bathroom was cramped enough for them to work in so Izzy needed to clear out those taking up unnecessary space. Eventually the other family members shuffled out until there was only the child and her parents remaining.

'Hi, I'm Doctor Cal. What's your name?' Cal knelt down beside the youngster, who was trembling and crying as she stood in the bath while her father was hosing her down with a shower head.

'This is Suzy,' her father volunteered, and shut off the water so they could assess her injuries.

'I hear there was an accident with a barbecue?' Although Cal took the lead, Izzy was there to back him up and give assistance where it was needed.

Dad nodded. 'The kids were running about, and she tripped and fell into the barbecue. She stuck her hand out to break the fall and I think that's where most of the damage was done.'

Whilst Cal was inspecting the upper-body burns that had left angry red marks across her chest and shoulders, Izzy gently took her hand to assess the extent of the burns.

'Where do you hurt most, Suzy?'

The child lifted her hand up and Izzy could see where it was beginning to blister.

'We're going to give you something to help with the pain, sweetheart. Cal, do you want to take a look at this?'

His brow furrowed too, and it was clear he wasn't any happier than she was at the sight. 'The chest and shoulder burns I would say are only two per cent partial thickness so we can dress those but I'd prefer a specialist to take a look at that hand. In the meantime, can we get a line in for some pain relief?'

One of the bonuses of transporting patients by helicopter was that they could take them directly to the best centre to treat their injury. In this case they could take little Suzy to the burns unit where plastic surgeons would be there to assess her injury and treat her straight away to limit permanent damage.

'Suzy, you're just going to feel a wee scratch in your hand. We need to give you something to help with the pain. Perhaps Dad can just hold you steady for me? Good girl.' Izzy administered the drugs as instructed by Cal, which would hopefully go some way to making the child comfortable again. It was difficult to watch her suffer and Izzy felt for the mother, who was standing nearby, whispering soothing words to comfort her child, though she must've been racked with guilt and anxiety herself.

Izzy understood motherhood wasn't an easy job when so many had failed her in her childhood, but she was looking forward to the challenges ahead. She wanted her child to know its mother would be there come what may and would relish that role of being needed, bringing a sense of security she'd never experienced herself.

'Dad, are you okay to carry her out to the helicopter? Then we're going to take a quick ride to the hospital. Have you ever been on a helicopter, Suzy?' Cal got them organised and on the move whilst Izzy checked in with the control room to update them on their progress and route.

'No, she hasn't, and neither have I.' Suzy's dad gave a nervous laugh.

'There's nothing to worry about. We'll be at the hospital in twenty minutes tops.' Half the time it would've taken an ambulance and it cut out all the transfers between departments. Izzy knew if it was her daughter she'd be only too glad to have Cal and the helicopter at hand to administer treatment. He was a calm, assured presence in the storm and Izzy hoped that remained true for the one he was about to enter with her.

Once they landed, Cal and Izzy worked together to unbuckle their passengers and get them out of the helicopter. They hurried with the stretcher towards the team waiting for the transfer, but the ground was greasy after the earlier downpour of rain and in Izzy's haste she slipped and landed on her back.

'Izzy, are you all right?' Cal hesitated and offered a hand to help her to her feet, but she was winded and a little disorientated.

'Go. Go.' She waved him on, their patient a priority here, but made no move to get up.

Instead, she lay back and rested her hands protectively on her belly. It was early days and she'd hit the ground hard, as indicated by the pain shooting up her spine.

Those darned hedgehogs were back, pricking her eye sockets and trying to make her cry again, as she wondered if she had been taking too many risks after all. If she hadn't been one hundred per cent sure about wanting this baby, the prospect of having harmed it confirmed it was all she wanted. She needed to know it was safe in there, protected from her stupidity and two left feet. At least she was in the best place possible to find out.

She heard a male voice utter an expletive and looked up to find Cal standing over her. 'You really hurt yourself, huh?'

He bent down and eased her up into a sitting position. That small act of support was enough to tip her emotionally over the edge. One crack in her defences and the dam broke, tears gushing down her face for the first time since Gerry's funeral.

'I'm pregnant, Cal.' She was finally admitting it now in the hope it made this baby real and lessened the possibility of something happening to it.

'Okay. Okay. We'll get you into the emergency room and I'm sure they can arrange an ultrasound for you to make sure baby's all right. How far along are you?' Cal did his best to remain calm, so he didn't freak her out more than she already was. Regardless, that was exactly what he was doing on the inside.

'Three months.'

Perhaps it was the shock of her news, but it took a moment for it all to sink in for Cal. Gerry had died over five months ago so the baby couldn't be his. On the other hand, he and Izzy had slept together more recently. Say, three months give or take a few days. His heart tried to take a flying leap out of his mouth. This was his baby. He was going to be a father.

There were a few seconds when he thought he was going to pass out from the sheer significance of what she'd told him. It was cruel timing to discover a one-night stand with his work colleague had resulted in an unplanned pregnancy so soon after the drama of his cheating fiancée and a baby that had turned out not to be his.

Not long ago this news would have made his day. He'd been looking forward to fatherhood since his own parents had died, but circumstances had changed. Along with his outlook on life. He was still reeling from Janet's abuse of his trust and he definitely wasn't ready to be thrown into another drama. Especially one as life-changing as fathering a baby.

He was still scarred by having his last family torn away from him and there was no way of telling how that could manifest itself as this pregnancy progressed. The trauma and loss wasn't something he'd get over easily and it was going to be difficult for him to get used to the idea of becoming a father again when Janet had forever tainted that picture of having a happy family.

It was important to remember this wasn't the ideal scenario for Izzy either after losing Gerry. They were going to have to work together to make sure this baby wasn't affected by the personal baggage they were both carrying from their pasts.

'I'm sorry.' As he got staff to help him transfer her to a stretcher and take her inside, she kept apologising, and he knew why. Izzy was such an empathetic person she was more worried about how the pregnancy would affect him than her.

'You have absolutely nothing to apologise for. We both messed up. The timing isn't the greatest, and neither are the circumstances, but the damage has been done.' He thought he saw her flinch at his choice of words, but he preferred to deal in the truth these days. This wasn't exactly a joyous occasion for either of them, rather something they were going to have to learn to live with.

They didn't love each other, and all indications would suggest she'd rather forget the night they'd apparently conceived this baby. It wasn't the family he'd planned on having but it wasn't one he could pretend wasn't happening either.

Later, as they transferred for the ultrasound it struck Cal how vulnerable Izzy looked. Once he'd got over his initial shock he could see how frightened she was, tears still falling from her red-rimmed eyes and her hands wringing her handkerchief into knots. For once she was the one who needed support rather than being the one who always provided it.

He squeezed her hand as the sonographer applied gel over her stomach to let her know he was there. If she hadn't wanted him with her she would've made it clear a long time ago.

'If this baby is as tough as its mum, it's not going to be bothered by one wee fall.'

His reassurance was rewarded with a crooked smile, but she was gripping his hand like a vice, further indication that she wanted him with her. It was survival instinct that made him want to disengage her hand from his and turn his back on the epic responsibility of becoming a parent after past experiences. They weren't even in a relationship, therefore giving her more reason to walk out the door when a better option came along. In the end it was his loyalty to Izzy that saw him stick around. This was a second chance for him to be a friend to her and give her the support she needed.

She turned her head to watch the screen as the sonographer moved the Doppler over her slightly rounded belly. Cal had been blind to the obvious signs of her pregnancy, which he would've spotted if he didn't spend so much time in his own head, wallowing in the past or trying to keep her at arm's length. The sickness, the unexpected emotional displays, not to mention the recent aversion to alcohol and greasy food, were blatant clues, along with her new curves.

Watching that hazy blob on the screen come to life brought up so many emotions he had to swallow before he started wailing. It should have been such an exciting time, seeing his baby for the first time, but this was the second time he'd been here. The memories of sitting here, holding Janet's hand, were too painful for him to enjoy the moment, even when the heartbeat sounded out around the room to let them know everything was all right. He was relieved, of course, but emotionally he was just kind of numb.

Izzy's sobs let him know she would love this baby enough for the two of them if it came to it. He lifted her hand to his mouth and kissed it, so she knew he wasn't angry at the situation they'd found themselves in and pleased that the baby was going to be okay.

Then he noticed the frown on the sonographer's face and the quick movement of the Doppler further over Izzy's stomach. She hadn't missed it either.

'What's wrong? I thought the baby was okay?' Her eyes were wide with panic and she almost cut off the circulation in his fingers with her grip. Cal's own breath stilled as they waited for a reply.

'You haven't had your twelve-week scan yet?'

Izzy shook her head. 'I didn't get around to organising that yet.'

The sonographer turned the monitor around for them to see, a smile now evening out her wrinkled forehead as the heartbeat rang out loud and clear once more.

'They'll be able to give you a more accurate reading and confirm dates with you, but I do have some news I can share with you.'

'What? What is it?' It was Cal's turn to voice his concern. He hadn't remained detached from this after all as a swell of nausea rose up inside him at the thought the baby was in any sort of jeopardy.

'I was confirming a healthy heartbeat, but I've found more than one. Meet baby number two.' She turned the screen round so they could see the evidence for themselves.

'You mean...twins?' Izzy's mouth fell open in a half laugh, half sob as it was confirmed with a nod.

'Wow.' It was all he could manage in the wake of the bombshell. Two babies at once. A ready-made family neither of them had planned.

He could see the second reality hit home for her too.

'What am I going to do, Cal?' Struggling for money and now with the prospect of having two children to support, she was turning to him for help. She wouldn't have asked unless she was desperate when she was always so single-minded about controlling her own life. It wasn't a plea he would ignore. These babies were as much his responsibility as they were hers. Neither of them had any family around, or had any intention of getting into another relationship anytime soon. It seemed to him there was only one logical solution to their current situation.

'You'll just have to move in with me.'

CHAPTER THREE

'IT WOULDN'T HURT to think about it. At least until you're back on your feet financially.' Cal was sitting in the chair opposite Izzy in the control room back at base with his feet on the desk, waiting for the next call and driving her to distraction in the meantime.

It was impossible for her to relax since he'd first made that ridiculous suggestion she move in with him to help solve her money problems. Of course, she'd eventually shot him down at the hospital, convinced it had been the shock talking after finding out she was expecting twins. The news had affected her so much she'd almost accepted in the heat of the moment.

It would've been easy to say yes and line up a partner to share the bills and parenting responsibilities but shacking up together for the sake of convenience wouldn't have been fair. Especially to her, when it would give her false hope they could pick up where they'd left off that night in his house. He'd made it clear that wasn't going to be an option, regardless of the new complication in their lives. Every time she thought that attraction between them was raising its head, he backed off, and she had to get it out of her head they could be anything more than friends or she'd never move on from that night.

Cal wasn't promising her that they'd live happily ever after together. In fact, he'd yet to acknowledge wanting to take on any sort of parenting role. This sounded more like offering a friend a sofa to kip on when they were down on their luck. She supposed she should be grateful for that much when he could hardly bring himself to touch her, much less declare his undying love for her, since they'd slept together.

'You know as well as I do it's a foolish notion. I'd appreciate it if you didn't bring it up at work where someone could overhear.' With sharp reflexes she shot out her hand to catch the rubber ball he was bouncing off the wall before the repetitive thud gave her a migraine. It was fair to say it didn't take a lot to rile her these days when she was so full of stress and worry.

'Uh…there's no one here. Mac's on his break.' Smartass had an answer for everything when he knew very well she didn't want him bringing this up again regardless of who was around. This wasn't a matter for gossip fodder or outlandish proposals born of a misguided sense of duty. It was her life.

Izzy unclenched her fist and the ball pinged back into shape. As it turned out, it was a pretty good stress reliever. It saved her wringing anyone's neck.

'You know what I mean. We spend half of our lives talking over headsets and I don't want anything accidentally slipping out. My private life is just that and I'll tell people about the pregnancy in my own time. As for moving in together, we're definitely keeping that between us before anyone gets carried away with the idea.' Her included.

He was saying all the right words but since finding out about Gerry's secret life she'd learned to look beyond mere lip service. Cal was the sort of man who would fulfil his obligations no matter what the personal cost was to him, but she didn't want him to feel trapped. Neither did she want someone else promising her the world and getting her hopes up about playing happy families, only to have them cruelly dashed further down the line.

Her reservations seemed justified when he wasn't giving off the same vibes he had when he'd announced Janet's pregnancy. It was understandable he wouldn't be as excited this time around after everything that had happened, but she didn't see that same desire in him to be a father any more. Her babies deserved the very best she could give them and that didn't include a reluctant dad. She knew what it was like to grow up somewhere you weren't completely wanted, and she vowed to do better by her children as a parent. Even if that meant raising them alone.

Cal's offer might be a temporary solution to her problems, but she knew it would be setting them up for future ones.

'I don't see why you're so against the idea.' He withdrew his long limbs from the desk and sat up in the chair, no longer appearing so relaxed.

'We'll start with the fact we've both recently lost the people we loved and neither of us are in the right state of mind to make a life-changing decision like this. Then there's the whole baby issue. You weren't even prepared for one baby, never mind two. Think of the disruption that's going to cause in your life on a practical level. I didn't tell you before now that I'm pregnant because I didn't want you to feel obligated. I'm not expecting anything from you.'

This wasn't about sparing his feelings, it was about

keeping things real. She could raise these babies alone because she would make them her whole world. To have two children at once gave her the family she wanted, and it didn't have to include a man.

'Are you done?' He leaned forward, his face and body rigid as he stared her down, and she knew she'd dented his pride. 'Yes, I'm thinking with my head instead of my heart but the whole love thing didn't work out for me. I don't like thinking of you in that flat with goodness knows who knocking on your door in the dead of night. My house is big enough to accommodate everyone and I've already got a nursery. We might have to double up on some things but that's easily arranged. I want to be a good friend to you as well as provide a stable home for you all.'

'What happens when you meet someone else and want to set up a home with them? Where would that leave me? Alone, penniless and out on the street with two children.'

After Gerry she knew she'd find it harder than ever to trust another man get close anyway, but her babies took priority over everything. Not that she'd be a catch, broke, with two children by another man. Cal might believe that he'd never get into another relationship, but he could change his mind over time. He was handsome, smart and too caring for his own good. There was no reason he couldn't have it all if he wanted. A woman would have to be a lunatic to turn him down. Or simply trying to save him from his own sense of chivalry.

'Think about it.' He edged his chair closer to hers and her heart picked up an extra beat.

He hadn't mentioned the babies in his argument but if Izzy was to entertain the idea of moving in she'd need some sort of assurance he was going to be a father to these babies. She couldn't live with him and pretend he was nothing more than a landlord to them. It was one thing being asked to forget what had happened between them but quite another if he thought she'd overlook that. Her children deserved a father who was crazy about them, so enamoured she'd be willing to forget everything she'd gone through in the past and risk it all again for their happiness.

She'd made the mistake of believing she'd finally found a forever home with Gerry, going all in and risking her heart in the hope things would work. The crash hadn't been his fault, but the debts and the gambling had proved he'd never put her first.

She couldn't commit herself to someone else who treated her babies the same way.

'We're friends who made a mistake, Cal, let's leave it at that. I hereby relinquish you from any responsibility.' Weary from the debate going on inside and outside her head about the subject, Izzy decided to put an end to it once and for all.

'I don't think that's your call. It took two of us to make these babies. Is that what's stopping you from letting me be involved? I mean, I wouldn't force you to be a *proper* wife, if you're worried about that?' The tinge of red flushing his complexion told him exactly what part of marriage he was thinking about.

Sleeping with Cal was something she was doing her best to keep from her mind. They had much more domestic matters to discuss, but now he'd mentioned it the image of the two of them rolling around in bed was suddenly on her mind. If they got married and planned a future together then that was something they would probably succumb to again. They both had physical needs and it would be, well, convenient as well as enjoyable. The idea held definite appeal for her, but she couldn't tell him that in case he thought she'd planned the whole thing.

'A *proper* wife? You mean like having dinner waiting on the table for you coming home after work, warming your slippers by the fire and generally losing my identity to keep my man happy? I don't fancy your chances, mate.'

'You know exactly what I mean, Fizz.' The lopsided grin and darkening eyes dared her to think about it again.

Now she was more uncomfortable than ever because she was imagining Cal as a permanent feature in her bed. A hot man who was offering her a bed and who'd already proved he could make her happy in that department made for an excellent sales pitch.

'Job! RTC. Two vehicles.' That was all Mac had to say to get the crew moving.

Cal jumped in the front of the helicopter with him to direct him to the crash site and waited for Izzy to get into the back.

'Check doors and harnesses.'

'Locked and secured.' Izzy followed his cue with the safety checks and they were in the air within minutes of the emergency call coming into the control room.

'Okay, land paramedics are on the scene and have requested our attendance. Patients are currently being assessed.' It wasn't long before Cal could see the site of the accident for himself as there was such a hive of activity going on around it. The flashing lights of the ambulance and the high-visibility vests of the crews al-

ready working to free the passengers were like a beacon
signalling the location.

From the air it was easy to see the car that had taken
the brunt of the damage on the passenger side. Although
they wouldn't be sure what they were dealing with until
they reached the ground.

The fire service on scene seemed to be concentrating
their efforts on that particular vehicle as the air ambulance landed in a field nearby and Cal and Izzy went to
join them. The other vehicle in the crash had damage to
the front but the driver was receiving treatment in the
back of the ambulance.

One of the paramedics came to update them on events
and as it had appeared from the outset, the girl still
trapped in the car, Stephanie, was the one they were
most concerned about. He and Izzy followed him over
to the patient and while Cal assessed any visible injury,
Izzy made strides to comfort the young woman pinned
inside the car.

'Hi, I'm Izzy, with the air ambulance. Now, the doctor's just going to take a look at your injuries before we
attempt to move you, Stephanie. Okay?'

'Okay.' She didn't sound convinced, but she was con-
scious and was a point in her favour.

'I want you to take nice deep breaths, Stephanie.' Cal
crouched down to get as close to her as he could. 'Can
you tell me where the pain is?'

'My left arm and left leg. They hurt so bad.' She was
crying now but it was Cal's job to determine whether
that was caused by fear or injury.

'I know they do and we're going to give you some
pain relief, but I can't see any blood so we're going to try
and get you out of here.' He gave the fire crew the nod

to start cutting the roof so they could get better access to her, but they still had to be careful. Although there was no visible bleeding, there was a chance she could be bleeding internally, and she had most likely broken her arm and leg.

'There's going to be a lot of noise and vibration while the crew work on cutting the roof of the car, Stephanie.' Izzy reached in and held her hand until the roof finally came off.

'Good girl. You're doing really well. I know it hurts, but we need to get you to the helicopter.' Izzy kept her vigil at Stephanie's side, reassuring her she would be all right and providing some comfort to the frightened girl. It struck him more in that moment than ever what a great mum she was going to make. Her compassion and nurturing side was everything a kid could want in its mother. He should know. He had his own parents to hold up as a shining example of how family life should be. It was a shame he apparently hadn't carried on that legacy when he was avoiding the subject of becoming a dad himself.

'I need some help here to get her onto the stretcher.' He concentrated on the job he was good at, administering some strong pain relief to the patient before they attempted extrication, and called the other paramedics and fire crew to assist with the transfer. 'Ready. Brace. Roll.'

They worked together to get her onto the stretcher, causing as little pain as possible in the circumstances. Izzy put a splint on Stephanie's injured arm and they put a pelvic binder around her to protect against any internal bleeding. Once she was stabilised as best they could manage, Cal again asked for assistance in carrying her over to the ambulance.

'Ready. Brace. Go.' They moved in synch, ensuring they didn't jolt her about too much, and Izzy radioed in a progress report and an ETA of their arrival at the nearest hospital.

When it came to work, and life-or-death situations, Izzy's confidence and decisiveness were exactly what was needed. In her personal life, however, that assertiveness that she could do everything on her own was ticking him off. He mightn't be the daddy-to-be she wanted for her children, but he wasn't Gerry either. Izzy should know him better than believing he'd walk away from this pregnancy because it was inconvenient. He had no intention of leaving her to pick up the pieces alone. As long as she dropped those defences enough to see the idea to move in was for her benefit, not his.

Janet had broken everything important in him beyond repair—his trust, his belief that he could replicate the happy family he'd grown up in, and, crucially, that urge in him to be a father at all. Still, she hadn't managed to take away the basic desire to be a decent human being. The mother of his future children was in trouble and he was going to do right by her.

If being broke, alone and pregnant with twins had been an illness, Izzy wouldn't have thought twice about finding a cure. Cal knew he wasn't perfect but as far as he could see he was the best option she had, and he would do his best to make her see that. They were in this together whether they liked it or not.

It was getting harder for Izzy to switch off after a shift. Stephanie was young, and she would heal with time, but that initial phone call to let Stephanie's parents know what had happened had been painful. She'd asked Izzy to make the call for her and to play down her injuries, but her mother's fear had been almost palpable. Izzy wasn't a parent yet, but this pregnancy was already changing her in ways she hadn't prepared for and she knew once the babies were here their safety would be the only thing that mattered to her. There were only six months before they arrived, and she had nothing in place for them except uncertainty.

To his credit, Cal hadn't pushed her any more on moving in with him and had been willing to talk over her concerns regarding their patient's prognosis in a debriefing session on the ride back from the handover at the hospital, leaving her free from any additional worries to keep her awake at night.

'Your usual?' Cal rested his hand on her back the second they made it back to base.

She nodded, having become accustomed to their sober chats. It wasn't as though they'd been in the habit of rolling home steaming drunk, but the nature of their relationship had changed along with their drinking habits. They'd become more than mates when she'd gone to him about the double life she'd discovered Gerry had been leading and now they had a connection that went beyond an emotional level.

Regardless of her vow to do everything single-handedly when that little blue line had appeared on the pregnancy test, Cal had made her realise how much she needed that level of support. His company alone reminded her she wasn't alone, even if she didn't intend forcing him to do it on a permanent basis.

'Tea and a chat is exactly what I need right now,' she said as she pushed open the office door.

'Good because that's exactly why I'm here.' It took

a few seconds for the sight of the blonde woman standing in the room to register with Izzy, and when it did she flung herself at her childhood friend.

'Helen? What on earth are you doing here?' she managed to sob out in the midst of the bear hug.

'Your friend Calum here persuaded me to pay a visit and clearly he was right. You're not yourself. What on earth is wrong, Iz? I've never seen you like this.' Helen prised her off to take a good look at her.

Izzy glanced at a sheepish Cal. 'But how…?'

'I thought you might need a friend.'

She did but she hadn't realised he'd been taking notes when she'd mentioned Helen, never mind take the time out to track her down. He'd obviously been concerned on more than a practical level about her welfare. Simply finding out he knew that much about her life and cared enough to make that contact instantly perked up her mood. Although he hadn't been gushing about becoming a father, his actions showed he was thinking very deeply about how this was affecting her. She hoped that was a sign he'd eventually warm to the idea of being a father beyond a superficial level, but he clearly hadn't shared their most important news.

'Thank you, Cal.' Izzy gave him a swift peck on the cheek to show her appreciation for his thoughtfulness and counted herself lucky to have these two special people in her life. Her babies deserved to have the same.

'I'm so happy to see you.' Izzy turned her attention back to Helen in case effusive thanks made Cal think twice about making such gestures in the future.

'I didn't come on my own.' Helen stepped aside to reveal a gorgeous pram with an even more gorgeous bundle wrapped inside.

'Oh, my goodness, you brought him with you?' Helen had given birth six months ago, just before Gerry's accident, but with everything going on she hadn't been able to find time to go and visit the new arrival. There was also a part of her afraid to see first-hand the trials she'd yet to face as a new mum.

'We thought we'd have a day out on the train to see Auntie Isobel and let Daddy catch up on some sleep.'

The thought that her friend had trekked the whole way here with a baby to surprise her overwhelmed Izzy with the fuzzy warmth of a love she'd forgotten existed. Helen was her bestie, a sister and a mother all wrapped in one. If it hadn't been for her, Izzy wouldn't have known love existed at all. She was the one good thing Izzy had had in her childhood and the only connection from that time she didn't want to lose. They'd kept in touch, but text messages and video calls weren't the same as a much-needed hug.

'And who's this?' Cal asked, peering into the pram where the baby was grizzling.

'This is Oliver and it's nearly time for his dinner.' Helen lifted him out of the pram as he made his impatience known at having to wait another second for his next feed.

'Feel free to feed him in here. We'll make sure everyone gives you some privacy.'

'I hope I'm not putting you out, Iz, by turning up here unannounced? I just wanted to see you.' Helen slung the changing bag over her shoulder and manoeuvred baby and pram out the door Cal was holding open.

'Not at all. I'm glad you came. Our shift's over so give us a minute to get changed out of our gear then we can go somewhere for a catch-up.'

'Will you be joining us, Calum?' As subtle as ever, Helen extended the invitation, no doubt in the hope she could pair him off with Izzy. Since she'd become a happy married she'd expected Izzy to join the club with her. Perhaps it was Helen's blissful experience of marriage that had convinced Izzy to stick it out with Gerry and hope they could eventually achieve the same idyll. Izzy hadn't told her about the pregnancy but that would likely fuel her search for a hubby for her and she certainly didn't need any more encouragement where Cal Armstrong was concerned.

'Um…'

'Of course he will. You haven't got anything else to do have you, Cal?' She knew he didn't and it was important he get used to being part of her personal life. Biology had dictated he was included in this family of hers, but she was going to make sure he was connected to these babies by more than duty to do the right thing. Love was a staple of a happy childhood and, as she knew too well, life was miserable without it. She wasn't prepared to enter into any sort of arrangement without a guarantee he was in for the long haul.

With Cal along for their coffee date she'd also be less likely to find herself telling Helen about his offer. The last thing she needed was someone egging her on to do something as outrageous as moving in with the reluctant father to her unborn children.

'Actually, I do. That's why I brought Helen here,' he answered with a scowl, dashing any hope he could be cajoled into being part of her life, or their children's.

It was typical that as soon as they got settled with coffee and cake, baby Oliver woke up from his afternoon nap.

Helen was trying to soothe him with one hand pushing the pram up and down whilst trying to inject herself with caffeine with the other. However, Oliver's wails continued to disrupt the other customers.

'Can I lift him out so you can finish your coffee in peace?' Izzy was itching to get her hands on the chubby-cheeked cherub for some cuddles. She couldn't wait for the time when she could do this any time she pleased.

'Go for it.' Helen seemed glad to have an extra pair of hands so she could have a break, and Izzy knew when she had two babies to take care of she'd have her work cut out for her. But she didn't care. Her life would finally have purpose and meaning, not to mention love.

Izzy scooped the wriggling bundle out from under his blanket cocoon and the screaming ceased once he was in the cradle of her arms.

'You just wanted to see what was going on, didn't you?' She was lost in those big blue eyes as he stared up at her, putting his trust in her to take care of him.

'Okay, now spill.' It took Helen a nanosecond to make it clear she knew there was something going on with her.

'I think someone might need a nappy change.' Izzy held Oliver out as a buffer, preventing his mother from probing for the truth.

'I changed him before we came here, so stop stalling and start talking.' Helen swatted away the feeble attempt to divert her attention.

'Huh?'

'Are you and Cal...you know?' Helen's eyes were bright with bubbling excitement at the prospect of uncovering a new romance. 'I wouldn't blame you. He's gorgeous and he was worried enough about you to phone me. It's obvious he cares about you a lot.'

'What? No. It's only been a few months since I lost Gerry.' She had to remind herself of that too since the memories of her time with him had got lost amongst recent revelations.

'You and Gerry were over a long time before he died, even if you didn't see it then. He was never going to be the man you needed.'

If Izzy had gone to Helen first when she'd discovered Gerry's betrayal she would never have found herself in this mess. It was only when things between her and Cal had subsequently become strained she'd turned to her friend about her troubles, omitting to tell her about Cal's role in her grief counselling. However, that visceral re-action to the circumstances Gerry had left her in, where she'd cursed him up and down, was ammunition Helen was sure to use against her should she believe Izzy was using his death as an excuse not to date again.

'I know there's something going on between you and Calum. I saw the looks you kept giving each other too. As though you were afraid one of you would slip up and say something you shouldn't.'

It was uncanny how well Helen still knew her, even though they only managed a meet up once or twice a year now. Unless she avoided all future contact with Helen she wasn't going to be able to keep the secret much longer. Especially when her bump had to accommodate two surprise bundles.

She put Oliver back in his pram and knocked back the remainder of her decaf coffee, wishing it was a shot of tequila or even an espresso to give her a jolt of bravado. 'I'm pregnant. With twins.'

The words burst out of her mouth before she could stop them, the pressure of keeping the secret to herself too great to hold back. The bombshell was accompanied by the appropriate sound of a crash as Helen dropped her cup on the table.

'Why have you waited this long to tell me?' She mopped up the spilled coffee with a paper napkin, never taking her eyes off Izzy.

'I'm still trying to come to terms with it myself.'

Helen was staring at her, her mouth open about a foot wide. 'Are they—?'

'Yes, they're Cal's. Do you remember I told you about that man who came looking for Gerry? Well, I went to Cal's that night because I knew I'd feel safe there and one thing led to another...' Izzy felt the need to justify what had happened because it seemed so quick after Gerry's death. Although Helen would never have judged her.

'It's no wonder you turned to him after everything you'd been going through. You don't have to explain yourself and Cal seems like a nice guy. I'm sure he'll stand by you.'

'I'm sure he will but that's not enough for my babies. You know what my childhood was like and I want more for these two. Cal is still hesitant about the whole parenting thing and I'd rather go it alone than have him only as a financial backer.'

'Well, if anyone's strong enough to do this on their own it's you, Iz. Wow. I can't believe you're really pregnant.' Helen reached across the table to give her a hug.

'Neither can I. It's a scary prospect.'

'I take it you're, what, two or three months gone? What are the plans?' She was vastly over-estimating Izzy's ability to process the situation and come up with a solution.

'I...er...haven't actually known for that long.'

'Have you told work?'

'Not yet.'

'Booked into prenatal classes?'

'Not yet.'

'Isobel… Have you even started taking your folic acid supplements?'

'I've been busy.'

It wasn't much of an excuse when she had no life outside work any more, but Izzy's way of dealing with her shock pregnancy had been not dealing with it.

'You're going to have to get organised,' Helen scolded, and immediately started scribbling a list of things for her to do in her personal organiser.

'You know I'm bad at this kind of thing.' She wasn't the type who pinned to-do lists to her fridge, or even marked appointments on a calendar. No, Izzy was more a spur-of-the-moment kind of girl who was used to thinking only about herself and doing what suited her.

'Well, you're going to have to get good at it pretty damn quick.' Serious-Helen face stared at her across the table until Izzy hung her head in shame.

'I know, but where the hell do I start?' She was so overwhelmed by the sheer magnitude of tasks and appointments that she'd avoided dealing with anything so far.

'Start with this.' Helen ripped out the page from her planner and slid it across the table. 'Your midwife will help you devise a birth plan. You *do* have a midwife?'

'Of course.'

'Good. What about after the birth? Have you given any thought to childcare?'

If Izzy had had a proper mother, she imagined she'd have received the same grilling as her friend was giv-

ing her now. A parent who cared might have been able
to help her out with childcare and hold her hand during the pregnancy. Given a chance, Helen would do the
same but she lived too far away and had a family of her
own to look after.

'Cal asked me to move in with him. I said no. We're
just friends. That night should never have happened.'

'It's sweet that Calum wants to take care of you. If
you had better taste in men you'd have snatched him up
a long time ago.'

'Yes, well, I'm done trusting men. I want to do this
on my own.' She didn't, not really, but it seemed to her it
was the only way to protect herself and the babies from
unnecessary suffering.

'Clearly you trust him, or you wouldn't have turned
to him for help in the first place.'

'I trust him in *that* way, it's just…' It was difficult to
put it into words when she wasn't entirely sure why his
interference frightened her so much.

'You're worried he'll hurt you the same way Gerry
did?'

'Yes. No. I don't know.' He could only cause her that
level of pain if she saw him as more than a friend and
that wasn't what he was necessarily offering. Although
there had been that nod towards a physical relationship,
which had shaken her to the core, but she wasn't sharing
that with Helen. The reason she was holding back was
because she was afraid she'd get in too deep when she
had even more to lose if it all fell apart.

'There's nothing to say you have to make a commitment beyond the rent to enjoy the benefits of what he's
offering.'

Izzy's mind leapt to those images of them exploring

each other's bodies again, but she decided to play the innocent. 'What do you mean?'

'You could do the fun stuff that goes with being a couple without the headaches. A housemates with benefits deal. If it doesn't work out you both move on without any baggage.'

'Wouldn't it seem as though I was using Cal by doing that? Besides, he hasn't shown any interest in me in *that* way since I spent the night with him.' It sounded feasible in theory, but Izzy was worried that was only because she was becoming desperate.

Helen shrugged. 'He offered, didn't he, with no strings? Trust me, I've seen the way he looks at you and I can read between the lines...'

This outside perspective on their situation no longer made Cal's suggestion as ludicrous as she'd first thought. They might be able to make this work after all.

CHAPTER FOUR

'CAN I GIVE you a lift home?' Cal didn't want to walk away and leave Izzy at the train station alone. She'd been very quiet since they'd waved Helen and Oliver off. Although the afternoon was supposed to help lift her spirits, he suspected it had been a huge dose of reality for her, seeing her friend struggle to look after the baby on her own for the afternoon. Not that she'd struggled per se, but it was very different trying to have a coffee and a quiet chat when you had a baby in tow. Something Izzy was going to have to get used to if she kept refusing all offers of help.

'Sure.' She barely glanced his way as she led the way to the car, deep in thought about something he wasn't privy to.

They buckled up in continued silence and Cal was afraid she was going to retreat back into her world alone. Izzy had been let down once too often and he wasn't going to add himself to that list by shirking his responsibilities.

'Helen seems lovely.'

'She is,' Izzy confirmed, her gaze fixed firmly on the road ahead. She was remarkably sullen compared to how buoyant she'd been in her friend's company and Cal knew it was probably because he'd refused to be dragged along with them. It was one thing offering her a lifeline but quite another getting involved in her personal life.

Left to his own devices, he'd batten down the hatches at home and prevent another woman from setting foot in his inner sanctum in case she broke his heart too, but these were exceptional circumstances. Given Izzy's reluctance, he knew she was every bit as wary about moving in together as he was, but they had to set their own comfort aside in favour of the babies. What they needed more than anything was a stable home environment.

'Olly's adorable too.' The baby had been a reminder of his sisters and their offspring, who were scattered across the UK now there was nowhere for them to congregate with the family home gone. He missed being an uncle. He missed being anything to anyone.

He started the engine, resigned to the fact that Izzy was never going to agree to anything unless he fully committed to parenthood. Something he wasn't ready to do and he wasn't going to make false promises.

Then she turned to him and said, 'Take me home with you, Cal.'

If she'd been any other woman and he any other man, that sentence could've been construed as a precursor to another night of passion. There was a part of him that still held a spark of hope that that was her intention, but he knew Izzy better than that. This was a sign of something other than a sudden overwhelming urge to bed him again.

He derailed the inappropriate train of thought, wondering if it was a sign he might not be able to take a vow of celibacy where Izzy was concerned after all.

'Any, um, particular reason?' He did his best to keep

his voice neutral, so she didn't guess where his mind had gone to.

'If I'm going to consider your proposal seriously, I'd like to see the goods on offer. I mean, your assets…the house…you know what I mean.' Her flustering combined with her heightened colour made him think he hadn't been alone in his less-than-pure thoughts.

He resisted the obvious teasing when they were beginning to make a breakthrough. This was the first hint he'd given that she was taking his suggestion seriously, so he didn't want to scare her off by turning it into something sordid. Whatever scenario his neglected libido had been conjuring up would have to give way to more important issues.

Cal had never been the type of guy to choose one-night stands over a meaningful relationship, but this wasn't about him. Sex wasn't something he expected in return for anything but if it was something they both decided they wanted as part of the deal, he wasn't going to say no.

Although he was still wondering what had brought her round to his initial way of thinking.

'Does this sudden turnaround have something to do with Helen?' He'd be surprised if Izzy had confided in her about his idea and even more so if her friend had advised her to proceed with it. From the outside it would've sounded absurd even to him, and he got the impression Helen was protective of Izzy and probably the closest thing to family she had. Apart from him of course. If their roles had been reversed he'd have been suspicious of him and his motives too. Still, if he'd won over her friend then he wasn't going to complain. Izzy would know Helen only had her best interests at heart, even if she doubted him.

'I told her about the babies.'

'Oh, okay. How did that go down?'

Izzy smiled for the first time since they'd been alone again. 'She's over the moon and insisted on writing me a pregnancy to-do list. It felt good, though, telling someone. Other than you, I mean. It's like I'm allowed to get excited about this now.'

She rested her hand on her belly, looking more at ease with the pregnancy than he'd seen so far.

'So you should. It's a special time.' Just not especially to him when it was a reminder of all the mistakes he'd made when it came to relationships.

'I suppose we could be housemates, landlord and tenant, whatever you want to call it, but I will be contributing to the household bills.'

'If that's what you want.' It stung a little that she wasn't interested in something more, but he'd take it.

'That's what I want. At least, I think it is.'

'I know, you still want to take a peek at the goods. I guess you can't have too much of a good thing after all.' He was rewarded with a playful nudge for his teasing.

He'd wasted time in a relationship with Janet when he could've been raising a family with someone who'd wanted to be with him. The whole idea of parenting to him had entailed being an active participant. From changing nappies and doing night feeds right through to playing football or driving to dance recitals, he'd been willing to do it all. Now, though, he could see the merits of being one of those back-seat dads. Izzy didn't really want to be with him either so getting attached seemed a pointless exercise, but he could offer these children a home. For however long it was needed.

He and Izzy weren't star-crossed lovers, but they had their feet on the ground and a more realistic view of life now they'd found out the hard way that love couldn't solve everything.

'I want to get a feel for the place and see if I can picture us all living there together.'

They'd be a modern family of convenience created by circumstance and friendship if not in the conventional sense.

Once Izzy saw the nursery and the potential space to raise her children he knew she'd agree to move in. His house would finally become a home. Just for someone other than him.

It wasn't that Izzy had never seen Cal's place before, they often called at each other's houses and sometimes shared a take-away, but she'd never taken much notice of the surroundings. This time she wanted to see it from a different perspective. She was viewing his house with the prospect of moving in. With him. And their babies. Possibly for ever. Well, it had to be preferable to spending the rest of her days in that poky flat at the top of a flight of stairs, which she could barely afford. If she'd ever pictured this scenario she might have chosen somewhere with access for a twin pram.

Although that would have demanded an even larger chunk of her wages to cover costs. She had to face it, no matter what decision she might have made, the minute she'd thrown in her lot with Gerry, she'd been in trouble.

It was probably a blessing that Cal had thrown her a lifeline and an opportunity to raise their children in a proper home. One she knew would be a supportive environment, even though they wouldn't be together as a couple.

As they pulled up outside the house she was already seeing the possibilities it offered in comparison to her own home. She got that fluttering in her chest as she imagined the green lawn littered with children's toys and opportunities for the babies to play outside. A garden wasn't something she'd had on her wish list when house hunting before, but now she could see how perfect it would be for family life. The detached house surrounded by trees and shrubbery with a driveway secured with high gates made it private and secure.

The size of the house, the grounds and the location made it a highly prized property but for a mother-to-be it was the scope for safe play and adventure that made it valuable. If she did a side-by-side comparison with the square of parched communal land littered with oddments of her neighbours' patio furniture Cal would have sold the whole idea to her based solely on the garden.

'Are you okay?' It was only when he spoke she realised he'd already cut the engine and had no idea how long they'd been sitting in silence whilst she plotted her imaginary playground. It explained why he suddenly sounded nervous about having her here when she hadn't showed him any sign she was happy about it.

'Yes. Sorry. I was miles away. You said something about a nursery?' She unclipped her seatbelt, keen to do her virtual interior decorating too.

Cal didn't waste any time opening up the house, probably worried she'd change her mind again. 'Obviously we'd furnished it for the babies, so you can use anything in there or you're free to put your own stamp on things.'

He led her up the stairs and she remembered the last time she'd followed him to his room at the end of the hall. That had been the moment everything had changed.

'So, er, this is the nursery,' he said, opening the door to a bright, beautiful room that took Izzy's breath away.

'Cal, it's gorgeous and bigger than my flat.' Which meant there was sufficient space for another cot to match the beautiful white cradle already there.

The white room highlighted with silver-star details mapped out an amazing bright galaxy on the walls and made a neutral space to suit any taste or gender. There were accents of pastel pinks, blues and yellows in the furnishings to break up the dazzling white, and the thick silver carpet underfoot was luxuriously expensive. Everything from the pretty star-embroidered blankets to the pine rocking chair in the corner festooned with plump cushions was tailored for comfort as well as appearance.

'I'm sure you'll want to change a few things to suit your own taste so let me know what you have in mind and I'll get on it.'

'Did you have an interior designer in to do this?' It looked as though someone had copied a page out of a magazine, everything was so perfectly matched and positioned.

Cal picked up a soft fuzzy sheep from a stack of toys on the dresser and laid it in the crib. 'No, it's all my own work.'

Izzy took another look around and could see how much love and care had gone into making this room baby heaven. He'd been so buoyant in those early months, planning for the baby he'd thought he was going to have with Janet, and she could picture him painstakingly painting every inch of this room in preparation for its arrival.

'I should've known something was wrong when Janet was happy to let me do this alone, without her input. I thought she was simply having a hard time accepting the pregnancy. How stupid was I?' The bitter laugh he gave was directly at odds with the caring man who'd put his heart and soul into creating this loving tribute to a baby who'd never been his.

'You weren't stupid. You trusted her, you were in love with her, and she betrayed you in the worst possible way. None of it was your fault.' She rested her hand on his shoulder to show him she was on his side. Who wouldn't be when a man this endearing had been left heartbroken and bereft, essentially grieving for a baby who'd never come home with him?

'Thanks.' When he covered her hand with his, his warmth enveloping her, she knew he was grasping for that connection he'd lost with Janet. An uneasy sense that there was more behind his motives to have her here other than being a good friend began to slither beneath her skin.

'Cal, you didn't ask me to move in just to fill the space Janet left behind, did you?' The one that had a baby-shaped void right next to it.

No amount of saving on her bills would convince her that this was a good idea if that was the reason, because she would never be a replacement for the fiancée he'd lost, and her babies weren't up for negotiation.

'Of course not.' He turned his head so violently to shoot down that theory that he jerked her hand away. 'I told you, you can do whatever you want in here. It's not some sort of shrine. I just thought it was a shame to let all of this go to waste.'

His defensive attitude suggested there might be more behind his reasons than he even realised. As long as she remembered the history here and didn't get sucked into playing the role recently vacated by his ex, they could hopefully cohabit without anyone reading something into the arrangement that wasn't there.

'It would be when I'm going to need two of everything. We could keep the furniture and redecorate, I suppose. It's beautiful, but I do think it might be better all round for something fresh. If you're on board with that?' It was a compromise intended to make things less weird.

'Does that mean you're moving in?' The Cal she recognised immediately wrapped her in a hug and Izzy let herself revel in that moment of intimacy. He was the only person who provided her with that sense of security she found in the circle of his arms.

To have someone who could do that for her on a regular basis, and she was going to need lots of hugs for the foreseeable future, was a definite point in Cal's favour. They were friends and soon to be housemates, with no one else close enough to provide this strength they seemed to find in each other.

She was certain that tingling sensation that travelled from her head to her toes and all the extremities in between when he touched her or held her was merely residual memory of their last, more intimate contact. It was tempting to burrow into his chest like a little dormouse seeking shelter for the winter, but she managed to keep herself in check and dragged herself out of his embrace before she got too used to using him as a crutch. She had to do this on her own. Cal was her back-up. Someone to give her a boot up the backside when she needed it, just as she'd done for him.

As soon as she stepped out of his personal space the sudden sense of loss slipped out of her mouth on a sigh. 'I'll need to see the bedroom before I make a final decision.'

The corners of his mouth tilted up as he deliberately misinterpreted her comment. It hadn't escaped her notice either that he hadn't attempted to end the too-long hug. Their previous conversation about exploring all aspects of marriage sprang to mind again and her pulse rocketed. Perhaps she should avoid all *double entendres* for the sake of her blood pressure from now on.

'*My* bedroom. The room where I'll be sleeping. Alone.' The emphasis was as much for herself as Cal when it would be far too convenient to jump into bed together should the mood strike them. That sort of blurry line would make things messy when they had to work and live together. Essentially that would put them in a relationship neither of them wanted. This new set-up was supposed to avoid the emotional uncertainty that came as part of a couple package.

'Spoilsport.' The wink he gave her sent shivers through her as though he'd danced his fingers along her spine and she followed him like a devoted puppy into another bright and spacious room.

'You really should think about a sideline as an interior decorator,' she said, taking in her proposed new accommodation. It had a modern appearance but with a lovely homely feeling.

'I'll give it some consideration when I get too old and decrepit for jumping out of helicopters.' He deflected the compliment with another self-deprecating comment, but

Izzy couldn't imagine him as anything other than in his prime at any age.

'You'll certainly save me a job, anyway. I won't have to redecorate or attempt to dismantle my flat-pack furniture to move in here. I assume fixtures and fittings are included?'

'Everything I have is at your disposal.' His exaggerated bow gave him the air of a handsome prince giving her the keys to his kingdom, which she liked to think included a secret library somewhere.

'In that case, I can cancel the removal van. Everything I want is right here.' She was referring to the solid pine furniture the entire contents of her flat could fit into but found herself staring at Cal instead.

'What about the bed? No one's ever used the one in here, but you might prefer to have your own.' He walked past her to sit on the end of the mattress, bouncing up and down to show her the obvious quality of the springs.

The lumpy, barely held together with chipboard thing she called a bed, which was also half the size of this sleep playground, couldn't compete.

'Are you kidding? I could live in this.' She threw herself on top of the bed so she was flat out, staring at the ceiling. Her bouncing knocked Cal off balance until he ended up lying beside her, only a hair's breadth away.

'I'm glad you're moving in.'

'I haven't agreed yet.' She was still clinging on to that one last thread of control.

'What else can I do to convince you?' Cal's husky voice was almost enough to persuade her to do anything.

That was it. The final tie to her logical brain pinged free and left her to the mercy of her hormones. They were lying so close to one another there was nowhere else to look but at his eyes, his lips… He was staring at her mouth too, clearly thinking the same thing—how nice a kiss would be right now. Breathtakingly slowly they were gravitating towards each other, closing those last few millimetres separating them from heaven, and insanity.

Izzy sat up, breaking the thrall of his hypnotic gaze. 'I think we should get one thing straight from the beginning, Cal. I want to move in and I appreciate everything you're doing for me, but I think we should take the, er, physical side of this relationship off the cards.'

With that bombshell Cal sat up too so they were both perched uncomfortably on the end of the bed. 'Certainly. I wouldn't dream of using this arrangement to take advantage of you. We'll keep things strictly platonic.'

The longer she spent in his company the more she'd anticipate spending nights in bed with him, but she knew the novelty of having her around would wear off as it always did.

'I think it's for the best.'

'So, we're free to date other people if and when we're ready for that?'

Izzy didn't know why that question shook her when he was a hot-blooded male, not a monk. She supposed it was because she couldn't imagine getting involved in another relationship and had thought he was of the same opinion. It wasn't fair to expect him to remain celibate for ever because she'd prefer it, but the thought of him bringing other women home with him was painful. Ridiculous, when she'd been the one drawing the line in the sand and deeming her side a sex-free zone.

She knew the one flaw in this plan could be if she fell for Cal, confusing his sense of duty for something more. Something that could only ever end badly.

CHAPTER FIVE

'You should be sitting with your feet up.' Cal marked out the light switch with masking tape so it didn't get splattered with paint and made sure the dust sheet was covering the whole floor.

'Why? You're not and unless I'm mistaken we've had exactly the same workload today.' Displaying her usual obstinacy, Izzy refused to take it easy after another hectic shift.

'Yes, but I'm not carrying two extra loads with me.' He pointed his paintbrush at her belly, which was noticeably more rounded in her form-fitting grey jersey top and black leggings.

'You promised you wouldn't mollycoddle me,' she reminded him, and began rolling on the pale turquoise paint she'd chosen to cover the nursery walls.

'There's a difference between mollycoddling and doing you a favour. I'm happy to do all the grunt work here.' That way he could make sure she had some down time. So far, since moving in with him, she hadn't shown any signs of slowing down. He had managed to convince her to let him carry the few belongings she had with her but only after an exhaustive debate. Eventually she'd accepted he was merely trying to be a gentleman and not treating her as an invalid. Despite his reservations about his suitability as a parent to these babies, he was doing his best to ensure they'd want for nothing, and that included a strong, healthy mother.

'I wouldn't call painting a wall particularly taxing.' Izzy proved her point by covering most of the mid-section in just a few strokes.

'The fumes can't be good for you.' He simply wanted her to take care of herself if she wouldn't let him do it for her.

It had been a huge part of Janet's pregnancy for him, fussing around and feeling useful in some capacity when he hadn't been able to help with any of the physical toll pregnancy had taken on her.

Seeing how active and reluctant Izzy was to let her condition become an excuse to slow down made him wonder if Janet had been laughing behind his back the whole time he'd been skivvying for her. Of course she had, the baby wasn't his and while he'd been preparing to become a father she'd been planning to leave him.

Izzy wouldn't take advantage of him in that way when he'd had to work so hard to get her this far.

Despite referencing the possibility of entering into a physical relationship, he knew it would never stay solely in the bedroom and he didn't want to jeopardise what they had here. It was simply a reaction to the attraction that had sprung to life rather quickly after their respective heartaches. Besides, apart from the scars they still bore from those ill-fated relationships, they'd be too tired dealing with two small children to think about dating or anything else.

'I promise if I start to feel faint or sick I'll hang up

my paint roller.' It was a concession he was willing to accept when she didn't often make them.

'Good. No stretching either. I'll get the ladder and do the top bits.' There was no need for her to overdo things when he was there to pick up the slack.

'I assume I'm allowed to do the bottom bits? I can sit on the floor to do that. You know, take it easy.' She was making fun of him, but it was better than bristling at him each time he attempted to do something nice for her.

'As long as you don't get under my feet.' She'd already worked her way over to the section he was covering so he let a blob of paint plop onto her head.

'For your sake I hope you didn't do that on purpose.' Izzy lifted her head to look at him, eyes narrowed and lips twitching.

'You know me better than that, Fizz.' He'd never been able to resist riling that temper of hers, such was their dynamic, and he was glad that spark was still there after all this time.

'Hmm.' She knew him too well and he laughed at the apparent scepticism.

Cal resumed painting his part of the wall, only realising he was in serious trouble when he saw her roller paint over the palms of her hands instead of the plasterwork. The next thing he knew those same hands were resting on his buttocks and with one squeeze he knew she'd wreaked her revenge.

'You haven't…' He tried to twist his torso around to see the evidence but the glee on Izzy's face was proof enough that she'd left two turquoise handprints on the backside of his trousers.

'You deserved it.' She was grinning up at him, her

eyes full of mischief, challenging him to do something about it.

'Isobel Fitzpatrick, you are in so much trouble...'

She let out a shriek as he dropped his paintbrush and tried to wrestle the roller out of her hands, but Izzy was too quick for him. With sleight of hand she hid her weapon behind her back, forcing him to reach around her to try and get it. Her laugh at his ear made him aware of how close their bodies were, and with the slightest turn of his head his lips were dangerously close to Izzy's.

He heard the hitch in her breath as she realised it too and he wanted so badly to kiss her it took all of his physical strength to back off before he did something stupid. The chemistry was there all right, but Izzy had made it clear she didn't want to repeat past mistakes. Instead he took a sidestep away and carried on decorating as though nothing out of the ordinary had transpired.

'It's just as well these are old clothes, or we'd have people talking about us.' As if. The only people they saw were their colleagues, and the crew had hardly batted an eyelid when they'd told them they were moving in together before they'd explained it was only as housemates. Mac, when Cal had tackled him about the lack of surprise, had explained they'd all thought the two of them had been at it like rabbits for years, despite having had partners for most of that time. Cal put him straight and asked him to pass on the information. The purpose, other than saving Izzy's reputation, was his own pride. He refused to let anyone believe he'd cheated on Janet and deserved what she'd done to him in any way.

It was a conversation he hadn't relayed to Izzy for fear of upsetting her. If he was annoyed there was any suggestion he'd played away on his treacherous ex, he could only imagine the effect it would have on her. The last thing Izzy needed stressing her out was malicious gossip that she'd somehow failed Gerry.

Cal had been blaming himself for months over what had happened between him and Janet, agonising over every disagreement that could have caused her to cheat on him. Izzy might have gone through something similar, wondering what she could've done to prevent the crash from happening, and she didn't need anything more to beat herself up over. Cal would rather put a smile on her face at his expense than give her cause to feel guilty about something she'd never had the power to control. It had taken all this time for him to learn that lesson.

It was only when Izzy had agreed to move in with him that he'd stopped blaming himself for Janet leaving. In some way he'd taken it as confirmation he wasn't as bad a person as he'd begun to believe, that he must've had some redeeming qualities if she was willing to live with him at this crucial time.

'I'll just tell them you're the father of my unborn babies and I'm marking my territory,' she said, following his lead in ignoring another heated moment between them.

The doorbell rang and gave Cal an excuse to leave the room before he took her comment seriously. The thought that Izzy wanted possession of any part of his body was arousing interest in certain areas that wasn't in keeping with their platonic agreement. 'I'll get it. It's probably the grocery shopping.'

With them both working and needing double the amount of food, they'd done their shopping online and left the front gates open for the home delivery to arrive.

Izzy required proper nutritious meals and his recent casual approach to cooking ready meals and a microwave was no longer going to cut it.

The buzzer went again before he made it down the stairs.

'I'm coming,' he yelled to the dark figure outlined in the frosted glass who was clearly impatient to get to the next delivery.

As he unlocked the door to the outside world again, the person waiting for him made him want to slam the door shut and lock himself away with Izzy again.

'Hi, Cal.' That was it. With just two words Janet was back in his world, blowing it completely apart.

'Aren't you going to ask me in?' Her audacity in thinking she could smile at him as though she hadn't ripped his heart out of his chest and stomped on it rendered him speechless.

Apparently, that was invitation enough for her to push past him. Easily done with the considerable weight she was now wielding with her heavily pregnant belly. She'd be due any day now, but the thought no longer brought the same sadness it once had.

'I hope they brought those cheesy cracker things I wanted. I have a hankering for something savoury and salty.' Naturally this was the moment Izzy's pregnancy cravings kicked in and sent her foraging for goodies. She stopped dead at the bottom of the stairs and came face to face with Janet. 'What do you want?'

There was no question that his ex was only here because she wanted something from him. Under the circumstances he didn't think he should be expected to waste time on pleasantries and small talk. He had nothing to say to her.

Janet looked Izzy up and down with the same undisguised contempt she'd always done. Only now Cal could see it for what it was—jealousy. He'd loved Janet body and soul but after how she'd treated him his eyes were open to the ugliness she wore on the inside. Izzy was honest, and kind, and all those things Janet wasn't.

'I've come for the rest of my things.' She made her way past Izzy as though she was perfectly entitled to roam where she pleased.

Cal took off after her, a frown burrowing into his brow as he envisaged her rifling through Izzy's belongings and upsetting her. 'I'm pretty sure you took everything.'

It had made quite an impact to come home from work to find empty closets and drawers and spaces where some of their joint possessions had once resided. He'd been one step away from calling the police to report a burglary when he'd found her note. The one ending their relationship and destroying the dream of having a family together.

'I want the baby's things,' she insisted, and walked on into the nursery.

'You're kidding.' Did she really not think how much this would hurt him by taking away that last connection, or did she simply not care? Given her past behaviour, Cal presumed it to be the latter.

The pressure of Izzy's hand at his lower back reminded him that someone did understand the significance of this to him and cared about it. Now he just wanted Janet to take any reminder of her out of his life for good.

'There's no point in wasting all this. It's not as though you're going to need it.' She went around the room, helping herself to the toys and bits and pieces dotted around the room and tossing them into the crib.

He was close to correcting her and informing her he did have a use for it, but he glanced at Izzy, who looked as horrified as he was, and she shook her head, making it known she didn't want a protest. Though Janet didn't deserve to walk away victorious, it was clear Izzy wanted Janet out at whatever price it took, instead of prolonging his agony.

The unwanted surprise appearance did prove one thing to Cal. He didn't, couldn't love her any more and he hoped that once she'd taken every last trace of their relationship away he'd forget all about her.

'Is Darren keeping a tight hold of the purse-strings? I don't blame him.' Cal had never denied Janet anything so perhaps she was missing being that pampered princess who'd once resided here. The thought of a possible rift didn't bring him any pleasure when their relationship had come at the price of his. Although he wasn't beyond making a dig.

'No,' she snapped, much too defensively for Cal to believe her. 'These were bought for the baby so I'm taking them for the baby.'

'Chosen by me and paid for by me.' More fool him for doing it and ending up here fighting over ownership of furniture for a baby that wasn't his.

'So you don't want him to have anything?' Janet cradled her bump and played a lament on his heartstrings. She was having a boy, a child he'd once seen himself playing football with and spending that father/son bonding time together as he'd done with his dad. He'd wanted that baby to have everything but that was when Cal had believed he'd be the one to see him make use of it all.

'I didn't say that, Janet.' If she was here for an argument he wasn't going to give her one because he no longer had the passion to fight. Not with her, anyway.

'In that case, you can start dismantling everything and take it down to the car. *She* can help you.' Janet's inclusion of Izzy in her demands was where Cal drew the line.

'No, she won't. Where's Darren? He can help with the heavy lifting.' It said a lot about the man that he'd let Janet come in here alone. Darren was a coward, along with the other names Cal had assigned to him over the months for not stepping up for the woman he'd got pregnant and allowed to carry on a relationship with someone else.

'He's waiting in the van. He didn't want a scene.'

'If he wants the furniture he can get his backside in here and help. I'm not doing it on my own and Izzy's not either.' He was already on his knees, unscrewing the sides of the cot for easier removal. The purchases he'd made when he'd been so excited for the future now held nothing but resentment for him. He was only sorry he'd promised it to Izzy and had to go back on his word.

Janet glared at Izzy, who was hovering in the doorway, then at the new pots of paint and finally at Cal's bottom where Izzy had left her mark.

'Oh. My. Goodness. You two are moving in together?' She laughed as she finally took in the scene.

'We are but it's not what you think.' Their set-up was none of Janet's business.

'That's priceless, making out as though I'm the bad person here when you two were carrying on behind my back the whole time. I knew there was something going on between you. Perhaps that's why I was driven to Darren.'

There was no way he was going to let her play the injured party and deflect the responsibility of her actions onto him and Izzy when they'd done nothing wrong.

'In case you've forgotten, you're the guilty one here. The decision to cheat on me and lie about the baby was entirely down to you. Now, I suggest that, to avoid any more unpleasantness, you go and wait in the van and send Darren in to collect whatever you believe you're still entitled to. After that I don't want to see or hear from either of you ever again.' He was trying to hold the emotion back and as a result he sounded menacingly in control. It was deceptive but hopefully effective because he didn't want to subject Izzy to any more of this toxicity.

Once Janet was gone they could start with a clean slate in whatever capacity she'd allow him to participate in her life. It had to be an improvement on being the sap Janet had taken him for when they were starting from a place of honesty.

This was the first time he'd had a chance to vent about what Janet had done to him and she simply puffed herself up with indignation and stomped away rather than admit to being in the wrong.

Cal set to work dismantling what was left of the nursery, so Darren could take it away without further discussion. There was nothing left to say except to apologise to Izzy for dragging her into this whole nightmare with him. His desire for a family had brought him nothing but trouble.

Izzy managed to hold her tongue until the furniture and unwanted guests had left the premises. She'd never been the woman's greatest fan but the nerve of Janet to come here and lay claim to everything ranked her the lowest of the low.

'I'm so sorry, Cal. That was just…' Heartless. Cruel. Cold. All of the above '…unbelievable.' It was heart-wrenching to see him slumped against the half-painted wall, sitting on the floor of the empty nursery. Janet's actions and manner tonight gave her some insight into how she'd treated him at the end of their relationship and it wasn't a pretty picture.

There was no justification for treating someone like Cal, who was kindness personified, in that manner. There wasn't a flicker of doubt in Izzy's mind that as a fiancé he'd been anything other than as loving and supportive as he was as a friend.

'You shouldn't have had to witness that, Iz.' He hung his head, clearly embarrassed at how things had panned out in front of her, but she was more concerned about how tonight's events had affected him.

'No, Janet should never have waltzed in here the way she did. I can't believe she had the audacity to turn up with Darren and take what didn't belong to her.' It was rubbing salt into the deep wound she'd inflicted, as though she never wanted it to heal.

Cal picked up a soft, cuddly sheep that had been left behind. 'It does look as though I've been burgled. At least she left Lamby behind. I've had him since I was a kid.'

He gave a sad smile that demanded she immediately hug him, but he couldn't manage to hug her back.

'I think he's had a lucky escape if you ask me. Who wants to live with a horror like that? Lamby will be much happier here with us. White furniture's too impractical anyway. Give it a week or two and everything she took will be permanently stained with puke and poo. She'll regret it someday.'

Nothing she could say would ever ease his pain, but she was here if he need her to jolly him along or keep him busy if he started to dwell on things again. It would've been so much worse if he'd have been left here in this shell of a nursery alone.

'I hope you're right.' Even so close she could sense him withdrawing from her when they needed one another more than ever.

'Next time we have a day off we could go shopping. I'm past the danger stage, touch wood, and I'd like to get organised. I'd appreciate your help in pointing me in the right direction to get what we need.' It was her attempt at including him more in this pregnancy, to give him something to look forward to, but she was taking a chance her good intentions might upset him further. The last thing she wanted to do was drag him around baby shops if it was all still too raw for him.

'I do happen to know of all the best recommendations when it comes to safety and quality.'

'I don't doubt it,' she said with a small laugh. He was so meticulous and thorough in everything he did. Assessing every possible risk was part of his job.

'She dumped me with a note taped to the fridge, you know. All those years living together, making plans for the future, and I wasn't worthy of a proper conversation. No apology, no explanation. "I'm leaving you for Darren. The baby's not yours, it's his." I mean, what could I have possibly done to deserve that? I spent weeks, months racking my brain, trying to figure out what I'd done wrong. Did I neglect her, had I become too clingy?

Was I too boring or working too much? I'm still none the wiser after tonight.' His eyes were glistening with unshed tears Izzy wished she could wipe away.

'If anything good can come out of this it's that you can see this is none of your fault. Janet wouldn't have hesitated in casting up your faults if she could've blamed you for her behaviour. She has no excuse. The cheating, the lies, using the baby to get what she wanted—it's all on her. You were unlucky to have ever met her.' From now on they should concentrate on the future, instead of looking back.

'It still happened and it's not something I can easily forgive or forget.'

It was so uncharacteristic of Cal to be so despondent, but she knew from experience you had to hit rock bottom before you could claw your way back up again. Surveying the abandoned nursery, surely, he'd found his.

'No one would expect you to but please don't let her continue to ruin your life. Think of this as a new start. Now you're completely free from Janet and everything associated with her. I appreciate you, even if she doesn't.' From tomorrow Izzy was going to do everything in her power to help him move on with her.

CHAPTER SIX

'CAL, WE HAVE enough stuff to open our own shop.' Izzy glanced around the newly refurbished nursery, imagining their two little ones here.

They'd left it a couple of days after Janet's surprise visit before venturing out to replace the items she'd purloined. Even then Izzy had waited until Cal brought up the subject, instead of pushing him into a situation that might have made him uncomfortable. He'd been her personal shopper, pointing out the best products to suit her requirements, and she'd chosen the colours and theme for the room.

Unsurprisingly, Cal had insisted on paying for everything, though she'd sworn to pay him back somehow. Retail therapy had helped him cast off the shadow that had fallen over him after a certain someone had briefly come back into his life.

It was important for her to include him in these decisions for the babies so he'd stop hovering on the periphery of this pregnancy and become more involved. He was good at the practical aspects, such as the redecorating, but he'd yet to express his feelings about the situation. He was bound to have doubts and fears for their future just as she had, and it wasn't going to do any good keeping them bottled up. She didn't want to find out there were problems too late, the way she had with Gerry. That had been devastating enough but now there were children to think about too.

It wasn't going to serve anyone well if Cal maintained that emotional detachment when the babies were born. Especially when Izzy knew how much love he had to give. She only had a few months to convince him she wasn't Janet and it was safe for him to open his heart again.

'We'll have to get used to it. Twins are going to come with a lot of baggage and mess.' His immaculate home was going to be disrupted by two demanding, messy little beings. She didn't want it to come as a shock after he'd spent every spare minute putting the furniture together to complete this showroom nursery of her dreams.

They'd gone for an underwater theme, the room now festooned with cartoon sea creatures featuring on matching mobiles above the cribs and on the bedding. It was the kind of lovingly put-together room she wished she'd had as a child, instead of the generic spare bedrooms she'd always been designated. When the children were old enough to choose their own décor, she'd make sure their rooms were tailor-made to suit their individual interests and personalities so they never felt like interlopers, the way she had. Their home had to be somewhere they felt safe, wanted and surrounded by people who loved them.

'You know we're going to take over this house?' She eyed the boxes containing the highchairs and baby-walkers they wouldn't use for a while but which were already taking up space.

'Trust me, I know exactly what chaos I've invited

into my home.' He didn't sound completely thrilled at the prospect but the smirk ghosting on his lips suggested he'd accepted the consequences.

After Janet's stunt she wouldn't have blamed him for changing his mind about sharing his house with anyone again. In the same position she might've decided it preferable to live on her own instead of inviting another pregnant woman to stay. To Cal's credit, he hadn't waivered in his decision to have her move in. He was reliable in that way and it was part of the reason she'd made a big decision regarding the twins.

'Cal? I have something to ask you.'

'Ask away.' He'd finished installing a night light that played a lullaby and projected moving images of seahorses and jellyfish around the walls. Izzy thought she might start sleeping in here herself if he made it any more appealing.

'Feel free to say no...you're under no obligation...but I was wondering if you'd consider being my birthing partner?' From the second that blue line had appeared on the pregnancy test she'd been determined to do it all on her own because she hadn't seen any other option. These past weeks Cal had shown her he was there for her day or night.

Although she didn't want to rely on him too heavily, with the twins on the way it was clear there were going to be more appointments, more risks involved, and these were times when it would be good to have someone holding her hand. It was also her plan to have him there to bond immediately with the babies and fall in love with them the second he saw them.

'You mean, like, be there at the birth?' Cal stopped tinkering long enough to come towards her, making her stomach flip. She couldn't tell if it was her hormones reacting to having him close or the babies letting her know they approved of the idea.

'Yeah. I thought you might like to be there.' She didn't have a partner or family member invested in her pregnancy, and Cal was the only person who had a right to be present in the delivery room with her.

'If that's what you want.' There was no indication that was what *he* wanted, but she was working on eventually teasing that information out of him.

'Just so we're clear, that doesn't entitle you to boss me about.' This role didn't give him carte blanche to interfere, and she'd remain the independent woman she'd always been.

'Okay, no pregnancy boot camp. I promise not to attempt to take over in any way. Although I hope that doesn't mean we can't discuss things like your birth plan or what sort of pain relief you'd prefer. It's good to look at all available options and work out what's best for you.'

At least he was thinking ahead on her behalf and it gave her hope that he wasn't going to leave her in the lurch when she'd need him most. Even if it was only on a practical level so far.

'You can help me draw up a suitable list of names too. Although I am putting my foot down now and saying no to suggestions of Bill and Ben, Pinky and Perky or any other such monikers.'

'I'm guessing that rules out This One and That One, too,' he said with a grin, but she knew he'd take the job seriously.

If there was one thing Izzy could guarantee her babies it was that they'd have somewhere to call home, and Cal had played a huge part in making that happen. No matter how reluctantly.

Cal walked into the office as Izzy was rubbing her hand across her chest with that pained expression on her face again. He set a tall glass of milk and a packet of antacids on the table before her. 'For the heartburn.'

She'd been getting a lot of that recently and particularly at night if the sounds of her pacing her bedroom were anything to go by.

As a result, she was becoming tired and irritable but as she refused to take time for extra rest, all they could do was wait for the symptoms to gradually ease as the pregnancy progressed.

It was difficult trying to look out for her best interests and avoid becoming a nag. There was a fine line between offering advice and interfering, and he knew he was currently straddling it. Especially since she'd asked him to be more involved as her birthing partner. She would've known he'd take that privileged position seriously and it wasn't something she'd assign to him on a whim. He was surprised when it had taken her so long to share the news about the pregnancy with him.

Cal wasn't the sort of man, or doctor, who thought pregnant women should necessarily be wrapped up in cotton wool but sometimes there was cause to be concerned. Multiple pregnancy carried a higher risk of complications anyway but as he spent the working day alongside Izzy he knew how hard she worked and the high-octane, high-stress-level environment she did it in.

'What would I do without you?' Izzy batted her eyelashes at him and accepted the prescribed treatment.

'I think you'd manage pretty well,' he muttered, refusing to get drawn back into that role of faithful servant he'd become during Janet's pregnancy. It had hurt that much more when it had all been taken away from him, knowing she'd been taking advantage of his devotion and making a fool out of him. He wasn't going to let that happen twice in his lifetime.

'It was a joke, Cal. We both know I could do this without you.' In case he'd doubted it, Izzy emphasised the fact he was dispensable and reinforced the notion that neither of them should get too comfortable about their situation.

'Have you spoken to Mac yet?' There was no point in being bitter about things now, so he moved them on to more practical, less emotive matters.

She'd been taking her time informing their bosses about the pregnancy, probably because she was afraid they'd ground her pretty soon. Working as ground crew overseeing hospital transfers might not be the job she'd signed up for, but there were too many health and safety risks involved professionally and personally to keep it secret for much longer.

'Yes. He's leaving it down to me to make the decision regarding when to take my maternity leave. Very sneaky, I thought. That way I can't complain when I'm forced to bail out. I suppose it depends on how huge I end up too. If I'm incubating two baby elephants in here, my bulk could stop the helicopter from lifting off the ground at all.'

Mac had been smart to put the ball back in Izzy's court because she would never jeopardise the safety of her crew over her pride. At least it was out in the open now and, bless her, her 'normal' clothes already seemed to be a bit snug. Her pride or denial that she was putting on weight couldn't last for ever. Eventually she'd have to cave in and buy some maternity wear for a little comfort. It was rare for a multiple pregnancy to go to full term so there was no predicting how this one would advance or what toll it would take on her. He did know he'd be relieved when she made the decision not to go up in the air any more, for her own good and his peace of mind.

'We've got a call.' Mac sounded the alarm for the rest of the crew to get moving, everyone pulling on their flight gear as they made their way to the waiting helicopter. Izzy had that familiar rush of adrenaline that came with every call, reminding her that she had an important part to play in every one of these life-or-death calls.

'Fifty-two-year-old woman thrown from her horse. May have sustained head and neck injuries.' Cal repeated the details of the patient requiring their assistance.

'We'll need to set down somewhere close to the site. There's an empty field next to the jumps there.' He gave instructions to the pilot over the headset for a suitable green space to land, clear of buildings, people and anything else that could impede their arrival.

Izzy was trying to focus on the ground rushing up to meet them, estimating how long it would take them to reach those in danger. However, the noise and vibration of the chopper as they raced to the scene was beginning to affect her. Before the pregnancy all the shaking and shouting that went on prior to landing had served to heighten the thrill of hitting the ground running.

Today, though, her body was responding altogether differently to the experience. Every shudder, every drop in altitude had her stomach lurching. She didn't know if it was a sudden and impractical bout of travel sickness or delayed morning sickness. One thing was sure, though, these babies seemed to be protesting about the current mode of transport. Unfortunate when it was also her place of work.

Izzy would never intentionally put any patient in jeopardy due to potential personal issues. She was hoping this was a one-off. If not, she was going to have to hang up her flight suit much earlier than she'd anticipated. She could hardly go running to someone's rescue if she was going to be violently ill every time she was on a call-out.

The wind generated by the chopper blades flattened the grass around them and Izzy and Cal jumped out. She let him run on ahead in the hope he wouldn't witness her vomit stop at the hedge and pulled the water bottle from the kit on her back to wash her mouth out. Except when she was ready to carry on he was glaring back at her. He didn't have to say anything for her to know he wasn't happy she was continuing to work as usual despite her discomfort. In other circumstances she might have accused him of pregnancy discrimination but given her current state she could see he had a point.

'What? Drinking a full glass of milk before getting shaken about was never a good idea.' She had an excuse this time but the next time he'd call her bluff. He could pull rank on her and play the doctor card to force her into co-operating. Anything more serious than some nausea and she'd put herself on bed rest. She was stubborn, but she was also a mum-to-be and she was learning what that entailed.

Cal opened his mouth to say something, probably to scold her, then took off again without saying a word towards the congregation in the adjacent field. It was almost worse having understanding colleagues trusting she knew her own body well enough to make the call when it came to cutting back on work, rather than have them making decisions on her behalf. Almost. Only because she'd have no right to rant and rave at anyone when the crew took off without her.

For now, she was making the most of still having the job she was trained to do, rushing towards someone relying on her and Cal to get them safely delivered to the nearest hospital.

He introduced himself to the gentleman kneeling on the ground next to the woman who'd apparently suffered the fall. 'Can you tell me what happened?'

Izzy knelt on the wet grass beside them and began to unpack the medical equipment they were liable to require.

'I found her like this. When she didn't come home for lunch I came to look for her.' It was clear the man was trying not to panic but he'd done the right thing by not moving her and phoning for help straight away.

'She hasn't gained consciousness since?' A sign that she could have suffered a head injury from the fall or that the horse might have kicked out at her.

'She's made the odd moaning sound, but she hasn't woken up.'

That was something at least. 'How long ago did you find her?'

'About fifteen, maybe twenty minutes ago.' The man was clinging to his wife's hand and Izzy prayed this had a happy ending. Since finding out she was going to have a family of her own she'd become much more sentimental concerning the partners and children involved on the cases. Now, with the love in her heart for the babies she was carrying and having Cal there for her, she better understood the impact of illness or injury on loved ones.

'What's her name?'

'Agnes.'

'Agnes, can you hear me?' Cal tried to garner a response as Izzy set about getting her ready to be moved.

There was a faint groan to reassure them that Agnes was clinging to consciousness.

'We think you've hit your head in a fall so it's very important you stay still until we get that neck stabilised. We're going to give you some pain relief then we'll put a brace around your neck to keep you immobile. You might be uncomfortable but the sooner we can get you stable here the quicker we can get you into the helicopter and on your way to the hospital. Okay?'

She gave another groan in response and though she tried to bat them away at times they managed to get the brace and backboard on her.

'We're going to take her to the local hospital if you want to meet us there. The trauma team already knows we're on our way.' Cal relayed their intentions to the husband.

It was at least forty minutes there by road, but they could do it in less than fifteen by air. Part of the reason they'd been dispatched for this call.

When Izzy got to her feet to transport the trolley over to the helicopter she stumbled, a tad unbalanced as the world around her began to spin. Thankfully she was holding onto the side of the stretcher, which prevented her from landing in a heap in the middle of the field.

The dizzy spell passed as quickly as it had begun but she could already feel Cal's eyes burning a hole into her.

'I'm fine,' she mouthed as they rushed towards the

chopper, but knew deep down this was the beginning of the end for her out in the field.

All systems were go as they hooked Agnes up to the monitors on board and radioed in their ETA.

'I've got this.' Cal nodded towards the jump seat, indicating he wanted her to sit this one out. There was nothing to be gained from arguing and detracting his attention from the patient when he was the medical lead and had the final say here.

Although she would challenge him if she categorically believed he was wrong, on this occasion she had to concede to his authority. She was no use to Cal or Agnes swaying on her feet and ready to pass out at any second.

'There's a protein bar and a juice in my bag. Take them.' Cal went back on his word not to boss her around, but she needed it. She might have been insisting she could carry on as normal, but some things had to change. Including skipping meals and risking her blood pressure dropping too low.

In the past all that had meant was having dinner later than usual. Now it could put their missions in jeopardy. They couldn't take the chance of her fainting in the middle of treating a patient or when they were in the air. From now on she was going to have to plan and prepare for all eventualities to prevent this from happening again. That was if she was ever allowed to fly again for the duration of the pregnancy when they'd have to log a record of this incident.

Regardless that she wasn't hungry or thirsty, she followed Cal's instruction so when they landed on the helipad on the hospital roof she was feeling more like herself.

'Okay, Agnes. That's us at the hospital now. The staff

know we're coming so they'll be waiting for us to transfer you into their care.' It was Cal who talked her through the proceedings as she continued to drift in and out of consciousness in the hope some of the information would filter through and the change in surroundings wouldn't be too much of a shock.

Izzy took her place on the other side of the stretcher from Cal and they wheeled her out to the waiting trauma team. Cal reeled off Agnes's personal details and his observations and once they'd handed over responsibility, the air crew was able to breathe again.

Not that Cal would let her get away with having a wobble on his watch without an investigation. 'You're going home for a proper meal and complete bed rest.'

It wasn't the worst proposition she'd ever had, and it was one she'd welcome. There wasn't a choice anyway when she was living with him. He'd insist on cooking her a nutritious meal and probably escort her to her room to make sure she followed his advice this time.

'Yes, sir.' She clicked her heels together and saluted, the teasing an attempt to reassure him he could stop fretting.

It was unfortunate that the sharp, sudden movement tilted the world around her all over again. That slight spinning sensation she'd experienced earlier evolved into a vortex sucking the oxygen out of the atmosphere and drawing her into its core. She couldn't keep her focus on any one point, including Cal's concerned face.

He sounded so far away as he called out her name. Then she was drifting away, the darkness that was calling her home. She was falling, her body crumpling under her as she gave in to unconsciousness, but the last thing she remembered was Cal's arms around her and a feeling of weightlessness as she was carried off into the unknown.

CHAPTER SEVEN

'Izzy? Fizz?' Cal called out to her the second he saw her wobble. He'd known something was wrong and wished he'd asked the hospital staff to send transport for her too.

He could see the unfocused gaze and reached her a millisecond before she passed out. With a volley of expletives to alert the rest of the air crew, he caught her in his arms and rushed her off in the direction the hospital staff had gone.

Everything in his training told him it was probably wasn't anything more than a faint. Nothing unusual for a pregnant woman, especially one who hadn't been eating properly and was overdoing it. It didn't prevent him from reacting on an emotional level as he witnessed her collapse. All those irrational fears that he was going to lose another loved one came rushing to the surface, making him act as though her life depended on it.

Even pregnant with twins, she seemed so fragile in his arms, completely dependent on him to get her to safety. Whatever past hurt had been preventing him from bonding with these babies was immaterial compared to what he was feeling now, faced with the possibility of losing them for ever. He was their father after all and resisting that connection was pointless when nothing in the world could alter that fact. Worry was simply a part of fatherhood he'd never outrun, and when it could all be snatched away from him at any moment he didn't know why he was trying. He should be making the most of every second of it.

By the time he'd whisked Izzy down to the emergency department she was thankfully beginning to come around.

'Sasha, I need some help here.' He commandeered an empty cubicle and called over one of the nurses he recognised from their transfers.

With a gentle hand he manoeuvred Izzy's head to rest on the hospital bed, grateful he'd caught her before she'd hit the ground and perhaps given herself a concussion on top of everything else.

'What's happened to Iz?' One of the benefits of rushing emergencies through was that at least they were familiar faces around here. Although given the capacity in which Sasha knew them she'd be forgiven for thinking some catastrophe had befallen the helicopter.

'She fainted up on the roof while we were doing a handover. I should probably tell you she's pregnant with twins, in her second trimester.' Cal could see the surprise on the nurse's face but as she didn't push any further he refrained from sharing any more of Izzy's personal information. Although he imagined people were going to find out he was the father sooner or later.

'Did she hit her head at any point?'

'No.' He was confident about that at least, thanks to his quick reflexes and the close eye he'd been keeping on her.

'Izzy? Can you hear me? It's Sasha in Accident and Emergency. It would really help us if you could open your eyes, sweetie.' Whilst she tried to rouse Izzy, Cal scooted over to the sink to wet some paper towels.

'Cal? Where's Cal?'

He heard her confused mumble and hurried back to her bedside to place the cold compress on her forehead. 'I'm here, Fizz.'

She was trying to sit up, but he placed a hand on her chest and gently eased her back. 'You fainted. We need you to rest up for a while.'

If she wouldn't listen to him, perhaps the staff here could convince her.

'The babies?' Her first thoughts went to her bump, along with her hands.

Cal understood that sense of terror, that utter feeling of dread and powerlessness because that's exactly what had happened to him when he'd seen her drop like a stone. He might not be Izzy's romantic partner, but he was still entitled to worry about all of them. It was clear he was the only one they had in their lives to rely on and he didn't want to let any of them down.

'I'm sure they're fine. You haven't been out long, and I brought you straight here.' He squeezed her hand, although he knew it wouldn't do much to reassure her in the circumstances.

Her chin began to wobble, her throat bobbed up and down each time she swallowed, and Cal could see how much she was desperately trying to hold back tears. With a cough to clear his throat he looked to Sasha for help. 'We can get an ultrasound to check everything's okay with the babies, right? Just to put Izzy's mind at ease.'

Sasha smiled at him in that way that said she knew he needed the confirmation too. 'Of course. We're going to check your blood pressure and take some bloods first, Izzy, so we can see if there's anything that caused you to faint. Have you been thirstier or needing to urinate more than usual?'

'No. Why, do you think it could be gestational diabetes?' Izzy was one step ahead of the nurse because of the symptoms she was describing, but Cal was sure it was something much simpler. Her blood sugar level was probably too low, rather than the opposite.

'We're just being thorough in our investigations but if you haven't noticed any symptoms then it's not likely to be GD. We'll do all the tests anyway.'

'She hasn't been eating properly.' He was ready for Izzy to call him a snitch, but she was waiting for Sasha's opinion on continuing her casual attitude to mealtimes during pregnancy.

'The thing to remember, Izzy, is that during pregnancy you're sharing your blood supply with your baby, and in your case two babies. I would recommend carrying snacks with you. Going without food will affect you more now.'

'Thanks, Sasha. I guess I'm going to have to start listening to my body more,' Izzy said, looking a little more reassured that there was no reason this pregnancy shouldn't go full term without any further complications. She probably just needed some rest and TLC, which Cal was always offering to help her with.

He knew their relationship had gone far beyond friendship, despite his intention not to get too close, but he was afraid to acknowledge it. There was so much on the line he couldn't risk what they already had together. The best he could probably hope for was that she'd continue to let him play a part in her life.

* * *

The whole event had given Izzy quite a fright. If it was a sign she should take things easier she was going to make sure she took heed of it rather than go through this again. Thank goodness she'd been given another peek at her little jellybeans to make sure they hadn't suffered during her dizzy spell. She supposed it was too much to ask if they could install one of those machines at home, so she could obsessively check on them for the next few months.

'We're going to move you onto the ward for the night, Izzy. The blood tests have shown signs of anaemia so we're going to have to get you started on some iron supplements, and your blood pressure's quite low too. I suspect that's what caused the fainting today and I'd like to keep you in overnight so we can keep an eye on that.' The doctor hadn't given her any chance to disagree and though she understood the precautions she simply wanted to go home.

'Can't you wheel me out the back door and take me home with you?' she suggested to Cal as he followed her to the ward, holding her hand as the porter manoeuvred her around corridor corner.

He was pale, she'd put him through a lot today. She was sure it had been no mean feat, carrying her dead weight down from the roof, and apparently he hadn't left her side since. That solid reassurance she wasn't in this on her own was priceless and made the whole ordeal slightly less traumatic. Although he hadn't said it, he'd obviously been as worried about the babies as she had been, and she considered that progress.

'Believe me, I would if I could, Fizz, but they're better equipped to monitor you here.' So far, he hadn't scolded her or insisted she would be on bed rest for the foreseeable future, but she would accept any conditions he might impose if she could be under his care at home, instead of being here. It wasn't going to happen, not tonight, but when she thought of home now it included Cal and the warmth and comfort she associated with his house. Their house.

'You should probably go and get changed, have something to eat. I don't want you getting sick on my account.' She didn't want him to go. Even on a busy ward full of other patients and staff, she could feel herself retreating, shrinking into the corner and building up those protective walls in the event he did go and leave her here alone.

As the staff busied themselves around her bed, getting her settled for her upcoming stay, Cal remained stubbornly in place. Once they'd gone and she was successfully hooked up to the machines checking her progress, Cal leaned in and whispered, 'I have contacts.'

'What do you mean?'

He tapped the side of his nose. 'As long as I keep out of sight and promise not to get you or any of your fellow patients over-excited I've got special dispensation to stay outside visiting hours.'

Izzy knew she should be magnanimous and tell him she was fine here on her own. In truth, she was relieved to have him with her a little longer.

There was a twinge of guilt every time Izzy glanced at Cal's flight suit draped over the back of his chair when she knew if it wasn't for her he'd be at home, relaxing after his shift.

'It's not what I'd call *haute cuisine*,' she apologised as they both finished the unappetising plate of hospital food they'd been served. It made her appreciate Cal's efforts in the kitchen every night even more.

'I'm just thankful she took pity on me and donated the unwanted meal to a good home.' He certainly hadn't turned his nose up at the free dinner offered to him from the trolley after being rejected by a more discerning diner. Izzy thought it was indicative of how ravenous he was when she'd had to force down every mouthful. Then again, she was too stressed and anxious about the babies to have any sort of appetite.

Despite the reassurances and precautions, there was still a long way to go and plenty of time for other, more serious complications to occur.

'Hey, don't you go getting all maudlin on me.' Cal set his empty plate beside hers on the table across her bed.

'Sorry, I'm not much company for you.'

'Would you prefer it if I left you alone?' The determined set of his jaw told her he seriously believed she might be better on her own than have him with her.

'No,' she said, much too quickly, and grabbed his hand. All that would do was make her even more miserable and give her more time to dwell on all the negatives of the situation when he was the only one who could give her a much-needed boost.

'Good. Otherwise there'd be no one here to make sure you eat up all of your fruit salad.' He lifted the dish of chopped fruit and pulled his chair closer to the bed. 'Now, are you going to open up or do I have to make aeroplane noises?'

When he began moving the spoon towards her mouth she complied by eating it, touched that he cared so much about her. She couldn't remember anyone nursing her when she was ill.

In the shared foster homes, the parents had been afraid of any viruses spreading to the rest of the children and at the first sign of sickness she'd been quarantined in her room. She'd thought all those images she'd seen in TV shows of worried parents mopping the brows of fevered offspring were pure fiction. Until Cal had refused to leave her bedside and she understood what she'd been missing. To have someone who cared about her well-being more than their own was alien to her but something she could easily become accustomed to.

'Do I get a prize if I finish it all?' she asked before accepting the last morsel. In normal circumstances she might have been liable to throw the food at someone trying to feed her like a baby, but Cal wasn't trying to patronise her, he was trying to lift her spirits and make sure she got some sustenance. Okay, she was enjoying the attention too.

'Why, is there something I can tempt you with?' He waggled his eyebrows suggestively at her and made her laugh. It was good to have someone around who was so good at distracting her when she needed it and, boy, was he a distraction. There had been a few moments between them when she'd been convinced they were going to give in to temptation again. She'd ached for it, but Cal was always the one to pull back from the brink. It had been on her say so, of course, one of the conditions of her moving in, but it seemed she was powerless against her own hormones.

'I want you in my bed,' she said, enjoying the shock on his face as she leaned forward and helped herself to the last spoonful of fruit.

Izzy patted the space next to her on the bed.

'The staff have been very accommodating, but I think

that might be pushing things too far,' he said with a cheeky glint in his eye.

'I won't tell if you don't.'

After years of knowing and teasing each other it suddenly felt more real. As though the flirting was going to lead somewhere. It was probably because they were both exhausted mentally and physically that they were letting this spark between them flare into life again. Beyond the comfort and support Cal represented, that attraction also lingered, on her part at least, but she knew nothing could come of it.

She was sure this fancy would pass once the babies were safely here and she didn't feel so vulnerable. More than likely she was confusing his kindness for something that wasn't there but had been lacking her entire life. Love.

Cal didn't wait for a second invitation, only pausing to kick off his shoes. The instant he climbed onto the bed beside her and put his arm around her she snuggled into his chest with a sigh.

Perhaps it was because she was feeling vulnerable, or that they'd become so close lately, but Izzy felt compelled to share how important it was to have him there for her.

'You know, I usually can't bear anyone near me when I'm sick. I'm not used to it.'

'Not even Gerry?' It was probably difficult for Cal to understand when he'd been so considerate. Plus, it was his job, his duty of care to look after the sick and infirm.

Gerry wasn't a subject she liked to discuss with Cal for obvious reasons.

'He was on the road a lot and I think it was better for us both that he wasn't around if I was ill.' She gave a little laugh because she could see now how unreasonable she'd been at times. It was fine for her to lecture others on self-care when they weren't well, but she had no time for lying around feeling sorry for herself. She wouldn't have thanked Gerry for pandering to her either, thinking he'd have an ulterior motive for keeping on her good side. That was on top of her already ingrained need to contain the possible spread of infection.

Now Cal had shown her the sort of nurturing she'd been missing out on since the day she'd been born, and she swore her own children would know what it was to be loved and cherished every day of their lives.

'That's one of the many things I miss about not having my mum around.' Cal was absent-mindedly stroking her hair and Izzy closed her eyes, gave herself over to his tender touch.

'If I was sick she'd give up her whole day, no matter what she'd been doing beforehand, to spend it looking after me. She made the best chicken soup and brought it to me in bed. Nothing was too much trouble and she'd spend hours reading to me or playing board games with me. Even when I left home she'd rush over a pot of soup at the first sign of a sniffle. I guess you could say I was spoiled.' He gave a self-deprecating laugh but the picture he painted was more about a very special mother and son bond than an over-indulged brat.

'More loved, I'd say. Your mum sounds as though she was a lovely person.' It was easy to understand where he got his loving nature from and Izzy wasn't jealous of his idyllic-sounding upbringing.

'She was, as was Dad. Nothing was ever the same after they died. There was no one there to keep the rest of us together and it felt as though I'd lost the rest of my family along with them. My sisters moved away with their husbands and children and suddenly I was no longer a son, a brother or an uncle. I lost my sense of identity along with them. When Janet told me she was pregnant I had a role again. I was going to be a husband and father, that's why the loss was so great when she left. I lost myself along with her and the baby and it took me a long time to rediscover my identity as just Cal. I think that's why I'm finding it difficult relating to the role of being a father again. I don't want it to completely define who I am.'

The sadness in his voice made Izzy reach out and wrap her arms around his waist. It was clear he was afraid of committing again in case she took it all away from him again, the way Janet had.

'I know the Cal you were before all this happened and I promise I won't let you get cast adrift in all the excitement. I want you very much to be a part of everything.'

He gave a brief nod before changing the subject. 'What about you? You don't say much about your foster parents except that they live some distance away.'

'I've never been able to think of them as Mum and Dad, although they were the last couple to assume the roles. I never knew my birth parents and I was passed around a series of foster homes until I was old enough to go it alone. Some of the foster parents genuinely wanted to help kids in the system, others you could tell were only in it for the money, and more than a few simply weren't equipped to deal with those of us who had serious issues about our start in life. I know I acted up, pushing the boundaries to test how willing they were to keep me, and as a result I never stayed in one place too long. Theory proved.

'Meeting Helen changed things for me. She lived next door and became a real friend, the first I'd ever had. I was welcomed into her home as part of the family and I probably spent more time there, eating their food and talking over my problems with her, than in any one of my foster homes. I think that's why having my own family is so important to me. I want my children to have that love and stability I'd never had. While I'm grateful to those people who did take me in, I was never treated as a *proper* daughter. There was no real affection there and I knew it when I saw how Helen's parents interacted with her. I didn't have anyone who cared when I was sick, and I'm not used to having it now. I guess that's why I get cranky around people when I'm ill.'

'My poor Izzy. Yet you're willing to put up with me. I'm honoured.' He dropped a kiss on her head and Izzy wanted to remain cocooned here in this cubicle with him for ever.

'You're different. I'm—' She stopped herself just in time before the words *I'm in love with you* caught them both by surprise. 'I'm used to you.' She managed to cover her back before she spoiled the moment by saying something daft enough to lose him, her home and her future when he'd admitted he didn't feel the same way.

'That's good to know.' He chuckled, the vibration of his chest beneath her cheek having the opposite effect on her from the judder of the helicopter. Instead of upsetting her stomach, it was comforting.

They settled into an easy silence but that thinking time soon led her into more anxiety.

'Cal? I'm scared.' She shared her fears, watching for reassurance even when she knew he'd never abandon her or lie to her the way everyone else in her life had done. He'd shown her that today and every day since he'd found out about the babies, when most would have run from the responsibility.

He leaned down until they were nose to nose and she could see the sincerity in his eyes. 'I will never let anything happen to you. You mean too much to me.'

She was tired of fighting this thing between them. When he was looking at her with such adoration and longing she no longer knew why she was resisting the inevitable. Especially when she knew how good it felt to give in to those impulses.

She closed her eyes and tilted her chin up, inviting him to make that final decision and seal their fate. Only a second later she felt that soft pressure of his lips on hers bringing her whole body back to life. For once she was being true to herself and to her feelings and could only pray Cal was doing the same.

There was the worry he was only kissing her to comfort her but as he tangled his hand in her hair and strengthened that physical connection between them she knew better than to doubt his intentions. He'd opened up to her emotionally about his childhood and his fears and he wouldn't have done that unless he was thinking seriously about their future. Cal wanted her. All of her.

Izzy freed her mind from everything except how good it felt to be touching him again. Everything she wanted was there in his kiss—comfort, security, but most of all the intense passion she'd convinced herself had only existed in that one night. How wrong she'd been when he was pulling her close to his body, telling her how much he wanted her without saying a word. His lips captured hers again and again, his tongue teased hers until she thought she'd expire if he didn't give her more.

It also sent her heart monitor into overdrive, so he knew exactly what effect he was having on her. She felt his smile against her lips before he pulled away from her again.

'I should probably go before the nurses throw me out.' His voice was thick with desire as he shifted his weight on the mattress, but Izzy wasn't ready for him to leave apparently any more than he was.

'Can't you stay a little bit longer?' It was unlike her to be needy, but she was done with being alone when she could be in Cal's arms.

'You need your sleep. I'm keeping you awake.'

'In the best possible way. There's plenty of room for two.' She tried to convince him, though it was doubtful whether either of them would have a comfortable night with four of them essentially packed into one single bed.

'Nice try.' He sat up and arranged the pillows for her to lie down.

'I'll stay here until you fall asleep,' he whispered into her ear, spooning against her with his arm draped so casually across her waist one might've believed this was a nightly occurrence. It was a pleasant thought, even though she wanted more.

Izzy closed her eyes, a smile on her lips as exhaustion claimed her. She hadn't realised how much she needed or wanted Cal in her life until she couldn't imagine one without him in it.

CHAPTER EIGHT

CAL HAD BEEN like a kid on Christmas Eve, unable to settle, waiting for the call to go and pick Izzy up from the hospital. He'd ignored the cramp in his limbs, which had set in as he'd been lying on that hospital bed with her because he hadn't wanted to swap it for the luxury of his spacious king-size bed.

Home offered him peace, space and comfort in comparison but without Izzy it was hard to find any of that. He'd have happily slept all night with her pressed against his chest, dead arm and all, just to be close to her a while longer. That's when he knew he was in way over his head.

This was supposed to have been a gesture that he was committed to raising the babies with Izzy. Moving in together was never meant to have been more than a favour. He'd certainly never intended to get as close to Izzy as he'd apparently become. It left him open to the same kind of emotional hurt he'd been through once too often. With her determination to include him every step of the way through this pregnancy she'd broken through those defences he'd imagined would keep his heart protected. When he thought losing her or the babies was a possibility he knew he'd become completely attached to the idea of their little family.

Yesterday had been stressful for them both but it must have taken a particular toll on Izzy for her to let him so close and to want him to stay. She'd always been a fire-cracker and independent to the point of being obstrep-erous, so it was an indication of just how much turmoil she'd been in for her to let him hold her.

Then there was the kiss. He'd been so overcome with compassion for her situation, gratitude for hav-ing her in his life and, well, love, there was nothing he could've done to prevent it from happening. When Izzy had kissed him back his whole body had sung out with sheer happiness that she'd wanted him too. It was only the rise in her blood pressure that had reminded him she was vulnerable, and he hadn't wanted to take advantage of that when he was the only person she had in her life. It would confuse her at a time when her whole world was in chaos and what she needed from him more was a sense of security and stability. Something she'd appar-ently been missing out on for some time.

She didn't have friends or family around and it was natural she should reach out for the nearest available substitute. He'd do well to remember that's all he was in the picture.

'Would you like me to hunt down a wheelchair to get you to the car?' Cal waited patiently as Izzy packed her newly prescribed medication and toiletries into the bag he'd brought for her.

She gave him a sidelong look. 'Would you like me to get a wheelchair to take *you* to the car?'

'Okay, okay. I was only trying to save you a walk.' He held his hands up in surrender. Secretly, he was pleased she was back to her fighting best. For him it was a better sign she was on the mend than her improved blood pressure and blood test results. Even if he'd miss his temporary position as chief hand-holder.

'I've been cooped up in bed too long. I need the exercise and some fresh air. Not to mention something to eat that doesn't resemble baby food. Can we stop somewhere on the way home?' She whispered the request, presumably to prevent offending anyone from hospital catering if they overheard.

'I can do better than that. I've stocked up on fresh fruit and vegetables and I'm going to cook you a veritable welcome-home feast. Anything your heart desires.' Cal bowed and grabbed her luggage before she insisted on carrying it herself.

From now on, he intended to provide her with wholesome, nutritious meals to ensure she wouldn't be lacking in any more essential vitamins or minerals. Avoiding any further upsetting overnight hospital stays.

'For now, I'd be happy if you took me home and put the kettle on.' Izzy softened a little towards him, slipping her arm through his and leaning against him for the duration of the short walk to the car.

'I think I can manage that.' He had worried that her defences had reassembled during the time since she'd last seen him and that she might have regretted their cosy bedtime cuddle session. On his return home, Cal's bed had suddenly seemed so vast and empty compared to that hospital trolley. Even more so than after Janet had left him. It was only with some considerable thought, comparing that one spooning session with Izzy against years of sharing a bed with Janet, he realised proximity to someone didn't actually constitute the nature of a close relationship.

They'd gone through the motions together as a couple, but they'd never had that bond he had with Izzy. Which was probably why Janet had never approved of their friendship.

Yesterday, experiencing that pain and worry together and finally expressing some of the emotions they'd tried to keep locked down, had finally cemented their bond. Their only worry now should be making sure these babies were safely delivered into the world.

He unlocked the car, which he'd parked as close to the entrance as he dared, risking a fine to save Izzy an uphill walk to the car park. Instead of climbing into the passenger seat, as he'd expected, Izzy suddenly turned around and said, 'Thank you for everything, Calum,' and kissed him full on the lips.

He drove on autopilot, in a loved-up haze, back to the home they shared. The only place he knew both of them wanted to be, where they could close the door and re-create that cocoon. Where all they needed was each other.

Izzy had spent the rest of the week under house arrest as per Cal's orders. She knew it wasn't a control issue, she'd worked alongside Cal long enough to know he wasn't the kind of guy who needed to exert his authority every second of the day. However, he was compassionate and well mannered. Not usually qualities a woman would find irritating unless she was used to being fiercely independent.

She was going stir crazy forced to stay in one place for so long, not permitted to lift a finger to do anything. It was alien to her, being so cosseted that she didn't know how to deal with it. So she'd gone back to being her bolshie self, giving Cal a hard time and accusing him of suffocating her because deep down she was afraid of jumping his bones for paying her a bit of attention.

Not that he'd have let her expend that sort of energy, even if he had reciprocated these new feelings she'd been harbouring towards him. She'd thought that night in the hospital and that wonderful sensation of falling asleep in his arms had been the start of something more between them. Except he'd turned into her carer since then with no inclination towards anything other than nursing her.

He hadn't reacted to the kiss she'd given him when they'd left the hospital and so she'd consigned it to the list of bad decisions she'd made regarding suitable men. She'd taken his kindness and understanding and tried to sabotage the relationship they did have by taking it somewhere he might not have wanted it to go. What else could Cal have done when she'd made him get into her bed and poured her heart except to make her feel better? She'd provided the awkward element by attempting to extend that moment beyond the hospital walls.

Unfortunately, this imposed relaxation was having the opposite effect it was supposed to have on her. Instead of keeping her calm and chilled out, it was giving her too much time to obsess about everything that had happened recently or could happen in the near future.

She'd tried everything to distract her thoughts from Cal and what he was doing without her at work. Including watching so much trashy daytime television she wanted to scratch her eyes out. Taking up knitting hadn't helped either. There were so many holes in the simple squares she'd attempted to piece into a blanket it looked more like crochet.

Izzy lit on him the second she heard the key in the lock, desperate for some human company instead of the virtual kind. 'You should have texted to let me know you were on your way home. I could have had dinner in the oven for you.'

She felt like a nineteen-fifties housewife, waiting barefoot and pregnant for the centre of her universe to come home from work and give her life some meaning. She really needed to get back to work and do something useful. Never in a million years could she have pictured herself in the role of the happy housewife because she'd never imagined it existed. Although she'd go mad if she spent every day tied to the kitchen sink with no outside interests, she had to admit there was a certain appeal in sharing dinner and chores with a man who would happily put her on a pedestal.

'I wouldn't expect you to do that. You're supposed to be taking it easy.' Cal hung up his jacket and rolled up his shirtsleeves, preparing to go into the kitchen and start making dinner. He was one in a million and easy to take advantage of if you were an unscrupulous user like his ex. On the other hand, this total pampering deal made her feel uncomfortable because she didn't know what to do with herself.

'Cal, I've been taking it so easy I'm practically comatose. I'm fine. The midwife confirmed that at my last appointment. My blood pressure is where it should be, as are my iron levels. Besides, you've cooked and labelled enough food to see out the entire pregnancy. All I'd have to do is microwave it.' Given his history it was no wonder he was used to doing his Florence Nightingale bit, but he couldn't carry on in this vein or she'd burst a blood vessel from pent-up frustration.

'You say that as though it's a bad thing.'

'It's not that I don't appreciate all your effort to take care of me, Cal. I'm simply not used to it. You know I'm not the type to sit on my backside and let everyone run around after me, no matter what the circumstances. I'm going back to work on Monday and before you say anything I'll make sure it's as ground crew only.' Then she wouldn't get in anyone's way and could still remain part of the team. She wasn't asking his permission, but she did respect him enough to inform him of her decision.

He nodded. 'It's one hundred per cent your choice, Iz. All I wanted to do was fulfil my promise to take care of you and the babies.'

'I know.' And she loved him for it. If only his actions were based on more than a misplaced sense of duty.

'Look, why don't we go out for a meal?'

Izzy was tempted to ask if he meant as a date, but it was more likely to be a compromise, so she had to dampen down her initial excitement that they were making progress on their personal relationship.

'It would be nice to leave these four walls and pay a visit into civilisation.' Izzy also realised it would be the first time they'd gone out to a restaurant as anything other than work colleagues. She couldn't help but hope for the day when they did it as a couple, or even a family.

'It's a date, then. Give me ten minutes to shower and change and we'll hit the town.' Cal bounded up the stairs to freshen up, while Izzy did her best to get her fluttering pulse back under control.

'I get the impression our waiter thinks we're having some sort of clandestine affair,' Izzy whispered across the secluded, candlelit table, which had obviously been set to create a romantic scene.

Cal grinned at her, clearly amused by being ushered towards the dark corner with her, away from business-men and noisy young families.

'Then maybe we should give him something to talk about.' He took her hand and lifted it to his mouth, brushing his lips across her fingers and making shivers dance their way across her skin. Her brain might have decided one or two kisses were probably best forgotten, but her body was keen to remind her of the intensity of sensations his touch alone could cause.

Whilst she tried to get her thoughts and rogue body parts under control, she noticed he'd gone quiet too. It really was time they were honest about what was happening between them on an emotional level.

'Cal, I think it's us who have something to talk about.'

For once he didn't pull away from her when they were veering towards the important issues affecting their relationship and held her hand fast in his.

'I know. We've kind of let things run away from us.' He was smiling, so it seemed he didn't totally regret those flashes of passion which kept flaring up between them.

'I just want to know where I stand. Where we stand, Cal.' She was putting everything they did have on the line by asking for that clarification, but they couldn't go on pretending they were able to suppress those urges for ever. The next time they gave in to them she knew she wouldn't be able to go back to being just friends. Not now love had become part of the equation for her.

It had come slowly, creeping in along with the friend-ship and passion they'd cultivated over time, but as she'd learned, ignoring her feelings didn't make them go away. If anything, it simply left them to spin out of control and with time running out before the babies came along, it was more important than ever to get some clarity on their relationship. She wanted to put down roots for her family but only if there was a strong, stable foundation available for them.

Of course, their waiter arrived back with their meals at the most inconvenient time, forcing them to break apart and lose that physical connection.

'Thanks.' Cal smiled politely at their server while Izzy did her best to hold her tongue until he left.

'I mean, we're going to be a family, whether you like it or not.' Weeks of pussy-footing around him in case she frightened him off by making him face the truth finally caught up with her and she ignored her delicious plate of Cajun chicken pasta to confront this head on.

Cal hung his head and sighed. 'I'll be the first to admit I haven't been the most excited father-to-be, but after Janet I'm a bit more cautious about the idea of family.'

'No kidding.' Izzy speared a piece of pasta and cursed that woman for making their lives more complicated than they needed to be. If it hadn't been for her cruel treatment of such a wonderful man, she and Cal might have settled down together by now and be looking forward to the birth of their children. Not fearing the event would trigger more betrayal or heartbreak.

They both ate in silence, but Izzy couldn't enjoy her dinner when it was overpowered by the taste of bitterness in her mouth.

Eventually Cal broke first, giving her some insight to the workings of his troubled mind. 'I did want it all at one time. You know, the wife and kids and the white picket fence. After my parents died all I wanted was to re-create that feeling of having my family around me.'

'And now? That's what's available to you but you're pushing us all away.' Izzy was tired of paying for someone else's mistakes. She and the babies deserved more than that.

'At first I was afraid you regretted our night together, that there was no real future for us. I tried to fight those feelings I had for you, which were about more than getting you back into bed again.' He grinned at her and she didn't know what had shaken her more, that smile, him opening up to her, or finally telling her he thought about her as more than a convenience. Whatever it was, she wanted more of it.

'I thought I could separate our relationship from the babies. A stupid notion, I know, but in my head, loving them could be my ultimate downfall. You never gave me any indication you wanted anything serious between us and I thought if you decided someday you could do better than me, I'd lose these babies the same way I lost the last one.' That pain was still so obvious in his eyes and in his quivering voice Izzy could understand why he was still trying to protect himself, even if it came at the price of her peace of mind.

'These are your babies too. I would never take them away from you. A family means more to me than anything because, unlike you, I've never had one, Cal. You don't know what it's like to grow up knowing your own parents didn't want you and people had to be paid to take you in. I've had so many foster parents I don't remember all of their names. I want better for my children. I need them to know they're loved every day of their lives. That means growing up in a house with a father who shows them that and, let's be honest, you haven't been thrilled at the prospect of becoming a dad, have you?'

If they were sweeping away the debris from the past to clear the path for a happy future together then they needed to be completely honest with each other.

'I've told you why I've been holding back. I'm sorry I can't give you more than that.' He was leaving it up to her to decide if she was willing to risk her heart again on a future with someone who couldn't commit one hundred per cent to her.

'I appreciate your honesty, but I need someone who's going to put me first, to make my children his priority. It might seem selfish, but after Gerry I'm done with being second best.' There was every chance Cal could tell her to get lost with her demands, but it was better to know now if she was asking too much from him than finding out when it was too late.

'Hey, I'm not Gerry.' He sounded angry at the comparison and it was no wonder after everything he'd heard about his predecessor, but this wasn't about soothing his ego. It was about protecting her babies.

'Was everything okay for you?' Their waiter with the bad sense of timing arrived back at the table, staring pointedly at the discarded plates still laden with food.

'Fine, thanks.' Izzy didn't mean to snap but she wanted to finish this conversation before Cal shut her out again and left her guessing about where they stood as a couple or as a family.

Suitably cowed, he cleared the table without further comment. Cal waited until he was completely out of earshot before he continued his defence.

'Gerry was selfish, not thinking of anyone but himself in the decisions he made. I like to think I'm doing the opposite. I want to take my time and make sure everything I'm doing is for the right reasons. I won't apologise for wanting to do right by all of us.' With that logic Izzy couldn't fault him. Perhaps it was a lot to expect him to outline all his plans for the future, including how he was going to feel about the babies once they got here, when it was clear he was still trying to adjust to the idea of being a father.

Cal got up to pay the bill, not waiting for it to be brought to the table, and Izzy had to hurry to catch him as he exited the restaurant without her. He was angry at having to justify himself to her yet again and she realised she had to make some concessions for the way he had let her stay with him in the first place, despite his reservations.

'Cal, stop. Please.' This evening could've been a chance for a romantic evening together, strengthening that connection she so desperately wanted. Instead she was in danger of pushing him away for ever by asking so much of him.

'It's just… I don't know what I'd do without you, Cal. I'm afraid of losing you.' Standing there in the street, with Cal refusing to even look at her, was sufficient to make her teary. She'd done the unthinkable and fallen for him somewhere along the way. It wasn't simply that she'd become accustomed to him being there for her, providing for her every need, but he'd become part of her life, part of her. Without him she knew she couldn't function properly and that wasn't a position she'd ever intended to let herself get into again when it meant depending on one person for her happiness.

He came back to her in a heartbeat, sliding his hands

around her waist and rubbing his nose against hers. 'I'm not going anywhere without you, Fizz, unless you ask me to.'

It wasn't a declaration of undying love, but she was sure it was there in his kiss as he claimed her mouth once more. He was tender and loving, as he was in all things, but Izzy demanded proof this time that this was more than him simply comforting or placating her.

She weaved her fingers into his mop of unruly hair and pulled him in deeper, seeking to find if the true nature of his affections transcended mere emotions. There was no mistaking the extent of his loyalty to her but she didn't want either of them to confuse it for something else that might never have been there in the first place.

She needn't have worried. Once she gave the green light that this was what she wanted from him, Cal pulled her hard against him, his passion leaving her legs weak at the knees.

Her skin prickled with awareness and the hairs on the back of her neck stood to attention as he showered her with kiss after kiss. He sought her with his bold tongue and teased her with little licks and flicks until she was grinding against him with longing.

Eventually they remembered to breathe, and she was glad to find she wasn't the only one panting after the unexpected encounter.

'We should probably go home,' he said half-heartedly, making no attempt to release her from his grasp.

'Mmm.'

Izzy was happy where she was but excited about moving their relationship forward. Cal had been as straightforward as he could be with her and it was up to her to decide if that was enough to base her future on. She had to ask herself if he was worth the gamble with her heart when there was no guarantee it was all going to work out this time either. Despite her whole body screaming, *Yes!*

CHAPTER NINE

THE JOURNEY HOME had given Cal some time to cool his ardour and think about more than what his libido was demanding. Izzy had told him in no uncertain terms what having a family meant to her, but he wasn't completely sure he felt the same as he once had about the idea. It wasn't fair to bed her and give her false hope that they were going to live happily ever after.

She deserved a partner who was totally committed to her and the babies, with no doubts about what he wanted. Until he found that certainty for himself he thought it best to cool things down between them again.

When they got back to the house he left her at the bottom of the stairs with, 'Goodnight, Izzy.'

This time his mouth barely grazed her cheek as he kissed her before going to bed. Alone. He hoped she understood he wasn't rejecting her on a personal level but taking precautions for both of their sakes.

There was a very real chance they'd both be lying awake tonight on either side of the wall separating their bedrooms, replaying the passion they'd given in to completely. He'd been doing that anyway since the very first time he'd laid his lips on her.

So much for taking a step back and focusing on being

a support to Izzy rather than being further cause for stress. She was vulnerable after her scare and didn't need him making a move on her when her hormones and emotions were all over the place. As were his. Especially since she'd kissed him back, her eyes and her body asking him for more.

Cal groaned, lifted the book he'd been reading from his nightstand in deference to the sleep that had been eluding him recently.

He managed a page or two before he realised not a single word had registered He was listening out for the sound of Izzy coming upstairs to bed.

'This is insane,' he confided to the fluffy sheep Izzy had made him keep on his bed. It was impossible to concentrate on anything but the creak of the floorboards as she crossed to her room and the thought of her getting undressed for bed. Despite only wearing his boxers, Cal was beginning to sweat.

He tossed the book back onto his nightstand, not even bothering to mark his place, and turned the bedside light off. Eyes closed, he tried to force himself into slumber, knowing tomorrow at work would be as physically demanding as ever. Gone were the nights when he'd slept fitfully on the sofa because his bed held such painful connotations of the woman who'd broken his heart. Only for them to be replaced with lustful thoughts of the woman who'd been right by his side for years.

In the too-quiet darkness he thought he could hear her tossing and turning on her mattress. If he was being kept awake by thoughts of how that bubbling chemistry between them was threatening to explode again, perhaps she was too. Or, as he'd predicted all along, was she too confused after Gerry's death and their twin surprise she didn't know what she was doing?

'Cal?' Suddenly Izzy's soft voice called to him in the darkness. At first he thought he'd imagined it, then he heard her footsteps cross his floor. He'd been so lost in his own head he hadn't realised she'd left her own room.

'Izzy? What's wrong?' By the time he managed to turn the bedside lamp on again she was sitting on the bed beside him. His brain was working overtime, trying to figure out what could possibly be wrong with her when she looked so calm. If there had been an issue with the babies she would've been in full panic mode by now.

Instead, she curled up in the foetal position beside him so their heads were side by side on his pillows. 'I don't want to sleep alone, Cal.'

She didn't appear to be in a hurry to go anywhere so he snuggled down beside her and pulled the covers over them. His heart was beating just as fast as it had when they'd kissed but he was doing his best not to misinterpret her meaning.

He couldn't help but reach out and touch her, brush the russet tresses off her shoulder to reveal the porcelain skin beneath.

'Are you sure you don't want to make the most of the peace while you've got it?' Cal tried to conceal his optimism that she was here for more than company with a lame attempt at humour. However, when she rested a hand possessively on his hip, the lower half of his body jerked wide awake.

'Don't make me beg, Cal. You know neither of us would venture into this lightly, but we don't seem to be able to stop it happening either. I don't want to stop it.'

Lying in his own bed, with Izzy saying everything

he wanted to hear, touching him with confidence that he was hers, Cal was completely undone.

Izzy was putting everything on the line by being here. By climbing into Cal's bed, not only was she risking further rejection but if he kicked her out now the last of her dignity would slink out the door with her.

An evening unsuccessfully dodging the sexual tension arcing between them, on top of the close relationship they already had, had been sufficient for her to act on. She knew he'd turned away from her tonight because he didn't want her to read more into his actions than he was offering.

For now, she'd be happy for him to acknowledge the attraction with more than a passionate kiss. It wasn't in her nature to throw herself at a man, but she knew Cal better than most. He wouldn't take advantage of her, quite the opposite. It wasn't difficult to tell he'd been holding back for her sake. If there was one thing preventing them from moving their relationship on to the next level it was liable to be because he was afraid of her getting hurt somewhere along the way. He'd already voiced his fears to that effect but as far as she could see it was too late, the kisses they'd shared were proof they were powerless to stop this runaway train anyway.

She ran her hand down his corded thigh, his skin hot enough beneath her fingertips for her to suggest he take off the last of his clothes.

His mouth kicked up at the corners, his eyes darkened and then his mouth was on hers, no longer constrained by concerns for her welfare.

Unleashed by his conscience, it seemed Cal was as eager to explore this evolving dynamic as Izzy. He took command of her lips, moulding them to fit his. His hand was in her hair, drawing her closer, unashamed to let her know how his body was responding to her touch.

With her eyes closed, giving herself over to the sensation of his hands and lips sweeping over her, she was already drifting away on a cloud of pleasure. Only the pure need for him she experienced when he slipped the strap of her night dress down her shoulder and cupped her naked breast grounded her again.

He brushed his thumb lightly over her nipple and she jerked back into her body with the sudden rush of arousal in response. Her reaction to that brief, intimate contact spurred him on to extract more of it from her. Cal moved his hungry mouth from hers, sucking and tasting her skin as he moved to her neck, her collarbone, and—*oh, yes*—her breast.

She sucked in a shaky breath of arousal as he slid the other strap down to follow its neighbour and flicked her nipple with the tip of his tongue. Izzy clutched his shoulders, arched her body further against his and demanded more. The first swell of ecstasy began to build inside her once he drew the responsive nub into his mouth. She'd forgotten how good it was to simply let herself go, enjoying the moment with him.

Cal grazed his teeth over her sensitive skin and sucked hard, ripping a cry of pure ecstasy from deep inside her very core. This time she didn't even waste time on the niceties of inviting him to undress, letting her hands do the work until he was fully naked beneath her fingertips. He did the same for her, sliding the rest of her nightdress excruciatingly slowly down her body and kissing every newly exposed inch of her skin until she was completely naked, and he was kneeling at her feet.

'You're beautiful,' he said, and though she felt a little bashful, with nowhere to hide her blossoming body under the glare of the bedside light, Cal's obvious appreciation was there for her to see.

'So are you.' She repaid the compliment with as much sincerity as it had been given to her. The nature of their relationship in the past, and up until recently, meant she'd tried not to recall what he looked like out of the padded flight suit. Now she was free to let her eyes feast once more on his impressive, solid physique and the majesty of his arousal.

Cal's smile was so big it crinkled the skin at the corners of his eyes and made him even more devilishly delicious as he covered her body with his. Her limbs were trembling with anticipation she wanted him so badly. With him nibbling the skin at her neck, his erection intimately teasing her, she was on the edge of flipping him over onto his back and climbing on top of him. Just when she thought his restraint was proving greater than hers he nudged her thighs apart and groaned a satisfied 'Oh...' as he entered her.

It was a moment of perfect joy and peace for her as they were finally joined together in body as well as soul. He paused, his eyes searching her face, and she could tell he was waiting for confirmation she was okay. She didn't want her condition or his fierce desire to protect her at all costs to inhibit this pivotal, much-longed-for moment in their partnership. They had to learn to trust each other's instincts as well as their own if they were going to have a future together.

'I need you, Cal.' She needed all of him with no holding back because she wanted to give him everything of herself in return.

Her plea, her surrender freed them both from the last threads of restraint and let them search together for that ultimate pleasure goal.

'My Isobel…' His husky voice in her ear, the sweet affection and the delicious fullness of having him inside her was too much for her to bear. She was at breaking point, desperately clinging on to prolong this feeling of ecstasy as long as possible.

With every grind of his hips, every thrust and using every trick he had in his locker to drive her wild, he made her cries more frequent, higher pitched until she was sure she'd shatter every window in the house.

Then the world was spinning somewhere far below her as she soared with one last push from her equally vocal partner.

They clung together for as long as their limbs held out, panting and grinning at each other like loons.

Izzy was so elated, if it wasn't for the obvious, one would've been forgiven for thinking this was her first time and she'd given herself to her first love. She'd had good sex before, and with him, but they were looking at each other with a certain smugness that said they'd both achieved a new level together.

'Why didn't we want to do this again?' Cal asked as he lay down beside her, still caressing her naked body and sending aftershocks of her climax rippling through her again and again.

'I think we were worried we'd burn each other out.' To illustrate the point that they'd have trouble keeping their hands off each other, she cupped his backside and squeezed.

The truth, they both knew, was much more complicated and painful than that. Although she couldn't speak for him, Izzy couldn't regret that time when it had given her so much to look forward to now and had brought her and Cal closer than they'd ever been.

'Hmm, I hope this isn't simply your way of guaranteeing the babies get a room each.'

It didn't escape her notice he was avoiding talking seriously about their future as a couple but as long as he continued to think of this as a permanent arrangement they were good.

As for Izzy, she knew she was in love with him and their epic lovemaking had confirmed it. Hopefully in time he'd come to feel the same, but it was too much to ask for now when the wounds Janet had inflicted were still raw. It was different for her when she and Gerry had had definitive closure. The same couldn't be said for Janet, who'd made her presence known so recently it still pained Izzy to think about it. With no discernible conscience about what she'd done, Izzy wouldn't put it past her to keep turning up like the proverbial bad penny.

That left a smidgen of doubt that Cal would remain committed to her should Janet decide she preferred his attentions and wanted him back. They had a long history together, Janet had been someone Cal had imagined having a family with, and that wasn't a thought easily dismissed. She, though, was always getting carried away on dreams of the family they could make once the twins were born.

'Just wait until I try to talk you into installing a swimming pool.' This wasn't the time for deep and meaningful conversations or displays of jealousy and insecurity. She wanted to keep things fun and flirty, not to mention irresistible, so he'd come back for more. 'I won't let you get out of bed until you agree to my every demand.'

'Do your worst,' he said, lying spread-eagled on the bed, his body ready to be persuaded by anything she said or did.

Always keen to show she was every bit as physically capable as the next person, Izzy rose to the challenge and took charge.

'Are you ready to go?' Izzy peeped her head around the bedroom door, but Cal simply pulled the covers back up over his head.

'No.'

She chuckled and plonked herself down on the bed beside him. 'You can't stay in there all day.'

'Why not? It sounds like a good idea to me.'

Izzy shrieked as he reached for her and tried to pull her under the covers with him. It was very tempting to climb back in with him when his bedhead hair and morning stubble made him look even more handsome than usual.

Now they knew how phenomenal they were together in all aspects of their relationship she could happily spend the day here with him making up for lost time. She'd heard an increased libido could happen at any stage of pregnancy, but she reckoned he'd have had this effect on her every time he touched her, long after her body was her own again.

'I. Would. Love. To,' she said, through his kisses along her collarbone, and he palmed her breast through her blouse to illustrate how keen he was for her to get naked with him again. 'But we have an appointment to get to.'

'We do?'

It wasn't fair to tease her like this, awakening that

ache for him inside her when they couldn't do anything about it.

'I booked us into a practical parenting class.'

'Isn't it a little early for that? I thought antenatal classes were for much later in pregnancy.' Cal frowned and seemed to withdraw to the far side of the bed. Obviously, they still had some work to do when it came to his role as a hands-on dad.

'True, but this isn't any ordinary class. It's a private course focused on parenting twins, and I hear it's very popular, so it books up early. I thought we could both use some tips.' She wanted them to be the best parents they could be for the children.

'I'll need all the help I can get,' he muttered as he pulled the duvet away.

'Cal? Are you sure you want to be my birthing partner? I don't want to force you into it if you really don't want to be there.' There was only so much she could do if he genuinely didn't want to be involved.

She wanted nothing more than to have him coaching her through her contractions as their babies were delivered into the world. Although they both had baggage they were dealing with, these babies represented their future together. She wouldn't have asked him to be part of the birth if she wasn't thinking of him as her real-life partner and the family they were going to make together.

Cal took both her hands in his and looked her deep in the eyes. 'It would be a privilege to be there for you.'

If Izzy could only believe his devotion extended to the little people they'd created together, everything would be just perfect.

CHAPTER TEN

'HI, EVERYONE. I'M SHARON. Help yourselves to tea and biscuits and make yourselves comfortable.' The woman holding the practical parenting class directed the anxious-looking couples huddled by the door towards the refreshments table.

Cal poured out two cups of tea and watched Izzy load a plate with enough chocolate biscuits to see them through the whole day. At last she was heeding the snacking advice. With any luck they'd get through this class without any fainting incidents. He hadn't been thrilled by the idea of coming here today but he supposed it would be useful to pick up some practical tips today on living with twins.

Janet hadn't even wanted him to attend the scans with her and she'd probably had Darren accompany her to the antenatal classes when the time had come. It no longer bothered him. He was just grateful Izzy was making such an effort to get him involved and feel part of this pregnancy.

They were embarking on an exciting new chapter of their lives, not only as a couple but they were about to be thrown into the deep end with the arrival of the twins too. Izzy had accepted him as her partner and that was enough for him. It meant he could be here to support her when she didn't have any family around to help. Cal hoped that through these classes he'd see exactly what he could do to make life easier for her. Even if it was just being there to mop her brow or have his fingers crushed during labour. It was better for Izzy's well-being to know she had someone who'd be by her side throughout this journey.

He glanced around the room at the other couples. There were married pairs, mothers and daughters and best friends. Every couple was different, but the common theme was that loving bond like the one he had with Izzy. It would've been tough for Izzy to have come here on her own and tougher for him if he had missed out. Some things a person could never get back and thankfully he'd realised that before he'd missed out on any more of their babies' important milestones.

The presentation began with a talk on what made multiple birth pregnancies different from single pregnancies. A lot of which he and Izzy were already aware of due to their medical experience but hearing there was a higher risk of complications and need for more health professionals at the birth was different when you were preparing for real.

There were plenty of helpful tips for them to take some of the stress out of coping with more than one baby. Including bathtimes and having all necessary supplies at hand before attempting to bath the babies, one at a time. A lot of the general advice was focused on support and making sure there was more than one pair of hands available when possible. Something he intended to do. In fact, he was looking forward to sharing the bathing and feeding with Izzy and forging a bond with their babies.

They were given a couple of dolls to practise changing nappies on and Sharon came to supervise their attempts.

'I can see Dad has done this before. Well done.'

There was a good reason he had his baby doll changed in seconds whilst Izzy was still grappling with the tapes on her twin's nappy. He'd had a lot of experience when his nephews and nieces had been young. Back then, when they'd all come together at his parents' house for special occasions, he'd made the most of his precious uncle time. As far as he'd been concerned, it was practice for the family he'd always expected to have, and his sisters had been over the moon when he'd volunteered for changing duty.

This practical lesson should have been overwhelming to someone who'd been doing his best not to get too involved beyond providing practical support, but it reminded him of the joy he'd once experienced being around children. Before life with Janet had attached negative connotations with the idea of being a father. Now he and Izzy were making moves towards being a real couple it was about time he stopped catastrophising, imagining the worst outcome, and enjoyed every moment life together would bring them.

He looked around at the other couples all mucking in together to change their pretend babies whilst he was standing back watching Izzy struggle do it alone.

'Let me help, Iz. We're a team, remember?' She gave him a wary look, and he knew it was going to take time to convince her he meant every word, but he had months left to prove himself. He was going to be the best father Izzy could ever wish to have for her children.

As they arrived back at the car after the class Cal caught sight of a couple exiting the maternity wing with their newborn in one of those carriers he'd had to buy for the twins. The pair were obviously new parents, that glow of unconditional love for the life they'd just created lighting them up like Christmas trees. Cal smiled, anticipating the day he and Izzy would experience walking out that door as first-time parents too.

The little family stepped out into the sunshine and it was then everything hit home. These weren't just random strangers he was watching start a new chapter of their lives together, it was Janet and Darren and the baby he'd been father to for its first weeks of existence.

They were oblivious to anyone's presence, in their little bubble of pure joy, and it was like a kick in the gut for Cal. Not because he was jealous of Darren but because he'd never seen Janet look so at peace. Leaving him had obviously been the best thing she could have done. He would never have made her this happy. Blinded by his desire for a family at any cost, he hadn't seen the flaws in their relationship at the time, but it was obvious now he'd never loved her the way he loved Izzy.

They'd never had the same connection or interests and, looking back, something had always been lacking in their relationship. It must have been for Janet to go looking for more with another man and for Cal to be happy for them walking away as a family. Izzy was the best thing to have ever happened to him and this encounter proved it.

* * *

'Is everything all right?' Izzy was sitting in the car, waiting for Cal to get in. His attention was elsewhere, and it hadn't taken long for her to figure out why. Janet was like a dead weight around her neck, dragging her down every time she thought she was making progress with Cal.

'Fine.' He got in and closed the door, making no mention of the scene across the road. If it didn't bother him he would've referenced the couple exiting the hospital with their new bundle of joy but clearly it was still hurting that he was no longer part of it.

It was difficult not to take that personally and have it pierce her heart until it felt as though her life blood was draining slowly and painfully away every time she thought of the longing on his face. He wanted his ex and her baby over Izzy and his own children. That was the family he was supposed to have, and they were simply the imposters he'd been landed with.

It wasn't fair to carry on pretending this was going to work out when she'd been forcing him into this relationship every step of the way. Perhaps she'd been trying to convince herself he only needed time to learn to love her and the babies because deep down she was afraid of doing this alone. She'd been out of her depth in that class even with their fake twins whilst Cal had been the calm, capable one. It was in that moment, holding that doll, not even knowing how to change a nappy properly, that it had hit home what a huge undertaking motherhood was going to be for her. There were going to be two precious mites totally dependent on her to protect and provide for them as well as guide them through life. Difficult to do when she hadn't had any role models who'd done the same for her. What if she couldn't handle it like all of those who were supposed to have parented her?

She didn't want to have children who resented her and rejected a relationship with her once they were old enough to leave home. Although she hadn't realised it, she'd been acting the role of parent as much as Cal. If they carried on pretending they knew what they were getting into they were going to end up resenting each other for getting trapped in a situation that would be much harder to get out of once the twins arrived.

They'd be taking a huge gamble on the future if they stayed together and she wasn't prepared to do that again. Cal deserved that same level of happiness he'd witnessed in Janet and she wasn't convinced she could give him that. Izzy didn't want either of them settling for second best.

So much for putting her mind at ease. Regardless of the information leaflets she had tucked in her bag and all the stress-relieving tips they'd been given, Izzy was more wound up than ever by the time they got home.

She'd been so caught up in that idea of her happy family coming together that she'd only today realised something capable of bringing her back down to earth with a thump. No amount of cajoling was going to make Cal love these babies.

Her crush and her bond with Cal had, on her part at least, evolved into real love. She was grateful to him for providing a roof for her and she wanted him to be part of her babies' lives but not if he didn't love these babies the way she loved them.

'Have you taken your supplements today?' It was a simple enough question but now when she was analysing every conversation Cal's focus on the pregnancy only ever seemed to centre around her health. His interest seemed limited to that of a doctor rather than a prospective father.

'Yes. You don't have to keep reminding me.' Now she was becoming vexed on behalf of her unborn children, memories of her own childhood made her snappy with him.

Those big eyes full of hurt at her tone might have made her feel as though she'd just kicked a puppy, but she'd fallen for that guilt trick too many times with Gerry. Time and again she'd been promised a life of her dreams only to find it was nothing more than an illusion. Foster families, her parents, even Gerry had conned her into thinking she'd found security, only to snatch it away again when they discovered life with her lacking in some way.

The circumstances might be different with Cal but they were also scarily similar. Despite promises to herself not to get too invested in a relationship again, or rely on any one person solely for support, she'd left her home and jumped into bed with him. If he didn't want this family as much as she did, wasn't completely and madly in love with all three of them, then her future was as rocky as ever.

With sleepless nights and double the mess a newborn usually brought, Cal would tire quickly of them all invading his space. Izzy wasn't prepared to expose her children to the same uncertainty she'd grown up in.

'What's wrong? Please don't feel too overwhelmed by it all. We can go through those information leaflets together later and work on your birth plan if you like.'

'As a matter of fact, I have been thinking about the

birth. I'm wondering if it's a good idea for you to be there after all.' It hurt to say it, even more to see him flinch as though she'd punched him in the gut. But theirs was a complicated relationship created mostly through circumstances. They needed some way to separate those feelings encompassing friendship, love and loyalty.

'I thought we'd already discussed this?'

After a brief lapse Izzy's barriers were back up, protecting her, and she needed the truth, not some fantastic version of it, before she'd let him bypass them again. In the long run, telling her only what he thought she wanted to hear now would cause greater distress later when it turned out not to be true. Her heart bore the scars of experience.

'Do you want these babies, or just me?' Cal had never made a declaration of love to her, never mind the babies, and it should be a requirement for a man who expected to be in their lives.

'Can't I have both?' He genuinely didn't appear to understand her concerns but that was half of the problem. If he had that nursery filled and someone in his bed, he'd be content to coast along. Whereas she wasn't prepared to let her family merely exist.

'You've done so much, Cal, but I worry you only want us to replace everything Janet took from you. I'm not getting any real emotional connection between you and the babies.' It was harsh, but she needed to figure out his true intentions. If this wasn't going to work out she'd have to make alternative accommodation arrangements and time was running out before the twins arrived. Izzy couldn't bring them back from the hospital to a house that was full of tension because she was afraid to trust the man they were supposed to live with.

He was pacing the room, hands on his hips, nostrils flaring—all the symptoms of someone trying not to lose their cool. Hardly surprising, she supposed, when it would seem as though she was turning on him after all he'd done for her. She should be jumping at the chance of having someone like that in her life but the string of liars she'd endured over the years had left her suspicious, even of a good man like Cal.

'You really think that of me? That I would offer you everything I had, make love to you, provide a home for you and our babies, all so I could pick up where I left off with a woman who'd clearly never loved me?' His gasp of disbelief did make her falter in her assumptions. He made it, her, sound crazy, but she'd been able to twist all his good intentions to fit some darker purpose because it suited her better than risking her heart again.

Izzy threw her hands up. 'I don't know any more.'

'You don't know any more...' His mumbling was punctuated with soulless laughter as he scrubbed his hands through his hair. The display of frustration at her lack of faith in him was as effective as if he'd burst into tears and she hated herself for putting him through this necessary test of his devotion.

'Don't get cross with me, Cal. Everything's just so... confusing.' Her head was beginning to hurt with all the back and forth going on in there. Everything in her heart wanted to believe they were going to have their happy ending but her head knew better and was working overtime to remind her of everything that could potentially go wrong.

He stopped pacing like a caged bear and came to stand in front of her, resting his hands on her shoulders and imploring her to look him in the eye. 'Why? I've been honest with you from the start about only wanting to do right by you. I never expected to fall in love with you. I know it's complicated things, but I thought we'd be able to work things out.'

He loved her, and she wished that was all she'd needed to hear from him. Wished that it made every misgiving she had about their future flap its wings and take flight.

'I'm sorry but it's not enough for me.'

'What have I done wrong?' In truth he'd been the perfect partner in every way imaginable. It was his potential as a father that made her wary of continuing their relationship if his heart lay elsewhere. The babies were never going to be good enough for him, just as she'd never been good enough for anyone in her life.

'Family is everything to me, Cal, but we both know this one doesn't include you.'

'I can only give you what I can but if it's not enough…' He faltered then, his hands falling from her shoulders as he let his true pain at the situation show. She'd been so selfish, thinking only of how she was affected by these great life-changing moments. Cal was every bit as insecure and damaged by his past as she was.

Izzy suddenly realised he was right, she was the one in the wrong here. He'd been bending over backwards to make her life easier, to make her feel wanted, and all this time she'd been looking for excuses as to why things couldn't work between them.

'I know. I'm so sorry.' It was a mess and all she'd done was destroy a relationship that could have stood a chance.

Izzy tried to reach out to him and he physically shrank away from her touch as though he couldn't bear her to touch him. She wanted to vomit.

'I told you everything Janet had put me through, you don't think that was humiliating enough for me?' It had taken him so long to open up to her again, Izzy knew how hurt and embarrassed he'd been by Janet's betrayal.

Arms folded, lips drawn into a thin line, his body seemed to close in on itself as he physically and emotionally withdrew from her, and Izzy realised she was about to lose everything.

'You saved me, Cal, and now I don't know what I, what we, would do without you.' The babies kicked her as though to remind her she was coming close to stuffing things up for all of them. In trying to protect herself from a man who'd never put her first, she'd lost sight of the man who always did.

Cal couldn't keep track of the emotional roller-coaster he'd been strapped into since last night when Izzy had climbed into his bed. He'd been delighted to jump on board then for the ride of his life. With her in his arms all night he'd believed it was the start of their rest of their life together. Now? It was like finding that note pinned to the fridge all over again.

'Yeah. I'm always good for picking up the pieces of the mess other men have left behind.' Janet had used him as some sort of back-up when Darren hadn't immediately stepped forward to be the father of her baby. She'd taken advantage of his desire to be part of a family again and milked him for everything he was worth in terms of money, love and attention. He'd never expected Izzy to do the same.

When someone, or something, better came along, she'd dump him quicker than a dirty nappy. It was his fault for getting into exactly the same situation again after vowing never to let any woman play him the way Janet had done. This was worse. Izzy had been his friend and confidante long before he'd fallen in love with her. Another one-sided love affair doomed to end in heartache for him.

After Janet, he hadn't thought he had anything left to lose. Now he was back in that same position with his heart, his home and his future on the line, and he had to take back some control. In another few months the babies would be here and there would be no going back.

'At the minute I feel as though I've been drafted in as a last-minute substitute to save the day, rather than someone you'd planned to be with for the rest of your life.' He was too angry, too hurt to hold back and save her feelings. He'd been doing that for too long with too many people and it was about time he was able to say what he really thought. Except getting it off his chest was doing nothing to make this any easier.

'To be fair, neither of us had planned for this to happen, Cal, and I'm sorry if you think I somehow tricked my way into your affections. If you knew me the way I thought you did, you'd realise I'm not that devious.'

'I'm beginning to think I don't know you at all.'

'So, what are you saying? That you want to put an end to this now? Do you want me to move out?' With her arms folded Izzy challenged him directly, instead of skirting around the problem the way he and Janet obviously had. If he'd known then what the problem between them had been, he wouldn't have hesitated in ending their relationship himself, but this situation with Izzy wasn't so clear cut.

He didn't want to act in the heat of the moment in

case he'd come to regret it. 'I need some time to think things through.'

'I—I'll pack a bag.' Izzy didn't argue, cry, shout or do anything to show she had any passion about what they did next and that made Cal question the whole nature of their relationship when his heart was breaking. He didn't want to split now with no way back until he had some space away from the situation to see it from a different perspective, but he wasn't sure Izzy was of the same opinion.

'No, I'll go.'

He wouldn't ask her to move out unless he was one hundred per cent sure that was what they both thought was for the best. With children involved they couldn't be that sort of couple who split and got back together whenever the mood took them. Stability was the key-word in a child's life and in that of a man who'd been burned once too many times.

'No matter what you think of me, I wouldn't ask you to move out of your own house.'

'You're not. It's my decision.' It was the last vestige of control he apparently had in this relationship. This time, if things were ending he wanted it to be on his terms.

CHAPTER ELEVEN

WHEN CAL HAD LEFT, Izzy had thought she'd never stop crying. Somehow she'd managed to throw away her one chance of a real family. Her own damn insecurities and inability to trust had caused him to cast her in the same mould as Janet. She couldn't blame him when he'd given her everything and all she'd done was take. The irony was that the second he walked out the door she knew exactly what she wanted. Cal. The babies. A family.

The only ember of hope she had left that that could still be a possibility was that he hadn't thrown her out on the street. It was typical of Cal to let her stay in his house and make himself temporarily homeless, even when he was mad at her. She didn't know why she'd ever doubted his integrity. Oh, wait, it probably had something to do with a series of unreliable guardians and one flaky boyfriend. Things that had absolutely nothing to do with Cal and everything to do with her personal baggage.

It had been days now since he'd walked out, and she felt every second of it. She'd grieved more over losing Cal than she had for Gerry. Which highlighted the differences between the two relationships and the two men involved. Not to mention the strength of the love in her heart for one over the other.

The relief and renewed sense of purpose she'd expected on her return to work had been overshadowed by the sadness at seeing Cal there, not being able to touch him or tell him how much she loved him. She didn't even know where he'd been staying because he hadn't stopped long enough to utter more than two words to her. He could barely look at her and she didn't know what she could do to fix everything she'd broken.

Every time she tried to initiate a conversation he'd simply say, 'Not here, not now,' and expect her to back off without complaint, and she had done until now.

They couldn't carry on avoiding each other for ever. She cornered him in the staffroom, which he had a habit of retreating into so he could avoid her in the radio room. One of her dagger looks in the direction of the other crew members he was using as cover and they scurried off, knowing where they weren't wanted.

Izzy stood in the doorway, blocking Cal's escape route, so he had no choice but to acknowledge her or attempt to push past her, and he was too much of a gentleman to do that.

'Cal, please talk to me. Shout at me, tell me to get out of your house or kiss me senseless and tell me we can work this out. Anything has to be better than this limbo we're in.' Okay, that last one was more of a fantasy than an option, but she'd spent these last days running through every scenario and that was the one she preferred.

'This isn't—'

'Don't tell me this isn't the time or the place when you haven't given me any choice. You can't stay away from your own house indefinitely and we can't go on ignoring each other at work. It's killing me.' It wasn't fair to leave her wondering if they still had a chance if he'd already made his mind up it was over. If they couldn't resolve the issues she'd caused she'd have to do something drastic, like leave her job rather than seeing him every day and realising what she'd thrown away. With the babies coming, job security wasn't something she took lightly but there was no way she could carry on here with a reminder of everything she'd lost staring her in the face every day.

'You don't think those things you said to me didn't almost destroy me? I don't think it's too much to ask for a little time out when you accused me of being some sort of conman simply because I loved you?'

He tossed the newspaper he'd been reading onto the chair as he got to his feet and slammed his coffee cup on the table, sloshing the contents everywhere. Cal had every reason to be angry and Izzy was almost grateful to see this blazing fire in his eyes that said all might not be lost after all. He'd said he'd loved her and that wasn't something a person could turn on and off at will. Whilst she was still able to rouse such a passionate display of emotion in him there was hope he hadn't stopped loving her altogether.

'I was scared, Cal, afraid history was going to repeat itself. That my dream of my little family was going to be taken from me again.' Her voice was cracking with the threat of tears, not at the memory of how people had treated her in the past but because she'd got it so wrong this time. She'd let the past steal away the one person who had actually loved her.

Cal took a step forward and for a moment she almost believed he was going to take her into his arms and tell her everything would be all right. Then the alarm rang out for all standby crew to head to the hangar and any notion of a reconciliation vanished.

'I have to go.'

There was never any doubt a call would take priority over Izzy, but she didn't want to let him go without some assurance that they'd made some progress today after she'd opened her heart to him. 'But you'll come and see me when you get back, yes?'

He looked as though he was about to refuse her, and she had to swallow the ball of disappointment lodged in her throat. Then he gave a quick nod before disappearing out the door.

That one spark of hope that she could salvage her relationship with Cal, along with the future for her and her children she'd been afraid was too good to be true, let her breathe again. Suddenly all that pent-up tension and worry ebbed away, taking with it what little energy she had and leaving her doubled over like a ragdoll.

Pain zipped across her belly, along with the feeling of being caught in a vice. Contractions weren't to be expected at this stage, it was too early. She tried to call out for Cal, but another sharp pain stole her breath away. Tears blurred her vision as she staggered over to grip the chair he'd vacated only moments earlier. Another spike of agony and with it a trickle of fluid running down the inside of her leg. Her waters had broken.

This was everything she'd feared come true. The twins wouldn't survive being born now and she was frightened and alone. She needed Cal.

'Isobel Fitzpatrick. Where is she?' Cal knew he'd probably broken all kind of rules in his desperate hurry to get to the hospital, but he didn't care about anything other than getting to Izzy.

'Are you her partner?' The woman at the desk didn't seem to understand the urgency of the matter as she kept tip-tapping away at the computer instead of immediately whisking him through to Izzy's bedside.

He leaned on the desk, trying not to act on the impulse to swipe everything on the floor. 'Yes. Her waters have broken.' *Get me to her now!*

Saying the words made his stomach roll again the way it had been doing since Mac had broken the news to him that she'd been taken to hospital. As soon as he'd heard that on his arrival back at base, he'd jumped to his car and high-tailed it to the hospital, cursing himself for not staying with her earlier. If he'd stayed to have that talk with her he would've been there for her. He would've been the one to get her the help she needed and comfort her when she would've been frightened about what was going to happen to the babies.

Then again, if he hadn't moved out in the first place he might've seen the signs something was wrong earlier, but he'd been too busy licking his wounds in a budget hotel for the past few days to notice. He hadn't even taken the time to check in with her at work to make sure she was eating properly and looking after herself because of his damn pride.

Yes, she'd questioned his commitment to their family, as he had done during his time out, but he hadn't stopped loving her. He wanted the best for her and the babies and should have prioritised their welfare over his bruised ego. Now the stress he'd put her through, thinking he was going to leave her, had probably caused her to miscarry, as the babies wouldn't be considered vi-

able at this stage and there would be no medical intervention to strengthen their lungs. They were already so
precious to him and Izzy. If it wasn't for those babies
the two of them would never have realised how much
they loved one another.

'Are you Cal?' A nurse at the desk seemed to take
more interest in his arrival than the woman he was talking to.

'Yes. I'm looking for Isobel Fitzpatrick. I was told
she'd been brought here.' If someone didn't take him to
her soon he was going to do a loop of the corridors yell-
ing her name until she answered him back.

'She's been asking for you. Come with me.' The
nurse exchanged a few words with the receptionist before marching him down towards one of the wards.

The fact Izzy hadn't sent out an alert to the staff, ban-
ning him from the premises, was promising that she was
willing to forgive him for walking out on her the way
he had. Although that could change if the babies came
early and suffered as a consequence. He would never
forgive himself if the worst happened so he wouldn't
blame her if she never wanted to see him again in those
circumstances.

'How is she?' He was running after the nurse, begging for more information like any other anxious partner or father-to-be.

'Frightened, tearful, and stubbornly refusing to let
these babies come early.' The half-smile gave him an
idea of how hard Izzy was fighting to stay in control of
this pregnancy.

Good.

'That's my Iz.' Those babies needed to hold on as
long as possible. If they couldn't stop the labour the

babies wouldn't survive, and it would be the same outcome if too much amniotic fluid had been lost. It was simply too early to do anything other than wait. There were so many things that could go wrong at this stage, but he knew everyone here would be keeping Izzy calm and comfortable until they had a clearer picture of what was going on.

'In here.' The nurse opened the door and led him into a side room where Izzy was lying on the bed. As soon as she saw him she burst into floods of tears as though she'd been holding them back all this time, waiting for him to come and be strong for her.

'Oh, Fizz, sweetheart.' He was on the verge of breaking down himself, seeing her lying there vulnerable and helpless and so unlike the woman he knew and loved.

'Cal? I'm so glad you're here...' She stretched her hand out toward him before lapsing into more sobs. He took the seat by the bed and smoothed her hair back from her forehead.

'Shh. It's all right. Everything's going to be okay.' It had to be.

'This is my fault. You told me I was overdoing it and I wouldn't listen. I'm just too damn stubborn for my own good and now we're going to lose the babies.'

'Now, if anyone's to blame, it's me. I shouldn't have left you on your own. I'm so sorry.' He kissed her forehead, refusing to let her feel guilty when he'd been the one who'd made her worry she might have to find somewhere else to live with their two children before they'd even been born. Now he'd happily hand over the keys to his house for ever if it would ease her mind and stop this nightmare.

'We've already talked about this, Isobel. This isn't

anyone's fault. It happens. Now, the scan showed that both heartbeats are strong and though baby number two is surrounded by less amniotic fluid than baby number one, there's still plenty there. We'll keep an eye on that but hopefully, if there's no further leak and no sign of infection, we'll be able to send you home soon.' The midwife did her best to comfort them, but Cal knew that was a lot of ifs. The statistics weren't in their favour for survival when the amniotic sac had ruptured this early, but Izzy Fitzpatrick was much more than a statistic.

'Thank you.' He was grateful they'd been here for Izzy when he hadn't, and luckily Mac had been the one to convince her to get to the hospital without delay. It meant they had every chance of getting the right outcome for Izzy and the babies.

'I'll leave her in your capable hands while I go and see about these test results and getting some antibiotics. Press this buzzer if you need any assistance in the meantime.' The attentive midwife unhooked the buzzer from behind the bed and left it on the bed for Izzy. It was a moment of privacy and a chance for a conversation he was no longer willing to avoid.

'Thank you for coming, Cal—'

'I'm so sorry for everything, Izzy—'

Their words tumbled over each other and he knew it was because of the seriousness of the situation. All the stuff that had caused the rift between them no longer mattered. They smiled at each other and she reached for his hand again.

'I thought I'd lost you.'

'Never. I was hurt but I meant it when I told you I'd never abandon you, Izzy. I love you. I don't care if you don't feel the same way about me, I just want to know you're all okay.' He was willing to put his feelings aside if that's what she wanted, if it meant he could remain in her life.

'Of course I love you, but I saw the way you looked at Janet with the baby. I thought you'd still rather be with them than us.'

He shook his head vigorously, unable to believe she could ever think that when everything he'd ever wanted was right here. 'Seeing them made me realise how lucky I was to have *you*. I never loved her the way I love you, Izzy. I can't wait to raise our family together.'

'Does this mean you'll move back home?' She was smiling now, those worry lines having faded away along with her tears.

'Is that what you want?' He daren't hope for anything beyond her health and happiness but it would be a relief if she genuinely wanted him with her after these past days convincing himself otherwise.

'Yes.' What Izzy wanted more than anything was to have her babies safely delivered at the right time and to go home, with Cal. She was grateful that Mac had been there at the base to make sure she'd got to hospital as soon as he had, but Cal was the only one she'd wanted.

Gone were the days when she'd expected to battle these difficult times alone. They were a team and if it hadn't been for their wobble after the parenting class he would never have moved out. She didn't want to go through any of this without him.

'Good.' He gave her an adorable half-smile that made her fall for him all over again. She knew she was in love with him, that was the reason she'd been so scared they weren't together for the right reasons. Now, having him here after everything she'd accused him of, she knew he was committed to this family. He'd told her he loved her, and this was the proof her twice-burned, baggage-carrying self had demanded before giving herself one hundred per cent to another man.

'I've missed you.' In case he didn't already know how much he meant to her, she was going to make sure to clarify things before they left this building. The time had passed for misunderstandings and skating around important issues. They needed to be a cohesive unit to face whatever the future held for them and the babies. Their babies.

'I've missed you too.' His voice cracked a little and he gave an embarrassed cough to clear his throat, but it was an emotional time for both of them. She could see he shared her worries about the twins and how close they'd come to losing everything.

'I'm sorry for questioning your motives for being with me. I guess I'm just wary of anyone who claims to love me but that's not your fault. You've done nothing but show me what true love is.' She'd pre-empted a disastrous relationship and almost willed it into existence because of her past experiences but all that had to change for the sake of her family. As long as Cal still thought she was worth the effort.

'I had a part to play in this whole mess too, thinking I could never make you truly happy and someday you'd walk out on me too. That's why I was afraid to let myself get close to the babies, thinking I'd never recover if you took them away from me. I guess it's too late for that anyway. The second I knew you were here I knew I loved you all, wanted to keep you all safe. I'm sorry it took so long for me to work it out, but I know my place is here, with you and the babies.'

That was everything she wanted to hear, and she could almost feel her body settling down to see out the rest of this pregnancy with him, free from further drama. 'Well, I'd prefer if we could do that doting partner thing at home.'

'You won't be allowed to lift a finger, you know. Do you think you can manage that?' His teasing came with a hint of genuine concern and it was little wonder when she'd been so difficult thus far, but she'd learned her lesson and hoped she'd get a second chance at this whole pampered pregnant lady thing. This time she'd take full advantage of everything Cal was offering.

'Complete bed rest. I swear.' She crossed her heart and promised to let him fuss over her. After these past days, wandering around that big house on her own, she didn't know why she'd resisted it this far. It was nice having someone worry about her and want to take care of her for once. A shame it had taken almost losing everything for her to appreciate that instead of fearing it.

'And after the babies are here? What happens then?' It was clear he was asking in terms of their relationship what would happen next, and though no one could predict the future she could be honest about her hopes for the future.

'I am hoping we live happily ever after. I love you, Cal, and I'm sure the babies will love you too. Can we think of this as our new start, our little family finally coming together?' It was something they'd both been missing out on and this pregnancy was a gift, giving them everything they'd dreamed about. With Cal in her corner she was optimistic they could persuade these babies to stay put until they were out of the danger zone.

A smile slowly crept over his face until he was positively beaming. 'You've never said that before.'

'What? That I love you? I think I was afraid to say it out loud and acknowledge those feelings myself. Now I've said it out loud, I can't take it back.' She gave a little laugh, still nervous about entering into another serious relationship, especially when there were going to be two more wee people affected by her every future decision, but leaping into the unknown with Cal was preferable to a lonely life without him.

'No, you can't, and I for one will never get sick of hearing you say it. Along with that "our family", thing you casually tossed in there. You don't know how happy that makes me, knowing that I'm going to be part of this.' He rested his hand on her bump and she couldn't imagine anyone else she would rather spend the rest of her life with, raising these precious babies. It was important he knew that because she didn't intend wasting any more of her life regretting things she did or didn't say.

'You're very much part of this, daddy Cal, and once we know for sure these two are going to behave and stay where they are until we're ready for them, I want to make it official. Calum Armstrong, will you marry us?' She hadn't known she was going to ask him until the words came out of her mouth, but it felt so right for all of them to make this relationship as solid as possible.

It was the first time she'd ever seen him lost for words as his jaw flopped open and shut without him making a sound. If he hadn't looked so utterly thrilled by the proposal she would've worried he was searching for the words to let her down gently.

'Is that a yes?'

'That's a yes to being your husband, yes to being daddy Cal and yes to spending every day of the rest of my life with you. On one condition.' His forehead crinkled and turned his handsome face serious again.

Izzy swallowed, concerned that he might impose some impossible demands, but had to trust that belief she had in him that he would never do anything to hurt her.

'Name it,' she said, feigning a bravery she would need to see her through the next months.

'You get some rest.' He kissed her all too fleetingly on the lips.

Now, that she could do. She snuggled down into the bed, exhaustion washing over her in waves now she'd laid herself bare emotionally, but knowing Cal was sticking with her gave her enough comfort to give in to slumber.

'Where will you be when I wake up?' she mumbled, refusing to let go of his hand as she drifted off to sleep.

'Where I belong. Right here beside you.'

She smiled with the soft pressure of his lips against her cheek and knew everything would turn out fine when she woke up because now she had a future with Cal to look forward to. This family of convenience had become one she was going to cherish for ever.

EPILOGUE

'I NOW PRONOUNCE YOU husband and wife.'

The registrar legally confirmed their commitment to one another, although Cal and Izzy had done that almost a year ago in the hospital.

'I can kiss the bride now, right?'

As if he would've let anyone stop him. Izzy would never tire of letting him either. Being able to kiss Cal any time she pleased was one of the many good things to come her way.

The registrar nodded her approval as Cal dipped his new bride back for a true Hollywood-romance-style kiss, which still had the ability to make Izzy spend the rest of the day walking around in a daze.

A chorus of whoops and cheers rang out from the congregated guests as they finally made their relationship official. They had planned an altogether different wedding from the one currently taking place, but seeing the sea of smiling faces cheering them down the aisle, Izzy was grateful at how things had turned out.

Originally, she'd envisaged a quick, quiet ceremony with no fuss so the twins would be born into a stable relationship but, as Cal had pointed out, they were going to have that regardless of a piece of paper. They'd also decided they didn't need the extra stress of wedding preparations when she already had an increased risk of going into premature labour.

She'd been true to her word and stuck to complete bed rest and Cal had gone above and beyond the duties of a loving partner and father-to-be. He'd taken time off work to play nursemaid as well as crawl into bed to watch movies with her and cook every meal for her to make sure she didn't die of boredom or malnutrition in the run-up to the birth.

That time together had been precious for them as a couple, getting to know each other again minus their baggage. She believed it was a major contributing factor to the babies hanging on until her thirty-fourth week. The amniotic sac had resealed itself after that terrifying episode and, although a little on the small side, their girls had been born healthy and able to come home after just a few days. Then the fun had really started, and those quiet moments together had become few and far between. There was never a dull moment in the Armstrong household now and she was thankful for it.

The extra time since the birth and announcing their intention to get married had given them a chance to share their special day with the important people in their lives. Mac and the guys from work were here to celebrate with them and Cal's sisters had travelled with their families to be with them. Perhaps it wasn't too late for any of them to be a real family.

'I love you, Mrs Armstrong, but I hate to break it to you: I'm leaving you for the other two special girls in my life.' Cal stopped halfway down the aisle and let go of her hand to reach for the beauties who'd caught his eye on the way past.

'Oh, well. It was fun while it lasted.' Izzy knew she could never compare to the other important people in this marriage but for once she was happy to come second in Cal's affections when she was equally enamoured with their daughters.

'Come here, Nelly Belly.' Cal reached for the cute bundle trying to wriggle out of Helen's arms to reach her daddy and Izzy did the same with Nell's sister, Rae. She had her best friend and her husband to thank for the twins' still pristine flower girl outfits as they'd juggled the childcare duties during the ceremony. But neither she nor Cal would be parted from them for longer than necessary. They'd named the girls after Cal's parents, Ray and Eleanor, and Cal was the most devoted father anyone could ever wish for. These girls would be as spoiled and happy as she was with him in their lives.

'Well, husband, I think it's time this family really got the party started. Everyone back to our place for champagne and cake.' Their home was their favourite place in the world and the natural choice for a venue in which to celebrate their big day with friends and family. On this occasion Cal had delegated the cooking to caterers so he could spend as much quality time with her and the girls as possible.

Izzy's heart was so full of love for this man she knew it wouldn't be long before the Armstrong family would be growing again…

* * * * *

COMING
SOON!

We really hope you enjoyed reading this book. If you're looking for more romance, be sure to head to the shops when new books are available on

Thursday 22nd August

To see which titles are coming soon, please visit
millsandboon.co.uk/nextmonth

MILLS & BOON

Coming next month

HEALING THE SINGLE DAD'S HEART
Scarlet Wilson

None of this had been planned. When Lien had appeared at the door it had seemed only natural to call her over to say hello to his parents. He'd half-hoped it might give them some reassurance that he and his son had actually settled in.

Instead, it had opened a whole new can of worms.

He felt his phone buzz and pulled it from his pocket. A text from his mother. Three words. 'We love her.' Nothing else.

Guilt swamped him. What was he doing? As soon as Lien had sat down she'd fallen into the family conversation with no problems and been an instant hit with his parents.

He couldn't pretend that hadn't pleased him. He'd liked the way they'd exchanged glances of approval and joked and laughed with her.

But it also – in a completely strange way – didn't please him.

Part of him still belonged to Esther. Always had. Always would.

He'd found love once. He'd been lucky. Some people would never have what he and Esther had.

How dare he even contemplate looking again?

His mother had pushed him here to start living again. Not to find a replacement for his wife.

The thought made his legs crumple and he slid down the wall, his hands going to his hair. For a few seconds he just breathed.

He was pulling himself one way and another. Guilt hung over him like a heavy cloud.

He knew why he was here. He knew he'd been living life back in Scotland in a protective bubble. It was time to get out there. That was why he'd accepted the tickets and climbed on that plane.

But what he hated most of all was that he did feel ready to move on. He was tired. He was tired of being Joe, the widower. It had started to feel like a placard above his head.

But part of him hated the fact he wanted to move forward. He was tired of being alone. He was tired of feeling like there would never by anyone else in his, and his son's life. He was tired of being tired. Of course, he had no idea about the kind of person he was interested in. The truth was, the few little moments that Lien had caused sparks in his brain had bothered him.

It had been so long and he couldn't quite work out how he felt about everything yet. Of course he'd want someone who recognised that he and his son were a package deal. He'd want someone who could understand his usual passion for this work. These last few weeks had mirrored how he'd been a few years before. Every day there was something new to learn. Someone new to help. It was what had always driven him, and he knew that, for a while, he'd lost that. But Vietnam was reawakening parts of him that had been sleeping for a while.

Continue reading
HEALING THE SINGLE DAD'S HEART
Scarlet Wilson

Available next month
www.millsandboon.co.uk

MILLS & BOON

THE HEART OF ROMANCE

A ROMANCE FOR EVERY KIND OF READER

MODERN
Prepare to be swept off your feet by sophisticated, sexy and seductive heroes, in some of the world's most glamourous and romantic locations, where power and passion collide.
8 stories per month.

HISTORICAL
Escape with historical heroes from time gone by. Whether your passion is for wicked Regency Rakes, muscled Vikings or rugged Highlanders, awaken the romance of the past.
6 stories per month.

MEDICAL
Set your pulse racing with dedicated, delectable doctors in the high-pressure world of medicine, where emotions run high and passion, comfort and love are the best medicine.
6 stories per month.

True Love
Celebrate true love with tender stories of heartfelt romance, from the rush of falling in love to the joy a new baby can bring, and a focus on the emotional heart of a relationship.
8 stories per month.

Desire
Indulge in secrets and scandal, intense drama and plenty of sizzling hot action with powerful and passionate heroes who have it all: wealth, status, good looks…everything but the right woman.
6 stories per month.

HEROES
Experience all the excitement of a gripping thriller, with an intense romance at its heart. Resourceful, true-to-life women and strong, fearless men face danger and desire - a killer combination!
8 stories per month.

DARE
Sensual love stories featuring smart, sassy heroines you'd want as a best friend, and compelling intense heroes who are worthy of them.
4 stories per month.

To see which titles are coming soon, please visit

millsandboon.co.uk/nextmonth

LET'S TALK
Romance

For exclusive extracts, competitions and special offers, find us online:

- facebook.com/millsandboon
- @MillsandBoon
- @MillsandBoonUK

Get in touch on 01413 063232

For all the latest titles coming soon, visit
millsandboon.co.uk/nextmonth